The Amethyst Heart

Penelope J. Stokes

WORD PUBLISHING

NASHVILLE

A Thomas Nelson Company

Library of Congress Cataloging-in-Publication Data

Stokes, Penelope J.
    The amethyst heart / Penelope J. Stokes
      p. cm.
    ISBN 0-8499-3721-5 (HC); 0-8499-4235-7 (TP)
    I. Title
PS3569.T6219 A8 2000
813'.54—dc21   00-026888

Printed in the USA
00 01 03 04 05 06 07 08 09 QWV 8 7 6 5 4 3 2 1

To my family in blood and spirit—
with appreciation for the rich legacy of love and grace.

And to the memory of Opal,
who shared her stories with me.

Prologue

———◦•◦•◦———

March 13, 1993

The old woman sat at her dressing table and peered into the mirror, working with one shaky hand to tuck a stray wisp of hair into the upswept bun. All her long life, that lock of hair had given her trouble, never staying in place, always tumbling out to sweep down and tangle in a necklace chain or get caught in an earring.

Just like me, she thought with a smile. *Never doing what other people expect or want me to do.*

She peered into the dim glass and wondered, as she had done countless times over the past forty years, whether she should go to the expense of getting the mirror re-silvered. But even ages ago, when she could have afforded a few extras, she had resisted. There was something appropriate about the yellowing, spotted glass. It fit with the ancient house, and with her.

She applied a bit of lipstick and sat back to survey the results. "You've got a few spots and wrinkles yourself, old girl," she murmured to her reflection. "But you've still got a good head of hair and all your own teeth. Not too bad for ninety-three."

Ninety-three. Was it possible? Could Miss Amethyst Noble truly be ninety-three?

She chuckled at the thought. Even though she had outlived two husbands and the vast majority of her friends, Southern tradition dictated that people still call her "Miss" and refer to her by her maiden name. As if she were still a debutante, a sweet Southern belle being courted by some handsome beau.

But Amethyst was far beyond those days—so far that any recollection of being a young girl had faded to a vague, hazy memory. She had weathered fourscore and thirteen years, survived two world wars, and come into the last decade of the twentieth century with all her marbles intact.

Or so it seemed. For here she was, still living in the ancestral home built by her grandfather in 1853, preparing herself for a birthday party.

Amethyst went to the big cedar wardrobe and selected a dress—her favorite, a soft lavender heather with a high neck and little pearl buttons down the front. She probably should have bought a new one for the occasion, but at her age the current fashions looked ridiculous. This would do just fine. Besides, her great-granddaughter and namesake, Little Am, had always loved it. As a tiny girl Little Am had climbed into her great-grandmother's lap, snuggled against the soft fabric, and stroked it with a gentle hand. The memory of that tender moment always brought tears to Amethyst's eyes. The child had been her joy and delight—and her single desperate hope for the future.

Amethyst sighed. The girl would be here today, no doubt, but she was no longer a child; and, sad to say, she was no longer anyone's delight. Puberty had transformed the gentle, sweet-natured little girl into a teenage mutant ghoul who dressed all in black, muttered in monosyllables, and wore four earrings in each earlobe. Not what Amethyst had hoped for the child. Not at all what she had prayed for.

Well, you can't change the times, she thought with a shrug. *You just have to keep on living and pray your life will have some kind of positive effect on the people around you.*

She slipped the lavender dress over her head and opened her jewelry box. It was cluttered with things she rarely wore: earrings and necklaces and rings—gifts, mostly, from family members who never knew what to buy for an eccentric old woman. Only one piece held any real significance for her, and she picked it up and fingered its surface lovingly.

It was a brooch, a single heart-shaped amethyst a little larger than a quarter, with small pearls set around the perimeter. Simple, elegant, and nearly perfect—except for the one missing pearl, lost years ago.

She turned it over and read the familiar inscription engraved on the back: *Sincerity, Purity, Nobility*. The motto of the Noble family for over a century, as far back as anyone could remember, and beyond. Generations of women before her had worn this heart of amethyst. But who after her would treasure it as she did?

With arthritic fingers she struggled to pin the brooch at her throat, then glanced at the clock on the mantel. Her family would be here in an hour, and she still had to set the table and arrange flowers for a centerpiece.

She got up from the dressing table and moved slowly into the parlor that adjoined her bedroom, pausing to stroke the keys of the hundred-year-old piano and basking in the comfort of the familiar. Across the foyer from the parlor was the log cabin room, the oldest portion of the house. Here the original log beams and massive stone fireplace had been preserved, and when she stepped down into the room, she felt it surround her with the welcome embrace of an old friend.

This house was her life. Its walls sent back the echoes of her dreams, her laughter, her tears. It had sustained her when times were bad and rejoiced with her in the happy years. Its corridors held cherished memories of her own nine decades and the legacy of generations before her. Here she had been born, grown up, learned to love, married, given birth, and mourned—and here she would die, when her time came.

But not quite yet.

Amethyst scrutinized her reflection in the mirror over the fireplace. She looked as good as anyone had a right to look at ninety-three—and a lot better than most, considering that most people her age were withering away their final years in some nursing home.

Against all odds, she was still alive—truly alive, not just existing in that nebulous place between this world and the next. And she meant to stay that way until they carried her out of Noble House in a pine box.

Part 1

INTEGRITY

———◆◆◆◆◆———

"You shall rise before the aged,
and defer to the old;
and you shall fear your God: I am the LORD."

Leviticus 19:32

1

Conrad

———◆✦◆———

*C*on! Hurry up, or we'll be late!"

Conrad Wainwright grimaced as his wife's shrill voice pierced through the study door. Why couldn't the woman speak in a normal tone?

Forty years ago he had thought it cute, that high-pitched squeal of hers. Mimsy. The perfect empty-headed Southern girl, who would keep his house, cook his meals, bear and raise his children, and be utterly satisfied to be known as "Mrs. Conrad Wainwright." The straight-C student who would never question his authority, challenge his decisions, or rock the domestic boat. The cheerleader who would devote her life to encouraging him. The prom queen who would entertain his clients and decorate his world.

Forty years ago Margaret "Mimsy" Hanover had been everything Conrad Wainwright had wanted in a wife. But back then she had been petite and blonde and beautiful, and when she had hung on his arm, simpering and fluttering her eyelashes and claiming that every word out of his mouth was nothing short of genius, he had thought her silly and sweet and utterly entrancing.

Over the years, however, the trance had worn off; now that voice could send him into a migraine without a moment's notice. She had fulfilled her part of the unspoken bargain—she had made a home for him, raised two children, entertained his clients, and always supported his decisions. But somewhere along the way, things had changed. The petite cheerleader had undergone a grotesque metamorphosis. Her hair had gone from blonde to brassy, her figure from lithe to lumbering, and that squeal of hers had grown so shrill, so insistent, that it could make a hyena cringe and run for cover.

Conrad closed his eyes and fought against the storm of emotions that assailed him. Fifteen years ago he had considered divorce, had actually gone to see a divorce lawyer to discuss his options. But before he had the chance to take any action, his son William and daughter-in-law Marlene had been killed in an auto accident. On the highway between Memphis and Nashville, a drunk driver had crashed head-on into their car, leaving them dead at the scene and their eighteen-month-old daughter orphaned.

The last thing Con had wanted to do at age fifty was to raise another child. But what other choice did they have? William's sister, Lauren, the child's only aunt, was totally worthless as a prospective parent. Still single and rootless, she was living with three friends in Greenwich Village. They heard from her two or three times a year, at Christmas and birthdays. The year before the accident she had called at four in the morning to tell them she had changed her name to Selina or Salmonella or some other odd thing Conrad couldn't remember. No. Lauren was not a viable option.

For once in her life, Mimsy, a veritable mass of motherly instinct, had taken over and insisted upon having her own way. The baby would come to live with them and be raised as their own daughter. She put her foot down and refused even to consider any other options. So, at midlife, he had found himself cast in the role of father to the infant Little Am, named Amethyst after her great-grandmother.

Mimsy was in heaven. Her empty nest had been filled again, her shallow life given depth and meaning by a senseless tragedy. Conrad, on the other hand, felt trapped, imprisoned by fate in a claustrophobic cell of responsibility.

Almost without realizing it, Con began to retreat into himself, to insulate himself from a world spun out of control. He started to drink on the sly, and his business began to slide. No one wanted a lawyer who couldn't keep up with his commitments, who didn't return calls, who misplaced files, got his clients confused, couldn't keep his billing straight.

Finally he had gotten a grip on himself and curtailed the booze, but it was too little, too late. In an attempt to get out of the hole, he had made some bad investments with money borrowed from the trust funds of several of his clients. At the point in his life when he should be looking forward to a comfortable retirement funded by ample stocks and bonds and IRAs, his practice was in the toilet, and his creditors were closing in. Bankruptcy loomed on the horizon.

Mimsy, of course, knew nothing of his dilemma. She had never taken an interest in his business dealings, always content to let him bring home the paycheck and control the finances. As long as she had a fine house, a gold card, her society friends, and Little Am, she didn't ask questions. And he certainly didn't volunteer any information.

Conrad raked a hand through his hair and shuffled the papers on his desk. If he didn't do something fast, he was going to lose it all—the Mercedes, the house in the country, everything. He could see only one option.

Mother.

"Con-rad!" The shrieking voice came again, this time accompanied by an insistent knocking on his study door. "Conrad, come on! We don't want to keep Mother waiting!"

Con gathered up the papers from his desk, folded them lengthwise, and shoved them into the inside pocket of his sports jacket.

It was a ninety-minute drive from their ten-acre estate in the countryside south of Memphis to Con's boyhood home in Cambridge, Mississippi. Cambridge was a small, compact university town, its streets lined with venerable antebellum homes and tall magnolia trees. At the center of the courthouse square stood the statue of a Confederate soldier, and the sight of it always evoked a wave of nostalgia in his heart. As a boy he had played under the watchful eye of that statue; as a youth he had painted his initials on its base. As a freshman at the university, his fraternity hazing included a long night chained to the soldier in his boxer shorts. As a law student he had attended trials in the courthouse and gazed out the window to see the soldier standing there, ever attentive, ever vigilant.

Conrad knew every street in Cambridge, every alley, every path through the woods that surrounded the town and the college. Even though his law practice forced him to live within commuting distance of Memphis, he still loved Cambridge and thought of it as home.

Today, however, the drive into Cambridge made Conrad unaccountably nervous. Usually he looked forward to the trip—the rolling green landscape, the sensation of power as the Mercedes accelerated around each bend in the road, the feeling of welcome as he drove up the long hill into the town square and made his way around the circle to Jefferson Davis Avenue, where Noble House sat as a monument to his family's longevity. All he could think of now as he pulled the Mercedes into his mother's driveway and parked it in the shelter of the hundred-year-old magnolia tree was that because of him, Noble House would soon become little more than a faded memory.

Reluctantly he got out of the car, took the presents from the trunk, and proceeded up the walk toward the front of the house with Mimsy and Little Am trailing behind.

"Do I *have* to go?" Little Am asked for the umpteenth time. She was seventeen, and Con was sure that visiting her ninety-three-year-old great-grandmother seemed like cruel and unusual punishment to the girl. But when she got out of sorts, which happened on a regular basis these days, her voice took on that shrill and strident tone she had learned as a baby at her grandmother's knee.

Conrad stopped in his tracks and turned to glare at her. "Yes, you have to go. Now stop whining." He looked her over and shook his head in dismay. Little Am was dressed in black jeans, a cropped-off black T-shirt that bore a Harley-Davidson logo and revealed five inches of her belly, and a black leather vest studded with silver spikes. His eyes locked onto an inch-long design just above her navel—a heart pierced by a thin blue dagger. A tattoo? Con sighed. He could only hope it was one of those temporary things that came off with baby oil and a good scrubbing. At least she looked clean and, except for that awful black stuff around her eyes, had toned down the makeup a little. Maybe he couldn't expect any more than that.

He turned and continued up the walk. The pink azaleas across the front of the porch were budding, and around the big magnolia tree, clusters of daffodils had already bloomed. In a couple of weeks, when crowds of people would be flocking to Cambridge for the annual pilgrimage tour, the place would be a riot of color.

Mother had finally conceded to taking Noble House off the pilgrimage. It was simply too much for her—dressing in a hoop skirt, having hordes of people coming through, standing on her feet ten hours a day to give "the tour." But folks still came by to see the outside of Noble House, which was the oldest historic home in the county. Sometimes Mother would still put on her rose-colored satin dress and sit on the porch swing waving to passersby, and if any of them had the nerve to get out of the car and come onto the porch, she'd offer them lemonade and regale them with her stories of Grandpa Silas and the War.

It was, he had to admit, a beautiful home—a rectangular two-story of planter design, with square columns and tall, narrow windows across the front, and a balcony on the upper level—a "courting porch," Mother called it. Noble House wasn't as large or as elaborate as some of the other stately homes in Cambridge, but it had a history, Mother said, that couldn't be matched. History, and a hundred and forty years of Noble love.

Con paused at the heavy iron-grilled doorway and rang the bell. This was Mother's one compromise to her passion for maintaining the historical accuracy of Noble House—the installation of a security system and iron grillwork on all the doors. Anyone who had ever been on the pilgrimage tour, after all, knew what kind of treasures the house held. Everything from Limoges china and Waterford crystal to an autographed portrait of Abraham Lincoln—an odd anomaly in a Mississippi antebellum, to be sure, but extremely rare and valuable. The carved, mahogany canopy bed in the Avery room upstairs had been appraised—twenty years ago—at $45,000.

Mother always said she was "house poor." She didn't have a lot of cash in the bank—just enough from pensions and social security to get by from month to month. But the house itself had been valued at well over half a million, and that didn't count the antiques. The truth was, the old woman was sitting on a gold mine.

Sooner or later, it would all come to him, of course. But he couldn't wait for *later*. Time was running out. Con could feel his life slipping away, as if he were trapped in the bottom of an hourglass while the sand sifted down around him and grew deeper with every passing minute.

Today. It had to be done today, or there might not be a tomorrow.

2
The Celebration

⎯⎯◆⎯◆⎯◆⎯⎯

Amethyst lifted the silver knife and looked around the long dining room table. "Who wants cake? I made it myself—three layers, coconut."

"I guess I'll take some," Con muttered, twisting his napkin in his lap.

"Just a little slice for me," Mimsy said with a titter.

"Yeah, okay." Little Am didn't look up, but slouched further down in her chair and stared pointedly at her watch.

Well, Amethyst thought, *this has turned out to be some celebration.* For the past hour and a half Conrad had barely spoken, and when he did it was with a forced cheerfulness. Mimsy frowned at her husband and tried to get him to talk, and Little Am spent the entire time slinking from one chair to the next, flipping through magazines and making her displeasure evident with exasperated sighs.

It was more like a wake than a party, and Amethyst had the uncomfortable feeling that she was the corpse.

Finally Conrad cleared his throat and pushed his cake aside. "Mother, we have to talk about something."

She raised one eyebrow. "All right."

"You're ninety-three, Mother. I think it's time for you to consider moving out of this drafty old house. You can't continue living here by yourself, struggling to keep warm in the winter, cooking for yourself. I—that is, *we,* all of us—are worried about you. Why, you could fall and break a hip, and nobody would know it for a week. You could—"

"I *could* keel over with a coronary tomorrow," Amethyst interrupted, "but I don't have any immediate plans to do so."

"And what do you need with such a huge house, anyway?" he persisted. "It's just so much to keep up."

"It's my *home*, Conrad." Amethyst felt a tightening in her throat and a hot flush of anger surging up from her belly. "I was born here, and I will die here."

"Look, Mother." His face reddened and his eyes narrowed. "There's a nice new development of retirement condos in the south end of Memphis, just minutes from our house. It's really beautifully done, with lots of lawn and a little pond with a gazebo. You'd be closer to us, and we could keep an eye on you—"

"Keep an eye on me?" Her temper flared, and she fought to regain control. "I'm old, Conrad; I am not a child, and I am not senile. I don't need supervision, and I don't need to be stuck away in a home for the aged and infirm. I'm perfectly capable of 'keeping an eye' on myself."

His tone mellowed, but his eyes turned to ice. "What if something happened to you?"

"Believe it or not, plenty of people here in Cambridge know I'm still alive and care about me. If something happened, someone would call you."

Her eyes drifted to Mimsy, who was perched on the edge of her chair, staring at her husband as if he had lost his mind. Clearly she had not been party to what her husband had been planning.

"We're simply thinking of your best interests," he protested. "We're the only family you have, you know. Little Am is growing up—don't you want to spend more time with your only great-granddaughter?"

Am heaved another sigh and rolled her eyes. Right now, the last thing Amethyst wanted was to spend another moment in the presence of this changeling, but she didn't say so. Something was up with Conrad, and she was determined to get to the bottom of it. She waved a hand in his direction. "Go on."

Evidently he took this as a sign that he was winning the argument, and he brightened. "The place is called Shady Brook, and it offers everything you could want. Nice apartments, trained medical personnel on the premises, three meals a day, plenty of company—"

"So I could sit around playing checkers and watching soap operas with the other inmates," she murmured. "How lovely."

He missed the sarcasm completely. "It really is nice, Mother. You'd have people your own age to spend time with—"

"The only place I'd find people my age is in the cemetery," she quipped. "I've outlived everybody."

"All the more reason you should spend your golden years in a place where you don't have to lift a finger. Everything you need would be provided."

"I'm way past golden, Conrad. I'm on my way to platinum." Amethyst caught Little Am's eye and winked, and the girl, clearly surprised, gave an admiring nod and suppressed a laugh. Maybe there was hope for this child after all. Maybe there was a spark buried under all that black leather.

Amethyst leaned back in her chair. One hand went to the brooch at her throat, and her fingers traced the outline of the heart. "And just how do you propose that I would pay for this life of luxury, do tell?"

Conrad ran a hand through his hair. "Well, I've been thinking about that."

I bet you have, Amethyst thought, but she kept silent and waited.

———

Conrad avoided his wife's incredulous stare and focused on his mother. She was beginning to play with the bait, he could see it. Now it was time to set the hook. "I took the liberty of doing a little preliminary checking, and I believe the sale of this house would provide all the financial resources you would need to—ah—make a change."

The whole truth was, he had gone far beyond "preliminary checking." He had, in fact, already contacted a real estate agent and signed a seller's contract in his mother's name. The agent had two very good prospects in the wings, just waiting for approval to see Noble House. One of them, a successful corporate lawyer in Memphis, had already begun drawing up plans to turn Noble House into branch offices. He wanted to purchase the property and all the furnishings, and then would select some of the antiques to complement the decor of the office and dispose of the rest.

"You would *sell* Noble House." His mother's tone was cold, controlled. "You would auction your history to the highest bidder."

"Well, yes," Con stammered. "It's only a matter of time, Mother. Mimsy and I can't live here, not if I'm going to maintain my practice. The house would be sold . . . ah, eventually."

As soon as the words were out of his mouth, he knew he had made a mistake, perhaps a fatal one. He watched as her hands, like talons, gripped the arms of her chair. Then she relaxed and gave him a faint smile—a smile that did not quite reach her eyes.

"And how much will Noble House bring on the current market?" she asked in a whisper.

Conrad felt his pulse accelerate. If he could arrange to sell the house, with all its furnishings, he stood to clear nearly $900,000 on the deal. But he needed her to think that she would barely get by on what they made from the sale. The rest of it—most of it, in fact—would get him out of hot water. And if he played his cards right, he could make back what he took from the purchase price, and she would never know the difference.

"Now, Mother, the financial part of it is very complicated. You don't really need to concern yourself over all the details. Suffice it to say that you can live very comfortably on what you'll make from the sale of the house. I'll handle everything."

"I'm sure you will, Conrad."

"It's a simple transaction," he rushed on. "We will establish a trust fund with me as executor of the trust. You won't have to worry about a thing."

"I'm sure I won't, Conrad."

He pulled the papers from his jacket pocket and spread them out on the table. "I've set it all up. All you have to do is sign, and then—"

He looked up at her and saw a strange look pass over her face—an expression of—what was it? Understanding? Compassion? No, not that. *Pity*.

"Just one thing, Conrad," she said softly.

"What is it, Mother?"

"You've been so efficient about everything else—I assume you've already engaged a real estate agent?"

Her gaze pierced into his, and for a moment he felt the way he had when, as a boy, he had been caught in a lie. Maybe it was instinct, some kind of maternal ESP, but she had always known when he had been less than truthful. If he evaded her question or tried to bluff her, she would nail him. Some things between a mother and a son never changed, not even in adulthood.

"Well, yes. A woman from here in Cambridge, actually. But she understands that nothing will be done without your approval."

It wasn't an outright lie, but it wasn't the complete truth, either. Buried in the sheaf of papers on the table was a power of attorney that gave Conrad the right to make any and all decisions on his mother's behalf. He'd rather convince her to acquiesce quietly, but if that failed, he was prepared to have her declared incompetent. She was ninety-three, after all, and more than a little eccentric. It was for her own good, to get out of this house and into a more controlled environment. Besides, if his business went into bankruptcy, what would that do to her—to all of them? What other choice did he have?

Still, invoking the power of attorney shouldn't be necessary. He almost had her convinced, and once her signature was on the documents and she had agreed to the sale, he would be on his way toward financial solvency again.

"Conrad?"

His mother's voice drew him back to the present, and he looked up.

"I want to talk to the real estate agent."

"What? Why?"

"Humor me. This is a major life change we're talking about. And, as you well know, I'm rather attached to this old place. I want to make sure Noble House is in good hands."

A surge of hope rose up in Conrad's heart. She was going to do it!

"Well, sure, Mother. Just go ahead and sign these trust documents, and on Monday I'll call her and we'll set up a time—"

"Now, Conrad. Before I sign anything, I want to talk to her."

"Now? But it's Saturday afternoon, and—"

"Real estate people work on the weekend, don't they? This agent of yours is in Cambridge, isn't she? Get in the car, drive over there, and bring her back."

"I—I guess I could do that, Mother. But why don't you just sign—"

"Now, Conrad. Take Mimsy with you. And pick up some vanilla ice cream on the way back, will you? I forgot to get it, and a birthday party is nothing without ice cream."

Ice cream. She wanted ice cream. And a face-to-face conversation with the real estate agent. Con sighed. All right. Whatever would get this over and done with in the quickest amount of time.

He rose and placed his napkin on the table. "I'll be back in half an hour. Mimsy, come on and go with me. Am—"

"Little Am can stay here," his mother said firmly. "She can help me clean up the dishes while you're gone."

The girl sighed and rolled her eyes, then picked up her fork and played with the remains of the birthday cake.

"Half an hour," Con repeated, herding Mimsy toward the door. He shut the iron-grilled door behind him and sprinted for the Mercedes, with his wife on his heels, shrieking questions. But this time he found himself less irritated with her shrillness.

He could put up with anything for half an hour. In half an hour he would be a very wealthy man.

3
The Hostage

Amethyst watched her son and his wife get in the car and drive away. When they were gone, she turned the key in the iron security gate, removed it, and dropped it into her pocket.

Con had insisted upon installing this security system—electronic sensors on all the windows, and wrought-iron grillwork on all the doors. The security gates were like storm doors, with screens and removable glass for ventilation, but covered by heavy decorative iron in a vine pattern. They had double deadbolt locks with keyholes on both sides. Once they were locked and the keys removed, no one could get in. No one.

Not even her only son.

Less than one minute into Conrad's frantic attempt to convince her that selling her house and moving to Shady Brook was a brilliant idea, Amethyst had seen right through his pitch. He had never been able to deceive her—he ought to know that after sixty-six years. But apparently he still thought he could pull the wool over his own mother's eyes. Or perhaps he just thought she was so old and senile that she wouldn't know the difference.

At any rate, she had suspected something was wrong even before he started talking; and the more he talked, the more she read between the lines. Something had happened, something even that simpering Mimsy didn't know about. He was in financial trouble—big trouble, if he would go to this much effort to get his hands on Noble House.

This wasn't about her welfare, but about his.

It was too bad he couldn't just be honest with her, tell her what his problems were. She might have been able to help him. She still had a little nest egg from life insurance payments, money she had squirreled away and never touched. It had been gathering interest for years, and although she didn't know the exact amount, it might have been enough to get Conrad out of whatever hole he had dug for himself.

But give up Noble House? Let him sell off her life, her history, to the highest bidder—just to salvage his own reputation? She didn't think so. She'd go down fighting, if she had to.

Amethyst made the rounds, locked the rest of the doors, and stowed away all the keys. Then she went to the hall closet, pulled out a step-stool, and shakily hoisted herself up so she could see onto the top shelf.

"Grandam?" Little Am's voice came from below her. "What are you doing?"

"Just getting something I need, child."

"Do you want me to get it?"

"No, I'm fine. Just help me down."

A hand reached up to steady her—a pale, young hand with fingernails painted black. A ghoulish hand. Amethyst grabbed on and stumbled back down the two steps. When she had her footing on solid ground again, she let out a trembling breath. Maybe she *was* too old to be doing everything for herself. But giving up Noble House and moving into an old-age home was out of the question.

"Grandam! What is that?"

Little Am's eyes sparked with excitement and a bit of fear. It was the most animation Amethyst had seen out of the child all day, and she peered at her namesake. The girl had striking eyes—dark brown, with long lashes—and strong, square-shaped features. If she would just get some of that shaggy hair out of her eyes and take off that garish eyeliner, she would be a lovely girl. She definitely favored the Noble clan, with her wide brow and stubborn jaw. And for the moment, that vacant, dis-interested expression had vanished, and her face had come to life.

"I said, what is that?"

Amethyst chuckled. "It's a gun, of course. Don't you watch TV?"

"I *know* it's a gun," the girl said, rolling her eyes. "It's a shotgun. Full-choke, double-barreled 12-gauge."

"Very good, Miss Marple," Amethyst said as she nodded. "How do you know that?"

"Who's Miss Marple?" Little Am countered. "And I know it because my friend Lenny has one. His daddy goes hunting with it. Lenny got into real trouble bringing it to school one day."

"Not the best choice for show and tell," Amethyst agreed.

"Hey, it wasn't loaded." She shrugged. "Besides, we're too old for show and tell."

"That was a joke."

"Oh." Am cocked her head. "Whatcha gonna do with it?"

"Don't schools teach grammar anymore?" Amethyst groaned. "What I'm going to do with it, young lady, is make sure your grandfather doesn't sell my house out from under me."

"You gonna shoot him?" The girl's eyes went wide with admiration.

"I'm not going to shoot anybody. Call it . . . leverage."

"Oh, I get it. When he comes back with the real estate agent, you're gonna tell him to hightail his butt out of here and never set foot in your house again."

"I was wrong," Amethyst muttered. "You *do* watch TV. Far too much of it, obviously. And didn't Mimsy ever teach you that it's not polite to use the word *butt?*"

Little Am ignored the question. "Hey, I saw a movie like this once. Some old geezer handcuffed himself to a bulldozer and wouldn't let this developer guy level his house. And then some little robot aliens came to help, and they restored the old house all in one night, and so they left it as a . . . I don't know, some kind of historical monument."

"Don't expect aliens to come to the rescue." Amethyst chuckled. "But you're getting the picture."

"And so you're gonna keep me here like . . . like a hostage? Cool."

Amethyst turned to look at the girl, this teenage aberration who bore her name. She wasn't sure exactly why she had wanted Little Am to stay with her. Company, perhaps. Odd company, but company nevertheless.

A sudden surge of tenderness rose up within her, and she reached out a hand to stroke the girl's cheek. "You're no hostage, child. You're my great-granddaughter. My namesake. Maybe I thought that somehow you might understand."

Little Am pulled back, just slightly, from the contact. She shoved her fists into her pockets and looked away. "I put the food away and stacked the dishes and stuff in the sink," she muttered. "Can't believe you don't have a dishwasher."

Amethyst smiled. "I appreciate the help. We'll wash them later. Let's go into the den."

The spark returned to the girl's eyes. "I can't wait to see the look on Grandpa Con's face when he finds out you've locked him out and are standing him off with a shotgun." She shook her head. "This would make a great story. I can just see it on *Dateline* or *60 Minutes*—Amethyst Noble's Last Stand."

Amethyst led her great-granddaughter into the den, where two over-stuffed chairs sat in front of the fireplace with a large ottoman between them. She sank into one of the chairs and hefted her feet onto the ottoman, then motioned for Am to take the other one. With the shotgun across her knees, she scrutinized the girl's face.

"You're interested in *journalism?*" It was hard for Amethyst to believe this girl was interested in anything except looking like a zombie.

"Oh, yeah. That's what I want to do—be a reporter on a newspaper. Or maybe a newscaster on TV. Or maybe write novels, someday when I'm really old—like forty, maybe. Like I said, this would make a great story. Human interest, that sort of thing." She snorted. "Con thinks it's a waste of time."

"And what does Con think you should do with your life?"

Am screwed her face into a scowl. "I dunno. Be a wife and mother, probably. He's such a chauvinist."

"You don't like your grandfather very much."

Am shrugged. "I dunno. It's like he's always so stressed out with his practice, and Mimsy, well, she kind of hovers, if you know what I mean. He was drinking real heavy a while back, only he tried to hide it and thought we didn't know. Uh, oh—"

"It's all right, Am. I knew, too. I was worried about him."

"I thought Mimsy was gonna have a nervous breakdown, I swear I did. You know how hyper she is all the time—and she got even worse. It was pretty scary."

"And now?"

"He's quit the sauce, but things are still pretty stressed. I don't know, something about some investments. I overheard him talking on the phone—yelling, really—at somebody he called Mario."

Amethyst nodded. Her instincts had been accurate. Conrad was in financial trouble, and apparently he had locked onto the idea of selling Noble House as an easy way out.

"And your grandfather doesn't approve of the idea of your being a journalist?"

"He doesn't approve of much." Am grunted. "When he found out I liked writing, he said I'd never be a success at it, and that newspapers are only good to line the birdcage."

"How did you feel about that?"

"I just shut up and quit talking about it. I'll be a senior in high school next year, Grandam. I know what I want to do. I want to go to the university here in Cambridge; they've got a great journalism program. But Con's determined to send me away somewhere, to some Ivy League college, someplace with status. I don't care about status, and my grades aren't good enough, anyway. Besides, I hate the way both he and Mimsy try to run my life and mold me into some kind of model citizen. Maybe they're trying to make up for what Mimsy calls 'my tragic loss,' but I wish they'd just give me some breathing room and let me decide for myself what's best for me."

"I know the feeling."

"Yeah, I bet you do." The girl chuckled.

"Something funny?"

"You are."

"Me?" Amethyst frowned. "What's funny about me?"

"Well, look at you. You're sitting here in a locked house with a hostage and a shotgun, refusing to budge. I figured you were just another weird old lady, you know, frail and senile. But you got guts, Grandam."

"I suppose that was meant as a compliment."

"Guts is good," Am said with a decisive nod. "Most people don't have the guts to stand up for what they believe, or to be true to themselves in spite of what other people think."

"So you don't believe your ancient great-grandmother is crazy for doing this?"

"Crazy? No way." Am pushed her hair out of her eyes and leaned back against the chair. "This is cool," she said. "Way, way cool."

4
Standoff

———◦•◦•◦———

The doorbell rang, and Amethyst struggled to her feet. She glanced over at Little Am, who gave her a broad grin and two thumbs-up.

Amethyst went to the tall, narrow window that looked out onto the porch. "Is that you, Conrad?" she called out.

"Who else would it be? Let us in, Mother. Your ice cream is melting."

"That's too bad, dear."

At an angle through the window, Amethyst could see her son's form as he pressed his face against the grillwork of the door. He had grown portly over the years, his flesh sagging into jowls around his jaw line. Through the wavering antique glass, he looked fuzzy and indistinct, as if someone had smudged his outline with an eraser. Perhaps it was an apt image, she thought. The Conrad she knew, the bright, energetic boy she had loved and raised, had certainly gotten lost—or at least blurred—along the way.

"Am!" Mimsy's shrieking voice came through the screen. "Am! Help your great-grandmother with the door and let us in."

"No can do!" Am yelled back. "Grandam's got the keys."

Amethyst could hear Conrad's heavy footsteps as he jogged around to the back of the house and rattled that door, then tried the one on the side next to the dining room. Panting heavily, he came back to the front.

"What's going on?" he shouted. "Mother, are you hurt? Is something wrong? Let us in!"

Amethyst propped the shotgun against the den wall and went to stand in the foyer. When Con saw her through the iron-grilled door, he smiled and held up a soggy paper bag. "Thank heavens, Mother. I thought you were . . . well, I don't know."

"Dead?" Amethyst put her hands on her hips. "Sorry to disappoint you, sonny boy. I'm perfectly fine."

"Well, open the door. I've got the real estate agent here."

She peered past him to see a tiny little woman with a huge head of hair dyed the color of carrot cake, holding a clipboard and looking anxious.

"This is Portia McMurphy, Mother. The agent I told you about."

"It's a pleasure to meet you," Amethyst said mildly, nodding her head.

"And you, Miss Amethyst," the woman returned, clearing her throat nervously. "I've long anticipated the opportunity to see this wonderful old house, and—"

"Are you going to make us stand out here all afternoon?" Conrad interrupted. "Open the door, Mother."

"I'm afraid not, Con."

"What do you mean, 'I'm afraid not'?" he stammered.

"I mean, I have no intention of letting that woman—or you, for that matter—into this house."

"But she has to see the house if she's going to list it for sale."

"Conrad, I have lived for more than sixty years under the delusion that I did not raise a stupid son. Today you have opened my eyes to the truth. But it's high time you realized that you do not have a stupid *mother*." She looked past him and smiled faintly at the agent. "I do apologize for the inconvenience, Mrs.—McMurphy, is it? I'm afraid you have been brought here under false pretenses. Noble House is not for sale."

The little woman paled and clutched her clipboard to her chest. "Not—not for sale? But Mr. Wainwright said—"

"My son says a lot of things he has no business saying. Now, if you'll excuse me—"

Amethyst turned her back on them, but when she heard Conrad utter a low curse, she wheeled around and glared at him. "What did you say?"

"I said, open the blasted door," he amended, "or I'll break in a window. You don't know what you're doing, Mother."

"I know perfectly well what I'm doing." She reached around the corner and retrieved the shotgun. "No one is coming into this house," she said in a low tone, cradling the shotgun like a baby. "Is that clear?"

Mimsy came up behind him, keening like a banshee, and grabbed his elbow. "Con, she's got a gun!"

"I can see that," he said in a level voice.

"She's gone crazy! And Little Am is in there! What have you done with my child?"

The girl appeared at Amethyst's side. "Chill, Mimsy. I'm here."

"Are you all right, sweetheart?" Mimsy's voice went up several decibels, and Amethyst wondered briefly if that screech might break the window glass without any assistance from Conrad.

"Yeah, sure. I'm great."

"Well, *do* something!" Mimsy squealed. "Get the gun! Unlock the door! Call the police!"

"I don't think so." Am gazed placidly at her grandmother.

"You're both crazy!" Conrad yelled.

"I think I'd better go," the real estate agent said, and bolted for her car.

"See what you've done, Mother? You've embarrassed us—and yourself—in front of a perfect stranger. The whole town will be talking about this by nightfall. Now come on, open up."

"It's one of the blessings of old age," Amethyst murmured to her namesake, "that you don't have to waste time and energy worrying about what anyone else thinks." She turned back to Conrad. "Go home, Con. Take responsibility for your own problems. You're sixty-six years old—it's about time you grew up."

His face flushed a bright red, and his tone turned nasty. "We can do this the easy way, or we can do it the hard way," he hissed. "I've got copies of those papers—"

"Which are completely useless without my signature," she finished. "Get the contracts," she said to Am. "They're still on the dining room table."

Little Am disappeared and returned in a second or two with the sheaf of papers in her hand. Amethyst took them from her, smiled, and with the shotgun still cradled in her elbow, ripped them in half. "Give these back to your grandfather."

Am moved forward and slid the papers through the mail slot. They fell in a scattered heap at Conrad's feet.

"Mimsy is right," Con growled. "You *are* crazy." He scooped up the contracts and tossed the ice cream onto the bricks of the front porch, then headed for his Mercedes with Mimsy on his heels.

"I'll be back," he yelled over his shoulder. "Trust me, you haven't heard the end of this."

Heaving a sigh, Amethyst watched him go. *Trust me,* he said. If only she could.

⸻

As he sped through Cambridge toward the sheriff's office, Conrad began to think about what had just transpired. And the more he thought about it, the more perfect it all seemed. It couldn't have gone better if he had scripted the scene himself. His ninety-three-year-old mother was garrisoned in her house, guarding the door with a shotgun and holding a teenage girl hostage. What judge in his right mind would refuse to declare her incompetent? Then, whether he had a signed power of attorney or not, he would be perfectly justified in settling her at Babbling Brook, or Stony Brook, or whatever the name of that home was. He could sell the house and its furnishings, and—

"Conrad, watch out!" Mimsy squealed as he ran a stoplight and careened the Mercedes around an oncoming pickup truck. "I know you're upset, but—"

"Upset?" he snapped. "Why the blazes would I be upset? My elderly mother has gone off her rocker, the girl we raised as our own daughter is being held against her will, maybe with her life in danger—"

"She didn't *look* like she was being held against her will," Mimsy whined. "She looked like she was—well, *enjoying* it."

"She's seventeen," he snarled. "She doesn't have sense enough to know better."

"My baby!" Mimsy howled. "What's to become of my baby?"

"Mimsy?"

"Yes, Conrad?"

"Shut up."

—•••—

Amethyst heard the siren before she saw the squad car pull into the driveway.

"Sounds like the S.W.A.T. team's here," Am snorted. "I can't believe he's doing this."

"He probably can't believe *I'm* doing this." Amethyst got up, clutched the shotgun to her chest, and went to the door.

"Miss Amethyst?"

"Is that you, Buddy?" She turned back to Am. "It's that nice young Buddy Rice, who just got elected sheriff last fall. He used to mow my lawn for me when he was a boy."

"Yes ma'am. That was a long time ago, wasn't it?" Buddy's voice, quiet and soothing, came through the screen. "Why don't you open the door, Miss Amethyst, so we can have ourselves a little talk."

"I'm afraid not. But don't you worry about us, Buddy; we're perfectly all right. How's that sweet thing you married? And those wonderful little twin babies?"

"Those twin babies started college last fall, Miss Amethyst."

"Do tell!"

"Yes'm. They're both freshmen at Auburn. Ross is majoring in chemistry, and Randy made the cut for the football team. They'll probably redshirt him, but—"

"Can the chitchat and get on with it," Conrad growled from behind Buddy's shoulder.

"Let me do this my way, all right?" Buddy muttered to Con. He turned back and smiled at Amethyst. "Now, Miss Amethyst, there's no call to lock your boy out of the house. And you don't need that shotgun. Just put it down real easy and open the door, and I'll be on my way."

"I'm sorry, Buddy. I can't do that. Are you going to tell me I'm breaking some law by keeping my own doors locked?"

"No ma'am. But I'm afraid it is against the law when you threaten somebody with a gun, and when you're holding a child in there against her will."

Little Am stepped forward. "Who are you calling a child? I'll be eighteen in September, and nobody's holding anybody against their will. Now get lost."

"Am, there's no call to be impolite," Amethyst chided. "Buddy here is only doing his job."

"Well, his job stinks. Who do you think you are, you fascist pig, harassing a little old lady like this?"

"Well, hey there, Little Am," Buddy said smoothly. "You're right grown up, aren't you? I haven't seen you since you were a little bit. Sorry, didn't mean to offend you. But you are under age, and your grandpa here is pretty worried about you."

"My grandpa is worried about himself," Am shot back.

"See what I told you?" Conrad said. "She's gone off her rocker. And now she's brainwashing Little Am."

Buddy held up a hand to silence him. "Miss Amethyst, I have to insist that you open the door."

"You can insist all you like," she answered. "But no one's coming into this house."

Buddy shrugged and turned to Con. "I can't do anything with her."

"Then break a window. Do something! You can see for yourself that she's incompetent."

"I don't think breaking in is the best idea," Buddy hedged. "And I'm afraid only a judge can determine whether or not your mother is competent."

"So what do we do?"

Amethyst leaned forward and strained to hear Buddy's answer.

"Well, if you're determined to go through with this, you'll have to wait until Monday to get an appointment to see the judge. Courthouse, Room 103. Her office opens at nine."

Con coughed and cleared his throat. "Since when does this county have a woman judge?"

"Since old Buford Renfroe keeled over with a heart attack," Buddy answered. "About a year now. Where you been, anyway?"

"I have better things to do than keep up with the local news," Conrad snapped.

"Well, there's nothing else I can do here," Buddy said. "I'll be on my way." He peered through the iron grillwork and waved. "Bye-bye, Miss Amethyst. Nice to see you again."

"Take care, Buddy. Give my regards to Alice and the boys. Next time you come, I'll be more hospitable. Maybe I'll make you some of my special ginger teacakes."

"Yes'm. I'd like that real fine. You be careful, now."

Amethyst could hear Conrad muttering and Mimsy screeching as they followed Buddy back to the squad car. "That's it?" Mimsy squealed. "That's all you're going to do?"

"That's all I *can* do, ma'am. She's well within her rights—she hasn't broken any laws, and she does have the prerogative of keeping her own doors locked. Con, you'll either have to let this go or see the judge on Monday."

Con let out a string of curses and stomped back up the walk.

"I'll be back on Monday," he yelled through the door. "Monday, you hear?"

"You don't have to shout, Conrad. I'm not deaf, you know." Amethyst smiled at Little Am and propped the shotgun against the wall of the den. "And I'm not incompetent, either."

"We'll see what the judge has to say about that."

When he was gone, Amethyst let out a sigh of relief.

"You did it, Grandam!" The girl laughed.

"*We* did it, child."

Little Am grinned sheepishly and looked away. "Hey, do you think it's a good idea to leave the shotgun here?" she asked, pointing to the gun leaning precariously against the wall. "Seems kinda dangerous. If it slipped and fell—"

Amethyst smiled. "Doesn't matter," she said with a chuckle. "It's not loaded."

5

Generation Gap

———◆·◆·◆———

By the time they had put together a dinner of leftovers and birthday cake, Amethyst found that she was exhausted. Miraculously, Little Am volunteered to do the dishes and then, while Amethyst sat in the den with her feet propped up, disappeared upstairs.

Half an hour later, just as she was about to doze off in the chair, Amethyst caught a glimpse of movement at the edge of her vision and looked up to see an angelic apparition descending the stairway in the foyer. She sat up and rubbed her weary eyes. She must be dreaming . . . or hallucinating. The figure floated down the stairs and into the den, settling itself into the chair opposite her own.

"I took a long bath," the apparition said. "Found this nightgown in the dresser upstairs. It's okay for me to borrow it, isn't it?"

Amethyst shook her head to clear her mind. "Little Am?"

The girl shrugged. "Yeah?"

"You look so—so—"

"Go ahead and say it. Different."

"A lot different. You look positively radiant."

It was true. The child had shampooed her hair and pulled it back so that it no longer draped over her face like a shroud. Gone was the pasty makeup and black eyeliner. Every trace of the ghoul had disappeared, except the black fingernail polish. She looked young, fresh . . . and positively lovely. Her brown hair shone with coppery glints in the lamplight, and the wide, dark eyes dominated an unblemished face.

"Don't make a big deal of it, all right?" Little Am said curtly. "I don't have any clothes or makeup here—I had to do something." She twisted in her chair.

"You look cool," Amethyst said with a little laugh. "Way cool."

Little Am giggled, and for the first time all day, she sounded like what she was—a teenage girl on the verge of young womanhood. A surge of pleasure and love rose up in Amethyst's heart. This was her great-granddaughter, her namesake. The zombie had vanished. Maybe there was hope for the girl yet.

"I washed my underwear and left it to dry over the shower rod. Is that okay?"

"Of course. Did you find everything you need?"

"Everything but a blow-dryer. I guess I can do without one for a couple of days." Am flung her legs over the arm of the chair and sighed. "Whew. This has been some day."

"The best birthday I ever had."

"Didja see Con's face when you came out with that shotgun? I thought he was gonna pee in his pants."

"You're really enjoying this, aren't you?"

"You bet." Am nodded vigorously. "It's about time he got what was coming to him."

Amethyst frowned. "You know that's not why I'm doing this, don't you?"

The girl leaned forward. "Not so you can get back at Grandpa Con for what he's trying to do to you?"

"Revenge is a poor motivation for any action," Amethyst sighed. "God doesn't put vengeance into human hands, and when we take it for ourselves—"

"I don't believe in God," Am interrupted.

"You don't?" Here was a twist Amethyst hadn't expected. "Didn't Con and Mimsy teach you about God?"

"Yeah, well, they tried, sort of. Dropped me off at Sunday school when I was little. Went to church once in a while—Christmas and Easter, mostly. But it didn't take."

"What do you mean, it didn't take?"

"All the God stuff. It was so . . . boring. And they sure don't believe it themselves. Con's god is his work, and Mimsy—well, I guess she's her own god. The universe revolves around her, anyway." She shook her head. "If I was God, I sure wouldn't want to listen to that whining all the time."

Amethyst stifled a laugh. The girl had a point about Mimsy's constant shrieking. But her heart sank within her to realize that Little Am was growing up without any spiritual foundation.

"Tell me what you think about God," she ventured.

The girl rolled her eyes, and for a moment the zombie appeared again. Then her expression cleared, and she looked straight into Amethyst's face. "I told you, I don't believe in God. I'm an atheist." She said the word proudly, as if it were a major accomplishment.

"It takes a lot of faith to be an atheist," Amethyst said.

Little Am frowned. "What do you mean?"

"Everybody needs some kind of faith to live by," she answered. "Faith in God, or faith in yourself. Faith in fate or destiny. I'd like to hear about this God you claim not to believe in."

"You mean like what I was taught in Sunday school?"

"Or what you learned from your grandparents. Whatever you'd like to tell me."

Am thought about this for a minute and then said, "Okay. Well, God is this big dude on a throne in heaven—a really, really old geezer. He says he loves everybody, but then you find out it's only the good people he loves—you know, preachers and nuns, people who do right, go to church all the time, that sort of thing. If you get out of line—wham! You're done for. Punished. Headed for hell." She paused. "Con and Mimsy say they believe in God, but they don't much act like it."

"Anything else?"

"Yeah. God hates teenagers."

Amethyst sat back in her chair. "Really?"

"Well, sure. God—if there is a God, and like I said, I don't believe there is—can't stand loud music and stuff. Or sex. Especially sex. God hates sex."

"That's odd. I thought God started the idea in the first place."

The girl gave Amethyst a curious look. "You sure don't talk like you're ninety-three."

"I'll consider that a compliment. Go on."

"I'm done, I guess. Now you're going to try to convince me I'm wrong, right?"

"No."

"You're not?"

"Why should I? If the Almighty really is like the deity you describe, I wouldn't want to believe in him either."

"But you do believe. You said so."

"I believe in God, but not in the god you're describing."

"So what other kind is there?" Just a hint of a sneer crept into the girl's voice.

Amethyst smiled. "A God who is loving and just and fair. A God who doesn't hate teenagers or sex or rock music. A God who cares deeply about the things that affect our lives."

"Like you trying to hang on to this old house?"

"Yes, I think God cares about that. But for me, there's a lot more at stake in this house than just a valuable piece of real estate and a collection of antique furniture. Those are just possessions. What's more important to me is the heritage this house represents—our family's history, and our family's faith."

Little Am leaned forward, and a glimmer of interest illuminated her dark eyes. "You mean like stories of stuff that happened here?" She gazed around into the darkened corners of the room. "Murders and ghosts and stuff like that?"

"Not ghosts, exactly, but stuff like that, yes." Amethyst peered at her great-granddaughter's face. "Didn't Conrad ever tell you about the history of this house?"

"He never told me anything except to turn the music down."

Amethyst laughed. "And you really want to hear this? It's rather a long story."

Little Am gave a shrug. "Hey, it's only eight o'clock. You don't have a TV. The doors are locked, and I'm a hostage. What else am I gonna do?"

"Maybe . . .," Amethyst mused. "Maybe it would help you understand why this house is so important to me—and to you."

"Go for it."

Amethyst took a deep breath and settled back into her chair. "Well, it all began right here, in this very room, almost exactly a hundred and forty years ago. . . ."

Part 2

LIBERTY

"Is not this the fast that I choose:
to loose the bonds of injustice,
to undo the thongs of the yoke,
to let the oppressed go free . . .
To share your bread with the hungry,
and bring the homeless poor into your house . . .
and not to hide yourself from your own kin?"

Isaiah 58:6-7

6
The Physician

April 1853

Silas Noble stood on the stoop of the run-down log cabin and gave an exasperated sigh. This wasn't what he had been led to expect. Not at all.

He reached into his leather bag and pulled out a copy of the letter he had received six weeks ago, shortly after he had completed his medical training in Baltimore:

Rivermont Plantation
Cambridge, Mississippi

To Dr. Silas Noble from Col. Robert Henry Warren, Esq.
5 February 1853

Dear Dr. Noble:
We have learned of you through correspondence with your school in Baltimore, an institution well known, even as far away as Mississippi, for the quality and dedication of its physicians. We understand you are nearing the completion of your medical training, and we wish to invite you to establish your practice in Cambridge County, Mississippi. There are numerous large plantations in the county and outlying areas, families with children, and we are greatly in need of the services of a young and energetic physician. You may not be aware of it, but you come highly recommended, and this county could do with a man of your caliber and commitment.

I understand that you are planning to marry within the year, and I anticipate
you may wish to purchase property in the area. I am prepared to offer you a
modest, fully furnished house with fifty acres of land for a reasonable price. It
was my grandfather's original plantation home, and it sits on an oak knoll on
the south end of my property. I am sure you will find it suitable for your needs.

If you agree to accept our offer, kindly apprise me of your intentions. When you
arrive, I will send a driver to the rail station to convey you to Rivermont and
will provide one of my best nigras as a personal attendant.

Sincerely yours,
Col. Robert H. Warren, Esq.

A furnished house at a reasonable price. Silas groaned inwardly. He
supposed it *was* a reasonable price, all things considered. But it had
been his life savings, money he intended to use to make a home for
Regina so he could send for her and they could be married.

Now his fate had been sealed. He had agreed to the bargain sight
unseen, but instead of the grand old plantation home he had envi-
sioned, he was faced with a log house with a plank floor and holes in
the chinking the size of his fist.

It wasn't that Warren had deceived him, exactly. Clearly these people
in Cambridge County needed a doctor and had been desperate to get
him. But when the carriage had pulled into the long drive that led to
Rivermont, he had entertained visions of his "modest" house being a
smaller version of that magnificent jewel, with its wide front porch and
fluted columns.

Robert Warren was an aristocratic gentleman with soft, pale hands
and an aura of refined elegance. He had greeted Silas at the door and led
him to an opulent parlor decorated in rose and green and cream. Mrs.
Warren, a bustling, effusive woman, had sent one of the house slaves for
coffee and pie and made over him as if he were a long-lost relative.

Silas sat in that parlor, sipping coffee and gazing in wonder at the display of wealth, convinced that he could send for Regina immediately. In
this place, with these lovely people, he could offer her the kind of life

she was accustomed to—a life of graciousness and hospitality, a life of ease and comfort.

Then he got his first glimpse of the house he had purchased from Robert Warren.

It was his, all right. He had the deed in his suitcase. A house and fifty acres. But what a house! One large rectangular room with a stone fireplace, a tiny sleeping alcove, and a rough kitchen with a small wood stove along one wall. With a bit of fixing up, it might be adequate for a bachelor doctor who needed only minimal accommodations. But he couldn't bring a wife here to live. Especially not Regina.

"Needs some work, don't it, Massah?"

Silas turned. The big colored driver, the same one who had picked him up at the depot and delivered him to Rivermont, stood behind him with a wide grin on his face.

"It's not exactly what I had hoped for," Silas admitted.

"Massah Robert's grandpappy, he built this place when he first come. Live here for a while, he did, whilst he was having the big house on the river done up."

"I take it Colonel Warren's grandfather didn't have a wife and children."

The black man threw back his head and laughed. "Naw sir, I reckon not—not when he lived here, anyways. Later on, though, he 'bout filled up that big house. Had hisself ten chillun, and nine of 'em lived. Law, there's prob'ly a dozen Warren grandchillun spread out all over the county, each one of 'em with his own big plantation, just like Massah Robert."

"You're privy to a lot of Mr. Warren's business, aren't you?"

The dark eyes flitted to the ground, but Silas saw the man's barrel chest swell with pride. "Yessir, Massah, I reckon I am. My daddy worked the land for Massah Robert's daddy. Massah Robert, he trusts me—I reckon that's why he lent me to you to help out some. I's born on this plantation—and I 'spects to die here."

Silas scrutinized the big black man. He stood well over six feet, with a solid, square jaw, clear eyes, and massive shoulders. "What's your name?"

"Sir?"

"I asked your name," Silas repeated.

"I's called Booker, Massah."

Silas smiled and scratched his head. "Not Master. *Doctor*. My name is Dr. Silas Noble."

"I knows, Massah."

"Seems to me like you know just about everything, Booker. But please, don't call me Master."

"Yessir, Massah Doctor."

Silas shrugged and gave up. "Where'd you get a name like Booker?"

A gleam of pleasure passed over the slave's countenance. "My mammy, she was a real smart woman. Taught me to read." He paused. "I can write my name and even do a little ciphering. Massah don't mind, so long as I don't raise no fuss about it and don't teach none of the others. Maybe that's another reason he give me to you, you being a educated man and all."

"What do you read, Booker?"

"Only got one book, Massah Doctor. My mammy's Bible."

"And you read that?" Silas gazed at the slave in wonder. Back in Baltimore, Silas had attended church with Regina—an ancient cathedral with high stained-glass windows and a massive pipe organ. He appreciated the ritual and loved the music, but that was about as far as his religion went. The few times in his life he had tried to read the Bible, he had found it mostly incomprehensible.

"Ever' day. Sun don't rise without me putting a few verses in my heart. Seems to me the Lord gots something to say to his chillun, and we's obliged to find out what it is."

"Do you understand it?"

"I understand enough to get by. Some of the words is real hard, but that don't matter. I get the hope, and that's what counts." Booker scratched his head and peered at Silas. "You a Christian man, Massah?"

Silas felt an uncomfortable chill run up his spine, and he fidgeted. "I guess I am, Booker. I try to be a good man, to do what's right."

A strange expression passed over the black man's face, and he averted his eyes. "Mmm-hmm."

For a brief instant Silas felt like one of the cadavers he had examined in medical school—cut open, with his innards exposed to scrutiny. He didn't like the feeling one bit. He cleared his throat and changed the subject. "So, I guess we'd better get my belongings into the house and clean it up a bit."

Booker didn't move. He just stood there, staring at Silas and jabbing the toe of his boot into the dirt. Finally he asked, "You really a doctor?"

"Yes, Booker, I am. That's why I came here, to serve as a physician to Colonel Warren's family and the other plantation families in the area." He shook his head. "I had planned to send back east for my fiancée as soon as I got settled. But I guess the wedding will have to be postponed. I certainly can't expect her to live here."

Booker's expression brightened, as if he had just been struck by an idea. But he kept silent.

"What is it?"

"Nothing, Massah."

"Are you sure?"

"Well, I's just thinking, and—"

"And what?"

"You sure you a doctor? You seem right young—meaning no offense, Massah—"

Silas laughed, relieved to be back on more comfortable ground. "None taken. Yes, I'm young—I'm twenty-five. But I'm sure I am a doctor. Very sure, Booker."

The black man's expression went grave. "My woman, Celie, she expecting a baby in a coupla months." He paused and took a deep breath. "She done had two babies, and both of 'em died. One of 'em was strangled by the cord."

"I'm sorry to hear that, Booker. If I can be of any help—"

Booker shrugged. "Massah, he pay for a doctor when a big buck gets hurt, so's not to lose a good field hand. But he don't pay for no nigra babies to be born. If Middie can't do it, well, the babies just go on and die."

"Who's Middie?"

"She's the one who helps with the birthin'."

Silas chuckled. "Let me guess. She got her name because she's a midwife."

Booker shook his head and smiled faintly. "Naw. Her name's Midnight, cause she real dark, and cause that's when babies seem to come around here."

Silas stared at the big black man, and his mind turned over all the changes in his life. Two weeks ago, he was in Baltimore, in the hub of city life, celebrating his completion of his medical training, making plans with his fiancée for their wedding. Now he was standing in the middle of an oak grove on the porch of a log cabin, having a conversation with a slave about a midwife named Midnight. What next?

"So I's thinking," Booker said, bringing Silas back to the present, "maybe we could strike us a deal."

"A deal? What kind of deal?"

"When Celie's time comes, you help her out. I can't pay, 'course, but I got something you need more'n money."

Silas found himself intrigued. "What's that?"

The Negro pointed to his head with his forefinger. "Know-how. You take care of my woman, and I'll build you a house. A real house. Not as fancy as Massah Warren's Rivermont, but a fine house, sound and sturdy, with big rooms and a curved stairway and a nice wide front porch for rockin'."

Silas's heart leaped within him. "You can do that?"

"'Course I can. Look." Booker strode across the covered porch of the cabin and out into the yard, pacing off a huge rectangle. "We start with the cabin, and build on from there. The porch where you are can be the front entryway. Over here"—he indicated the area where he stood— "can be a parlor, and here a bedroom, and then three more rooms upstairs. We'll do it up real nice for your lady. White clapboard and tall columns and green shutters."

As Booker talked, the house took form in Silas's mind. A glorious two-story home, sparkling in the spring sunlight, surrounded by oak trees and overlooking acres of rolling land. His land. His house. The place he and Regina would call home.

Booker went back to the carriage and started unloading Silas's trunks. "We got us a deal, Massah Doctor?" he asked over his shoulder as he set one of the trunks down on the porch.

"A deal." Silas extended his hand to seal the bargain with a handshake, but Booker stood there, arms at his sides, staring at the outstretched hand with wide eyes and looking as if he had just been snake bit.

"Oh, I—well—" Silas dropped his hand and felt his face flush. Of course. A white man didn't shake hands with a slave, even to confirm a bargain. "Sorry."

When he recovered from his faux pas, Silas followed Booker back to the carriage. "But you can't do this all yourself," he protested.

"No, sir. But lots of it I can do on my own, when I'm not drivin' you round or helping with your doctoring. And when I get to needing help, there's plenty of nigras on this here plantation who'd 'preciate a real doctor from time to time." Booker looked at him pointedly. "We needs you, too, Massah Doctor."

"Of course." Silas stood there awkwardly for a minute or two. When he was just a boy, his best friend, Gerald, a lad from the poorer quarter of Baltimore, took sick and needed an operation. Gerald's parents couldn't afford the hospital fees, but a benevolent doctor performed the surgery without compensation and saved Gerald's life. Silas remembered with startling clarity how he had begged for his friend to live, and how he had promised God—or fate, or whoever—that he would work hard to become a doctor like that, so that he would be able to help people who could not help themselves.

Against his father's wishes—and against Regina's, if truth be told—Silas had turned down the opportunity to join his father's law firm, where he would have been ushered into a life of wealth and privilege among the Baltimore elite. It had been a hard-fought battle, convincing Regina that she would not have to live in destitution. When the invitation had come for him to begin a practice among the plantation owners of Cambridge, he had spent countless hours painting for her a scenario of gracious Southern living in the company of educated and genteel folk. At last she had given in, kissed him, and promised that as soon as he was settled, she would join him. Silas suspected that Regina considered Mississippi as half-swamp, half-wild Indian territory, but once she got here, she would see. It would be a different kind of life from Baltimore society, but she would adjust.

If he managed to get this log cabin turned into a livable home, that is.

Suddenly a surge of remorse washed over Silas. What was happening to him? What was he thinking? Against formidable opposition, he had made good on his promise and begun his medical training. He had given up a life of luxury for his dream of becoming a doctor. And now, not six weeks into his career, was he already succumbing to a vision of ease and comfort with the beautiful Regina at his side?

The memory of the physician who had saved Gerald's life churned uncomfortably in Silas's mind, and his conscience began to nag at him. Was he really going to barter his services as a physician for the sake of a house? This wasn't what his calling as a doctor was all about.

"Booker?" he said softly to the Negro's back.

"Yessir?"

"I feel I have to tell you—I'm obligated by my oath as a physician to help anyone who is in need of medical attention. You and your . . . your people don't have to trade extra work for my services. I'll help you whether you build me a house or not."

There. It was out, and Silas felt better, even as his vision of the fine white house and Regina at his side began to fade into oblivion.

Booker turned to him, and his dark face brightened in a wide grin. "I reckon I knows that, Massah Doctor. But I 'preciate you telling me, truly I do."

"When we're done here, you can drive me over to take a look at Celie."

"Yessir. And after supper, I'll get some stakes in the ground." Booker gave a determined nod. "We gonna start on this house first thing tomorrow morning."

7
Celie

———◆◆◆◆———

As soon as Silas stepped into the dimly lit cabin, he felt a wave of shame crash over him. His own "modest house," as Colonel Warren had described it, was not what he had been accustomed to in high-society Baltimore, but neither was it a hovel. Booker's cabin was one sparse room with a dirt floor, mud chinking, and a fireplace made of river rock. In one corner lay a sleeping mat covered by a thin, moth-eaten gray blanket, and the only real furnishings were a rough-hewn table topped by an oil lamp, and two backless stools. On the far wall, under a single window, a sagging wooden counter held a rusted tin sink with a small pump.

Silas took in the details with a single glance, and his heart plummeted like a lead weight at the sight of such crushing poverty. His mind flashed to the opulence of Rivermont, the way Warren and his family lived, with their mahogany furniture and imported hand-loomed rugs. How could a man with any soul at all allow people to live this way? And then he remembered: Warren, like most other plantation owners, did not consider "his nigras" to be human. They were livestock, needing only the most basic accommodations. Warren cared for his slaves the way he cared for his horses and cattle. A bed of hay, a roof over their heads, some feed in the manger, and they would survive another day to work his cotton and bring in his profits.

Silas shuddered at the thought. Still, the cabin was clean, and even amid the destitution, he could sense a certain level of pride in the place. The floor had been swept smooth, the tabletop scrubbed, and flour-sack curtains at the window fluttered in the evening breeze.

At the table, a young woman sat snapping peas and tossing them into a black kettle. When she saw the men, she jumped to her feet, and the pea strings that filled her apron scattered to the floor.

"Oh! I's—I's sorry, Massah!" She tried to kneel and clean up the mess, but her swelling midsection made the task nearly impossible.

Booker took two steps and was at her side. "It's all right, Celie," he crooned in a low voice. "I'll get it." In one swift motion he scooped up the pea strings in his massive hands and dumped them into the sink. "This is Massah Robert's new doctor," he explained as he turned back to her. "Massah Doctor, this is my woman, Celie."

Silas took a step forward. "It's a pleasure to meet you, Celie."

The girl shrank away from him and cowered at Booker's side. Except for the unborn baby that jutted out like a watermelon under her ragged shift, she was small and thin, with skin the color of molasses and huge dark eyes.

"Don't be afraid, honey," Booker whispered. "Massah Doctor's a good man. He's come to help with the baby."

She laid a protective hand over her abdomen and peered at Silas. "My baby?"

Her voice, when she spoke, was high and soft, a tinkling sound that reminded Silas of the wind harp his mother had hung outside his bed-room window when he was a child. The memory was a pleasant one, and he smiled. "That's right, Celie. Booker's told me about the babies you've lost. If you'll allow me, I'll see what I can do to make sure this one is born healthy."

She lowered her eyes. "We can't pay no doctor, Massah," she muttered.

"I know. Booker and I have that all worked out, haven't we, Booker?"

Booker nodded. "Yessuh, we done got that agreed on." He pushed Celie gently in Silas's direction. "Go on, girl. He won't bite."

Celie let out a shy laugh and moved closer to Silas. "What I needs to do?" she asked.

"Just let me examine you. It won't hurt. And Booker will be right here the whole time."

Celie nodded, and at his instruction lay down on the sleeping mat. Silas knelt beside her, and she flinched when his stethoscope touched her belly.

"Sorry." Silas removed the stethoscope and warmed it between his hands, then listened for the baby's heartbeat. "Sounds strong. That's a good sign," he said when he was finished. "But you're too thin, Celie. You're eating for two, remember?"

"Yessuh. I try to do better."

Booker helped her up from the mat, ushered her over to the table, and stood behind her with his hands on her narrow shoulders.

Silas sat in the other chair. "What do you do, Celie?"

"Sir?"

"What's your job? What kind of work do you do for Colonel Warren?"

"I works in the kitchen," she answered proudly. "I's a good cook—Massah Warren, he says so." A smile lit her face for the first time—a bright flash of white against that smooth brown skin.

Silas grinned in return. "I'll bet you are. But you really should be doing something less taxing, some job where you don't have to be on your feet all day. Doesn't all that lifting and standing hurt your back?"

Celie slanted a glance up toward Booker, and he nodded as if to say, *Tell him the truth.* She turned back to Silas. "Well, yessuh, I does get terrible pains in my back and legs. I can't hardly sleep some nights." She paused. "But I don't serve at the Massah's table. Least that way I get off my feet before dark."

"I'll talk to Colonel Warren about it, see if I can't get you some lighter duty until the baby is born."

A look passed between Booker and Celie, something Silas didn't understand. But a twist in his gut told him that he might be treading on dangerous ground.

"Naw, Massah Doctor, you don't have to do that," Booker protested. "We be fine."

"Booker," Silas countered, "we made an agreement, didn't we? You do your job, and I'll do mine. And my job, as a doctor, is to see to it that my prettiest patient is well taken care of."

Celie grinned shyly and ducked her head at the compliment, and Silas felt a rush of pleasure in the awareness that he had won her over.

"Massah Doctor," she said at last, "if you's a mind to, we'd be pleased for you to share our supper. I got a mess of real nice pole beans, and cornbread, too."

Silas looked into Booker's eyes and saw an affirmation of his own instinct: it had taken a monumental effort and an enormous risk for this young Negro girl to invite a white doctor to supper. He wondered briefly if they had enough for three, then pushed from his mind the temptation to refuse. "Thank you," he said at last. "I'd be pleased to join you."

After supper, Booker drove Silas up to the big house. They rode in silence for a while as Silas digested his dinner of beans and potatoes and cornbread and thought about his new patient. It was, he had to admit, the best supper he had enjoyed in ages. Celie's cornbread could lift a man right to heaven. And despite his initial misgivings, there had been plenty to go around.

But he couldn't still his doubts about the baby. He hadn't said anything, because he couldn't be certain, but if she had already lost two babies, there was a good chance that this one might die, too. He wondered if the one strangled by its own umbilical cord had been a breech birth. And what if this one was breech, too? It was possible the infant would turn when Celie went into labor, but if it didn't, she could be in for a difficult birth. Well, he would just have to ford that stream when he came to it. He couldn't do anything about it—except pray.

Like a sudden splash of icy water, the thought startled Silas. The last time he remembered praying was as a child, when his little friend Gerald was sick and needed surgery. In general, Silas wasn't a praying man, and rarely thought about God. But here at Rivermont Plantation, the concept of a Divine Being seemed to be cropping up on a regular basis. Maybe it was Booker's influence—the man seemed to have a simple and genuine faith in the Almighty, and it was a good bet *he* would be praying for the safe delivery of his child.

"Booker," he ventured, his voice sounding loud against the silence of the early evening, "how long have you and Celie been married?"

Booker gave him a curious look, then laughed out loud. "Massah Doctor, where you get such ideas? Celie and me, we jumped the broom 'bout six years ago, I reckon. In our minds that's as good in the Lord's eyes as gettin' married all legal-like, like the white folks do. But no Massah's gonna allow his slaves to marry."

Silas gaped at him. "Why on earth not?"

Again Booker laughed. "That'd be like marrying the Massah's prize stallion, Lightning, to his best mare. Or havin' a legal ceremony for the bulls and the cows." He paused, and Silas saw an expression of barely controlled fury pass over his face. "Nigras ain't *human,* Massah Doctor, leastways not in the white folks' eyes. We's livestock, just like that stallion and that bull."

Silas shook his head. This was not news to him, of course—he had thought about it just this evening, when he saw for himself the conditions in which the slaves lived. But he had never considered the ramifications where marriage and families were concerned.

"So at any time, Colonel Warren could sell either you or Celie—or your children—to someone else?"

"Yessuh, he *could.* I don't think he *will*—Massah Robert is a pretty good owner in that way. He don't often break up families. But plenty of other owners do it all the time—specially if they want to use a big strong buck to breed new workers."

Silas felt bile rise in his throat, and he swallowed it down. Suddenly he wondered if he had made a huge mistake, coming here to Rivermont Plantation. He'd had no other offers, of course, but in time, and with his family's connections, he probably could have found a position in Baltimore. Maybe even a position that would have brought him status and some level of financial security. But here he was, in Mississippi, and at the moment he couldn't think of a single good reason why.

Booker reined the horses to a stop in front of the huge double doors of Rivermont. "You want me to wait, Massah Doctor?" He squinted at the sky. "I prob'ly got near an hour of light left. I could start steppin' off that addition for you."

"All right. Pick me up in an hour—or whenever you're done. If I get finished sooner, I'll start walking back. It's a nice evening for a stroll."

"Yessuh." Booker waited until Silas got down, then turned the horses around and started back toward the oak grove.

Silas watched the big Negro drive away, and as the buckboard receded into the distance, he felt an unaccountable stab of loss. He turned toward the big house and stepped up onto the wide front porch, and suddenly the difference struck him like a blow. In Booker's cabin, sharing a simple meal, Silas had felt comfortable, at home, almost as if he were . . . with *friends*. Here, on Robert Warren's massive veranda, he felt like an interloper. An employee whose presence might or might not be welcomed.

But welcome or not, he had a job to do. He lifted the enormous brass door knocker and let it fall.

———•·•·•———

At the other end of the massive expanse of dining room table, Robert Warren and his wife, Olivia, looked like miniatures, little dressed-up Southern dolls at a tea party. Silas craned his neck to see around the floral arrangement. At this distance, he'd have to shout to be heard.

Much to his surprise, he had been invited to stay for dinner, but after Celie's succulent beans and melt-in-your-mouth cornbread, the lavish fare offered at Colonel Warren's table, served by a slave in a white jacket and gloves, seemed bland and unappetizing. Out of politeness, he had managed a few bites of the *boeuf bourguignon* and tried a little of the potatoes au gratin, but he simply could not manage a single spoonful of the rich, cognac-laced flaming dessert. Did they eat this way every night? If so, that could explain Olivia Warren's ample figure, which even now seemed to be straining against her well-corseted bodice.

"Colonel Warren," he called at last, "I need to talk to you about something. May I come down to that end of the table?"

Warren peered around the centerpiece. "What's that, Noble? Something wrong at the stable?"

This is ridiculous, Silas thought. He got up and stalked to the other end of the dining room and positioned himself in the chair at Robert Warren's left. Olivia Warren fanned herself as if she might faint at this breach of etiquette, but Warren patted her hand. "It's all right, dear." He turned back to Silas. "You needed to speak to me, Doctor?"

"Yes, if you don't mind discussing business at dinner. Otherwise I can come back tomorrow."

Warren waved a manicured hand. "Go on."

"It's about one of the slaves," Silas began.

"Booker giving you trouble? If he's getting uppity, just tell me. I'll have him lashed, and he'll be back in the fields by morning. He's been with me a long time, but he's not above a little discipline if—"

"No sir, Colonel. Booker's just fine. I need to talk to you about his—" The word *wife* was on the tip of Silas's tongue, and he bit it back. "His woman. Celie."

"Ah, you've met Celie. Fine girl. Great cook." Warren patted his non-existent belly, and an ancient memory flashed through Silas's mind—a picture book he had owned as a boy, showing Jack Sprat, who could eat no fat, and his wife, who could eat no lean.

He suppressed a smile and avoided looking in Olivia Warren's direction. "Yes, Celie is a delightful young woman. I assume you know she's pregnant?"

Olivia Warren gasped, fanned frantically, and reached for her water glass.

"Forgive me, Mrs. Warren. I mean, she is with child."

"Of course," Warren answered. "It's rather obvious." He shook his head. "She's such a pretty young thing—I considered moving her into the house to serve at my table. But given her condition, I didn't think it would be appropriate." He glanced at his wife and then winked in Silas's direction. "Can't risk offending the ladies, you know."

Silas took a deep breath and pressed on. "I examined her this afternoon, and although her child seems healthy, she has already lost two babies. I wonder—" He paused, trying to choose his words carefully. "I wonder if it might be possible to give her some lighter work until after the baby is born—something, perhaps, where she doesn't have to be on her feet all day."

When Silas glanced up, he found Warren staring at him as if he had just grown two heads. "Excuse me?"

Silas frowned. Had he not been clear in his request? "It's hard on her, having to work in the kitchen," he repeated. "I'll be there for the delivery, but I'd hate for her to lose another child."

Mrs. Warren fanned harder, and all the blood drained from her face. She looked as if she might be about to faint.

"Let me get this straight. You *examined* her?"

"Well, yes—"

"And you intend to deliver her baby?"

"I, uh—"

"And you want me to let her sit around with her feet on a pillow, eating chocolates and sipping mint juleps until she finally gets around to dropping the little pickaninny?"

Silas fought to control his temper. "I just thought—"

"No, you didn't." Warren cut him off with a snarl. "You didn't think at all. You come down here from your high-society Baltimore culture and want to start telling me how to deal with my own *property*? Who hired you in the first place?"

"You did, sir."

"And what was our agreement?"

"That I would, ah, provide medical services to your family and the other plantation families in the county, and—"

"Exactly! Plantation families. *White* families. Until the nigras are paying your bills, *Doctor* Noble, you're working for me, not for them. This is business, not charity. You understand? *Business!*"

Something in the way Warren emphasized the word *business* triggered an idea in Silas's imagination, and he latched onto it. "Yes sir, I *do* understand business. In fact, that's exactly what this is—a business arrangement."

The colonel sat back in his chair and crossed his arms over his chest. "You want to explain that, son?"

Silas nodded and tempered his voice. "Well, sir, you see, I have a fiancée back in Baltimore—a lovely young woman named Regina. She comes from a very fine family, and—"

Suddenly Olivia came to life, her hands fluttering and her eyes shining. "Oh, Robert, won't that be wonderful! To have another *lady* on the place. A real lady! Right here at Rivermont! Why, we can plan teas and parties and—"

Warren smiled indulgently and pushed a wayward curl away from his wife's temple. "Yes, dear. Now let's just let the young man finish, shall we?"

"So," Silas continued, "when I saw the house I had purchased, I knew—" He stopped mid-sentence. He needed to phrase this just right, so as not to offend the Warrens while still getting his point across. "I thought I might like to add on to the house. The oak grove is such a magnificent location, and I could just envision a beautiful two-story on the top of that hill—a place Regina and I could call home. A house that would, well, be in keeping with her station in society."

"Sounds like a good idea to me," Warren commented.

"It's perfect!" said Olivia. "Absolutely perfect! And having a lady here would be just—"

"Yes, dear." Warren raised an eyebrow and motioned for Silas to continue.

"Anyway, Booker indicated to me that he and some of the other slaves would be glad to help me out . . . in exchange for occasional medical services."

"Ah. A business arrangement."

"Exactly. And I want you to understand, Colonel Warren, that this would be entirely separate from the slaves' other duties. They'll work after hours. And I—I'll cover all the costs of materials myself." The truth was, Silas didn't know how he would manage to pay for the materials on his salary. But somehow he was determined to make it work.

Warren looked over at his wife, who was nudging him in the ribs and rolling her eyes at him. "Nonsense," he said amicably. "Olivia is so excited about the prospect of having another lady around the place. Just get Booker to tell you what he'll need, and order everything from Avery's Lumber Mill." He held out his hand and shook Silas's vigorously. "Didn't think a doctor would have that kind of business sense. I'm proud of you, son." He clapped Silas on the back. "Just remember that the plantation owners and their needs come first."

"Don't worry. I won't forget who hired me."

"That's good to hear. And one other thing, Noble."

"Yes sir?"

"I know you're not from these parts, so I can give you a little leeway on account of not being familiar with our ways. But be wary of getting too involved with the nigras. They're like children or hunting dogs. They don't know what's best for them. They'll want a lot of attention, but what they need is a strong hand of discipline to keep 'em in their place. Let down that discipline, and you've got chaos. You gotta let 'em know who's boss, all right?"

Silas almost choked on his response. "All right, Colonel Warren."

"That's a good lad. Now, be off with you. I know you want to get settled in."

———•—•••—•———

Booker drove back toward Silas's cabin without a word.

"Don't you want to know what happened?" Silas asked after a while. He didn't really want to tell Booker, but he figured he owed him that much.

"Guess I pretty much know, since you ain't said a word. Massah don't have no intention of giving Celie lighter work, does he?"

Silas shook his head sadly. "I don't think so. But I did try."

"And I appreciate it, Massah Doctor. I also appreciate you looking after Celie."

"I'm glad to do it, Booker. I think everything will be all right. We'll just have to hope for the best."

"And pray," Booker added quietly.

"Yes, that, too."

Booker pulled to a stop in front of Silas's cabin. "You need anything else, Massah Doctor?"

"Not tonight. Midmorning I thought we might go into town and see about getting some lumber and supplies for the house."

"See you in the mornin' then. Night, Massah Doctor."

"Good night, Booker."

For an hour after Booker left, Silas labored over a letter to Regina. He tried to tell her about the house Booker was going to build, but all he could think about was Celie, due this summer and undoubtedly worried. One thing he knew for certain—no matter what Robert Warren believed, Celie was not just another mare about to foal, nor was Booker just a breeding sire. They were human beings, with human emotions and concerns, human passions and desires.

Silas laid aside the letter to Regina and put his head down on his arms. Something inside nagged at him, telling him that he was here for a reason. It felt true, but he wasn't sure he could make his mind believe it.

After all, he was only one man. What difference could one man possibly make?

8

The Abolitionist

June 1853

Silas awoke exhausted, vaguely aware that for hours he had been disturbed by the sounds of voices and hammering and Booker's booming instructions, telling people to hush so as not to wake Massah Doctor. He pulled on his trousers, snapped the suspenders over his shoulders, and stepped out onto the front stoop of the cabin.

"Mornin', Massah Doctor!" Booker grinned at him and laid down the two-by-four he held in his massive paw. "She's comin' right along, ain't she?"

Silas let his gaze wander over the clearing around his cabin. It looked for all the world like a Pennsylvania barn-raising, only with black faces instead of white ones, and ragged slave clothing rather than the stark dress of the Amish.

"What are all these people doing here, Booker? It's well past dawn—why aren't they in the fields?"

Booker threw back his head and gave a hearty laugh. "Why, Massah Doctor, it's Sunday! Even black folks don't chop cotton on Sunday."

Silas shook his head. The truth was, he had been working so hard and keeping such late hours that he had trouble remembering what day it was. Just yesterday he had spent seven hours traveling around to four plantations in the area to treat colds and lance boils and doctor colicky babies. And then after supper he had been in the slave cabins until nearly midnight. No wonder he couldn't get his days straight.

"But you *are* working," Silas protested.

"Yessuh. I reckon we is. But this here's a different kind of work. We's workin', but we's also worshipin'. Fact is, we's thanking the good Lord for sending you to us."

From somewhere behind the house, a deep baritone voice began singing, and other voices joined in: *"Soon I will be done with the troubles of the world. . . . Goin' home to live with God."*

"Come see, Massah Doctor, what we done."

Silas turned back into the cabin, pulled on his boots, and followed Booker.

"See," the big slave said proudly when they had gone ten paces out and turned around. "Over there's the front entrance, parlor, and a nice big bedroom. Upstairs, three more bedrooms, and above that, the attic."

Silas took in a breath. He *could* see it, the framing rising high above his head. A fine brick chimney going up on the right. A gabled roof, not yet closed in but clearly visible. And in the front, six massive square columns and what looked to be a small second-story porch.

"Booker, I can hardly believe my eyes. You're really doing a wonderful job."

Booker's chest swelled, and he put his big hands on his hips and grinned. "I done told you, Massah Doctor. Come fall, you'll have yourself a house fit for your fine Baltimore lady."

An unaccountable twist of dread knotted Silas's gut for a moment, then released. Surely Regina would be pleased with such a house. Surely she would get along with Olivia Warren, find a place for herself among the society of plantation owners. He would send for her, they would be married, and his dreams would be fulfilled.

"Morning, Doctah Silas." Celie's soft voice captured his attention, and he looked down. She stood there, smiling up at him, holding out a plate of food and a tin cup filled with steaming coffee. "Thought you might like some breakfast."

Silas positioned himself on a tree stump and took her offering. Fried ham and grits as thick as mashed potatoes, with something that looked like flat cornbread.

"Hoecakes," she explained. "I made 'em myself, but"—she laughed and ducked her head—"in a skillet, not on the flat of a hoe." She pointed toward an open fire, where a dozen or more slave women gathered around, cooking and gossiping.

"Lily's got a real bad infection in her foot," Celie told him as he ate. "Cut herself chopping cotton. Do you s'pose—"

Silas nodded. "I'll take a look at it as soon as I finish." He waved the tin fork at her. "This is very good, Celie. I didn't know how hungry I was." He pointed to a stump a few feet away. "Sit down. I don't want you on your feet any more than necessary."

"Yessuh." She lowered herself onto the stump with a sigh.

"You feeling all right?"

"I reckon so, sir. Baby's kickin' all the time."

"It shouldn't be long now."

Celie placed a hand on her stomach, and her eyes took on a faraway expression. "We been prayin' ever' day that he'd come through healthy and strong."

"He?" Silas grinned. "You know it's going to be a boy?"

"I just got a feelin'. Middie hung a ring on a thread over me, and she says it's a boy."

"Middie's going to help with the delivery, right?"

"Yessuh. And Pearl, too."

Silas frowned. He didn't remember meeting any slave by that name. "Who's Pearl?"

Celie pointed. "That's Pearl. Over next to the fire, talkin' to Middie."

Silas's eyes followed the direction of her finger. Midnight, the big black slave woman, stood with her back to him, her hands waving animatedly as she carried on a conversation with someone Silas couldn't see. He got up and handed his empty plate and cup back to Celie. "I'll get my bag and go tend to Lily," he said. "And maybe I should meet this Pearl before your time comes."

Lily's foot was bad, but not as bad as it could have been without treatment. Some of the slaves, Celie included, had watched him intently when he treated cuts and lacerations, and already they knew how to clean a wound and bind it to reduce inflammation. Apparently one of them—maybe even Celie herself—had washed Lily's wound and kept a clean covering on it.

Lily was a fieldworker, and she was tough. She never flinched when he poured alcohol into the deep gash. The skin around the angry wound was dark and swollen, infected, no doubt, by the dirt on the hoe that had caused the lesion. Whoever had treated her initially had probably saved her from losing the foot to gangrene.

"When did this happen, Lily?" he asked as he put salve on the cut and bandaged it.

"Couple, three days ago. I don't rightly remember."

"Did you clean and bandage it yourself? Because, you know, you could have lost this foot if you'd let it go without treatment."

"Naw suh, I didn't do it. I's hurtin' too much at the time. Bled real bad, it did. But Pearl stopped the bleedin' and took care of it for me."

Pearl again, Silas thought. Who was this woman who was going through the slave camp practicing medicine without a license? She obviously knew the rudiments of medical treatment, knew how to make a pressure bandage and clean a wound properly. And according to Celie, she knew a thing or two about midwifing as well. Pearl, whoever she was, must be an exceptional slave. He was more determined than ever to meet her. Maybe with some additional training, she could serve as a nurse when he wasn't available, and as an assistant when he was.

"I think that'll do it, Lily," he said as he finished tying the bandage. "Stay off of it for today, and keep it propped up. You have to go back to the fields tomorrow morning?"

"Yessuh. Massah Robert, he don't take to slaves shirkin' their duty."

"I'll see what I can do about that." Even as he said the words, Silas remembered his futile attempt to keep Celie out of the kitchen. Lily was right—Robert Warren didn't have much patience for sick or injured Negroes. He wanted everybody working, giving him his money's worth, keeping Rivermont Plantation the richest, most profitable industry in the county.

Silas sighed and packed up his bag. "I'll check on you tonight. Meanwhile, don't go running around on that foot."

By the time Silas was finished with Lily, the sun was almost directly overhead, and Midnight was standing over the fire, stirring a pot of stew for the men's dinner. He walked up beside her and set his medical bag on the ground.

"Smells good, Middie," he commented, inhaling a deep whiff of the savory steam.

She turned and grinned at him, her round face dominated by a wide mouth full of large white teeth. "Well, Massah Doctor! How you be this lovely spring day?"

"Just fine, Middie. Even better if I can get my hands on a bowl of that stew." He reached for the spoon, and she playfully slapped his hand away.

"Now, don't you go messin' in my stew," she reprimanded with a robust laugh. "If you want some, I reckon you'll have to wait like ever-body else."

"I reckon I will, Middie," he retorted, "especially with you guarding the pot."

"Booker's doin' a right nice job on your house," she observed. "Guess it won't be long 'fore you can bring that fine lady of yours down here and get yourself hitched."

Silas shook his head and chuckled. "Does everybody on this planta-tion know my personal business?"

"Why, sure, honey. Ain't no secrets here. We's family."

An unexpected rush of pleasure surged through Silas at her words. *Family.* And he felt it, too—that inexplicable sense of connection that binds people together, even people who seem to have no common ground. It had only been three months since he had first set foot on Rivermont soil and met Booker for the first time. Now he was surrounded by people who cared for him. People who welcomed the sight of him. People who—could he think it without presumption?—needed him.

And the truth was, he needed them, too.

Robert Warren had warned him about getting too involved with the slaves. They were like children, Warren claimed, wanting their own way and needing a firm hand of discipline to keep them in their place. But Silas had experienced nothing of the kind. He had found them gentle and compassionate, hard-working and humble. And among them he had experienced a taste of something else, something totally unfamiliar to him: faith.

How these people could have faith, Silas couldn't imagine. They were enslaved, worked practically to death, treated like farm animals, and yet they looked beyond the difficulties of this life to the promise of the next. He had never once heard any of them blame God for their captivity. Instead, they identified with the oppressed people in what they called the Good Book—with the Israelites, whom the Lord liberated from servitude to the Pharaoh of Egypt, with Daniel in the lion's den, and the three children in the fiery furnace. According to the Good Book, the Lord had miraculously delivered those ancient believers, so the time must be coming when God would set the captives free on plantations all across the South.

The faith and hope of Booker and his people stirred conflicting emotions in Silas's heart. On the one hand, he desperately wanted to trust in a God who would liberate the oppressed. In the past few months he had looked into the eyes of those forced into slavery, touched them with his own hands. He had lived among them, bound up their wounds, comforted them in sickness, and wept with them in death. At times he almost found himself agreeing with their deep faith, believing that God loved them and wouldn't leave them in bondage forever.

But Warren had given him a different perspective on the Almighty's view of slavery, quoting verses from the very same Bible about slaves being faithful to their masters and content with their lot in life. Silas could barely tolerate Robert Warren's smug presence anymore or listen to his superior attitudes when he spoke about "my nigras." Yet every time Silas went to the big house, he came away confused and frustrated. Who was right about God—the slaves, who trusted that the Lord loved them and would set them free, or the slave owners, who justified their tyranny over the Negroes with well-selected scriptures?

Silas didn't know. And until he knew, he couldn't take the risk of accepting a God who might turn out to be as self-righteous and despotic as Colonel Robert Henry Warren, Esquire.

"We's gonna have a service after dinner," Middie said. "You want to join us, you's welcome. Shepherd's gonna preach, and there'll be some real good singin'."

"Thanks, Middie," Silas answered absently. "I'll think about it. But I've got something to do first." He picked up his medical bag. "A while ago, you were talking to somebody called Pearl. Celie says she's going to help with the birthing, and I need to talk to her."

Middie let out a huge sigh, and her broad face filled with an expression of sheer admiration. "That Pearl—she's some girl, I tell you. You right, Massah Doctor, it's high time you met her." She jerked her head in the direction of the cabin. "I think she's 'round back, talking to Booker and Celie."

Silas made his way around the workers, marveling at the design of his new house. In the back, more framing jutted out from the original cabin, forming a large dining room and attached kitchen. Next to what would eventually be a back porch, Booker stood with Celie, blocking Silas's view of the third person.

He approached, and Booker turned. "Massah Doctor! Just the man I's lookin' for. This here is Pearl—she's the one going to help you and Middie with Celie's deliverin'."

Silas's gaze locked onto the face, and for a moment he couldn't breathe, couldn't speak.

"Doctor Noble," the young woman said, coming toward him and extending her hand. "I've heard so much about you; it's a pleasure to finally meet you. I'm Pearl Avery."

She shook his hand with a firm, solid grasp, not the dead-fish finger-grip of most Southern belles. This was a woman confident in her own abilities, sure of herself.

And she was white.

"Mrs.—Mrs. Avery," he finally managed. "Well. You're not what I expected, not at all."

She threw back her head and laughed. "I imagine not. And it's *Miss* Avery, not Mrs. But please, call me Pearl."

Silas knew he was staring, but he couldn't stop himself. Pearl Avery was not only white, she was unlike any woman he had ever seen in his life. She wore men's trousers, rolled up at the cuffs, sturdy boots, and a blue chambray shirt that matched her eyes. Her hair, long and wavy, was a soft shade of brown, pulled back into a kind of horse's tail at the nape of her neck. Her skin was tanned to a glowing bronze, and a streak of soot marked her chin.

"*You're* the Pearl I've been hearing so much about?" he blurted out.

"I'm afraid so." She smiled crookedly, and a single dimple creased her left cheek. "I hope I haven't invaded your territory."

"Not at all," he managed. "Lily would have lost that foot to gangrene if you hadn't tended to it right away. But—"

"But who am I, and what am I doing here?" she supplied. "Well actually, Dr. Noble, this is not the first time we've met. My father is Harmon Avery, owner of Avery's Lumber. You came in with Booker to order supplies for your house."

"Yes." Silas sorted frantically through his memory, trying to recall. There had been a young woman behind the counter, but he hadn't paid her much mind. Booker had handled the order, and he had simply waited, woefully ignorant about anything that concerned construction. "I'm sorry. I'm afraid I don't remember."

"I wouldn't expect you to. You looked a little . . . well, lost."

Silas's first reaction was to take offense at this veiled denigration of his manhood, but he stifled the impulse. She was right. He had been lost. Totally out of his area of expertise. He uttered a short laugh. "Well, Miss Avery, I see you've got my number."

"Pearl," she corrected for the second time. "And when I found out you were the new doctor, I didn't expect you to know much about manual labor."

Silas liked her immediately, this audacious young woman who spoke her mind so freely. But he had many questions about her.

"I suppose you want to know why I've been around here doctoring your patients," she said, as if she'd read his mind. "My mother died a few years back. Shortly afterwards, my father and his brother inherited some timberland in Cambridge County. They had both worked in the timber business as a young boys in Upstate New York, but never thought they'd have the opportunity to own their own mill. Then the inheritance came through—from an uncle we barely knew—so they both took a chance, and here we are, starting a new life. I had some medical training up north, and I wanted a change, too, so I joined him. I keep the company's books and do what I can to help when somebody needs emergency attention."

Silas turned to Booker. "So why, if there was a nurse already here, was Colonel Warren so insistent that this county needed a doctor?"

Booker stared at him. "Pearl's a woman," he said, as if the answer should be obvious. "None of the plantation owners is gonna let a woman touch them, not if they're dying. Besides, she's a *Yankee* woman."

"Well, I come from up north, too. I'm from Baltimore."

"Maryland's a border state," Pearl interjected. "Apparently people in your neck of the woods haven't read *Uncle Tom's Cabin*, or if they did, decided to keep quiet about it."

Silas considered her words. It was true, Maryland was divided on the issue of slavery. He knew that some people in the state owned slaves, but he had never had to face the reality of slavery personally, as he had here in Mississippi. And Pearl was right in her assumption—most of his family, and those in their social circles, did keep their opinions to themselves. His father had often commented that he wished those wild-eyed revolutionaries would just shut their mouths and quit stirring up trouble.

Silas had never met an abolitionist—at least not that he knew of. If Pearl Avery was one, she didn't fit the picture his father had painted. Not in the least.

"Pearl's been helping us out for some time, now," Booker added. "She's a fine woman, a godly woman—"

"But I'm not a doctor," Pearl interrupted. "These people need you. We all do. And if you're willing, I'd be honored to assist you in any way I can."

Silas's mind barely registered the words, so taken was he with the modulated tones of her low-pitched voice. Like honey. Like silk. Like . . .

"Oh," he said, recovering his composure. "Certainly, Miss Avery—ah, Pearl. I'd appreciate your help. Between the slaves and the plantation owners, I've got my hands full."

A clanging sound arrested his attention.

"That'll be Middie, callin' us all to dinner." Booker grinned at Silas. "Reckon you and Pearl ought to join us."

"I—I reckon so," Silas stammered.

Pearl caught Silas's glance and winked boldly at him. "Why thank you, kind sir," she said in her best imitation of a Southern accent. She took his arm and batted her eyelashes at him. "I'd be downright delighted."

9

Death and Life Are in the Hands of the Lord

Later that night, Silas sat at the table in his cabin, poring over Pearl Avery's copy of *Uncle Tom's Cabin*. Harriet Beecher Stowe's novel had been released the year before, and already, Pearl told him, had sold over three hundred thousand copies. No wonder people were up in arms about slavery. Yet here he was, on a slave plantation in Mississippi, and he had never seen the extreme horrors Stowe described in her book. Colonel Warren was firm—he believed in discipline. But he always made a point of boasting about how fair he was to his nigras, how well he treated them. Maybe Stowe had exaggerated the situation to make a point; or maybe there were just a few plantations—certainly not the majority—where slaves were treated with viciousness and cruelty.

But for all his rationalization, Silas could not rid his mind of images he *had* seen with his own eyes. Warren's refusal to relieve Celie from her heavy duties during the final months of her pregnancy. The festering infection in Lily's foot, which surely would have gone untreated had it been up to Robert Warren. The sneering overseer, Otis Tilson, who rode his horse through the fields, flailing his whip at any slave who seemed to be lagging behind. And most of all, the sad, haunted look that filled Booker's countenance in unguarded moments, an expression that, for all the man's hope and faith, communicated the unbearable burden of perpetual enslavement.

Silas laid the book aside and rubbed his eyes. This wasn't at all what he had expected when he responded to Robert Warren's invitation to come and serve as a physician in Cambridge County. He had always considered himself a moderate man, a man more interested in the wellness of the individual human being than in politics or social action. He was a healer, not an activist. Moral enigmas wearied his mind and confused his heart. And he hadn't the faintest idea how to sort all this out.

"Massah Doctor!" Booker's voice boomed through the closed door. "Massah Doctor!"

Instantly alert, Silas slung his coat around his shoulders, grabbed his medical bag, and threw the door open. "What's wrong, Booker?"

"Massah Robert says to bring you up to the big house right now!"

"Do you know what's wrong?"

"Naw suh. He jus' says come, and quick!"

By the time they reached the circular driveway in front of the plantation house, a crowd had gathered—Olivia Warren, surrounded by a bevy of weeping house servants. One of the slaves, a light-skinned girl of perhaps seventeen, ran toward the buckboard pointing and shouting.

"They's at the barn, Massah Doctor!" she screamed. "Hurry!"

Booker jerked the horses around and careened down the dirt road that led to the barn and stables. He pulled to a stop so fast it made Silas's neck pop.

"Come on, come on!" someone called.

Dozens of slaves stood milling around the barn door, and Silas had to shove them aside to get in. When he finally entered, the scene spread out before him revolted him, and for a moment he thought he was going to retch.

There was blood everywhere.

A black man lay sprawled on his side in the straw, a big, muscular man with skin as dark as pitch. But that was as far as the identification went. His face, what was left of it, was beaten beyond recognition. His back and shoulders had been whipped to a bloody pulp, and his right foot was—well, gone.

Beside him stood Otis Tilson, the overseer, with a whip in one hand and a bloody ax in the other. Robert Warren stood to one side, his face averted, his skin pale as paper, even in the yellow light of the two lamps hanging from opposite stalls.

Silas ran to the man and knelt beside him. Puddled blood seeped into the knees of his trousers, and he felt the warm wetness oozing onto his skin.

"What happened here?" He craned his neck and looked up at Warren.

Otis Tilson answered. "Runaway," he spat out, raising the ax as if that was all the explanation Silas needed. "Guess he ain't gonna run no more."

Silas jerked a pressure bandage out of his bag and applied it to the stump. The ax had severed an artery, and blood was pumping like a fountain. "He's not going to do anything anymore," he muttered.

Robert Warren came to life and grabbed Silas by the shoulder. "You've got to save him. He's my best horse trainer."

"Marcus?" Silas choked out. Marcus was Lily's man, a big bear of a fellow with a kind and gentle soul. He would never have run away and left Lily alone.

"He weren't runnin'," one of the bystanders muttered.

Tilson stepped forward and raised his whip. "You keep your mouth shut, Nigger," he snarled. "'Less you want double of what that boy got."

"But he weren't!" the young slave protested. "I saw it all. He was just disagreein' with you about how to break that new stallion, and you lit into him."

Warren moved closer to Tilson and narrowed his eyes. "Is that right, Otis?"

Tilson spat at the master's feet. "He had it comin'. That buck's been trouble since the day you bought him."

"Shut up, both of you!" Silas snapped. "Get me a blanket."

Warren motioned to one of the slaves, who retrieved a horse blanket from the tack room and spread it on the bloody straw. Gently, Silas turned Marcus over onto his back. "Hold that pressure bandage in place—tight!" The slave complied, turning his eyes away from the gushing of blood.

Marcus's eyes fluttered open. "Massah Doctor?"

Silas knelt beside Marcus and cradled the man's head in one arm. "I'm here, Marcus. I'm going to take care of you."

Marcus shook his head slowly from side to side. "Ain't no use, suh."

"Don't talk that way, Marcus. I need you to fight." Tears sprang up in Silas's eyes.

"I know it's my time. I ain't afraid." His breath came in ragged gasps. "Tell Lily . . . I loves her."

Then, with one final rattle as his last breath escaped, Marcus's big head lolled against Silas's shoulder.

Silas looked up. "You can let go of the bandage now," he sighed. "It's over."

Colonel Warren, his eyes blazing with fury, moved toward Tilson until they were nose to nose. For a minute Silas thought that the master was going to kill the overseer, or at least fire him for this unnecessary cruelty. Instead, Warren said, "I paid a hundred dollars at auction for that buck, Otis. Don't expect any salary until I get it back."

Tilson was about to protest when a small Negro boy ran into the barn, panting and out of breath. For a minute he just stood there, his eyes wide and white as he took in the carnage, and then he pulled frantically on Silas's bloody sleeve. "Massah Doctor, Middie says you gotta come *now*! Celie's havin' her baby!"

With the help of three other slaves, Booker wrapped Marcus's body in the horse blanket and hurriedly loaded it into the buckboard. "Come on!" he yelled.

Silas started for the rig, but Otis Tilson's hand grabbed his arm. He looked down at the filthy paw, brown with Marcus's dried blood, and then up into the sneering face.

"Just a minute," the overseer snapped. "You ain't done yet."

"Thanks to you, he's dead," Silas shot back. "My work here is finished."

"Naw it ain't. Remember why you was hired, sonny boy. I got this big boil"—he pointed to his backside—"and it really bothers me when I'm in the saddle." He gave a leering grin, showing a mouthful of crooked, tobacco-stained teeth.

Silas narrowed his eyes, jerked the ax from Tilson's hand, and threw it on the ground at his feet. "Lance it yourself," he snapped. "And swing hard."

Silas looked at his pocket watch. It was nearly four in the morning; Celie had been in labor for more than seven hours. The coolness of the night air came in on a breeze through the open window of the cabin. Still, sweat covered the girl's body and fear filled her eyes.

"It's going to be all right, Celie. Just hang on." Silas had waited as long as he could, hoping the baby would turn, but to no avail. If he didn't do something immediately, he might lose them both.

"Pearl, get up there beside her head and hold her hand." Pearl moved into position, and Silas squatted between Celie's knees. "I need the lamp closer."

Middie moved the lamp to the floor beside Silas. "Now, Celie, your baby is coming out feet first. This is going to hurt, but I'm going to try to turn it so that it can be born headfirst. When the next contraction comes, don't push, no matter what. Take shallow breaths—pant like a dog—but don't push. All right?"

Celie nodded and gripped Pearl's hand.

The contraction came. "I can see a foot!" Silas shouted. He reached in and slid his hand along the leg, gently pushing on the baby's bottom to try and turn it around. In some far distant place, he could hear Middie praying and, even farther away, the sound of mourners singing: "*I want to meet my Jesus. . . .*"

Dear God, he pleaded silently, *we've had enough death tonight.*

Suddenly he felt a movement, an almost imperceptible shift, and the baby turned in the womb and righted itself. "All right, now, Celie, push!"

Celie pushed. The crown of a head appeared, covered with downy black hair. One shoulder, then the next, and—

"God, no," Silas muttered under his breath. The infant's face had a bluish cast, and the umbilical cord twined around its neck like a serpent. "Celie, stop pushing if you can." He reached with trembling fingers and released the cord. "Now!"

The child—a boy—slid out into the lamplight, slippery as a river rock, and just as lifeless. As soon as he was free, Silas grabbed him by the ankles and swatted his bottom. Nothing. Frantic, Silas laid him on the blanket between Celie's feet and cleared his mouth, then began compressing his tiny chest. A motion—a heave—and, finally, a squall loud enough to be heard all the way up to the big house.

Silas picked up the infant, cut and tied the cord, and wrapped him in a small blanket. "Atta boy." He lifted his eyes toward the soot-stained beams of the cabin. "Thank you."

Despite her exhaustion, Celie raised her head and laughed. "He all right, Doctah Silas?"

"He's just fine," Silas choked out. "Got a good set of lungs, once we got them working."

Silas laid the baby on Celie's chest and watched as she inspected him. "He's beautiful," she murmured. "But ain't he a little pale?"

"He'll get his color soon enough," Silas assured her. "It takes a few days."

"Tha's right," Middie confirmed, coming to kneel at Celie's side. "You done real good, chile."

Pearl got up and went to join Silas at the rough-hewn table. "He would have died," she whispered. "Maybe both of them, if it hadn't been for you."

"I couldn't have done it without your help."

"Sure you could have. The point is, I couldn't have done it at all."

"I prayed," Silas admitted. "For the first time in ages, I really prayed."

Pearl ran a hand through her hair and patted his shoulder. "We all did. And, wonder of wonders, God answered."

Torches lit the slave cemetery with a wavering, eerie light and cast dancing shadows over the rustic grave markers. A sliver of moon sat high in the sky, and a stiff breeze stirred the cedars that stood in a circle around the clearing.

Silas stood next to Pearl Avery and tried to focus. It was difficult, with her so close. The warmth of her shoulder, touching his arm, penetrated through his jacket and kept him conscious of her nearness.

Shepherd, the slave preacher, was talking about resurrection, about the freedom that could come either through liberation or through death. In his low, singsong cadence, he continued:

"The Good Book says that all who live in righteousness will stand in the presence of the Lord."

"Yes, amen!"

"And those who put their faith in God will nevah be disappointed."

"Say on!"

"I say, those who put their faith in God will nevah be put to shame!"

"That's right!"

"Those who put their faith in God will RISE to eternal life!"

"Amen!"

"Those who put their faith in God will forevah be FREE!"

As if on cue, someone began singing: "*Soon I will be done with the troubles of the world, the troubles of the world, the troubles of the world. Soon I will be done with the troubles of the world, goin' home to live with God. . . .*"

The unfinished pine box was lowered into the hole, and Lily, still limping gingerly on her wounded foot, moved forward to drop a handful of dirt into the grave. Tears streaked her face and shone in the torchlight, but she held her head high and nodded with dignity to those who had come to mourn with her.

At last Booker stepped forward, holding his newborn son in his arms. He stood at the foot of the grave and held the child up for all to see. "Life and death is in the hands of the Lord," he declared sagely. "One brother was goin' out, even as another was comin' in."

"Hallelujah!" someone shouted. Silas thought it was Middie.

Booker pulled back the blanket and held the naked infant in his two big hands. He extended his arms and lifted the child over his head. The baby flailed his fists in the dim light.

"His name," Booker said in a solemn voice, "will be Enoch. The one who done walked with God."

"Enoch," everyone repeated.

"May he have his mama's goodness and his daddy's strength," Booker went on. "And may he live to see the day when all folks will be free at last."

"Free at last," the crowd echoed. "Free at last."

Silas watched, and felt tears sting his eyes. When he looked down, Pearl Avery was holding his hand.

10
The Baltimore Belle

March 1854

Silas Noble stood in the foyer of the house and looked to the left, into the old cabin room with its stone fireplace and low-slung beams, and to the right, into the front parlor with its high ceilings, double French doors, and gleaming oak floors.

It had taken eleven months, but it was finished. And it was all his.

His and Regina's.

Today she would arrive by train from Baltimore, and he would present her with this lovely new home and the amethyst and pearl brooch given to him by his grandmother on his twenty-first birthday. Their engagement would be sealed, their wedding date set.

Silas's eyes moistened as he remembered Grandmama Noble. She had been the only person in the entire family who had understood his calling to become a doctor. The day he turned twenty-one, she had called him into her room and held out a hand to him.

"Silas," she had said in a quavering voice, "I won't be around much longer, but before I go—"

"Don't say that, Grandmama!" he protested. "You're not going to die. You're not!"

"Everyone dies, son," she countered with a smile. "The only question is when, and how." She had fixed him with a fierce and tender gaze. "Make sure that when it's your time, you go out gracefully, and with integrity. Don't spend your last moments wondering about what might have been."

Silas had been too young—perhaps he was still too young—to understand fully what she was saying. But he had nodded and waited for her to continue.

"I want you to have this," she said, extending a small velvet box. "It was mine, given to me by your grandfather on the day we married. When you marry, it will be your gift to your bride."

Silas took the box and opened it to find a heart-shaped amethyst brooch surrounded by small pearls. The gemstone glinted a deep purple in the lamplight.

"Amethyst for sincerity," Grandmama murmured. "Pearls for purity." She motioned to him. "Look on the back."

Silas looked. In cramped, tiny lettering were engraved three words: *Sincerity, Purity, Nobility.* For generations past, it had been the motto of the Noble family. Silas turned the brooch over in his hand. "Is it valuable?" he blurted out, then immediately regretted the question.

But Grandmama did not rebuke him. "As priceless as the one who wears it is to the one who gives it," she answered cryptically. She latched onto his sleeve and pulled him close, showing surprising strength for one so ill. "Make certain you choose wisely," she whispered.

Grandmama had not lived to see her only grandson turn twenty-two. And now, more than four years after her death, Silas wondered, just for a moment, if his grandmother would approve of his choice.

Of course she would, he reprimanded himself. Regina came from a fine Baltimore lineage, a family of impeccable breeding and taste. She was gracious and cultured and elegant. She would make the perfect wife.

And she would make Noble House into a beautiful home. A lovely, peaceful place to live together and raise their children.

For months he had been anticipating this day with a strange feeling in his gut. It had to be excitement, he reasoned. Excitement, and perhaps just a little touch of fear. All new bridegrooms got cold feet, or so he had been told. This was a major change in his life, a watershed moment. Once he and Regina were married, nothing would ever be the same.

But of course, it would be *better.* Silas would have stability in his life with the woman he loved. He would have children, a meaningful career, a place in society.

Silas let his mind dwell for a moment on Regina—the beautiful, refined girl he had fallen in love with nearly three years ago, long before he had completed his medical training and come to work at Rivermont. His life—and his thinking—had changed so radically since then. For all his initial confusion and inner torment, everything had fallen into place the night he delivered Booker and Celie's son, little Enoch. He knew he belonged here. He just wasn't completely sure Regina would understand his place of belonging.

He stepped down into the log cabin room—still his favorite room in the large planter house. The rest of the place was formal in design, the kind of home where Regina would hold teas and dinner parties and ladies' sewing circles. But this was his room, with its masculine oak furnishings and big roll-top desk.

Silas went to the desk, seated himself in the swivel chair, and drew out a packet of Regina's letters. He untied the ribbon, sorted the letters by date, and began to read back through the correspondence she had sent to him in the past year.

Most of the letters were full of news from Baltimore—the coming-out of her debutante friends, the balls, the dresses, the celebrations, the financial success achieved by his old friends from college. Chatty letters, containing little information of any personal nature, and even less response to the ones he had written to her.

He had told her all about his life here—about the slaves, about Booker and Celie and their infant son Enoch, about the Warrens and the other plantation owners, about Olivia and her mounting excitement at the prospect of Regina's arrival. She *had* responded to that one, now that he thought about it—asking a multitude of questions about the society scene in Cambridge, questions he hadn't the faintest idea how to answer.

But she made no mention whatsoever of his philosophical musings about the humanity of slaves, or his understanding of his calling as a physician. She had only commented that she hoped the nigras knew what they were doing in building the house, and she would be glad when it was finished and Silas would be freed from this harebrained agreement to doctor the slave families.

She just doesn't comprehend what my life here is all about, Silas rationalized to himself. *When she gets here, meets these people, and sees in person how much good I'm doing, she'll be proud of me and supportive of my work.*

It wasn't the first time Silas had tried to convince himself that everything would be perfect once Regina arrived. Nor was it the first time he came away unconvinced.

"Daisy!" Olivia squealed at the top of her lungs. "Get up here, right now!"

Robert Warren went to the foot of the stairs and peered up at his wife. "Olivia? Is everything all right?"

"I should say not!" she shouted down to him. "Miss Regina will be here at any moment, and her room is not ready! Daisy was supposed to put fresh calla lilies and roses in the vase, and the pitiful bouquet she brought in is all wilted and brown around the edges. DAISY!"

The diminutive slave girl almost bowled Robert over as she raced around him and up the stairs. "'Scuse me, Massah," she gasped. "I's comin', Miss 'Livia!"

Robert heaved a long-suffering sigh and went back to balancing his accounts. He would be glad when Miss Regina, the belle of Baltimore, finally did get here and get settled. Maybe his wife would calm down a bit, not be so frantic to have everything just so. And maybe Regina's presence would knock some sense into that addlebrained doctor.

More than six months ago he had been ready to fire Noble and be done with him. The man couldn't seem to get through his thick skull that his job was to tend the plantation families, not the nigras. Robert had to admit, albeit reluctantly, that everybody who needed the physician's attention had eventually been treated, but Noble still had his priorities all out of whack. The young man apparently didn't understand—or didn't want to—that his white patients came first, and the slaves got any time that was left over. Noble seemed to have it set in his mind that the most serious cases should be treated first, whether that was a little pickaninny baby, a dying field hand, or the plantation owner himself.

And Noble had made a formidable enemy when he had refused to

lance Tilson's boil the night that big buck Marcus died. The overseer had
been gunning for the doctor ever since, calling the man all manner of
uncomplimentary names and pestering Warren to "fire the nigger-lover."

But Robert hadn't fired him—not yet, anyway—and the main reason
was Olivia.

"Please don't let him go," his wife had pleaded. "His fiancée will be
here soon, and he'll straighten out, you'll see. A good woman, an aristocratic woman, will make all the difference in setting things right."

Warren had his doubts, but he had agreed, for Olivia's sake, not to
take any action against Noble for the time being. Olivia had her heart
set on having another genteel female at Rivermont, someone of her own
social status, someone she could take under her wing and introduce to
the rest of Cambridge society.

And who knows? he thought. *Maybe it will work out.* He couldn't deny
that Noble was a good physician. If he could just find a way to get the
man's attitudes in line. . . .

Silas stood next to Booker on the depot platform and watched as the
train squealed to a halt in a cloud of steam. He craned his neck, searching for Regina as the passengers began to disembark.

Then he saw her, emerging like an angelic vision from the smoke, an
apparition of loveliness and grace. The sunlight reflected from her
auburn hair, done up on top of her head with wisps escaping around
her face and neck. Her satin dress, the same color green as her eyes, rustled as she walked toward him. Booker leaned in close and whispered,
"Is that her, Massah Doctor? I declare, she is one fine—"

Booker stopped suddenly and lowered his eyes. *Of course,* Silas
thought. It was totally inappropriate for a slave man to notice, much less
comment on, the charms of a white woman. He clapped Booker on the
back. "Don't worry about it, Booker," he said under his breath. "And yes,
she is a fine woman."

Booker grinned and stepped to one side as Regina approached and held
out her arms toward Silas. In one hand she carried a small train case, in
the other a satin parasol that matched her dress. Any kind of embrace—

even a handshake—was impossible under such conditions, so Silas leaned forward to receive a phantom kiss, first on the right cheek, then on the left.

"Silas, darling!" she cooed, stepping back to look him over. "My soul, you look absolutely . . . rugged." She set the train case on the platform and reached a lace-gloved hand to stroke his face. "You're so tan! And that beard!" She slapped him playfully on the cheek. "Well, that will have to go, now won't it?"

Silas felt himself beginning to blush. The beard had initially been a concession to convenience—it took so much time to shave every morning, and he was always cutting himself in his rush to get out to the slave cabins or up to the big house. In the end, he had just let it go, and by the time it had grown in completely, he found that he liked it. It made him feel more masculine, more powerful, as if he had finally taken control of his own destiny. He had never felt that way, not once, while he lived in Baltimore.

Now, with Regina standing here in front of him, all those old memories came flooding back. He saw, as clearly as if he were there again, how she and all her girlfriends governed the men in their lives—their fathers, their brothers, their beaus. They didn't try to hide it, either; they constantly joked about how men didn't know what was good for them and needed a feminine hand to keep them in tow. On one occasion, even though he had worked an eighteen-hour shift at the hospital and they were already late, Regina had sent him home to change, complaining that she simply could not be seen with a man so inappropriately attired for the opera.

Silas ran a hand through his beard and smiled down at his fiancée. "No," he said softly. "I think I'll keep it. It suits me."

Her green eyes went icy, and she forced a smile. "We'll see about that," she answered with a chilly laugh. "Shall we go?"

Silas was just about to introduce her to Booker when she picked up her train case from the platform and shoved it in the slave's direction. "My other things are there." She pointed to a wheeled cart piled high with trunks and boxes. Without even so much as a glance at Booker's face, she pivoted around and stalked toward the waiting carriage, her high boots making a definitive clicking sound across the boards.

Booker caught Silas's eye and grinned. "Looks like we shoulda brung the buckboard 'stead of the carriage."

On the drive to Rivermont, Regina oohed and ahhed over the beauty of the landscape. The azaleas were on the verge of blooming, and all along the river, dogwoods and redbuds blossomed profusely, and daffodils lined the banks with yellow and white.

"You didn't tell me it was so lovely here," she gushed, gripping Silas's arm as they sat together in the rocking carriage. "Who planted all these flowers and trees?"

"Well, uh, nobody," Silas stammered. "They're all wild." He recovered himself and squeezed her hand. "But wait until you see Rivermont. Miss Olivia—that's Colonel Robert Warren's wife—has fabulous gardens. She grows roses and calla lilies and hyacinths—"

"We *are* going to Rivermont first, aren't we?" Regina interrupted. "I'm very anxious to meet the Warrens."

Silas frowned. His plan was to take his fiancée to their new home, to show off what he had done for her, and to present her, in a proper and formal manner, with the amethyst brooch that felt as if it were burning a hole in his jacket pocket. "You will be staying with them, of course, until the wedding. We're both invited for dinner tonight. But I thought that first we might stop by our house. I want you to see—"

"Oh, there's plenty of time for that." She dismissed him with a wave of her hand. "I'd rather see Rivermont and meet Colonel and Mrs. Warren."

Silas reached past the opposite seat, piled with trunks and suitcases, and tapped Booker on the shoulder. "Change of plans, Booker. Take us to the big house first."

Booker turned his head and rolled his eyes. "Yessuh, Massah Doctor. Whatever you say."

Regina was clearly impressed with the opulence and grandeur of Rivermont. After Olivia had given her the tour, the two women settled themselves in the parlor with coffee and pie, chattering like squirrels, while Silas and the master retreated to Warren's study and tried to make uncomfortable small talk.

"Well, Noble," Warren finally said after several aborted attempts at conversation, "I guess your life is about to change significantly."

"Yes, sir, I suppose so." Silas shifted restlessly in his chair.

"Nothing like a good woman to keep a man on the straight and narrow."

"Yes, sir."

Warren lit a fat cigar and leaned back in his chair. "You got any experience with women, Noble?"

Silas jerked to attention. "Excuse me?"

"Any experience. You know. . . ." The older man grinned salaciously and waved one hand.

Silas balked at this intrusion into his privacy. But Warren *was* his employer, and he didn't know how to avoid answering without offending the man. "Well, of course," he stammered. "I *am* a physician, after all. I've delivered babies, and—"

"I'm not talking about *professional* experience," Warren interrupted. "I'm talking man to man here. You know what it takes to please a woman?"

Silas felt a hot flush creep up his neck and into his cheeks. "Colonel Warren, forgive me, but I'm not very comfortable with this line of conversation—"

"What it takes to please a woman is—" Warren paused dramatically. "Money!" He threw back his head and laughed uproariously at his own joke. "Money, my boy! Elegance. The good life. And looks to me like you've got yourself a girl who appreciates fine things."

"Yes sir, I suppose I do," Silas responded miserably.

Warren slammed a bony fist down on the table next to his chair, nearly upsetting the marble ashtray. His thin face held an expression that could only be interpreted as *victory*. And Silas didn't have to wait long to find out what Warren's triumph was all about.

"I'll make you a deal, son." The master laid his cigar on the side of the ashtray and sat up straight. "You're going to need a lot more than you've got right now to keep that little Baltimore belle of yours happy. Am I right?"

"I guess so, sir."

"You got yourself a nice house, and that's a good start, but trust me, it's not enough."

"It's not?"

"Of course not. Olivia's got big plans for your little girl, now that she's here. Balls and parties and hobnobbing with every plantation family within a hundred-mile radius. Our own children are grown and gone, but now that Olivia's got somebody to mother, she'll make the most of it, mark my words. You'll need money for ball gowns—custom-made by the best dressmakers in Memphis, probably—and a nice carriage of your own, and a thousand other things. Where do you plan to get the finances to support that kind of life?"

"I—I don't know, sir. I hadn't really thought about it."

Warren leaned back in his chair. "Figures. I suppose you thought your Miss Regina would be perfectly content to move to Mississippi and become"—he turned up his lip in a sneer—"a *doctor's* wife."

"What's wrong with being a doctor's wife?" Silas blurted out.

"Nothing, boy, nothing at all." He gave a sly wink. "It's just not the same as being a *master's* wife."

For all the fury that was churning inside Silas, he knew that what Warren said was true. He had seen the look on Regina's face when she got her first glimpse of Rivermont. The house he had built for her, nice as it was, would pale in comparison. It had no hand-loomed rugs from England, no custom-crafted mahogany furniture. His pathetic savings would barely purchase the basics. And he hadn't even considered the expense of parties and balls and gowns—all the things he knew instinctively that Regina would insist upon.

"So here's the deal," Warren went on. "I'm prepared to double your salary."

Silas shook his head in disbelief. He couldn't have heard correctly. "What?"

"That's right." Warren gave a benevolent nod.

"And what must I do in return for this generous gesture?" Silas realized that his voice was laced with sarcasm, but he couldn't help himself. After almost a year, he knew Warren too well. The man never offered anything without strings attached.

"Not much," the master hedged. "All I ask is that you remember who you're working for. Fulfill the original terms of your contract. Concentrate on the plantation owners and their families, and stay out of the slave cabins. If I want you to treat a slave, I'll tell you who and when and under what circumstances. Understand?"

Silas didn't answer. Shortly after Marcus had died, his woman, Lily, had discovered she was with child. She was due to deliver any day now, and although she was a healthy, robust woman, Silas knew the birth could be difficult for her. He had promised her he would be there when her time came, along with Middie and Pearl Avery, and that no matter what, he wouldn't let anything happen to the baby.

"Noble?" Colonel Warren prompted. "Did you hear me?"

Silas forced himself to look at the master. "Yes, sir. I heard. I'm just not sure I can comply with your conditions."

"Why the blazes not?"

Silas took a deep breath. "Remember Marcus, the slave Otis Tilson claimed was a runaway? Tilson beat him to a pulp, cut off his foot, and let him bleed to death?"

"Of course I remember." Warren nodded. "That buck was the best horse handler I've ever seen. I'll probably never find anybody to replace him."

Silas stifled his rage. "His woman, Lily, turned up pregnant shortly after his death. She's due to deliver soon, and I promised I'd help her."

Warren bit his lip and thought for a moment. "If it's a boy, and he grows up to be like his daddy, he'd be some fine asset around here."

"Yes sir, he would." Silas hated himself for agreeing with Warren, who was talking about the baby as if it were a new foal sired by his prized stallion. But if that line of argument would persuade the Colonel, he was willing to take it.

"I'll tell you what," Warren said at last. "When Marcus's nigra woman goes into labor, you have my permission to take care of her, unless—and I repeat, unless—you're needed elsewhere. And from now on, you'll go where you're told and treat the people I instruct you to treat. No arguments. Got it?"

Silas nodded mutely.

"Good." Robert Warren went to his desk and retrieved a small strong-box. He drew out a wad of bills and handed them to Silas. "The first installment of your new salary," he said. "Plus a little wedding gift."

With a trembling hand, Silas reached out and took the cash.

A memory flashed across his mind—an image from his days in medical school, when after classes he would make his way into the less savory parts of Baltimore to treat the sick at the charity clinic. All along his route, scantily clad ladies of the night stood posed in doorways, urging the men on the street to come in and sample their wares.

Back then, Silas had wondered what could possibly motivate a woman to prostitute herself, to do something so shameful just for the sake of money.

Now, with Warren's payoff searing his palm like a live coal, he knew.

11
A Matter of Conscience

───◆◇◆───

Silas stood facing Regina in the downstairs bedroom, which adjoined the parlor. He had waited to show her this room last—it was already furnished, if sparsely, with a wide bed and an elaborately carved dresser crafted from solid oak.

"Booker built the dresser and bed with his own hands," he explained, running a palm over the satiny finish. "He did a wonderful job, don't you think? He's quite the artist."

When Regina didn't respond, Silas pressed on. "Celie and Lily made the mattress and quilted the comforter. It's beautiful, isn't it?"

And it was. A wedding ring quilt, with interlocking circles in soft pastel hues on a background of unbleached muslin. Each stitch tight and even. The two of them had labored for weeks, Silas knew, quilting by lamplight long into the night. Where they got the fabric, he had no idea, but here and there he recognized snippets of some of the house slaves' better clothes, and a hand-me-down or two from Olivia Warren herself.

A labor of joy. A wedding gift from people who loved Silas and valued his presence in their midst.

Still Regina offered no response.

Silas couldn't take the suspense a moment longer. "Well, darling, what do you think? If you could have seen it before—"

Regina managed a wan smile and sank down onto the bed. "I think—"

she began, then paused. "I think you've done rather well, considering what you had to work with."

The words dropped like lead pellets into Silas's heart. He swallowed, hard, to push back the choking lump in his throat, but before he could say anything, she spoke again.

"It isn't Rivermont, of course, but it is very nice, all things considered. I know a seamstress back in Baltimore who makes lovely cutwork duvets and draperies—" One long fingernail pulled at a knotty place in the muslin. "I'm sure she could fashion something more appropriate than a . . . a slave patchwork." Her nostrils flared just slightly, as if she had caught a whiff of something distasteful.

Silas fought to stem the rising tide of his emotions. He knew, of course, that his fiancée was accustomed to the finer things in life, and the master's big house would be exactly the kind of place that would appeal to her refined sensibilities. But once he had seen the magic Booker had worked in transforming the original log cabin into this large and impressive home, he had been so sure that Regina would be elated. It appeared to him now that he had grossly overestimated her response.

Make certain you choose wisely.

Grandmama's words echoed in his memory, but Silas pushed them aside. He couldn't let his initial disappointment rule his future. Regina was here, and that was what mattered. Olivia Warren was already in the middle of planning a large wedding for the end of April—in the formal gardens, with every plantation family within fifty miles in attendance. And besides, once Regina had the opportunity to choose the furnishings, surely she would be pleased with her new home. It was best to just let her have her head and do what she wanted with the place.

Silas took her hand and led her into the parlor, where they sat together on the single love seat. "Regina," he said quietly, "I'm sure this isn't quite what you expected or wanted, but I've left most of it unfurnished so that you could choose whatever you like, whatever will make this house feel like home to you." He thought of his unexpected raise in salary, and the sour taste of bile filled his throat. "I've got some savings set aside, and—"

Regina wasn't listening. Her eyes wandered around the room, as if already she were imagining a rug here, a settee there.

Somewhere in the back of his mind, he heard Grandmama whisper again: *Choose wisely.*

Then suddenly Silas remembered: the brooch! He reached into his pocket and drew out the gray velvet box. "I asked you to marry me before I left Baltimore," he whispered, looking into her sea-green eyes. "But I had no token to give you." He extracted the brooch from its casing and held it out to her. The heart-shaped amethyst glowed a deep purple, as if it beat with a living pulse. "This brooch has been in my family for generations," he said in a low voice. "My grandmother gave it to me to present to the woman I would marry."

Regina looked down at the brooch and then up at him. "Why, isn't that a pretty little bauble," she said, with a smile that did not reach her eyes. "Is it quite valuable, do you think?"

Silas winced. "Grandmama said it was as priceless as the one who wears it is to the one who gives it."

Regina gave him a blank stare. "How sweet. And you're sweet, too." She patted his arm and gave him a perfunctory kiss on the cheek. "Thank you, Silas." Then she stroked a hand across his beard. "You will shave that off before the wedding, won't you, darling?"

⁕

Lily's cousin Jute set a steaming tureen of soup on the table in front of Silas and smiled at him. "Chicken an' rice," she said, then dipped a curtsy in Regina's direction. "Hope you likes it, ma'am." She backed out of the dining room and paused in the doorway. "I be in the kitchen if ya'll needs anything."

Silas ladled the soup into a bowl and passed it to Regina, then served up a second one for himself. He slid the tureen aside, picked up his soup spoon, and dug in. It was wonderful—a thick, hearty chicken stock laced with big chunks of meat and the wild mushrooms that grew down by the river.

Regina pushed hers around for a moment and finally sipped daintily at the broth. "Hasn't anyone taught that nigra girl how to wait a proper table?" she complained. "A slave is supposed to *serve* the food, not just slap it down in front of the master."

Silas felt himself grimace. Regina had been here more than a fortnight, and in all that time he had barely had a moment alone with her. She was spending every day up at the big house with Olivia Warren, planning the wedding, ordering furniture and draperies and rugs, and every evening Silas had been forced to endure the Warrens' company at elaborate dinners. At last, thanks to Lily and Jute, he had managed to get her alone for a quiet meal in their own house. Couldn't they just have a few minutes of pleasant conversation?

"I'm not a master," Silas countered. "And Jute is not a house servant. She's a field hand who's already worked ten hours today chopping cotton. She prepared this nice dinner for us as a gift."

Regina ignored the part about Jute's hard work and generous offering. "You're the master of your own home," she retorted. "And why couldn't you be a master—a real one, I mean? Olivia says Colonel Warren would sell you a hundred acres of good cotton land adjacent to the oak grove, and even help you build slave quarters—"

His self-control failed him, and Silas watched as his hand formed into a fist and slammed down on the table, rattling the silverware. "I am not now, nor will I ever, be a master! I am a doctor, a physician, whose lifework is to heal people, not enslave them!"

Regina gazed at him in surprise, but she didn't appear a bit disconcerted. "Now, Silas," she soothed, "you know perfectly well that when we're married—it's only a week away now, can you imagine?—we will have to have a few slaves, whether you want to continue this obsession with medicine or not. We'll need a cook, and a driver, and someone to clean the house—" Her dainty brow furrowed into an expression of disdain. "Surely you don't expect me to do all that?"

Silas hadn't really thought about it, but now that she had brought up the subject, he knew that deep in his heart he did not have any expectation that his beautiful Regina would give herself to household drudgery. "We'll get you the help you need," he conceded. "But they will be employees, not slaves, and they will be paid a fair wage."

"You can't be serious!"

"I'm perfectly serious. Why not?"

"Because it will ruin everything, that's why not! Think about it, Silas. What's going to happen if you begin to pay Negroes for doing what they've already been purchased to do? It can only result in chaos, and in dissatisfaction for everyone. And how, pray tell, do you intend going about acquiring such 'employees,' as you call them?"

Silas scratched his beard and waited, and at last the answer came to him. "I suppose I'll buy their freedom."

"You'll buy their freedom? And then pay them wages?"

"Yes." Silas smiled at the brilliance of the plan. "That's exactly what I'll do."

"It's insane."

"No," he countered, "it's humane. Negroes are not animals, Regina. They're human beings with hearts and souls, with minds and gifts and dreams."

She stared at him. "Silas Noble, you're a—a—an abolitionist!"

Silas was about to respond when he heard a noise behind him. He turned to see Jute, standing in the doorway with a platter of roast pork and sweet potatoes in her hands. "Beg pardon, Massah Doctor," she said as she set the food on the table. "I come to take the soup away and bring the entry."

"Entrée," Regina corrected icily.

"Yes'm." Jute tested the word: "Ahn-tray." She gathered up the soup bowls and tureen, and then stood in front of Silas with her head down.

"Is there something else, Jute?"

"Yessuh." She nodded. "I jus' want you to know that I'd be right proud to serve you and your missus in this fine house."

"She was eavesdropping!" Regina hissed.

Jute's eyes went wide. "No ma'am! I mean, I didn't plan to hear ya'll talking. It jus' happened, accidental-like."

"It's all right, Jute. And thanks for the offer. I'll keep that in mind."

"My freedom wouldn't cost much, Massah Doctor. I ain't much good as a field hand. And I be real loyal to you and your lady. Yessuh. Real loyal."

When Jute had disappeared into the kitchen, Regina turned on Silas with an expression of triumph. "You see? What did I tell you? You'll have nigras lining up from here to Memphis trying to get you to buy their freedom. What does that tell you?"

Silas bit his lower lip. "It tells me," he said quietly, "that no human being is content being a slave."

———◆◆◆———

Regina pulled on Silas's arm. "Stop this immediately!" she demanded. "I have no intention of going in there!"

Silas looked at her. The door to the cabin stood open, and inside he could see the slave midwife and Pearl Avery preparing Lily for delivery.

"Come on." He jerked Regina inside and shut the door behind her. "You'll be amazed. The experience of birth is nothing short of a miracle."

Silas believed his own words. Every time a new life came into the world, every time a helpless infant slid into his hands squalling and squirming and so vitally alive, he felt as if he had been born again himself. Delivering babies had made him a believer—in God, in hope, in the future.

"I'm going to need your help, Regina," he said. "I can't do this without you."

The truth was, he didn't need her assistance. If she hadn't been there, someone else would have volunteered to hold the lamp, to hand him equipment from his medical bag. But he had other reasons for wanting his fiancée present at the birth of Lily's baby. She needed to see, firsthand, why his "obsession with medicine," as she called it, was so important to him. It was time for her to experience what it meant to be a doctor's wife. And he hoped, deep in the recesses of his soul, that participating in this birth might change her mind about the humanity of Negroes.

"I—I can't."

"Yes, you can. Stand here beside me and hold the light."

With obvious reluctance, she obeyed, and waited silently, her eyes averted, while Silas examined Lily.

"How far apart are her contractions?"

Pearl came and stood behind him, placing one hand on his shoulder. "About five minutes, Silas. It won't be long."

"Who is this woman?"

Silas turned to see Regina frowning. "Sorry—guess I wasn't thinking about introductions. This is Pearl Avery, Regina. She's trained as a nurse. I don't know what I'd do without her." He looked up at Pearl. "This is my fiancée, Regina Masterson, from Baltimore."

"Delighted to meet you," Pearl said pleasantly, offering a hand that Regina did not take. "I've heard a great deal about you."

"And I, on the other hand, have heard nothing about you," Regina responded coolly.

"I wrote you about Pearl," Silas protested. "Didn't I?"

"Not a word."

"Oh. Well, I thought I did." He turned back to Lily. "I'll explain it later. Lily, you doing all right?"

"Yessuh, Massah Doctor. I jus' be glad when he comes."

"I'll bet. My best guess is that you're a couple of weeks overdue."

"He a big one, ain't he? Like his daddy."

Silas nodded. "I think you're right, Lily. You sure it's a boy?"

"Don't rightly know. Don't matter to me, long as it's healthy."

Lily was a big woman herself, muscular and strong from working the fields, with wide hips and powerful thighs—the kind of figure people often identified as "plainly built for childbearing." Under other circumstances, Silas wouldn't be worried about a successful delivery. But the baby was large—and late. Besides this, the child was Lily's only living connection to Marcus, the man she loved, and Silas had vowed to her that, no matter what, he would help her through this.

Regina stood rigid and stoic, saying nothing, while Lily labored for two hours. Then, just as the final contractions were coming, Celie rushed into the cabin.

"Doctah Silas!" she gasped. "Massah Warren sent a boy down to get you."

"I can't come now," Silas muttered, his attention focused on the child about to be born.

"He say you gotta come to the stables. Mister Tilson, he got throwed from Massah's new stallion and his leg is broke."

A surge of satisfaction rose up unbidden in Silas's heart, and he stifled a smile at the irony of the situation. Silas could never forget, as long as he lived, the image of the slave Marcus, Lily's man, beaten to raw meat and bleeding to death from a severed artery. The overseer had killed Marcus without a moment's remorse, and now, on the evening when Marcus's child was being born, he needed help. Well, Tilson had it coming to him. This was payback for his cruelty.

But that wasn't how a doctor should react, Silas argued with himself. No matter who, no matter what the circumstances, he had a responsibility to save lives. To heal, not hurt. And what had Robert Warren told him? *Whites come first. Remember who you're working for.*

Silas remembered. How could he forget, when Warren had raised his salary contingent upon his promise to comply with his employer's orders? Without that money, Silas could never afford to provide Regina with a life of luxury and social acceptability.

"Massah Doctor," Lily pleaded. "Don' leave me now."

"Do you want me to tell Massah Warren I couldn't find you?" Celie suggested.

In that instant, Silas made his decision. Tilson wouldn't die from a broken leg. When he had seen Lily's baby safely delivered, he would go and set the man's bone. He doubted that he could save his income, but maybe—just maybe—he could salvage what was left of his integrity.

Silas shook his head. "No. Don't lie to him. Tell him Lily's baby is on the way, and to keep Tilson's leg immobilized. I'll be there as soon as I can."

Celie ran out, and Silas glanced up at Regina. Her lovely face had been transformed into a mask of disbelief, and her green eyes glittered with unspoken anger.

━━━━◆━◆━◆━━━━

Regina held the lamp high and didn't move. Nor did she turn away from the disgusting bloody mess Silas had called a miracle. What was so miraculous about a nigra woman dropping her bawling infant onto a mattress stuffed with straw? She had seen a foal born once, a thoroughbred. That process was neater and considerably more efficient than what she was witnessing tonight.

And besides, how could Silas decide that birthing a slave baby was more important than tending to one of his own? The man had no concept of what was proper in polite society. He was a doctor, yes, but didn't a doctor have some choice in the matter?

With a curious detachment, she watched Silas as he worked. And gradually the truth dawned on her: he *had* chosen! He loved what he was doing. He would actually rather be in a slave cabin pulling a little pickaninny out of a big black mammy than in the Warrens' Rivermont mansion setting the white overseer's broken leg.

She had accused him, point-blank, of being an abolitionist, and he had never responded to the charge. But no matter what he said, she could see the truth for herself. It was in his eyes, the way he looked at the nigra woman who sweated and strained on the mat. It was in his hands, the way he touched her with comfort and encouragement. It was in his voice, as he urged her to push or hold back, as he spoke to her in low, compassionate tones.

"More light!" he called out. Regina held the lamp a little closer and watched as a nappy-headed infant pushed its way out into the world. It was a girl.

Regina gave an involuntary shudder as Silas lifted the baby up and cuddled it against his chest. He was getting his best shirt all messy; those stains would never come out.

And then, something totally unexpected happened. The white woman, Pearl Avery, reached out to take the infant and wrap it in a blanket. Her hands touched Silas's, and she froze for a moment, looking up at him. In the yellow gleam of the lamplight, Regina saw the naked truth.

It wasn't possible—she must be imagining things. After all, who was this Pearl Avery? More man than woman, to all appearances, in her dungarees and boots and chambray shirt. She wasn't attractive, and she certainly did not possess a single ounce of breeding or gentility.

Still, Regina couldn't deny what she had witnessed, the look she had seen in Silas's eyes.

Her fiancé was in love with another woman.

"Do you mean to say that he stayed with that slave woman when Robert had expressly ordered him to come here?"

Regina nodded. Silas was out in the stables, setting Otis Tilson's broken leg, and in the meantime, over tea and finger sandwiches, she had told Olivia everything—or almost everything. "Yes, just as I said. He forced me to go with him to the slave cabins. I resisted, of course, but now I'm glad I went. I saw it all, with my own eyes."

"It must have been horrible for you." Olivia patted Regina's hand and poured more tea.

"It was." Regina closed her eyes and shuddered. "The smell! I can hardly believe I survived it without fainting. And the blood and mess—"

"There, there, dear," Olivia cooed. "You're here now, back where you belong."

"But Silas doesn't belong here."

"Whatever do you mean, child?"

"I mean," Regina answered fiercely, "that he likes it! He'd rather be with the slaves. He even told me at dinner tonight that he was thinking about buying freedom for some of the nigras."

"He said what?"

"We were talking about how many servants we would need for the house. I was encouraging him to take Colonel Warren up on his offer of the land, to begin developing a plantation of his own. But he said he would never own a single slave as long as he lived, and that if we needed servants, he'd buy their freedom and then pay them a wage, as employees."

"Good heavens, no!" Olivia put a hand to her heart and fanned herself with a linen napkin. "Does he know what he's saying?"

Regina took a sip of her tea and set the cup down with a shaky hand. "Apparently he's serious about it. If you could have seen the way he acted tonight, as if those nigras were—I don't know . . . his *family*."

"He can't go around freeing slaves and then paying them—not in Mississippi! It's preposterous. We'd have an uprising on our hands."

"That's what I told him." Regina nodded. "I insisted it was a crazy idea—completely insane. But after what I witnessed tonight, I don't think it's just a notion he's recently gotten into his head. I think—"

"Think what, dear?" Olivia prompted.

"I think he may be—" Regina took a deep breath. "I think he may be an abolitionist."

"No!" Olivia Warren's expression of horror mirrored the feelings that were churning inside Regina herself. "Oh, my poor dear! Whatever are you going to do?"

Regina hesitated. She had known the truth the moment she had set foot in that hodgepodge of a house Silas was so proud of, the second she had gotten her first glance at the pitiful old amethyst brooch she now wore at her neckline. But she had yet to say the words. Slowly she unclasped the brooch and laid it on the table. "I'm going back to Baltimore."

"You can't!" Olivia wailed. "The wedding is in one week. And I've grown so fond of you! What will I do without you at Rivermont?"

"I'm sorry," Regina responded. "You've gone to so much trouble to make me feel welcome here, and I do apologize for the inconvenience. I'll miss you, too, but—"

"But what? Isn't there some way we can make this right? Surely your influence will help Silas see the error of his ways—"

"The error of what ways?"

Regina looked up to see Silas standing in the doorway. She didn't know how long he had been standing there, but the expression on his face told her that he had heard enough to be angry.

———•◦•◦•———

"Talking about anyone I know?" Silas walked over to the table and poured himself a cup of tea. He picked up two sandwiches and settled himself in the chair across from Regina. "I've set Tilson's leg. He'll live."

"You sound disappointed."

"And you sound as if you've been unburdening yourself to the Master's wife." He shook his head. "What did you tell her?"

"She told me," Olivia said, "that you disobeyed a direct order from my husband, and that you've been talking like an abolitionist."

Silas heaved a deep sigh but said nothing.

"Now, Silas," the woman went on, "I think we need to have ourselves a little chat. I have considerable influence with my husband, and I do believe I could convince him to give you another chance, if only—"

Silas held up a hand to silence her. His mind flashed back over his dinner conversation with Regina, how she wanted him to be a plantation owner in his own right, with a big mansion and hundreds of slaves. But he could never convince himself to do it—not in three lifetimes. Not for Regina Masterson. Not for anybody.

It was time for him to stand up for who he was—as a man, and as a physician. No one, not even the Master who paid his salary, was going to tell him whom he could and could not help. He stood to lose everything—his job, his income, the woman he was engaged to marry. His family back home in Baltimore would probably never speak to him again. But he would not lose himself.

"No," he said finally. "I don't want another chance. I want to be given the liberty to treat those people who most need my medical services, no matter who they are."

"And that's your final word on the matter?"

Silas turned to see Robert Warren enter the room. Every muscle in the man's wiry body was taut, as if for a fight. His eyes glittered with fury.

"Yes sir." Silas stood to face him. "If I do any less, I'll be denying my oath as a physician."

Warren's jaw clenched. "We have had this discussion before, have we not? And you have repeatedly disobeyed my orders. I have no choice but to—"

The master stopped abruptly as a white-coated slave entered the room, followed by a flushed and breathless Pearl Avery.

"Who is this woman, and what is she doing in my house?" Warren demanded.

"Forgive me, Colonel Warren. I didn't mean to barge in. But Silas—ah, Dr. Noble—is needed at the slave quarters."

"And you are—?"

Silas stepped forward and put a hand on Pearl's elbow. "This is Pearl Avery, Colonel Warren. She—"

"Avery? Harmon Avery's daughter, from the mill?"

"Yes sir. She's also a nurse, and she has been assisting me—"

"From what I've seen, she's been doing quite a bit more than assisting," Regina blurted out. "Just look at her! I can see it in her eyes, and in his." She let out a gasp and reached for Olivia's hand. "He may be engaged to me, but he's in love with her!"

Pearl took a step back, and Silas watched as a bright red flush crept into her cheeks. He could feel heat climbing up his own neck, and he tore his gaze from hers.

"That's nonsense!" he protested. "We just enjoy working together, that's all. Pearl has been invaluable to me, and—"

Suddenly words failed him, and Silas stopped mid-sentence. No matter how he tried to deny it, there was something between him and Pearl. Something special. The way she looked at him—the way she was looking at him now, with a softness in her eyes. The way he felt charged with vitality whenever her hand brushed his. Every time he left her, an empty space opened up in his heart, a space not even Regina's presence could fill.

Then he looked at Regina, and he saw what he had refused to see before this moment: a spoiled child, whose constant selfish demands would drain him, divert him from his purpose. She hadn't the faintest understanding of his call to medicine and his desire to heal, nor did she make any *effort* to understand. And life with her, for all her beauty and elegance, would be a constant battle of wills.

Choose wisely, his grandmother's voice whispered in his heart.

"Is this true?" Warren demanded, his eyes fixed with disdain on Pearl Avery, still clad in her dungarees and boots. "Are you in love with this— this—?"

Silas sighed. "I don't know. But I do know I don't have time for this discussion right now." He turned back to Pearl. "What's the problem?"

"Celie's boy Enoch. He turned a pot of coffee over on himself. Celie's tending to him, but he needs a doctor."

"All right, let's go." Silas grabbed his bag from the doorway.

"If you leave now, Noble, you'll never set foot in this house again," Warren snarled. "You'll never collect another dime of salary. And I'll expect you off my land by nightfall."

Silas turned. "I believe, Colonel Warren, that I hold the deed to my house and land."

"Maybe so, but you'll never work in this county again."

Silas lifted one eyebrow. "I'll still have plenty of patients."

"You'd throw away our whole life?" Regina howled. "You'd give up everything to tend those—those nigras?"

Silas looked at her and saw in her eyes not regret, or even pain, but pure rage. She didn't love him; she was only upset that he had not surrendered to her will. "I'm afraid so, my dear," he answered. "And I'm afraid it's something you'll never understand as long as you live."

Regina picked up the amethyst heart from the table and hurled it at him. "Then keep your pathetic old brooch. And that house the slaves built for you. I'll have no part of it!"

The brooch clattered against the wall, and he reached out his hand and scooped it up. "That's probably for the best," he sighed. "Good-bye, Regina. I'm certain the Warrens will see you to the station. Give my regards to everyone in Baltimore."

12
Strange Guidance

As the buckboard bounced along the road toward the slave cabins, Silas stared straight ahead and avoided looking at Pearl, who sat behind him in the bed of the wagon. A tangle of emotions wrapped around his heart—concern for little Enoch, guilt over breaking his promises to Regina, fear of what might happen to him and his practice now that he could no longer depend upon Robert Warren's financial support.

He had gotten himself into a real mess this time. His beautiful, aristocratic fiancée was on her way back to Baltimore, armed no doubt with a trunkful of stories about what a despicable cad Silas Noble had turned out to be. His parents would be furious; this marriage to Regina was the single redeeming factor in what they considered an otherwise unremarkable, even embarrassing life. The Noble name would never recover from this blow, and he'd never be able to show his face in Baltimore again.

In addition, his benefactor had turned against him. He had a house and land, but no money with which to support himself, and a raft of patients who needed his services but couldn't pay the first dime. One moment, one decision made out of conscience, had suddenly thrust him into a situation that would most likely lead to his downfall.

But it wasn't just one decision, Silas reasoned. It was the culmination of months of self-evaluation and transformation. He was no longer the same man he had been when he left Baltimore to come to Cambridge

County, Mississippi. He had seen the dark reality of slavery for himself, and he had formed a strong bond with Booker and Celie, Marcus and Lily, and the others. They had become his family. He had wept with them, rejoiced with them. With Pearl at his side, he had tended their wounds, delivered their children, buried their dead. He had made a place for himself here, and he couldn't imagine leaving. What would he do without them? What would he do without Pearl?

Regina had made the accusation, and he had denied it. But now he wasn't so sure. Could it be that he was in love with Pearl, and she with him? Regina said she could see the truth in his eyes. And he had to admit that he felt something for Pearl. Whenever he looked at her, whenever she was near, he had sensed—what? Wholeness. Completion. Peace. He had called it admiration, appreciation. It couldn't be more than that . . . could it?

Still, the moment Regina declared her intention to go back to Baltimore, one overwhelming sensation had risen up in his heart: relief. Despite the questions and confusion that filled his mind at this moment, he was experiencing a curious sense of liberty—as if, for the first time in his life, he had stood up and taken charge of his own destiny.

Silas felt a gentle hand touch his shoulder, and he turned to look at Pearl. Her eyes were shining, and a wide smile graced her lips. She leaned close and whispered into his ear, "I'm proud of you, Silas."

A thrill ran through him, and the hairs on the back of his neck stood up. He couldn't speak for a moment; then his hand closed over hers. "Thank you."

There was no time for more conversation. Booker reined the horses to a halt, and Celie motioned to them from the door of the cabin. Silas got down, helped Pearl clamber out of the wagon bed, and headed inside.

Little Enoch lay sprawled on the sleeping mat, one hand swathed in a bandage. Carefully Silas unwrapped the bandage and examined the burn. With a puzzled frown, he turned toward Pearl.

"I don't understand."

"He pulled a pot of coffee over on him, Doctah Silas," Celie explained.

"Yes, I know. That's what Pearl told me when she came to get me. But—" He rose to his feet. "This is just a minor scald. It won't even leave a scar." He turned to face Pearl. "You doctored and bandaged this hand?"

"Yes," Pearl admitted, her eyes downcast.

"Then you knew I wasn't really needed."

"I suppose I did." She looked up and grinned at him, lifting her hands in an attitude of surrender.

Booker came forward and slapped Silas on the back. "We all talked 'bout it, and we thought maybe you'd need rescuin' from the Massah's—what's that word, Miss Pearl?"

"Inquisition," Pearl supplied.

The truth sank into Silas's heart, and he began to laugh. "Do you mean to tell me that the three of you cooked up this scheme to get me out of Robert Warren's house? That you called me, knowing Enoch was not seriously hurt, so that I wouldn't have to face down the dragon in his den?"

Pearl nodded sheepishly. "But Silas, we had no idea you'd get fired, or that Regina would break off the engagement. We never planned for that to happen. I'm sorry if we got you in deeper trouble."

"Jus' a second," Booker interrupted. "What's this about gettin' fired?"

"Colonel Warren gave Silas an ultimatum—" Pearl began.

"What's that?"

"He said that if Silas didn't agree to do things his way, he was to get off the plantation by nightfall," she explained. "Silas told him that the house belonged to him, and that he intended to stay, even if he didn't get paid."

A troubled expression passed over Booker's broad face. "An' what about Miss Regina?"

"Regina broke off the engagement and said she was returning to Baltimore."

Silas was relieved that Pearl left out the part about Regina accusing the two of them of being in love. It was something they would need to talk about eventually, but he preferred to do it in private.

A look passed between Booker and Celie, and Silas saw Booker wink at his wife and suppress a smile.

"So you ain't got no money comin' in now?" Booker asked.

"Not a cent."

"But you's gonna stay?"

Silas grinned and shrugged. "I've got a nice house, thanks to you, Booker, and a deed that says it's mine. Somehow I have the feeling that I'm not finished with what I'm supposed to do here. It won't be easy, but I'll manage."

Once more, Silas felt a sense of liberation rise up in his soul. A taste, just a tiny sliver, of what it meant for a slave to finally be free.

"So you're not upset with us at what we did?" Pearl asked for the third time that evening. Even with that miserable expression on her face, Silas thought, she looked lovely by lamplight.

He pushed his dinner around on his plate. "It was a sneaky thing to do," he answered candidly. "But I honestly think the outcome is all for the best."

"For the best? When you no longer have any income, and the woman you were engaged to marry has left you?"

"How many times do I have to explain it?" he countered. "I would never have been free as long as I was under Robert Warren's thumb. I don't understand it all myself, but I do know that I feel better than I have in months. I feel like I can breathe again."

"And what about Regina?"

"What about her?"

"Well, I was thinking. I might be able to stir up some work for you in town. My father's friends—"

Silas lifted an eyebrow. "Do you really want to do that?"

"I—I feel responsible for . . . well, you know," Pearl muttered. "If you had some paying patients, Regina might consider coming back, and—"

"And what? Grace me with her presence? See to it that I was reinstated into social acceptability?" He leaned his elbows on the table and gazed at her. "Regina never wanted me to be a doctor. She thought I should be a master," he said. "Wanted me to buy land from Warren and plant my own crops, purchase my own slaves, build my own plantation."

"She said that?"

"I'm afraid so." Silas let out a sigh. "Even if I had agreed to live by Warren's terms, she would never have been satisfied."

"Then she's a fool!" Pearl blurted out. "Any woman would be fortunate to have a man like you for a husband."

Silas chuckled. "Regina would no doubt say that any woman who would have me for a husband is the fool." He looked into her eyes. "I feel bad about it, of course. A gentleman does not break his promises to a lady. But neither does a gentleman marry one woman when he might be in love with someone else."

Pearl started to say something, then clamped her mouth shut. Her eyes went wide. "What did you say?"

"I said, it's possible that Regina's accusation might be true. I might be in love with another woman."

Even as he uttered the words, Silas felt a grip in his gut and a trembling in his heart. It was a huge risk, making such a declaration when he didn't know how Pearl felt about him. She could reject him, say it was all a misunderstanding. For all he knew, she might have a beau in town. She might admire him, or enjoy working with him, but there were a thousand reasons for her to distance herself from him, not the least being that he was on the verge of complete financial disaster. If he ever did get paid for any of his services, he would probably be reimbursed in chickens and cornbread and pots of beans.

"Are you saying you're in love with me, Silas?"

"I don't know what I'm saying," he admitted. "But I'd sure like to find out."

She leaned across the table toward him, drawing so close that he could feel her warm breath on his cheek. "It's a subject I might be willing to explore," she whispered.

As their lips met, Silas felt a shock run through him, a vibrating sensation as if every nerve in his body had awakened. The kiss was long and sweet, and when it was over, Pearl sat back in her chair and gazed at him, her eyes large and soft.

"So," she said at last, "what do you think?"

"I think," he responded in a low voice, "that your wardrobe will never be the same."

Pearl looked down and began to laugh. In a wide stripe across the front of her blue chambray shirt, dark gravy soaked into the fabric. The roast beef from the platter had been pushed onto the table, and a brown stain puddled on the tablecloth.

"Guess I'll never be a society lady," she said with a shrug.

He grinned. "Well, as Booker would say, ain't that a load off my mind?"

13
Pearl of Great Price

———◆◦◆◦◆———

Spring 1855

Silas watched as Pearl, on her father's arm, made her way down the walk toward the front porch of the house. She wore a long white dress, with Grandmama's heart-shaped amethyst at her throat, and dogwood blossoms twined in her hair. In a semicircle around the yard, the slaves—along with Pearl's Uncle Deke, who looked distinctly uncomfortable—had gathered to witness their union.

Silas and Pearl had waited more than a year to marry, and although Silas had grown increasingly impatient over the past couple of months, he was glad they had agreed to a long courtship. Both of them wanted to take their time, to get to know each other, to be sure they were making the right decision. And the delay had served them well. They had grown more and more in love during the past year, had learned to accept each other and honor each other's gifts.

The wait was worth it. Tonight, when they shared a bed for the first time, they would come together as a couple completely devoted to one another and to their mission in life. Two whole people, committed not to changing each other, but to changing the world in which they lived.

For the first time in his life, Silas truly believed he could make a difference—with Pearl at his side. He was beginning to acknowledge, much to his own surprise, that God—or fate—had been leading him, that all this had been planned from the beginning. And he was glad someone else seemed to be guiding him, for this certainly was not his idea of how his medical career should take shape.

When Robert Warren had cut off his financial support, Silas hadn't had the faintest idea how he would make ends meet. Fortunately, he had been able to cancel all of Regina's orders for expensive furnishings for the house. The money saved would buy him some time. But when those resources were gone, then what?

It was Pearl, ultimately, who helped him set aside his fears and find the faith he required to listen to his heart rather than his mind. Unlike Regina, she had simple tastes and the readiness to sacrifice for the sake of a dream. "Silas," she had told him, "I don't need diamonds or ball gowns or fancy furniture. All I need is a husband who is willing to follow his calling. Everything will work out; trust me."

And it had. Pearl had set up a chicken house in the backyard, and within a year they had a good stock of frying hens and rich brown eggs. Harmon Avery had rounded up a few patients in town, folks who were willing to pay, albeit modestly, for the services of a physician. The slaves bartered goods for doctoring—cornbread and pies and big pots of turnip greens, lovely patchwork quilts and, thanks to Booker, a houseful of finely crafted furniture that cost Silas no more than the wood from which the pieces were made. And although there was never any money, he always had food and shelter and the love of good friends.

And he had Pearl. He had never expected to find the woman of his dreams in a slave camp, dressed in boots and dungarees. But there she had been, as if waiting for him to come to her. And whatever the future held, from this day on, she would be his forever. Silas couldn't ask for much more than that.

Last night, after dinner, he had presented Pearl with the amethyst and pearl brooch he had been given by his grandmother. As he told her the story of how Grandmama had passed it on to him with the exhortation to choose wisely, tears pooled in her soft blue eyes.

"I wish I had known her," Pearl whispered.

"And I wish she had known you," Silas responded. He paused for a moment, remembering. "But then again, perhaps she does know. Maybe she's looking down on us now, smiling. I have no doubt she'd approve."

Pearl took the heart-shaped stone and turned it over reverently in her hands. "It's beautiful," she breathed. "I'll treasure it forever."

Silas squinted at the brooch. "There's a pearl missing. It must have fallen out when Regina threw it at my head." He grinned wryly. "I'll have to get that fixed."

Pearl thought about that for a moment. "No," she said at last, "I'd rather leave it as it is. It's like the human condition—precious, yet flawed. And priceless, even in its incompleteness."

Silas gazed in wonder at the woman who was to become his wife. *Sincerity. Purity. Nobility*.

"Make certain you choose wisely," Grandmama had said.

And despite himself, Silas had.

Booker stood at Silas's side as his best man. Had Robert and Olivia Warren known of this plan, they would have been horrified, but to Silas's way of thinking, Booker was the only choice for the honor. This man had become his best friend, his supporter and encourager, and, in an odd way, he was the one who had brought Silas and his bride together.

Silas took Pearl's hand, and together they stood before the befuddled minister as he led them through their vows of lifetime love. His voice shook when he said, "I do," but the tremor was derived from intensity rather than fear. Silas was not afraid to make this commitment; it was the truest thing he had ever done in his life.

More quickly than he had anticipated, the brief service came to a close. "I now pronounce you man and wife," the minister intoned solemnly.

Silas leaned toward Pearl, and just as his lips met hers, she whispered, "No gravy today," and dissolved into laughter.

A mighty cheer arose. They were just about to step off the porch and make their way around to the back of the house, where tables full of fried chicken and cornbread and wedding cake were set up in the yard, when Booker produced a broom. With a wide grin, he laid it on the ground in front of them.

"Now it's o-fficial," the big black man said.

Silas took Pearl's hand, and the two of them jumped the broom together. And amid hugs and handshakes and congratulatory kisses, they made their way to the backyard to celebrate with their family.

———•◦•———

He awoke at dawn with that blasted rooster crowing loudly enough to raise the dead. For a minute Silas looked around, dazed, then realized that a warm body lay next to him in the bed.

Pearl. His wife.

She was curled up on her side with the wedding ring quilt tucked around her shoulders, and Silas felt his heart melt with love for her. How beautiful she was, with her hair spread out like a fan across the pillow!

Tenderly he reached out and brushed a tendril away from her ear. She stirred and turned toward him. "What time is it?"

He looked at his pocket watch on the bedside table. "Almost six."

"Too early," she moaned, covering her head with the quilt. "We didn't go to bed until after midnight."

"Go back to sleep," he murmured.

Cautiously, so as not to disturb her, Silas got out of bed and went to the kitchen. He stoked the fire in the stove, put on a pot of coffee, and then, still in his nightshirt, headed outside to the chicken coop. The morning dew chilled his bare feet, but he didn't mind. He felt exhilarated, at one with the entire world. Yes, he decided. He liked being married. Liked it a lot.

He gathered two handfuls of fresh eggs and returned to the kitchen. While the bacon was frying, he went back outside and cut a single red rosebud from the bush next to the kitchen door. Within a few minutes he had a tray loaded with coffee, bacon and scrambled eggs, and the rose.

"Breakfast in bed?" Pearl mumbled sleepily when he came into the bedroom. She sat up and pushed her hair out of her eyes. "Is this going to be a regular habit?"

Silas laughed. "I wouldn't count on it."

"Then I'd better take advantage of it while I've got it."

When they finished eating, Silas laid the tray aside and put his arms around Pearl. "You are such a gift to me," he murmured in her ear. "I only wish I could give you more."

Pearl sat up and glared at him. "What on earth are you talking about?"

"Well, sweetheart, every man wants the woman he loves to have the very best. I know that life with me is likely to be difficult. We don't have much money, and probably never will, and—"

She put both hands on his chest and pushed him so hard that he fell back against the pillow. "Don't ever let me hear you talking like that again!"

"What did I do?"

"I married you for yourself, you idiot, not for anything you can give me. We're together, we have a wonderful house, good friends, a purpose in life. Have I ever given you any indication that I want more than that?"

"No, but—"

"No buts." Her eyes pierced his with a steely gaze. "I am not Regina Masterson," she said with deliberation. "I don't care about the 'finer things' in life. I care about what's in here—" She poked a finger into his breastbone. "Understand?"

Sheepishly, Silas nodded. "I understand."

"Good. Don't forget it."

He moved closer to her. "Have we just had our first fight?"

"Maybe."

"Is it over?" He reached out a hand and gently stroked her cheek.

"I guess so."

"Then we can make up?" Silas drew her into his embrace and felt her warmth seeping into him. She relaxed against him and lifted her face to his. The kiss, when it came, was gentle and sweet at first, becoming increasingly passionate as her lips lingered on his.

No, Silas thought, Pearl was not Regina Masterson. She was a fiery, opinionated, stubborn woman with a heart big enough to hold him forever. She would always stand by him, always support him, always tell him the truth, even when he didn't want to hear it. She was, indeed, a gift. A pearl of great price.

"Maybe we should fight every morning," he murmured into her hair.

She smiled up at him with an expression that held a world of love. "Only if you bring me breakfast in bed."

14
Traitor Hero

October 1862

They were just finishing breakfast when a knock sounded at the front door.

Silas checked his watch. It was a little before seven. "Who on earth could that be at this hour?"

He went to the door, with Pearl close behind him, and opened it to reveal a ragged soldier in a tattered blue uniform. The man was supported by a crutch rudely crafted from a tree branch. His face was filthy, but beneath the dirt, the skin was as pale as paper. Reddish circles ringed his blue eyes.

"Name's Trevor," the man gasped. "Trevor Howard. One of the slaves told me I could find help here."

Pearl reached out a hand toward him. "Of course. Come in. This is Silas Noble, the doctor; I'm his wife, Pearl."

"Mighty glad to meet—" the soldier began, but his eyes glazed, and as he collapsed, Silas caught him.

"Let's get him inside."

Pearl ran ahead and dumped the breakfast dishes in the sink. Silas dragged the man in and laid him on the long oak dining table.

"How bad is he?" Pearl asked.

Silas unwrapped the rags that bound the man's right leg and winced. "Pretty bad. Direct hit to the kneecap. It's already gone into gangrene." He looked up at her and shook his head. "The leg will have to be amputated."

A booming voice sounded behind him. "You the doctor?"

Silas looked over his shoulder to see a strapping, broad-shouldered man in a blue uniform much cleaner than Trevor Howard's. "I am. And you are—?"

"Captain Thaddeus Malone."

"Is this one of your men?"

The officer nodded. "We're passing through on our way to Memphis. Howard got shot by some Rebs hiding out in the woods. You going to help him?"

"His leg will have to come off," Silas answered bluntly. "You might as well move on; he won't be any use to you from now on."

"He's one of my men," the captain countered. His eyes narrowed. "You're the one who doctors the slaves, aren't you?"

Silas nodded. "I doctor anyone who needs my help. Black, white, slave, free."

"Union or Confederate?"

"Anyone," Silas repeated, "who requires my services."

An expression of relief broke over the officer's face. "Good. I've got a bunch of men who need treatment."

"More wounded?"

Malone shook his head. "Dysentery, mostly. Typhoid. Malaria. Don't know what all. But one thing's for sure—we're not moving on until we get some of these men on their feet. They can't march, can't fight. Some of them can barely stand up."

Silas looked at Pearl, and she nodded. "Where are they now?"

"We've taken over the plantation house. The owner has apparently gone off to fight. The wife and some of the house slaves vacated when they saw us coming, and that coward of an overseer took a horse and hightailed it out of here like the devil was on his heels. The house is empty." He raised an eyebrow. "Fortunately for us, the smokehouse is full."

Silas winced inwardly. He had heard how the Union soldiers moved through the South like locusts, raiding plantations and stealing food, then burning anything that was left. It was the reality of war, he supposed, but it didn't seem very humane. Even the slaves they claimed to be freeing were left without food and shelter. "I'll help you, but you have to promise you won't take it all. We still have people to feed."

"Not for long," the captain said. "Emancipation's on its way—it'll be official, come January. The slaves will be free, and this plantation will be a ghost town."

Silas turned on him. "Oh, really? And where do you expect the slaves to go, once they're freed? I believe in emancipation—I've been waiting and praying for it for years. But it's a lot more complicated than just saying, 'All right, you're free now, go on.' Most of the black folks here were born on this land—it's the only home they've ever known. They're not educated, don't have skills beyond plowing and planting and hoeing. The Slave Codes have seen to that."

Pearl shot him a glance, and he realized he was ranting. "Sorry. I know it's not your fault," he added. "You're just doing your job, and you don't have any control over what happens after the war is over. But you've got to guarantee that you'll leave us *some* provisions at least."

"You have my word that we'll take what we need and leave the rest."

"Fair enough." Silas turned to Pearl. "Did you know Robert Warren had signed up?"

She shook her head. "No, but I wish I had. We might have been some help to Olivia."

"Maybe. If she had allowed us to help. But that's water over the dam now." Silas turned back to Malone. "Captain, can you assist me here?"

Malone nodded.

"Leave my surgical tools, bandages, and a couple of packets of morphine," Silas instructed Pearl. "And take my bag up to the big house. There's quinine, and some laudanum, cinchona for the malaria, and more morphine. Do what you can. I'll be up as soon as I finish here, and—"

"Does she know what she's doing?" Malone interrupted.

"She's had medical training, and she's as capable as most doctors," Silas snapped. "Do you want our help or not?"

"Sorry, ma'am." The captain tugged on his hat and lowered his eyes. "Didn't mean to offend."

"It's all right." Pearl laid out Silas's instruments, took the bag, and headed for the door. "I'll send Booker back for you as soon as I can."

———•••———

Fortunately for him, Trevor Howard did not regain consciousness during the surgery. Captain Malone held the young soldier down as Silas removed the gangrene-infected leg just above the knee. When the procedure was over and the stub bandaged, Malone lifted his eyes to Silas with a look of admiration.

"I've seen plenty of amputations in the field," he said in a low voice. "Most times, the doctor simply lops off the limb and tosses it into a hole in the ground. It's horrible. You did this so. . .well, so *neat*. Looks like that stump will heal over just fine."

"He'll live," Silas responded. "Help me get him upstairs and into bed. I've given him enough morphine to make him sleep until tomorrow. Then we'll go up to the big house and see how Pearl is doing with the others."

———•••———

In early November, Captain Malone and his men left Rivermont Plantation. Most of the soldiers, now healed from various diseases, were able to march out on their own two feet. Trevor Howard rode out in the bed of a wagon, waving to Silas and Pearl and thanking them for saving him.

"He's so young," Pearl sighed as they drove off. "A pity he had to lose his leg."

"If he hadn't lost his leg, he would have lost his life," Silas answered.

Pearl linked her arm through his. "I guess we finally know why you stayed here."

"I guess we do." Silas smiled down at her. "Do we get a little rest now?"

"Maybe for five minutes or so." Pearl pointed. A middle-aged Negro was coming down the road toward the oak grove, supporting a filthy, bedraggled white man in a gray uniform.

"Massah Doctor!" he yelled. "We needs help!"

Silas hesitated and looked into his wife's eyes. Long ago he had made his decision, coming down on the side of the enslaved. He believed in emancipation, in freedom for all men and women, no matter what their race or social status. But he also believed in his oath as a physician. Suddenly the two principles conflicted. Could he treat this Confederate soldier, knowing that by doing so he was helping to prolong the abomination of slavery?

"Go inside and lock the door," he said to Pearl.

She didn't move. "No."

"Do it! I'm not going to help this man. It goes against everything I stand for."

Pearl took his hand, and he could feel her fingers caressing his. "If thine enemy hungers, feed him," she whispered. "If he thirsts, give him drink. . . ."

Silas sighed. "It's too much to ask."

"It's not only your job," she responded, "it's your calling."

Reluctantly, Silas motioned for the black man and his charge to approach. "Body slaves," he muttered. "A rich Southerner goes to war and takes his servant with him." He let out a snort of disgust. "But I don't suppose you can expect the Massah to polish his own boots."

The black man came closer, practically dragging the white officer. Silas shielded his eyes from the sun and peered at him. "Cato?" he asked. "It can't be."

The slave stopped in front of him. "Yessuh, Massah Doctor." He nearly collapsed under the weight of the gray-clad soldier. The Confederate's midsection was covered with blood, and Silas's eyes focused on the gaping belly wound. "Please, suh. Help us."

Silas put an arm around the wounded man and held him up. "Let's get him into the house."

With Pearl's help, they lifted the man and carried him inside. He wasn't a large fellow—thin, and rather wiry, but in his present condition he was dead weight and not easily handled.

"Let's put him on the table where I can take a look at him. Pearl, get my bag, will you?"

Carefully Silas ripped open the officer's uniform and saw what he dreaded: a Minié ball shot, directly into the man's gut. His intestines were torn to shreds.

"Dear Lord," Pearl murmured. "What happened?"

"A Minié ball," Silas explained. "It has a hollow base, and explodes on impact. Causes much more damage than a conventional lead bullet. Captain Malone told me about them."

"Can you help him, Massah Doctor?"

"I'm going to try, Cato. But what were you doing out there?"

"I went with him, suh. Where he go, I go."

A sick feeling rose up in Silas's stomach, and he ripped the officer's hat off and peered into his grime-covered face. "Lord, help us," he muttered. "It's Robert Warren."

Warren's eyes fluttered open, and he squinted, trying to focus. "Noble?" he slurred. "Silas Noble?"

"It's me, Colonel Warren. You're in my house. Cato brought you here so I could help you."

Warren's head lurched back and forth drunkenly. "No. Not you. Get another . . . doctor. I won't have you . . . touch me."

"Massah Robert, *please!*" Cato begged. "If Massah Doctor don't help you, you's gonna die!"

"Then let me . . . die." His eyes rolled back and his head slumped to one side.

"He dead?" Cato asked frantically. "Massah, no!"

"He's not dead; he's passed out." Silas motioned to Pearl. "Hand me the small forceps. I'm going to try to get the remains of this ball out of him."

Pearl handed over the forceps and looked at him intensely. "He said he didn't want your help," she whispered.

"I can't let him die," Silas shot back. "I won't."

He removed the fragments of lead ball piece by piece, trying to stem the bleeding. "Cato," he ordered over his shoulder, "go find Booker. Tell him what's happened, and send him to the surrounding plantations to look for the missus."

"Ain't she at the big house?"

Silas shook his head impatiently. "The big house was taken over by Union soldiers a month ago. Mrs. Warren and some of the slaves left, and I expect they're hiding out with relatives. Now go! Bring her back here as fast as you can."

"Yessuh!" Cato sprinted out the door and slammed it behind him.

"He's not going to make it, is he?" Pearl asked.

"I doubt it. Still, I have to try. I just hope Olivia gets here in time."

"Robert?" Olivia Warren gripped her husband's fingers, and her tears fell onto his hand. "Robert, it's me, Olivia."

Pearl watched as the man's eyes opened slightly. His gaze cleared for a moment, and he focused on his wife. "Olivia?" he moaned.

"I'm here, darling. Don't try to talk."

"What happened?"

"Doctor Noble took the bullet out of you. You're going to be just fine."

Pearl turned her eyes away. Robert Warren wasn't going to be fine, and Olivia knew it.

"Noble? Noble worked on me? I told him—"

"Fortunately," Olivia interrupted, "he hasn't learned, even in all this time, to obey your orders."

Warren managed a weak smile. "I guess I should thank him."

"You certainly should." Olivia squeezed his hand.

Warren's eyes wandered around the room until they locked on Silas. "Thank you," he said, "for keeping me alive long enough to say good-bye."

"Robert, don't talk that way!" Olivia cried. "You're not going to die."

"Yes, I am," he sighed. "And we all know it."

Olivia began to weep, and with great effort Warren lifted his free hand to stroke her hair. "Noble told me the house was taken over by Yanks," he gasped. "You're all right?"

"I've been staying with Sophie. Her husband's gone off to fight, too."

"Stay there," he whispered. "Don't come back."

"Of course I'm going to come back," she protested. "It's my house, after all. And once you're well—"

"Stay there," he repeated. "There'll be nothing here to come back to." He reached out and grabbed Silas's arm. "Is Cato here?"

"He's right outside."

"Send him in, please."

Pearl caught Silas's nod and went to the front door. Cato was holding vigil, along with Booker, Celie, and several other slaves, in the rocking chairs on the porch. "The master wants to see you," she said.

Cato rose and followed Pearl into the house. Robert Warren motioned him over to the bed. "You took good care of me, boy," he murmured. "Now, I've got one final job for you to do." Warren crooked his finger at the slave, indicating that he should draw closer, and whispered something into his ear.

"Massah! You can't mean it!"

"I do mean it. It's my last order. Do it, and then—" he gasped for air. "Once it's done, you're free."

"Free, Massah?" Cato's eyes grew wide.

"In front of all these witnesses, I give you your freedom. Now go, and be quick about it."

Cato left the room at a run, and Robert Warren took his wife's hand again. "Forgive me, dearest. It's the only way." He grabbed at his belly and writhed in pain.

"Robert!"

"It's over," he groaned. "It's all over. Nothing will ever be the same again."

Pearl watched through her tears as Olivia Warren leaned down to kiss her husband for the last time. She had witnessed death, but never until this moment had she thought about how she would respond if Silas died. A tremor ran through her—not fear, for she knew she could manage without him, just as she had managed before she met him. It was, instead, a vicious stab of loss and loneliness. Silas stood here beside her, alive and well, and yet she could feel in her deepest soul what it would be like to say good-bye to him.

Perhaps he was feeling it, too. At any rate, his arms went around her, and she leaned against his solid warmth.

"Good-bye, Olivia. I love you. I always have."

Through her sobs, Olivia managed, "I love you, too."

Warren looked up at Silas and Pearl. "I was wrong," he said. "I'm—"

Before he could finish his thought, his breath caught in his throat, and his wiry frame went rigid. The last sound they heard from Robert

Warren was the hissing, rattling noise of his final breath leaving his body.

"Fire! Fire!"

Silas raced to the window in the upstairs bedroom, where he had been preparing Warren's body for burial. It was nearly dark, and from this vantage point upstairs, he could see an odd crimson glow beyond the trees in the direction of Rivermont Plantation.

He took the stairs two at a time, with Pearl and Olivia Warren on his heels, and flung open the front door to see Booker reining the horses to a stop in front of the house.

"Massah Doctor! The big house is on fire!"

Silas helped Pearl and Olivia into the buckboard and climbed up beside Booker. "Let's go!"

When the wagon careened around a bend in the road and headed up the drive toward Rivermont, Silas could see that the whole place was engulfed in flames. The nauseating odor of kerosene permeated the air.

A bucket brigade was forming from the well to the front porch. Silas and Booker stepped to the front of the line and began receiving buckets. But before they could throw the first drop of water onto the conflagration, Cato ran forward and stood in their way. The wavering light from the fire cast an eerie, dancing illumination over his features.

"No!" he shouted. "We's gotta let it burn!"

Silas ran to him and shook him by the shoulders. "What are you talking about? Step aside, man, and let us do something!" Even as he spoke the words, he knew it was hopeless. Already the flames were licking through the roof. With a resounding crash and a shower of sparks three stories high, the second floor fell in.

Olivia and Pearl ran up beside them. "I's sorry, Missus," Cato went on. "But it was Massah's last order. Burn the place to the ground, he say. He weren't gonna have no more Yankee soldiers plunderin' Rivermont."

"That's what he meant when he asked me to forgive him," Olivia sobbed.

"Yes'm. He axed me to say he was sorry, but he couldn't fight no more, and it were the only thing he could do now to stop the Union army."

"It's all right, Cato," Olivia said quietly. "With Robert gone, there was nothing left for me here, anyway."

She turned and began to walk away, then came back and looked into the slave's eyes. "Master Robert promised you your liberty," she whispered. "Come see me tomorrow, at Miss Sophie's place, and I'll write up your papers. You're free to go."

"Go where?" Cato lifted both hands helplessly. "I got nowhere else to go."

"Go, stay," Olivia responded without emotion. "It makes no difference to me." With a dazed expression she wandered off into the crowd of slaves gathered around the house.

Silas motioned to Booker. "Go get her. Take her back to Miss Sophie's place."

"Yessuh." Booker's eyes fixed on the destruction of Rivermont. "It's a crime, ain't it?"

Silas let out a heavy sigh. "Most everything that happens in this war is a crime, Booker."

Booker wagged his head. "Now ain't that the gospel truth."

15
Day of Jubilee

———◆◆◆◆———

January 3, 1863

Silas sat at his roll-top desk, his eyes fixed on Booker, who was pacing back and forth in the log cabin room. In the distance, down toward the cabins, they could hear the sounds of music and laughter—a celebration of the Day of Jubilee. As of two days ago, the slaves had finally been set free.

"They can sing and dance all they want, but it don't mean nothin' Massah Doctor. It don't matter that the big house is burned down, Massah Robert be dead, and Missus done gone to live with Miss Sophie. Mister Lincoln can proclaim all he likes, but it don't make a dime's worth of difference south of the line."

Silas sighed. His heart objected to the slave's reasoning, but his mind told him that Booker was right. The Emancipation Proclamation had given all slaves their freedom, but the law hadn't changed the reality of life below the Mason-Dixon line. The war still raged. Men from both sides were still dying. And the local patrollers, whom the slaves called *pattyrollers*, would shoot Negroes on sight, or capture and lynch them, leaving their bodies to rot in the trees as a warning to others.

Noble House, as people had begun to call it, was still standing—but only because Silas's reputation for doctoring both Union and Confederate soldiers had become widely known. Every few days, someone else would come limping in—once an entire company arrived, brought to their knees by dysentery. There wasn't enough room in the house for them, even stacking them side by side on corn-shuck mattresses on the floors. In the end, they had to be housed in the Rivermont barns, which had escaped the fire.

"We's safe here, at least for now," Booker went on. "Long as the Rebs and the pattyrollers think of us as your slaves, they'll leave us be. But we step one foot off this land, and you know what's gonna happen."

Silas knew. Two nights ago, four slaves had taken their women and children and made a run for it, hiding out in the woods. They figured that if they could get to Memphis, they could catch a boat up to Cairo, Illinois, and into free territory. But they never even got close. The pattyrollers tracked them down with dogs, shot the men, raped the women, and made the children watch. When the bodies were found, there wasn't much left of them—the dogs had finished them off. The details were widely publicized, and the intimidation worked. No one wanted to risk that kind of end, even for the sake of freedom.

"I know, Booker. But consider the alternatives. You can't stay here. The missus' daughter Sophie and her family, as well as the other children, intend to take over their daddy's land. For the past few months you've had the place to yourselves, and managed to feed everybody by working the gardens and slaughtering what's left of the pigs and chickens. That's not going to last forever."

Booker frowned. "Massah Robert was a hard man," he mused. "He worked us nigh to death. But least we was fed and clothed and had a warm house to sleep in. We didn't get whupped too often. Maybe slavery ain't so bad after all."

Silas went over and put a hand on the big man's shoulder. "You won't convince me of that, Booker. I saw it in your eyes from the moment I met you that first day at Rivermont Plantation. You longed to be free. You still do. You're just afraid."

Booker pushed his chest out. "You saying I'm skeert, Massah Doctor?"

"I'm saying you have a right to be scared. But some things are worth risking your life for. You just have to decide whether freedom is one of them."

An expression passed over Booker's face—a look of determination. "It is, Massah Doctor. I knows that."

"Besides, Booker, you can *read*. You can teach the others, help them to make a better life for themselves. But first you have to get out of here."

Even as Silas said the words, the truth twisted around his chest, nearly suffocating him. Booker was the best friend he had ever had—a man he could depend upon. Silas loved him, and the other slaves as well. They had become his family, and life without them would be miserable.

Still, he couldn't be selfish. He cared too much about Booker and the others to encourage them to stay. If they were ever going to make a life for themselves, on their own terms, they had to leave. And despite the pain in his heart, he had to encourage them to go.

If only, he mused, sending the thought forth as a desperate prayer, *if only they had someone to help them.*

"What's wrong, Daddy?"

Booker looked up to see his son, Enoch, gazing into his face with an expression just short of despair. He scooped the boy up and set him on his lap. "Nothin's wrong, son. I's just thinking about what we's gonna do."

"'Bout what, Daddy?"

Booker smiled down into Enoch's wide brown eyes. The child was the light of his life, a miracle sent from God. Since the day the boy came into the world, Booker only had to look at him to renew his faith and trust in the Almighty. If the Lord could send him a gift like this, Booker reckoned God could do most anything—even give him direction and courage when he needed it most.

"I's thinkin' about what it means to be free," Booker answered candidly. "And where we's supposed to go from here." He looked over the child's head and saw Celie at the fire, stirring a pot of soup. The expression in her eyes held deep love, and absolute faith that he would decide what was best for them all. *Two gifts,* he thought. *The two best gifts a man could ever have.*

He motioned for Celie to come and sit beside him, then let out a deep sigh. "I been talking to Massah Doctor," he began. "I could tell he didn't want to say it, but he thinks we ought to try to leave Rivermont and make a life for ourselves up north, where our freedom would mean something."

"He wants us to leave?" Enoch asked. "Don't he love us no more?"

"Of course he loves us, honey," Celie soothed. "That's why he wants us to go to a better place, where we'll be treated equal with the white folks."

"Equal? I don't understand." The boy frowned.

Booker hugged him close. "We's free now, son. We ain't slaves no more."

"What's it mean to be free, Daddy? Nothin's changed."

The question stung, and Booker couldn't answer for a minute. "Out of the mouths of babes," he murmured at last. And his son was right. Nothing had changed, and nothing was likely to change unless they—himself, Celie, all of them—took the risk to make it happen. They could go on as if Mister Lincoln's Emancipation Proclamation had never been enacted, living on Rivermont land, working Rivermont's fields and gardens. They could live in fear of the pattyrollers, dreading the day when Massah Robert's children would either evict them or set them to sharecropping. Or they could summon up all their courage and take a stand for themselves and their dignity.

A tug at his sleeve caught Booker's attention. "I think I figured out what it means, Daddy," Enoch was saying. "What it means to be free. It's in the story."

"What story?"

The boy reached across the table and laid a small brown hand on Booker's well-worn Bible. "The story from the Good Book, about Moses settin' the people free."

Celie smiled and nodded. With trembling hands Booker picked up the cracked leather volume and flipped its pages until he came to the passage he had read to them just the night before. His eyes scanned the verses, and then, for Enoch's sake, he decided to tell the story in words the boy could understand:

"That's right, son. God's people was held in slavery, in Egypt, under the rule of the Pharaoh."

"That's like the Massah," Enoch put in.

"That's right. And the Massah Pharaoh, he was hard on the people. Made 'em work day and night, with never enough to eat. Then God called Moses and said to him, 'Go down, Moses, and tell ol' Pharaoh to let my people go.' But the Pharaoh, he said no. So the Lord called down plagues on the folks in Egypt—"

"Hail and fire and frogs and grasshoppers!" the boy squealed, bouncing on his father's lap.

"That's right, son. But who's tellin' this story?"

Enoch giggled and settled down.

"Then finally," Booker went on, "Massah Pharaoh give in—them plagues were just too much for him. He agreed to let them go. So Moses took his staff in his hand and led the people out into the desert, headin' for the land the Lord had promised them, a land flowin' with milk and honey."

"Milk and honey?" the boy echoed.

"It's like all the ham and grits you'd ever want," Celie supplied. "Biscuits and cornbread and real blackstrap molasses."

"And fried chicken?"

"Yes, fried chicken, too." Celie suppressed a smile.

"But it wasn't all easy," Booker continued. "Soon as they was gone, ol' Massah Pharaoh had hisself a change of heart. Sent his armies after them, to bring them back—"

"The pattyrollers!" Enoch yelled.

"Yep. Just like the pattyrollers. They caught up with Moses and the people just when they was gettin' to the sea. Had the sea in front of them and the pattyrollers behind them and no place to go. Until—" He winked at his son. "What happened then?"

The boy's eyes shifted back and forth, and he scratched his head. Then his little face cleared, and he grinned. "God opened up the water, and they walked across on dry ground!"

"'Deed they did, child. 'Deed they did!"

"And the Lord led 'em to the land of fried chicken and biscuits."

Booker nodded. "Eventually."

"Daddy," Enoch said, a plaintive tone filling his voice, "I want to go to the Promised Land, too."

Celie was gazing at him with an odd expression. "I can't read," she said softly. "But I can hear. Seems to me the Lord's sayin' maybe Doctor Silas is right. Maybe we oughta think about it long and hard."

Booker started to protest, to say that you couldn't pick a story out of the Good Book and take it as the Lord's direction. But something inside—a warning, maybe—stopped him. Celie was right. Just because she couldn't read the words for herself didn't mean she couldn't hear the voice of the Almighty. And it might be that she was hearing better than he was right now.

"It'll be a hard road," he murmured. "A dangerous road."

"The Lord done drowned the pattyrollers for Moses," Enoch put in. "Ain't he gonna do the same for us?"

Booker sat there in silence, thinking about it, considering what the Good Book had to say about the faith of a little child.

Maybe God was speaking, even without a burning bush. But where was Moses?

The barn was dark, lit by a single lantern hanging from one of the stalls. Booker went about his nightly chores, forking up fresh hay for bedding, brushing down the last of the mares, putting feed in the mangers. Massah Robert was passed on, and Otis Tilson had hightailed it out at the first sign of trouble, but that was no reason to let the animals suffer. The cows had been milked, and the milk taken down to the slave cabins. The new calf was asleep in the stall next to her mother. Even the massah's big stallion had grown quiet.

A stirring behind him prickled the hairs on the back of Booker's neck. *Pattyrollers?* They had been known to steal stock—especially prime horses. And they wouldn't think twice about shooting a nigra where he stood.

Slowly his hand gripped around the hay fork. He waited, his breathing coming harder and faster. Then he whirled, pulling the fork up in front of him. "Who's there?"

A shrouded figure stepped from the doorway into the lamplight, and Booker felt a huge breath of relief whoosh out of him. It was a woman. A small colored woman.

"You can put the fork down, sonny," she said, her voice low. "I ain't come to kill you. I come to help."

Booker watched as she took another two steps forward. Her skin was dark, her face misshapen as if she had, at one time, suffered some terrible beating. One leg dragged a little.

His hands still gripped the hay fork, his muscles tensed. "Who are you?"

"Name's Harriet," the woman answered.

Booker peered at her face. He didn't recognize her from any of the surrounding plantations; he was certain, in fact, that he had never seen her before. "What you doin' here?"

She gave a crooked smile. "Like I said, I come to help."

"Help how?"

"You ever hear of the Underground Railroad?"

The questioned stunned Booker. Everybody had heard the rumors about such a thing—not a real railroad, but a system of safe houses run by abolitionists and sympathizers who provided food and shelter and protection to slaves escaping to the North. But he had never met anyone who had dealings with the railroad firsthand, and he sometimes suspected it might just be wishful thinking.

"I heard of it," he said finally.

"Folks tell me you're the one to talk to, the one who has most influence over the slaves here."

"Don't rightly know about that. I been here a long time, though, and I reckon most folks respects me pretty good."

"If your people want to leave, I can get them out."

Booker shook his head. This little bitty woman, all beat and battered up, thought she could help slaves escape past the pattyrollers? She had to be crazy. "Who'd you say you was?"

"Harriet," she repeated. "Harriet Tubman."

"Lord, have mercy," Booker breathed. This woman—if she was Harriet Tubman, as she claimed—was practically a legend among the slaves. The woman who had singlehandedly aided in the escape of more than three hundred Negroes in Maryland and Pennsylvania. Even in Mississippi, people knew her reputation. Everybody called her—

His heart skipped a beat, and his mouth went dry.

Moses.

Silas gaped at the women who stood before him. "It is a pleasure to meet you," he managed at last, reaching out to shake her hand. "We've all heard about you, of course, but—"

"But you thought I was some kind of spirit?" Harriet Tubman laughed. "Some phantom somebody worked up out of their imagination?" She took a seat in a chair and accepted the cup of coffee Pearl offered her. "Naw sir, I be real enough. Just not what anybody ever 'spects."

"What are you doing here?" Silas asked.

"I been in Alabama for some time," she answered. "It's tougher to get folks out of the deep South, but we's doing all right. Ain't lost nobody yet."

"And you say you can help Booker and his people escape? You know about the pattyrollers? They're always on guard, and nearly impossible to get around."

Harriet gave a little snort. "Pattyrollers—humph! Just a bunch a crazy redneck boys who got bullets but no brains." She took a sip of her coffee and nodded at Pearl. "If you can't fight 'em, you gotta outsmart 'em."

Silas looked over at Booker, whose eyes had widened in an expression of admiration. "And you can do that?" he asked.

"Not without help," she countered. "And not without commitment. Your people gotta be ready for a long journey, and they gotta have faith. But like I said, I ain't lost a single one yet—" She reached into her waistband, pulled out a pistol, and waved it in Booker's direction. "And I ain't had nobody turn back, neither."

Booker took a step backward. "I hear tell somebody want to quit, you shoot 'im."

Harriet's eyes danced. "Haven't had to yet. But I would." Her expression sobered. "The cause is too important to be ruined by one or two cowards. We got a big job to do, and we gonna do it. Now, you in or not?"

Silas went and put an arm around Pearl, who was trembling. "It sounds dangerous."

"It *is* dangerous," Harriet agreed. "Most everything worth doing involves some danger. But not doing it is a bigger risk."

"So what's the plan?"

"It'll take some months to get everybody out, and we can't start till spring, when the leaves are on the trees. Can't take more than ten or twelve at a time, and the trip north is a long one. You'll need to decide who goes first; maybe the doctor here can help you make a list. And we'll need to find a place where people can hide until the coast is clear. We can't just go marching out in broad daylight."

"I got that part covered," Booker declared. "Follow me."

He got up and led them into the downstairs bedroom, where two closets filled the space on either side of the fireplace. Silas slanted a glance at Pearl that asked, *What is he doing?* But she just shrugged. When everyone was gathered around, Booker pushed the clothes to one side and slid a panel open to reveal a ladder going down into a narrow passageway.

"It leads to the root cellar," he explained. "There's a tunnel that goes out into the woods. Don't go but a little ways, but unless you're right up on it, nobody can see anyone going in or out."

"Booker!" Silas interrupted. "When did you do this?"

Booker grinned crookedly and scratched his head. "When I's building the house, Massah Doctor. Jus' thought it might come in handy someday."

"Perfect," Harriet declared. "You can gather your folks in the house, and if the pattyrollers get wind of it and come looking, they can hide down there."

They returned to the log cabin room, and Booker plopped into a chair. Celie stood beside him, and little Enoch clambered onto his lap. The boy gazed at Harriet Tubman with open curiosity and wonder. "She don't look like Moses, but she'll do," he declared at last. "Now we can go to the land of chicken and biscuits."

Booker smiled. "The land of milk and honey," he translated.

"That's where we're going, son," Harriet affirmed. "To the Promised Land. You ready?"

Enoch nodded firmly. "Yes'm. I'm ready. Ready to see the pattyrollers get drownded in the sea."

Booker looked at Celie and shrugged. "I reckon we're all ready."

The woman called Moses stood, picked up her small bag of belongings, and nodded. "I'll be on my way then. Be ready with the first group by early April. Dress warm and travel light. I'll send someone for you as soon as the time is right."

With that, she opened the door, limped out, and disappeared into the darkness.

16
Free at Last

April 1865

Silas awoke to find Pearl bending over him, kissing his eyelids. He lay there for a moment, accepting her kisses, savoring her nearness. After all this time—nearly ten years of marriage—he only had to look into her deep and tender gaze to be transported back to the moment he had stood with her on the porch and promised to love her forever.

It hadn't been a difficult vow to keep. Pearl was, in every way, his soul mate. He adored her, couldn't imagine life without her. And now, at last, after years of disappointment, she was about to become the mother of his child.

He opened his eyes and reached up to embrace her. Her swelling body pressed against him, and he laid both hands on her abdomen. "Good morning, little Abe," he murmured to her belly.

She pulled back and playfully swatted his hands away. "And how, pray tell, are you so sure this child will be 'Abe'? She might be 'Abby,' you know."

Silas laughed and pulled her close. "True. But either way, he—or she—will be our offspring, and the finest child ever to bear the Noble name."

When Pearl had discovered that—after two miscarriages—she was once again with child, they had determined that their firstborn would be named after President Lincoln, in honor of the man who had freed the slaves and changed the nation forever. This baby would live, Silas was certain. He would see to it, no matter what it took. This baby would be the son he had longed and prayed for.

He had tried, at first, to make sure Pearl took care of herself, determining that he would strap her to the bed and make her stay there, if necessary. But it didn't work out quite the way he had anticipated.

Harriet Tubman had put into motion a method of escape for the Rivermont slaves, and nothing could stand in the way. And that plan took a good deal longer than they had expected. Because Rivermont was so deep in Confederate territory, Harriet's people could only take slaves out in small groups—ten, at most. A larger group would prove too dangerous, too easily tracked. And since there were fifty-seven slaves on Rivermont land who once belonged to Robert Warren, that meant six groups, and long waiting periods in between. During the winters, there could be no safe passage, so it had taken eighteen months to get them to freedom. Eighteen months fraught with fear and apprehension.

No one—not even Booker—had ever laid eyes on Harriet Tubman after that first meeting, but the reports from her slave-smuggling operation were encouraging. The word came back: not a single soul lost. All resettled north of the Mason-Dixon line.

Tonight the last group would slip out through the root cellar and into the woods on their way to freedom: Booker and Celie, with Enoch; Lily, with her daughter Marissa, and her cousin Jute; and Cato, who had stayed to the very end.

Booker had begged Silas and Pearl to come with them, and at last they had relented and agreed to leave Noble House and make the journey. Silas, of course, was worried about the baby, but they should be able to get to Cairo before Pearl delivered. It was a daunting prospect—a new life in a new place with a new child. Still, Silas was convinced he'd be able to find work among the relocated, and there wasn't much left for them in Cambridge. And he had to admit that he did want his child to grow up in an environment where all God's people stood on equal ground. It was a huge risk, but one he thought he was willing to take.

Pearl nudged him. "Drink your coffee before it gets cold."

Silas sat up. "Breakfast in bed? Does this mean we're about to have a fight? Or did we already have one and I didn't notice?"

Pearl smiled. "I don't think so. Besides, it's just coffee. Then you need to get up. We've got a lot to do to prepare for tonight."

He propped up on a pillow and reached for the coffee. "Are we doing the right thing, do you think?"

Pearl stroked his hand and smiled. "It will be difficult, leaving Noble House. So many wonderful memories. But we have to trust that if it's not the best decision, God will somehow give us a new direction."

Silas nodded. Despite his apprehensions, he felt a sense of peace wash over him. What mattered was not where they were, but that they were together. Wherever they went, as long as Pearl was at his side, everything would be all right.

At six that evening, as Pearl packed up the last of the food she had prepared for the trip, Silas sat at the kitchen table watching her. "You need some help?"

She turned and smiled at him. "I'm almost done. But we've got half an apple pie left, and I'm afraid it won't travel well."

He grinned. "Then I guess we'll have to do something about it. Come, sit down."

She brought the pie and two forks to the table, along with two glasses of milk. As he started in on the pie, Silas realized he felt like a child raiding the kitchen in the middle of the night—a delicious sense of rebellion. "This is going to be quite an adventure, isn't it?"

"I'm glad you can look at it in that light," Pearl responded. "For a while there, I was beginning to think you'd back out at the last minute."

"I just don't want to take any chances with you and the baby."

"We'll be fine—both of us. And I've got everything packed, including the quilt Lily made. I didn't have the heart to leave it behind."

Silas chewed thoughtfully. "Pearl, I don't have any idea what kind of life we're going to have when we get to . . . well, to wherever we end up. I'd like to be able to promise you that we'll have a nice house and that I'll make a good living, but—"

"I know." She put a finger to his lips to silence him. "You can't make such a promise, and I'm not asking for it. All I want is for us to be together."

He gazed into her face. "I love you, you know—with all my heart and soul."

She started to respond, but before she could get a word out, the back door slammed and Booker rushed into the kitchen.

"You're here a little early, aren't you?" Silas laughed. "We don't leave until after dark." Then he looked at Booker's face.

The big black man was trembling, and shiny tracks ran down his cheeks.

"Booker!" Pearl reached out and touched his arm. "Booker, what's wrong?"

"Is somebody hurt?" Silas asked. "Pearl, where's my bag?"

"Your medical bag ain't gonna do no good this time, Massah Doctor." Booker leaned over the table and dropped a newspaper in front of them. "Found this in a trash bin in town."

Silas stared down at the headline, and his heart sank.

LINCOLN ASSASSINATED.

"He dead," Booker whispered through his tears. "Mister Lincoln, he dead."

Silas felt something shrivel in the depths of his soul. "When did this happen?"

"What the paper say is three nights ago. Mister Lincoln, he went to a place called Ford's Theatre to see some big play, and a fella shot him in the head."

"Who would do such a thing?"

"Southern sympathizers, of course," Pearl snarled. Silas looked at her and saw an expression of raw fury in her eyes. "People who thought that if they got rid of the president, the Confederacy would live on."

"Man's name was Booth," Booker answered. "An' Pearl ain't far wrong. All them pattyrollers is out with a vengeance. They's roamin' the woods with guns and ropes and dogs. There's gonna be trouble—big trouble."

Silas closed his eyes and fought back tears. They had come so far, and now this. "Maybe tonight isn't the best night for us to go," he suggested. "Maybe we should wait a while."

"Naw sir, Massah Doctor," Booker countered. "We gotta get out now."

"Booker's right," Pearl added. "Who knows what will happen now that President Lincoln is dead? Up till now, Noble House has been spared because we helped Confederate soldiers as well as Union ones, and because Master Robert's slaves stayed put. But if they come and find all but a few of the slaves gone, they'll know we've helped. There's likely to be retribution."

"All right," Silas sighed. "Booker, gather everybody up and get them over here as quickly as possible. I don't want any Negroes roaming around in plain sight. Tell them to be packed and prepared to go on a moment's notice. Our guide will be here shortly after dark, and we need to be ready."

Booker nodded, picked up the newspaper, and left without a word.

"I'm scared, Papa Silas."

Pearl watched as Silas held Enoch on his lap and cuddled him close. "I know, son. We all are. We just have to wait until it's safe to go."

The clock on the mantel chimed ten. For the past three hours, the remaining seven slaves of Rivermont Plantation had been huddled in the log cabin room of Noble House, with the shutters closed and only a single lamp lit. The guide sent by the Underground Railroad, a big, burly fellow named John Carver, paced back and forth across the rug.

Outside, the noise continued as if some kind of bizarre celebration were in full swing. Gunshots, dogs baying, shouts echoing through the woods, and every now and then a bloodcurdling Rebel yell that made Pearl fear that the pattyrollers had begun another lynching party.

She went into their bedroll, retrieved the handmade quilt, and laid it out on the rug as a pallet for Enoch and Marissa. After a while, despite the noise and commotion, the two children settled down and fell asleep at the adults' feet.

If only we could be that trusting, Pearl thought as she watched them. *To lie down and sleep, and believe that no matter what, we'd be safe, because Someone is looking out for us.*

Was it any wonder that Jesus told adults they needed the faith of a little child? But grownups always seemed to have a difficult time with simple faith. *We always try to figure things out for ourselves,* Pearl thought. *We trust our own reasoning, our own plans, and our own schemes, instead of putting our faith in the protection of the Almighty.*

Well, they would have no choice but to depend upon the Almighty's protection this night. When the right time came—if there was a right time—they would have to trust God to blind the eyes of the pattyrollers and keep them at bay. Otherwise, they might all end up swinging from the nearest tree.

"It's time," John Carver said. "Let's move."

Silas stirred in his chair and strained his ears. The gunshots had died down, and the baying of the dogs seemed to be getting farther and farther away. He checked his pocket watch: twelve forty-five.

Lily awakened the children and herded them into the bedroom. Cato and Jute followed. From the parlor, Silas caught a glimpse of the closet door standing open, revealing the secret passage that would lead them into the root cellar and then to the woods. And—he hoped—to safety.

"Get your coats on. It'll be chilly out there," Silas instructed. "And make sure you don't leave anything behind." Out of the corner of his eye, Silas saw Pearl bend down to roll up the quilt. Then, without warning, she collapsed to the floor, gripping her stomach.

"Pearl! Are you all right?" He ran to her and started to lift her up, then saw the stain beneath her on the quilt.

"No," she moaned. "Not now!"

Booker came to his side. "What's wrong?"

"Just lie back, honey. It'll be all right." He turned to Booker. "Looks like she's going into labor."

"It's too early," she protested. "It's probably false pains. Give me a minute, and I'll be fine."

Silas shook his head. "Apparently it's not too early. Your water broke." He knelt beside her and took her hand. "There's no turning back now."

John Carver appeared in the doorway. "That's exactly what I was about to say. Booker, Celie, come on. Lily's already got Enoch and Marissa down in the cellar. It's now or never."

Booker turned and faced Carver as if tensing for a fight. "We still got plenty of darkness left," he argued. "We ain't leavin' without Massah Doctor and Pearl."

"That's right," Celie put in. "We's staying 'til that baby is delivered and strong enough to travel."

Pearl clutched Silas's hand and motioned for him to help her to a sitting position. "Celie, you know better. This is my first pregnancy—at least the first one I've carried to term. And I'm not so young anymore. This is likely to be a hard delivery, and a long one. But you can't wait. You've got to go now. We'll catch up with you. Wherever you are, we'll find you." She gave a wan smile, then winced as a contraction gripped her. "We're—we're family. Don't worry—we'll be together again soon."

Celie and Booker exchanged a glance, and Booker put his fists on his hips. "No ma'am."

Silas eased Pearl back onto the quilt and stood up. "Booker, you listen to me. This is your chance—it's what you've waited for all your life. Now, take your wife and son and go. Please."

Booker looked at him, and his dark eyes held a curious expression. "If you was me, Massah Doctor, would you leave?"

Silas narrowed his eyes and gritted his teeth. "Yes. Yes, Booker, I would."

Booker stepped forward and enveloped Silas in a massive bear hug. "You's a bad liar, Massah Doctor," he whispered in Silas's ear. "Now you take good care of that gal of yours," he added. "And that baby. I 'spect to see all of y'all real soon."

"Come on!" Carver insisted. "If we don't go now, we won't be far enough along by daybreak."

"Wait!" Pearl gasped. She motioned for Silas to bring her the canvas bag that held their meager belongings. She reached in and drew out a small velvet box.

"Sweetheart—" he protested.

But her eyes stopped him cold. "The night before we married, I told you I'd treasure this forever," she said softly as she drew out the heart-shaped amethyst. "But if it can help save the lives of people we love—"

Silas nodded. "You're right." He took the brooch from her and handed it to Booker. "If you get into trouble, maybe you can find some sympathetic white folks who will sell this for you."

Booker's enormous, pale palm dwarfed the amethyst. "I can't take this, Massah Doctor."

"Yes, you can. And you will. We can't go with you right now, but—"

"We've got to hurry," Carver interrupted. "We don't have time for this."

Booker heaved a huge, shuddering sigh and slipped the brooch into his pocket, then swiped at his eyes. "Pray for us," he said as he turned to go. "You be right here"—he pounded a hand against his chest—"in our hearts."

Silas nodded and laid a hand on his own chest. But tears choked him and he couldn't speak. By the time he found his voice again, the big slave he had come to love so deeply was gone.

Just as dawn was sending rays of orange and pink over the horizon, Abraham Lincoln Noble pushed and kicked his way into the world. Silas cleaned him up, tucked mother and son into the big poster bed, and went out onto the back porch with a steaming cup of coffee.

Father. Daddy. Papa. Pa.

He tried out the names in his mind, and breathed a prayer of thankfulness into the morning air.

An early rain had washed the world clean, and scattered clouds reflected back the light of the rising sun. Unbidden, his gaze wandered toward the woods. Were they all right, the friends who had fled in the dark hours of the morning? Had the patrollers found them, or were they now on their way toward the liberty for which they had waited so long?

Thousands had fought and died for that freedom—indeed, were still fighting, still dying. President Lincoln lay dead because he dared to stand up and declare that no one should have to endure a lifetime of enslavement. And from the deep recesses of his memory, Silas called up Booker's profound words the night of Enoch's birth: *Life and death is in the hands of the Lord . . . One brother was goin' out, even as another was comin' in.*

Through the screen door, Silas heard the reedy cry of his infant son and the soft murmuring of his wife as she cooed the child back to sleep. How could he feel so fulfilled and, at the same time, so empty?

"Let there be an end to the dying," he prayed. "Dear God, keep them safe."

Early June 1865

Abraham Lincoln Noble was little more than a month old when his father's prayers were answered. The war was finally over. The fighting had ended; the Confederate surrender had been signed. And this time when troops of both colors marched over Silas's land, they didn't ransack or burn or pillage. They just walked on, exhausted, trying with the last of their strength to get back home.

Some of them stopped, asking for food or water or quinine or bandages, and Silas and Pearl gave freely of whatever they had. But nobody stayed, not even the sick ones. The medicine they needed most was the first glimpse of home, the long-awaited embrace of a loved one.

"Are we going to go or not?" Pearl asked one morning as she sat at the table nursing Abe. "He's very strong. In another month or two he should be able to make the trip without any problem at all." She smiled down at the baby. "Besides, now that the war is over, traveling will be a good deal easier. At least we won't have to sneak through the woods in the middle of the night."

Silas sighed. He didn't know how to answer her. As the time approached when they could finally leave and go north, he sensed a powerful resistance in his soul, as if they should stay in Cambridge. But why? Pearl's father had died of influenza the previous winter, and she rarely saw her cousins who now ran the mill. Everyone they loved was gone. And although Silas expected he would be able to rebuild his practice, nobody's money would be worth anything—just more of the useless scrip that had been floating around during the war. Once again, they'd be taking chickens and hams and potatoes for payment, and for what cause?

He felt lost, as if all sense of mission had vanished from his life. He had his wife and son to look after, but he had spent so many years with a larger purpose than just caring for his family. He loved them, but he needed more—something beyond himself and his own to give his life to.

How could he explain this to Pearl? Would she think that she, and their son, and their life together weren't enough for him? And how could he tell her that he had a feeling he wasn't supposed to leave when he could not give her—or himself, for that matter—a single reason to stay?

Pearl stroked little Abraham's downy head and looked beyond him to Silas. Something was wrong; she could tell as certainly as if he had said it out loud. And she suspected she might know what it was: They would not be leaving Mississippi.

In many ways, she was torn by the idea of staying. On the one hand, she wanted her son to be raised in a place where equality and acceptance were a way of life. But where was that place? Were the slaves who had fled north any better off? She had read a newspaper or two that told stories of the horrible overcrowding in the cities, the living conditions that were often no better—and sometimes worse—than slave quarters. Freed slaves who expected a better life must be terribly disappointed. They had no skills and could do only the most menial jobs. Thousands were unemployed and near starvation. They might be liberated, but they were still on the lowest rung of society's ladder. What kind of equality was that?

On the other hand, if she and Silas stayed here, what purpose would their lives serve? What influences would shape the kind of man little Abraham would become? What would happen if—?

She stopped suddenly and smiled inwardly at her own foolishness. No matter what the logic of the situation, there was only one real question to be considered:

What was God calling them to do?

They had been ready to go, ready to risk everything. But in the final moments their path had been blocked by an unforeseen event—the untimely arrival of this baby she held in her arms.

Was the Lord trying to tell them something? And if so, what?

She looked up into her husband's face and saw a wistful, faraway expression. She had known him long enough and loved him well enough to know what it meant. God was speaking to him, too.

———————

When Pearl spoke, Silas had a hard time drawing himself out of his reverie to hear her words. "I'm sorry. What did you say?"

"I said, is it possible we're not supposed to leave?"

He shook his head to clear it. "Not leave? But I thought you wanted to go as soon as—"

"I did," she interrupted. "Or at least I thought I did."

His heart did a little flip. "Go on."

She smiled. "You need a purpose, a mission in life. We both do. And I'm not sure quite how I know this, but I have a feeling that our purpose is here, not somewhere up north."

As soon as she had said the words, a sense of relief rushed over Silas like an enormous wave. For a minute he couldn't catch his breath. And in that moment he became fully aware of the truth. He had no idea why, or how, or what form it would take, but he knew that for some reason he couldn't fathom, he and his wife and child were to stay put. The purpose would be revealed in time.

He grinned at Pearl and reached out to take little Abe's flailing fist. "I love you," he whispered.

"And I love you," she responded. "I guess we'll find out eventually what this is all about."

"I guess so. But for now, it's sufficient to know what we're *not* supposed to do. The rest will fall in place soon enough."

———————

"Pearl! Come quick!"

Pearl took the pan of potatoes off the stove, scooped up Abe, and followed Silas's voice to the front porch. The sun was setting, and in the distance she could see the silhouettes of three figures on the road, back-lit by the colors of dusk.

"Who does that look like?" Silas asked.

Pearl squinted. "It's hard to make out in this light. A man—a big man. A girl, maybe, or a small woman. A little child." Her eyes widened and she clutched Abe closer to her breast. "It can't be!"

"I think it is. Stay here." Silas took off running down the road, and Pearl watched as he stopped, then ran ahead a little farther, enveloped the male figure in a hug, and leaned down to kiss the girl on the cheek. He turned back and waved in her direction, and tears formed a lump in Pearl's throat.

Booker, Celie, and Enoch had come home.

Pearl hurried to set three more plates at the table, and they all sat down in the dining room. Dinner was simple—cornbread, black-eyed peas, and potatoes—but there was enough to go around, and everybody seemed to be enjoying it.

Booker shook his head. "Lawd, you jus' wouldn't believe it. Two, three families in a house no bigger than our old cabin. Chinks in the walls you could put a hand through. I reckon we do better down here, where we belong."

"'Sides," Celie murmured, rocking little Abe against her bosom, "we jus' couldn't stand not seein' what become of this child."

"Oh," Booker said suddenly. "I near forgot." He reached into his pocket. "Reckon I oughta return this to you."

He pulled out the heart-shaped brooch, and the deep color of the amethyst captured the light and sent back rays of warm purple.

Pearl's breath caught in her throat, and her pulse quickened. "I thought for sure you had sold it!"

"Wouldn't rightly do that unless I had to," he responded quietly. He pushed the brooch in her direction. "It belongs with you, Miss Pearl. With you and Massah Doctor and young Abraham."

"There was one time we thought a bit about selling it," Celie added, "but we got by all right. I told Booker that unless it was a matter of life or death, you had to have your heart back."

Pearl put a hand on Celie's arm and felt a warm rush of love rise up within her. She had no idea what Booker would do to earn a living or how they would all get by, but their family—at least part of it—was together again.

"With it or without it," she murmured, "I do have my heart back."

And for now, that was enough.

17
The Birth of Hope

Summer 1899

Silas leaned back in the rocking chair and shaded his eyes. Heat shimmered from the cotton rows, and on the edge of the nearest field a muscular, well-built young man leaned over to inspect the crop. Enoch had grown into a handsome, intelligent, responsible adult. He looked up, saw Silas, smiled, and waved. When Silas waved back, his hand jerked unsteadily, a palsied tremor.

He dropped his hands into his lap and stared at them. Spotted, ancient hands that shook when they moved. When had he grown so frail? He hadn't remembered the process at all. It was as if one day he awoke to find himself in the body of an old, old man.

It was the cancer. He knew it, although he didn't want to admit it. He might hold out a year, but not much more than that. His time was coming, and he wasn't ready.

Oh, he had accomplished plenty with his life. He had built a wonderful home, lived for years basking in the love of a good woman, and done what the Good Lord placed in his hands to do. He had brought a number of folks into the world, and helped others to go out gently. He had given more than forty years in the service of healing—fulfilling years, happy years. He had fought the good fight, had run his race well. He just hadn't anticipated having regrets when he got to the end.

Correction. One regret.

His son, Abraham.

Silas closed his eyes and heaved a weary sigh.

He must have dozed. When he opened his eyes, he saw Enoch's smiling brown face gazing down at him. "Thought I'd come get a cold drink," he said. "It's pretty hot out there."

"Sit down." Silas motioned to a chair and called over his shoulder, "Pearl, could you bring us some lemonade?"

In a moment the screen door opened and Pearl came out bearing a tray with a pitcher and several glasses. She was thin and stooped, and walked with a little shuffle, but to Silas she was still the most beautiful woman on the face of the earth. A prize. A gift. His Pearl.

His eyes wandered to Enoch, and he remembered that night, so long ago, when Booker had lifted his infant son to the heavens and named him "The One Who Walks with God." If only Booker had lived long enough to see how his boy had turned out. He would have been proud. Enoch Warren carried himself with dignity and faith, a man of conviction, a free man who bowed his head to no one but the Almighty.

Years before, shortly after Booker and Celie returned to Rivermont, Silas had managed to purchase part of the old plantation acreage, and Booker had run the place. They had hired freed slaves to work the land, raising cotton and corn and soybeans. Under Booker's direction, the farm had quickly become a paying proposition, and now Celie lived in a fine house of her own just beyond what used to be the slave quarters. When Booker died, Enoch returned from the Negro college up north with an agricultural degree and took over. Bright and ambitious and a genius when it came to numbers, the young man had expanded their holdings and made quite a name for himself.

And Abe was green with jealousy.

"You treat him better than you do me," Silas's son had accused him more than once. "Sometimes I think you wish he was your son instead."

The criticism, Silas had to admit, had some basis in truth. The two families had been together so long that Silas *did* consider Enoch as one of his own. But there was more to it than that—much more. The truth was, Abraham had turned out to be a bitter disappointment. Self-absorbed and irresponsible, Silas's only son would have run the place into the ground inside a year had he been given the chance. Any money he made, he spent—frivolously, without regard to the future. Abe seemed to think that the world owed him a living, and he was more than content to live off the proceeds of other people's labors. He was the Prodigal, while Enoch was the faithful Elder Brother.

It had caused him great pain to do so, but Silas had determined long ago to let Abe live with the consequences of his actions. Maybe the boy would learn a lesson or two in the process; maybe seeing Enoch's success would motivate him to be more responsible.

It hadn't worked. Abraham simply grew more arrogant, more convinced that he never got what he deserved. He expected the fatted calf every day of his life, without once considering that for the Prodigal, repentance came before restoration.

Silas couldn't for the life of him figure out where Abe came by his haughtiness, his contempt for hard work and diligence, his presumption that the world should be handed to him on a silver platter. Certainly he and Pearl held different values, values they had tried to teach their son and live out before him. But almost from the beginning, the boy had rejected their principles of living. He wanted a life of ease and wealth rather than hard-earned respect and spiritual fulfillment.

And ironically, it seemed as if he was finally about to get it.

After years of sowing his wild oats as a handsome and available bachelor, Abe had finally set his sights on one girl—a young woman for whom Silas could feel nothing but disdain. A girl named Patricia—Pansy, they called her—the spoiled, wealthy daughter of Bick Littleton. Bick ran a huge spread called Nine Willows, on the far north end of the county, a plantation that had changed little since the end of the war. To be sure, Bick's Negroes were no longer slaves, but they might as well have been. He kept them on the land as sharecroppers, paying them so small a percentage that all of them were perpetually in debt for the most basic necessities of life. Bick was still a master, climbing to ever-increasing wealth on the backs of his workers.

Silas despised Bick's way of life, but to be fair, he couldn't hold Pansy responsible for what her father did. He could only blame Pansy for her own faults—and she had many. She was one of those brainless, sickly sweet Southern belles with a high, tittering laugh and such a penchant for fainting that she carried smelling salts wherever she went. Pansy fawned on Abe as if he were divine, and of course Abe, in Pearl's words, "ate it up with a spoon." They were made for each other, but Silas suspected it wasn't exactly a match conceived in heaven.

"Papa Silas, are you listening?"

Silas smiled slightly and returned his attention to Enoch. At least he had one son who made him proud, even though it wasn't the child of his own body.

"I got the figures worked out," Enoch went on. "With the kind of crop we've got this summer, we'll be able to put in two more forty-acre sections of cotton next year. But we'll need extra help. I got an idea, though it'll cost us a little money up front."

Silas waved a hand. "Go on."

"I been talking to some of the sharecroppers over to Nine Willows. They want to come work for us, but they're deep in debt to Littleton and figure they'll never get above water. They know when we have a good year, we share profits with the fieldworkers. I've been thinking that maybe we pay off their debts to Littleton, and then give them a chance to earn it back—not from their wages, 'cause they'll need that to live, but from any bonuses that might be coming their way. That way they get out of debt, start working for themselves, and get to keep their dignity—and we get the help we need."

Silas nodded and slanted a glance at Pearl, who was beaming. "It's just the kind of plan Pearl and I might have come up with a few years ago," he said. "Let's do it."

"I thought you'd go for it." Enoch nodded, then frowned. "But there's one hitch."

"What's that?"

"Mister Bick isn't going to be too happy about it. We'll be taking some of his best hands."

"It's a free country," Silas said. "Finally."

Enoch grinned and stood up with his clipboard under one arm. "I'll get on over there, then, and take care of it. You think this might put a damper on the little romance Abe's got going with Pansy?"

Silas rocked back in his chair and lifted his glass of lemonade in a shaky salute. "We can always hope, son. We can always hope."

———

For the first time in weeks, Abe appeared at the dinner table and sat in silence as Pearl and Silas carried on a guarded conversation about the weather, the crop, and the prospects for the future. Neither mentioned Enoch's name or his plan to buy out some of Bick Littleton's best field-workers, but it probably wouldn't have registered anyway. Their son obviously had something on his mind—something that had nothing to do with the current cotton and soybean markets.

Finally, over Pearl's fresh peach turnovers, he broke the suspense. "I need to talk to you about something."

Silas put down his fork and rested his hand over Pearl's. This sounded important, and a serious conversation coming from their son always made Silas nervous. What kind of trouble was the boy in this time? Gambling? A girl?

They didn't have long to wait.

"It's about Pansy," Abraham said with a sigh.

"Are things not going well between the two of you?" Pearl asked. Silas thought he heard a tiny glimmer of hopefulness in her voice.

"Actually, they're going very well. Sorry to disappoint you."

Silas bristled. "Son, there's no cause to talk to your mother in that tone of voice."

"I know how she feels about Pansy," Abe countered. "I know how you both feel. But it doesn't matter. We're going to be married, and that's all there is to it."

Silas watched as Pearl tried to put on an expression appropriate for a doting mother who has just received the news that her son is betrothed. "Well, congratulations, Abraham," she managed at last. "Of course we're happy for you."

"Happy that I'm finally settling down?" he muttered. "Or happy that I'll be out from underfoot? We will, as you might expect, be living at Nine Willows—Bick is planning to build a house for us." He looked around the dining room. "A much finer house than this, although I don't suppose that would impress the two of you."

Silas narrowed his eyes. "What would impress *me,*" he responded, "is showing a little respect for your parents. We've worked hard to bring you up right, and even though you obviously do not share our values, we try to be supportive."

"Your values? You mean giving everything away—mostly to those nigras—without a thought to leaving anything behind as an inheritance?"

Ah, Silas thought. *The inheritance again.* Ever since he found out about his father's cancer, Abraham had been pressing them about the future, asking repeatedly if all their papers were in order. As their only son, he clearly expected to inherit all the land his father owned. He didn't know—and wouldn't, until the time came—that the farming business and most of the property, except for the house itself and the oak grove, had already been transferred to Enoch's name. It was only fair. Enoch had worked hard for it and deserved it. Abe would only squander it. But now was not the time for that issue to be raised.

"Please," Pearl interjected, "can't we have a civil discussion without arguing?"

Abe sighed. "All right. Let's call a truce."

Pearl leaned forward. "Have you set a date? Next spring, perhaps? Nine Willows would be lovely in April, with everything blooming—"

"Right away," Abe interrupted. "Next Saturday."

Pearl nearly choked on her turnover. "So soon? Son, we can't get a wedding together in that short a time. Surely Pansy's mother would agree. Does she know about this?"

Abe nodded. "She does. So does Bick."

"But if you waited until spring, the house Mr. Littleton is building might be ready—"

"We'll live in the big house temporarily. It's all settled, Mother."

Silas watched the play of emotions that ran across his son's countenance. He was getting what he wanted—a wealthy wife, marriage into a prominent family, a father-in-law who would support him. But he didn't seem happy about it. He seemed—nervous, somehow. Fidgety. He was hiding something, and Silas was pretty sure he knew what it was.

"When's the baby due?" he asked softly.

Pearl squeezed his fingers until they turned white. "Silas! How could you even suggest such a thing?"

"He suggests it, Mother, because he's right." Abraham let out a shuddering sigh. "Face it, Mother—real life does not always turn out the way you believe it should. Maybe it has for you and Father. You had this great romance, this rich heritage of doing good for the downtrodden. And it's no secret you expected better from me. But I'm not like you. And I never will be, no matter how much you pray for me to change."

The word *pray* came out with a sarcastic sneer, and Silas saw an expression of pain flash over his wife's face.

"So we won't be waiting until spring," Abe went on. "We're getting married right away, before the truth becomes too obvious. The Littletons have been told, and now you. No one else will know—unless they go to the trouble to count backward when the baby is born." He shrugged. "Don't take on about it, Mother. It happens all the time."

Pearl blinked back tears, and Silas did his best to set aside his own feelings and resign himself to the reality of the situation. He was too old, too sick, and too tired to waste energy on his son's foolishness. Abe would just have to live with the consequences. He only hoped that the baby wouldn't suffer from its parents' irresponsibility.

The thought arrested him. The baby!

Silas had birthed enough children in his life to know that every newborn infant brought fresh hope into the world. No matter how reckless and self-centered Abe and Pansy were, there was now another life to think about and pray for—the unborn child that was even now developing in the womb.

His grandson . . . or granddaughter!

————•✦•————

March 1900

The new century had dawned, but Silas barely had the energy to notice.

His body had weakened steadily since fall, as the cancer spread. But it was not just the cancer that was eating away at him; it was also the perpetual tension in the household. When Bick Littleton had discovered that Enoch had paid off the debts of his best field hands and taken them to work on Noble land, he flew into a rage and refused to complete the house he had promised to Silas Noble's only son. With nowhere else to go, Abe and Pansy had come to live at Noble House, and the burden had fallen upon Pearl to care for the two of them, along with nursing Silas as the disease doled out his final days.

Abe, of course, did little besides ride his horse into town to drink and gamble, and Pansy hadn't lifted a finger in months. Always dependent, pregnancy had rendered her even more helpless. Shortly after the wedding, she had taken to her bed, panicked that if she did the least bit of work, something might happen to the baby. Never mind that women had for ages done grueling manual labor right up until the time they delivered, with few ill effects. Pansy was the exception.

Abe, in typical form, had adjusted poorly to no longer being the center of his wife's attention. They argued, often loudly and long into the night, especially after Abe had been drinking. Sometimes he would leave in the middle of the night, stalking out and slamming the door and not returning until morning. No apology would follow, nor a word of explanation. Just a sullen moping about until he and Pansy made up, or until some real or imagined slight sparked the next argument.

Meanwhile, Silas's illness had progressed to the point that he barely recognized himself when he looked in the mirror—which wasn't often, for he rarely had the strength to get out of bed. His arms and legs were bony and drawn, and his skin hung in pasty gray folds.

It wouldn't be long now. He was simply waiting. Holding on with a fierce grip to the last moments of life.

In spiritual terms, Silas was ready to die. He had no question about his eternal destiny. He looked forward, in fact, to being released from the pain that racked his body and the fatigue that drained his soul. And he was certainly ready for a little peace and quiet. But there was one thing he had to do before he let go.

Upstairs, in the bedroom she shared with Abe, Pansy was in labor.

Pearl came down regularly to inform him of her progress and ask his advice about the birthing. She would deliver the child herself, with the aid of a local midwife. Abe was nowhere to be found.

Silas lay on the big four-poster bed in the downstairs bedroom and listened to the sounds of labor, sounds he knew well from years of delivering babies. Pansy shrieked a lot more—and a good deal louder—than most of the women he had helped, but that was to be expected. He waited and prayed.

At last he heard the sweet sound his old ears had been longing for—the lusty, bawling cry of a newborn. He could see it in his mind's eye—the child wriggling, protesting heartily at the injustice of being removed from its warm womb and forced out into the cold, frightening world. Tears filled his eyes, for he knew, as the baby could not, what a splendid world it could be, full of light and love and promise and purpose.

With great effort he struggled to his feet, reached for his cane, and went to open the dresser drawer.

The amethyst and pearl brooch lay in its accustomed place, nestled inside the velvet box. Years ago, he and Pearl had discussed giving the brooch to Abe as a wedding gift for his wife, according to Noble tradition. But given their son's penchant for gambling and drink, they had decided to wait, to pass it on to their first grandchild, if they ever had one. And now that child had been born.

Silas pulled the amethyst heart from its casing and turned it over in his bony hands. His eyes could no longer see the inscription on the back, but he knew what it said: *Sincerity. Purity. Nobility.* "Lord God," he whispered, "let this child live up to the Noble name."

With a shaky movement he dropped the brooch into his sweater pocket and slowly made his way up the stairs. When he reached the doorway and grasped hold of the doorpost for support, Pearl turned and saw him.

"It's a girl," she whispered through her tears. "We have a granddaughter!"

Silas shuffled toward the bed and reached down to take his daughter-in-law's hand. Her hair, usually perfectly coiffed, was plastered in damp strands against the pillow. Her nightgown was stained with sweat and blood.

She gazed up at him with a vacant expression. "Where's Abe?"

"I don't know," he answered honestly. "He'll be back, I'm sure."

"Eventually." She turned her head away.

"What is her name?" he asked.

"Whose?"

"The baby. It's a girl, you know."

"Oh. Yes, I know." The emptiness in her eyes tugged at his heart. "Doesn't matter. You name her."

Silas frowned. "That's not for me to decide. Haven't you and Abraham come up with possible names?"

Pansy shook her head. "No."

"Well, what would you like her name to be?"

At last a little life came into the girl's face—but it was anger, not interest. "I said, it doesn't matter," she responded. "You do it." She pushed the baby in his direction and closed her eyes.

Silas reached out and took the child in his arms. Supported by Pearl, he gazed down into the tiny face and looked into his granddaughter's eyes, and his heart stirred. "I feel like Simeon," he murmured. "Lord, now let your servant depart in peace." He smiled at his wife. "But not quite yet."

With Pearl following behind, he shuffled down the hallway and out onto the small balcony above the front door—the courting porch, Booker had called it. It was a perfect night, cool and clear. The moon had risen, casting a pale light over the yard. The scent of dogwoods and azaleas wafted to him on the evening breeze.

In a brief moment, it all came back—all the feelings he had experienced over the years in this house. His deep love for his Pearl of great price. His sense of fulfillment at doing something with his life that counted—not just for time, but for eternity. The liberty that had come to his soul in this place.

He leaned against the wall for support, cradled the child in one arm, and with some difficulty pinned the heart-shaped brooch onto her blanket. From a lifetime ago, his grandmother's answer came back to him: *It is as priceless as the one who wears it is to the one who gives it.*

Looking into the face of his infant granddaughter, Silas knew that Grandmama's words were true. His ancient eyes fixed on the brooch.

The amethyst glittered dimly, and the pearls that surrounded it glowed with a faint luminescence, like little moons. One of the pearls was still missing. Human nature, his wife had said. Precious, yet flawed. Priceless, even in its incompleteness.

Silas nodded in Pearl's direction and summoned the last ounce of his physical strength to raise his newborn granddaughter over his head, as he had long ago seen Booker do with Enoch. "We commit this child to the purposes of the Almighty," he whispered, "and name her Amethyst Pearl Noble."

Breathless, Silas slid down the wall to a sitting position, still holding the baby in his hands. Pearl sat down next to him, weeping as he prayed: "May she draw from her heritage the faith and love of her ancestors, and may she live a life worthy of her name and her calling. . . ."

The infant made no sound. She gazed into her grandfather's eyes as if she understood every word he uttered. Perhaps, as Silas had long suspected, the newly born did come into the world bearing the wisdom of the ages.

Silas drew the baby close to his chest and held her there. "Live, my little Amethyst," he murmured, "live under your grandparents' blessing. Find your way to truth, no matter what it takes. . . ."

The child's tiny hand closed around his finger, gripping it as if she would never let go. Then her head nodded against his shoulder, and his lolled back against the wall.

"One goin' out, while another's comin' in," Silas murmured.

And as he breathed his last, the baby slept on.

18
Legacy

———◆◆◆———

March 14, 1993

And that was you, Grandam?"

Amethyst looked up at her great-granddaughter. Since yesterday evening, off and on, she had been telling Little Am the story of Silas and Pearl. Now tears glistened in the girl's brown eyes, and a wistful smile crept over her face.

"Yes, child. I was that baby. The day I was born, Grandpa Silas died. One was going out, while another was coming in."

"So you never got to know him. That's so sad."

"I knew him, all right." Amethyst shook her head. "Just not the way you mean. His blood runs in my veins, and his blessing influenced my life in some rather miraculous ways."

"But where did you get all this information?" Little Am persisted. "Did you grow up hearing these stories from your grandma Pearl?"

"No," Amethyst sighed, an old familiar regret washing over her. "My grandmother Pearl died the following year."

"What happened to her?"

"I'm not certain. My suspicion is that, with Silas gone, she simply decided it was time to go. It's not unusual, you know—true love has a powerful draw on people."

Little Am's eyes took on a faraway look. "I hope someday I find that kind of love."

"I pray you do, too, child. Love is what makes each day special and unique. Love gives purpose and meaning to life."

"Have you ever had that kind of love, Grandam?" The girl lifted one eyebrow. "You know, real passion?"

"It's probably hard for you to believe, since you've only known me as a decrepit old woman, but yes, I've had my share of love. More than my share, if truth be told."

"Well," Little Am declared, sitting back and folding her arms, "you can bet I want to hear *that* story."

Amethyst chuckled. "Why? Because you can't imagine your old Grandam as a wild young thing?"

"You? Wild?" Little Am's eyes wandered to the den wall, where the unloaded shotgun leaned against the fireplace. "Come to think of it, it's not too difficult to think of you as wild, Grandam. I mean, you showed a pretty wild streak when you stood up to Grandpa Con and locked him out of the house."

"Your grandfather would probably say that I showed an *insane* streak," Amethyst corrected. "And it may get me into trouble."

"I think we're already in trouble," Little Am countered. "But it sure is fun." She sat in silence for a minute. "Silas was a real hero, wasn't he?"

"Yes, child, he was. Not in the sense of winning the Medal of Honor or being famous, but simply by being faithful to what he was called to do." Amethyst got up from the chair and stretched her arthritic limbs, then walked to the wall that separated the log cabin room from the dining room and took down a picture. She handed it to Little Am. "Do you know who that is?"

Am stared at the photograph. "Of course I do. I make A's in history. It's Abraham Lincoln."

"Can you read the inscription?"

"It says, '*To Silas Noble, with appreciation for your contributions to the cause. A. Lincoln.*' I suppose he means the abolition of slavery, and the help Silas gave to the wounded soldiers?"

"That's my assumption. From what we know, Grandpa Silas was a great man, in a very quiet way."

"That brings me back to my original question, Grandam. How do you know all these details about Silas's life?"

"See that bookcase on the right side of the desk?"

Little Am nodded.

"Bring one of the books from the top two shelves over here."

Little Am went to the bookcase and returned with a faded red leather volume. "What is it?"

"This," Amethyst answered, stroking the cover lovingly, "is one of nearly fifty journals left by Pearl Noble."

The girl's eyes grew wide. "Really? Cool."

"*Cool* doesn't begin to describe the contents of these books," Amethyst said. "Pearl kept records of everything—the daily events of their lives, the crises, the slaves' experiences. And not just what happened, but her philosophy—her thoughts about the times, about the Emancipation, about the confusing and difficult struggles that followed the war. Her journals are a treasure trove of history—and they give a lot of insight into her heart and mind as well."

"May I see it?" Little Am reached out a hand.

Amethyst smiled to herself. Clearly, the story of Silas and Pearl was working on her granddaughter. The zombie hadn't reasserted itself since she had begun to tell the tale, and now Little Am was asking politely rather than demanding what she wanted—and in proper English, no less.

"No," she said, pulling the book away with a teasing smile. "You may not see it. You may *have* it."

"To keep? For good?" Little Am's eyes flashed with anticipation.

"For good. And all the others as well. But if you don't mind, I'd prefer them to stay here, in the house."

"Oh, sure," Am replied distantly. "Whatever." Her attention was riveted on the pages. After a minute or two she looked up. "I just had the strangest feeling, Grandam. Like these journals are about *me*."

"In a way, they are." Amethyst nodded with satisfaction; the girl was beginning to understand. "We're not born in a vacuum, child. We're the product of our genetic makeup, our environment, our influences. And although I don't quite comprehend it myself, I'm convinced that somehow we can be affected by the spiritual legacy left to us by ancestors whose names we've never even heard."

"You mean like in China?" Little Am put in. "I've read about how people in Oriental countries worship their ancestors."

"You *did* get A's in history," Amethyst commented. "But I'm not talking about worshiping those who have gone before us. I simply believe we can be influenced by the heritage of the people we carry inside of us. The way I was influenced by Grandpa Silas."

"Great. So I'm going to become like Con and Mimsy?" Am twisted her mouth up in a grimace.

"Not necessarily. If you have the insight, you can choose who your spiritual mentors will be."

Amethyst watched the wheels turning as her great-granddaughter considered this. At last Little Am closed the journal and sat up straighter. "The story doesn't end with Silas and Pearl, Grandam. I want to hear more."

Amethyst glanced at the clock on the mantel. "Not tonight, child. It's nearly midnight, and tomorrow is Monday. You know what that means."

"Yeah. Grandpa Con will be back."

"I'm afraid so. I think we should both go to bed and try to get a good night's sleep."

Little Am got up and came over to Amethyst's chair. "All right. But if it's okay with you, I'll take Pearl's journal with me."

"Just don't stay up all night reading."

Little Am leaned down and gave Amethyst a kiss on the cheek. "I won't." She turned to go, but when she reached the doorway, she looked over her shoulder. "Grandam?"

"Yes, child?"

"Thanks."

"For what?"

"For the stories. For the journals. For everything." She paused. "Mostly, for being my Grandam."

Amethyst smiled. "I love you, child."

"I love you, too." Am muttered the words under her breath and disappeared up the stairs.

———•◦•———

Settled in the big four-poster in the downstairs bedroom, Amethyst gathered the quilt around her shoulders and relaxed into the down pillow.

She was exhausted, but it was a satisfied kind of tiredness.

Her great-granddaughter was showing more promise than she had ever dreamed possible. The girl was intelligent and insightful, and truly seemed to be captivated by the stories of her ancestors. That was a good sign. A very good sign.

Perhaps the Noble legacy wouldn't die, after all, when Amethyst made her exit from this world.

As her eyes drifted shut, Amethyst breathed out the prayer she knew by heart, the blessing Pearl had written in her last journal. *"May she draw from her heritage the faith and love of her ancestors, and may she live a life worthy of her name and her calling. . . ."* But this time she prayed it for the teenage girl who slept upstairs

"Find your way to truth, Little Am," she murmured, *"no matter what it takes."*

19
Judge Dove

———◆◆◆———

March 15, 1993

Conrad Wainwright stood in the judge's chambers with Mimsy on one side and the sheriff, Buddy Rice, on the other. He glanced at his watch—a gold Rolex, with diamonds marking the hours—and wondered how long it would be before he had to hock it and go back to wearing a thirty-dollar Timex from Discount World.

The Rolex said 9:15. The judge had kept them waiting for a full fifteen minutes. A power play, most likely. A ploy to make him increasingly nervous.

Harriet Dove, the judge's name was. Probably one of those women's lib types who loved lording it over males. Conrad couldn't stand feminists. Their primary goal in life, it seemed, was to emasculate men, to use whatever authority they could muster to make him feel like a fool. All the lady lawyers he knew kept telling him it was time for him to get with the program, to come into the nineties and stop acting like a chauvinist pig. He had learned, over the years, to put on a good front so as not to irritate them or get himself accused of harassment, but privately Con still held to the belief that a woman's place was in the kitchen—definitely not in the courtroom or the operating room, and most certainly not on the judge's bench.

He cleared his throat and shifted nervously from one foot to the other. He would have to watch himself with this Judge Dove—would probably have to grovel and say "Your Honor" and "yes ma'am" to her.

It made him sick. Who on earth had come up with the insane idea that a female—a *girl*—could ever be rational enough to serve as a judge? The law demanded clearheaded reasoning, not mushy emotionalism.

Still, his future—his solvency—was in Harriet Dove's hands. He'd have to be careful, all right.

At 9:23, the side door opened and a woman walked in and seated herself behind the desk. Con had to restrain himself from laughing—or at the very least, from gaping. The tiny woman with short blonde hair, a narrow chin, and huge horn-rimmed glasses looked like Tweety Bird in a black robe. A child playing court. The front panel of the desk blocked his view of her legs, but Conrad could imagine that her feet were swinging free, unable to touch the floor.

When she spoke, the Tweety Bird image vanished from his mind. "Be seated."

They sat.

"All right, Sheriff," she said in a low-pitched, commanding voice, "what do we have here?"

Buddy Rice took a step forward. "This is Conrad Wainwright, your honor, and his wife, Mimsy. He's the son of Miss Amethyst Noble."

Judge Dove peered over the top of her glasses. "I understand you seem to be having a bit of trouble with your mother?"

Conrad took his cue, nodded, and responded in his best lawyer-voice, "Yes, Your Honor. My mother is quite elderly and has become, well, intractable. She needs care, but refuses to be moved from the family home."

The judge shuffled some papers on her desk, then looked up again. "You say that she kidnapped your granddaughter, a teenager over whom you have custody, and drove you and your wife off the premises at gunpoint?"

"She did, Your Honor. The sheriff here witnessed everything."

"Buddy? What's your take on this? Is Miss Amethyst incompetent?"

Rice hooked a thumb in his belt and considered his answer. "Her behavior is, well, a little eccentric. But the girl is seventeen, and claims that she is not being held against her will."

"Anybody get shot at?"

"No ma'am."

"Any crime committed?"

"Not that I can tell," Buddy answered. "As Miss Amethyst said, she has the right to lock her own doors."

"Against her only son?" Conrad interrupted. "She's ninety-three years old, Judge! Anything could happen in there!"

Judge Dove cast a withering look in Con's direction. "Mr. Wainwright, we may be in chambers rather than in a courtroom, but this is still my territory. You will not interrupt, nor will you give an opinion until you are asked for it. Understood?"

"Yes, Your Honor." Conrad lowered his eyes, not out of humility, but so that she couldn't see the rage that was building in him. This judge was just what he expected—a women's libber who took delight in cutting a man down to size.

"Go on, Buddy."

"Well, Your Honor, I told Con and Mimsy here that Miss Amethyst was perfectly within her rights to refuse them entrance to the house. And the girl is nearly of age; she's intelligent and obviously knows what she wants. As far as I can see, it's a family disagreement, nothing more."

Judge Dove turned back to Conrad. "I want to know what started the dispute. What happened, Mr. Wainwright, to cause your elderly mother to lock you out of her house?"

Conrad said nothing.

"I am giving you permission to speak, Mr. Wainwright. Now."

Con pushed down the sarcastic reply that rose to the surface of his mind. "I was trying to convince my mother that she would be much happier and safer in a retirement home. I have a lovely place picked out near my home outside of Memphis."

"But she doesn't want to go."

"She thinks she can still take care of herself in that big house," Con hedged. "But, Your Honor, she's an old woman. She's getting frail, and no longer coherent. What mother in her right mind would threaten her only son with a shotgun? I'm—I'm afraid for her."

Judge Dove pushed her glasses up her nose and stared at him in silence, as if she were looking right through him. "Yes. The good son," she muttered under her breath. "What about you, Mrs. Wainwright? What do you think?"

Conrad cringed inwardly. *Please*, he begged. *Please, Mimsy.*

"Well," she began, "I suppose I understand, just a little, why Mother doesn't want to sell her house. But—but—" She broke down and began to wail. "But my little girl! She's locked in there all alone, and—and—"

"There, there, honey," Conrad soothed. He turned back to the judge. "You can see how devastated my wife is over all this."

"Hmm. Yes, I can see." Judge Dove's expression clearly indicated that she wished she had never turned the valve that opened Mimsy's floodgates. She turned her gaze back to the sheriff. "Buddy, do you think the girl is in any danger?"

Buddy shook his head. "No ma'am."

"Mr. Wainwright, you need to know that I have no intention whatsoever of declaring your mother legally incompetent on your word alone. This seems to me to be a simple case of misunderstanding. Can you give me one reason—any reason—to run legal interference in a family matter?"

Conrad racked his brain, and finally came up with a stroke of genius. "Isn't it illegal for her to be kept out of school without her guardians' consent?"

Mimsy looked up. "Oh, no, Conrad. Don't you remember? They're on spring break, starting today. She doesn't have school this week."

He could have throttled her. But murder in the judge's chambers wasn't the kind of offense he wanted on his record.

Judge Dove gave a knowing smile. "All right. Here's my decision. You"—she pointed toward Conrad—"will go back and try to reason with your mother. If you haven't settled this in one week, I'll issue an order that Miss Amethyst appear before me and that your granddaughter be released back to your custody."

"A week?" Conrad sputtered. "Another week? But it'll be too late by then—" He stopped himself before he said something incriminating.

"You have a problem with my decision?" Judge Dove asked. "Or with me?"

"No—no ma'am," Con replied, infusing all the false contrition he could muster into his voice.

"Buddy, you go with them. But no hard-handedness, understand? Just a quiet discussion."

"You got it, Judge."

"Fine. I will hope *not* to see you next Monday. The truth is, I don't like meddling in family situations that could be handled with a modicum of reason and compassion. Now if you'll excuse me, I have work to do."

The dismissal couldn't have been clearer. Conrad got up and, stifling a curse, stalked out of Judge Harriet Dove's chambers.

20
Round Two

———◆◇◆———

"Mother? Mother, are you in there?"

Conrad's shouting and frantic pounding, muffled by the closed door, sounded like a television cop show coming from a great distance. Amethyst looked up at the clock, then smiled at her great-granddaughter, who was seated in the opposite chair.

"Right on time."

Little Am nodded. "Like clockwork."

Amethyst struggled to her feet and motioned for Am to follow.

"You want the gun?" Little Am pointed to the shotgun that was resting against the fireplace.

"Not right now. You can come get it if need be."

Amethyst opened the front door and peered at her son through the iron grillwork.

"Open up, Mother! This nonsense has gone on long enough."

"No, Conrad."

"I've been to the judge, Mother. She said—" He stopped suddenly and looked over his shoulder at the sheriff, who stood directly behind him. Clearly, he had been about to concoct some outrageous story, but Buddy Rice's presence kept him honest.

"Said what, Conrad?" Amethyst threw a smile over her shoulder at Little Am.

"She said we need to work this out like civilized people."

Amethyst nodded. "I couldn't agree more."

"Finally!" Con heaved a sigh of relief and tempered his tone. "Let us in, Mother, and we'll talk about this."

"I don't think so."

Conrad let out a string of curses.

"Does that sound like civilized conversation to you?" she asked Little Am.

The girl shook her head. "I think he needs to have his mouth washed out with Drano."

"I taught him better," Amethyst sighed. "I really did."

"Mother, listen! You've got to let us in, and that's all there is to it."

Amethyst peered at Buddy. "Is that all there is to it?"

Buddy grinned. "No ma'am. It's entirely up to you."

"Then good-bye, Conrad. Come back when you've given up this idea of carting me off to the home. And when you can keep a civil tongue in your head."

"But Mother, you cannot stay here by yourself any longer. It's just not reasonable."

Little Am stepped forward and pointed her finger at her grandfather. "Alone? What do you think I am, anyway?"

"You're an idiotic teenager who doesn't know what's good for her."

Mimsy stepped forward and laid a hand on her husband's arm. "Conrad, there's no cause to insult people. Am, are you all right?"

"I'm cool, Mimsy," Am replied. "No problems here."

"You're going to leave this house and come home with us right this minute," Con ordered.

"No, I'm not." Am planted her hands on her hips. "I've got spring break, and teacher's meetings come after that. I don't have to be back to school for two weeks. And I plan to spend them right here with Grandam."

"I brought you some clothes, honey," Mimsy said. "And your CD player and a portable TV. I thought you might be bored."

Con turned on her. "You did WHAT?"

"Well, the girl needs clothes, Con."

"You already determined you'd let her stay?"

Mimsy shrugged. "A good mother anticipates."

"Thanks, Mimsy," Little Am said. "I would like the clothes, but you can forget about the TV and CD player. I won't be needing them. The last thing I am right now is bored."

Con stared at his granddaughter as if she had just morphed into an alien being. "You—you don't want rock music or television?" he stammered.

"Nope."

He turned on Amethyst. "What are the two of you doing in there?"

Amethyst smiled benignly. "Girl stuff. You wouldn't understand."

"And you won't let us in to talk? Not even for a few minutes?"

"Not a chance. Not until you come to your senses."

Con's face turned a bright red. "Mother, you're the one who needs to come to her senses. I've done what I'm supposed to do—I tried to talk reasonably to you. We'll just let the judge decide what happens from here on."

Amethyst began to shut the door. "Fine, Conrad. Leave Little Am's suitcase on the porch. And be sure to let me know how it turns out."

While Con was still shouting at her, Amethyst locked the door in his face. She turned to Little Am. "Now what?"

Am grinned. "First, I'll wash up the breakfast dishes. Then you have a promise to keep."

"More of the story?"

"Much more. I can't wait to hear about your wild and reckless youth."

When the dishes were done, Amethyst settled in the den with a second cup of coffee. "All right. Now where were we?"

"You were born. Silas just died."

"Of course. One going out while the other was coming in," Amethyst mused. "But I'll have to skip a few years. We'll pick up when I was—oh, just about your age."

"Cool." Little Am settled into her chair and popped the top on a can of Diet Pepsi. "I'm ready."

"All right. It was 1917—"

"World War I," Little Am supplied.

"Ah, yes, the A in history." Amethyst nodded. "I didn't expect the war to affect us much, but it did. . . ."

Part 3

DIGNITY

———◦◆◦———

"I will restore you to health and heal your wounds,"
declares the LORD,
"because you are called an outcast . . .
for whom no one cares."

Jeremiah 30:17

21
Dishonest Abe

———◆◆◆◆———

June 1917

Abraham Lincoln Noble peered at his face in the looking glass and scowled. As had become his habit throughout his fifty-two years, he cursed his name. Cursed his life. Cursed the attachments that held him in bondage to this land, this house, these people. And cursed his dead father for chaining him to an icon, a cherished martyr cut down by an assassin's bullet.

No matter what he did, he would never fulfill other people's expectations of him. All his life, his name had caused him to be compared to Lincoln, who had, in his father's glowing terms, "selflessly laid down his life in the battle for freedom." An accident of birth and geography had sentenced him to be compared to Enoch Warren, the man who walked with God—and who, for all practical purposes, was a god. An agricultural genius, a divinity who had stretched out his hand over the land and made it fertile and prosperous.

Every time Abe saw the muscular black man striding across the fields or riding his horse into town, his gut twisted with jealousy and rage. Clearly, Abe had turned out to be a bitter disappointment to his father. Why else would Silas Noble have willed most of the farmland to the son of a slave, leaving his own son with only Noble House and a small percentage of the yearly proceeds from the crop?

The injustice stabbed at his heart like a blade. *He* should have been the landholder, the prominent citizen of Cambridge County. *He* should have been given the chance to make a name for himself, a future for his family. But all he had to show for his heritage was this house, this prison without bars that kept him incarcerated with a simpering, mindless wife and a headstrong seventeen-year-old daughter.

Enoch had *sons*. Tall, strong sons who worked with him and made him proud. And one daughter as well—the beautiful Silvie, just turned twenty-one, whose very presence aroused in Abe a lust that would not leave him in peace. Pansy had seen the look in his eye, he was certain, but had never confronted him about it. She never would. She was too weak to take the risk. But someday—someday soon, if her multitude of medical complaints had any basis in reality—she would be gone, and he would have the opportunity to act on his fantasies.

His time would come. And when it did, he wouldn't give a second thought to the consequences. He deserved some pleasure in life, didn't he?

The problem was, he couldn't wait. The walls were closing in, suffocating him. He had to get out. And finally, after all these years, he had stumbled upon a way to do it without seeming like a cad.

Abe didn't keep up much with current affairs, but he did know enough to realize that three years ago, somebody had assassinated some archduke over in Europe, and the result had been a conflict of monumental proportions—a war bigger and more complex than the world had ever seen. And now, finally, the United States had gotten into the fray. In April, President Wilson had declared war on Germany and last month had instituted something called "Selective Service."

Most of the men being conscripted were much younger than himself—in their twenties and thirties. But word was that the army would take volunteers up to the age of forty-eight. Abe was beyond that, of course, but his wife and daughter wouldn't know the regulations, wouldn't know that he was too old to enlist.

This war, whatever it was about, would give him the perfect excuse he needed. He wouldn't be viewed as a despicable husband abandoning his family; he would be a hero, marching off to battle to save the world for democracy. A protector of home and hearth.

Never mind that he had no intention of joining the army. He made it a practice never to put himself in danger without a very good reason—

a nice bottle of bourbon, for example; or a rich faro game with a table-ful of patsies; or that shapely new barmaid at Colby's Tavern. Now, *that* was a risk worth taking.

Abe left the bedroom, went into the kitchen, and sat down at the table to glance through the newspaper. A Selective Service office had been set up in Memphis. The train schedule for new inductees was printed in the paper.

But where would he get the money he needed? Vanishing into thin air and creating a new life for himself wouldn't be cheap. Enoch had already advanced him most of the profits due him from the summer's harvest, but he'd had a run of bad luck lately, and it was already gone. Still, a good gambler could feel it when his luck was about to change. This was his chance, and he had to do whatever was necessary to take it.

Then he remembered—the brooch! Before she died, his mother had made it clear that the heart-shaped amethyst was to be given to his daughter on her wedding day. Except for this prison of a house, it was all she had as an inheritance from her grandparents. One of the pearls was missing, he remembered vaguely, but if Mother had treasured it that much, the stone itself had to be valuable.

Abe went back into the bedroom and rummaged in his wife's drawers until he came up with a small, worn velvet box. He opened it, placed the brooch on his open palm, and watched as the sunlight from the window glittered on the table of the gemstone.

For a moment he gazed, mesmerized, as the amethyst glowed in the ray of light. It seemed almost alive, like a tiny heart beating in the palm of his hand. Then he shook off sentimentality and shoved the brooch into his vest pocket. This was his transfer out of hell. No one would miss it, at least not until he was long gone.

He would leave on the first train out in the morning. That was time enough to tell Pansy, pack his gear, and prepare for his departure.

Abe heaved a deep sigh of relief. This time tomorrow, he would be on his way.

With a ticket to freedom in his pocket.

Amethyst stared at her father. Her dinner had grown cold, and the juice from the turnip greens had seeped into the mashed potatoes and congealed into an unappetizing mess. But it didn't matter. She couldn't eat anyway, not after the bombshell he had just dropped.

"Abraham, no!" her mother wailed, reaching into her bag for smelling salts. "You can't just leave us here alone!"

Amethyst wanted to tell Mama to shut her mouth, but as a dutiful daughter she could only think the words, not say them. Still, her eardrums vibrated painfully with the shrieking, and her stomach twisted into a knot.

"Pansy, sweetheart," her father was cooing with uncharacteristic tenderness, "don't you understand? I have to go." He paused and puffed his chest out. "It's my—" He groped for words. "My patriotic duty."

Amethyst tasted bile rising in her throat, and she choked it back. She loved her father, but she didn't like him very much. She could see through him as her mother never could, and up until this moment she had never detected so much as a grain of patriotic loyalty in the man. He was trying to paint himself as a hero, but Amethyst knew better. He was doing this for himself, not for the two of them or for the sake of his country.

"You'll be fine," Father was saying. "Amethyst is nearly grown, and she can take care of things. Besides, Enoch and his family will be close by. I'm sure Silvie can help out, too. Isn't that right, Ammie?"

Amethyst looked at him and took a deep breath to get control of her emotions. The truth was, he wouldn't be missed much at all, considering the way he spent most of his time. Abe Noble considered himself a "gentleman farmer," a country squire. Apparently that meant that his primary responsibility was to swagger around town with a brass-headed walking stick and wager every dime of his earnings on the card games in the back room of Colby's Tavern. The growing acceptance of prohibition laws supposedly made liquor more difficult to come by, but that didn't seem to have much effect upon Father or the rest of his cronies down at Colby's. Amethyst often heard him come in late at night drunk and angry, and several times recently her mother had come to the breakfast table with bruises on her face and arms. Mama made excuses for him, of course, but Amethyst knew the truth.

Yes. Despite her mother's tearful protests, it would be better for all of them if he were gone for a while. Maybe the army would instill some adult responsibility in him. She had heard that men often returned from war radically changed. Perhaps such a miracle would happen to her father, as well—even at his age.

They could only hope and pray.

Silvie sat in the rocking chair with her embroidery while Amethyst lay on the bed reading Carl Sandburg's "Chicago Poems" aloud. Silvie liked to hear Amethyst read; her voice was so animated, so passionate—especially when she was reading poetry. Sandburg was a rough kind of poet, and as a country girl, Silvie didn't identify with a lot of what he wrote about the city. Still, his words were powerful and stirring and, like all good poetry, left her with the feeling that anything was possible.

Out of the corner of her eye she watched the expressions on Amethyst's face as she read. The girl seemed so much more at peace, now that her father was gone. Yesterday he had boarded the train, bound for Memphis to sign up for the war. He had been out of the house barely one day, and yet the change in Amethyst was remarkable, as if a storm cloud had lifted from her soul.

Silvie, too, was glad he was gone. She had felt uncomfortable around Mister Abe for nearly as long as she could remember—the way his eyes followed her, the way he smiled at her and stroked his mustache with a kind of leer tugging at his mouth. She had told no one about her feelings, and she wasn't entirely certain that anything bad would have happened if he ever did manage to get her alone, but she kept her guard up nevertheless. Now she, like Amethyst, relaxed in the assurance of his departure.

How sad it was, that her friend was more comfortable in her father's absence than in his presence! Silvie couldn't imagine such a situation for herself—she adored her daddy. He was a wonderful provider, a doting father, and, when her mother was alive, a devoted husband. In Silvie's mind, Enoch Warren had to be the most wonderful man on the face of the earth. Her only question was whether any man she married would ever measure up to him.

Amethyst had stopped reading and was staring curiously at her. "Silvie, are you listening?"

"Yes. At least I was. I guess I got to woolgathering for a minute or two."

"I want to ask a favor of you."

Silvie smiled. "Go on."

"Mama's going to be out of her mind with grief, now that Father's gone."

"Don't I know it." Silvie gave a shrug. She and Amethyst had been best friends for years. Neither their racial difference nor their age difference mattered—in fact, the four-year span between them had seemed to shrink as they grew up. They were more like sisters than friends, and were completely candid with one another. "I have to admit I don't understand it. I'd think your mother would be relieved not to have to deal with his drinking and gambling and . . . well, everything else."

Amethyst nodded. "Yes, but you know how Mama is. She's always turned a blind eye to his faults, as if a bad marriage to a foolhardy man is better than no marriage at all. I'd rather be an old maid all my days than put up with what she's endured." She let out a deep sigh.

"The favor?" Silvie prompted.

"I'd like you to stay here with us while Father's gone. Mama's going to be a handful to deal with, and I'm going to need all the support I can get."

"I'll ask Daddy, but I reckon it won't be a problem." Silvie raised one eyebrow. "What you *really* want is a live-in cook."

"Silvie! You know I don't think of you that way!"

"I'm just kidding."

"You'd better be. What I *want* is the company and assistance of my best friend." Amethyst grinned. "Of course, if you'd like to make your fabulous custard pie now and then, I wouldn't object."

Amethyst and Silvie were in the kitchen fixing dinner when they heard the knock on the front door. Mama had taken to her bed with a fit of vapors, so the meal was going to be a simple one—fried pork chops with sliced tomatoes and butterbeans.

"I'll get it." Amethyst laid down the knife, wiped her hands on a dish-towel, and went to the front door. On the porch, hat in hand, stood a tall, thin stranger in an army uniform, a grave expression on his face.

"I'm looking for Mrs. Abraham Noble," he said. "I'm Captain Wolfe."

"I'm sorry," Amethyst responded. "She's—ah, incapacitated right now. I'm her daughter. May I help you?"

The officer averted his eyes. "No ma'am. I mean, I must speak to Mrs. Noble on a private matter. It's essential that I see her."

"Come in." Amethyst opened the door and ushered the man into the parlor. "I'll just be a moment."

She went upstairs and roused her mother, and in a few minutes the two of them, along with Silvie, sat opposite the stranger, staring at him.

Amethyst watched as Mama ran a hand through her scraggly hair and forced herself to focus. "You must understand," she murmured, "I'm not well. My husband has just left to enlist in the army, and—" Tears overcame her, and she put her face in her hands and sobbed.

"It's all right, Mama," Amethyst said. "Try to pull yourself together."

"I'm afraid I have some bad news." Captain Wolfe shifted in his seat. "About your husband."

A fist closed around Amethyst's heart, and she reached a hand toward Silvie. "What is it? Has something happened?"

The man nodded. "He took the train to Memphis yesterday morning?"

"Yes."

"There was an accident, a derailment. I'm sorry to tell you this, ma'am, but I'm afraid your husband is dead."

Mama let out a wail, and Silvie gripped Amethyst's hand so tightly that her knuckles cracked.

Amethyst gaped at him. "Dead?"

"Yes, miss," the officer affirmed, finally giving up on Mama and addressing Amethyst directly for the first time. "A loose rail on a trestle. It gave way as the train passed over the Tallahatchie River. We have his name on the manifest, but—" He looked up with a sorrowful gaze and shrugged. "His body must have washed downriver. They're still searching, but so far it—ah, *he*—hasn't been recovered."

The officer paused for a minute and shifted uncomfortably while Mama wept at the top of her lungs. At last he asked, "How old was your father, miss?"

Amethyst thought for a minute. "Fifty-two."

The officer shook his head. "It's a terrible tragedy. I'm afraid the army wouldn't have accepted him anyway. He should have known that."

Amethyst tried to take in the devastating nature of the news, but all she could feel was relief. The same relief, multiplied tenfold, that she had felt the morning before as she had watched the train pull out of the station. He was gone. Not just for a few months or a year, but forever. Her father was dead.

The relief vanished, however, when she looked at Mama. A temporary separation had been hard enough on her. What would this do to her? In that instant, Amethyst felt the weight of the world settle on her shoulders, and any remnant of peace dissipated.

While Mama keened on, Silvie gripped Amethyst's fingers and gave her a knowing look.

"We'll make it," she whispered. "We'll get through this. I promise."

22
The Final Straw

December 1917

Amethyst sat at the big roll-top desk in the log cabin room and shuffled the papers in front of her. She could sit here forever and not be able to decipher the mess her father had called "his books." The only two items she had found that made any kind of sense to her were the original deed to the property, signed by Col. Robert Warren and Silas Noble, and Grandpa Silas's will, which left the majority of the tillable land to Enoch Warren.

It had been six months since Father's death. What little money they possessed had run out, and Mama had yet to lift a finger to help in any way. Mostly she just kept to her bed during the daylight hours and wandered the house at night, a ghostly figure in the darkness.

According to a dog-eared cashbook she found in the bottom drawer of the desk, Grandpa Silas's will allowed for a small percentage of the crop profits to come to Father. But evidently the summer's profits had already been advanced to him in May. Maybe he took the money with him. Maybe he hid it somewhere. Whatever he had done with the money, Amethyst couldn't find it, and as the immensity of the situation became clear to her, panic rose up in her chest so that she couldn't breathe.

She didn't know how long she sat there, tears splattering the pages on the desktop. At last she came to herself, blotted the smeared ink, and took a deep breath. The numbers in the cashbook swam in front of her

eyes, and in her mind she could see her father waving jauntily as the
train pulled out of the station.

Fear and anxiety slowly melted away, replaced by an emotion Amethyst
was all too familiar with: rage. Once again, her father had abandoned
them. Once again, he had put his needs ahead of everyone else's. But this
time it wasn't just a temporary setback caused by his drinking and gambling and carousing. This time it was permanent. Abraham Noble had
pulled the ultimate disappearing act, leaving his wife and daughter alone
and penniless. If he hadn't already been dead, she might have killed him
herself.

"How could you?" she screamed, pounding her fists on the desk.
"What kind of man does this to his family?" Fresh tears came—hot, vio-
lent tears of anger and scorn—and Amethyst put her head down and
sobbed.

A gentle touch roused her—Silvie's hand on her shoulder. "Are you
all right, hon?"

Amethyst looked up. "What do *you* think?"

"I think you got too heavy a load for a gal your age."

"I'm almost eighteen, Silvie. I should be able to handle this without
falling apart. I *should!*"

"What you *should* be doing is attending college over at that Columbus
Female Institute, getting an education, like you always planned. What
you *should* be doing is going to dances, meeting some nice beau—not
sitting around here taking care of everybody else."

Amethyst grimaced. "Well, that dream is dead. And you can bet I
won't be looking for some man to sweep me off my feet anytime soon."

Silvie drew up a chair and sat down beside her. "I know. Mister Abe
pretty much ruined all that for you, didn't he?"

A deep sigh shuddered up from Amethyst's soul. Silvie was right, and
it was just one more reason for her to be furious at her father. For three
years she had been planning and waiting for the day she could enroll at
the Columbus Female Institute. The school, founded before the Civil
War, was practically a legend throughout the South. A college for young
ladies, which provided its students with an excellent education and the
opportunity to become professional career women—teachers, social

workers, nurses. Some of its graduates had even gone on to become doctors.

But not Amethyst Noble. In her room upstairs, an acceptance letter lay gathering cobwebs in the bureau drawer. If Father hadn't gone off and been killed, she might be there today. Now she had missed her chance—her one opportunity to leave Cambridge behind and make something of her life.

"I have no choice," she answered after a while. "Mama can't do for herself, and there's no one else to take charge."

"So it all comes down to you."

"I'm afraid so, Silvie. It's not so bad, really. I can do this. What bothers me most, I think, is that I have no alternatives." She shook her head and pointed to the papers on the desk. "And apparently no money, either."

Silvie peered over her shoulder. "Your daddy's books?"

"If you can call them that. He didn't keep very good records. The best I can figure, he took an advance on last summer's profits, and the money has simply disappeared."

"You've got nothing?" Silvie's eyes widened.

Amethyst let out a ragged breath. "Not a dime. And taxes on the house are due in January."

"Maybe you oughta talk to the bank."

"Apparently Father didn't believe in banks. Kept everything in cash, here in the house. But you know how he was, Silvie. Every dollar that made its way into his pocket in the morning ended up in the cash register at Colby's Tavern before nightfall."

"I hate to mention this, Am, but—"

"But what? If you've got an idea, girl, let's hear it!"

"The—the brooch," Silvie answered hesitantly. "Your grandmama's amethyst. I remember when we were little, your mama used to show it to us sometimes, telling us how you would be wearing it on the day you got married, and—"

"I could never sell that!"

"Course not. But maybe you could use it as—" She groped for the word. "As collateral. For a loan, you know."

Amethyst thought about that for a minute. "Maybe you're right. Silvie, you're a genius—an absolute genius!"

The two of them went to the downstairs bedroom—the room Mama had steadfastly refused to enter since the day her father boarded the train and began the journey that ended his life. Amethyst looked around. Nothing had been touched in over six months. The wardrobe door stood open a crack, and she could see the sleeve of her father's dressing gown sticking out. The book he had been reading lay facedown on the table next to the bed, covered with dust.

"Do you know where she kept it?" Silvie asked, prodding Amethyst into action.

"In the bureau." Amethyst went to the dresser and began rifling through the top drawer. "It was in a little box—gray velvet, if I remember correctly. Oh! Here it is."

She retrieved the box and opened it. Nothing.

"It's empty," Silvie said.

"I can see that." Amethyst felt her last hope crumble, and her shoulders began to shake.

"Don't fall apart now, girl. Keep looking. Maybe it came out of the box and is loose down in the drawer." Silvie pushed past Amethyst and continued the search.

"It's got to be here!" Amethyst dumped out the second drawer, then the third, kneeling on the floor to sort through the contents. "It can't be gone!"

"Where else could your mama have put it? Think, Amethyst!"

"Nowhere. She always kept it right there, in the top drawer. She was very particular about it, I recall. Wouldn't let me take it to my room for fear it would get lost, and—"

Suddenly Amethyst sat back on the rug, and her heart sank like a lead weight.

"Well, we'll just have to go up and ask your mama," Silvie was saying. "Surely she knows where it is."

"No, she doesn't," Amethyst muttered woodenly. "But I do. And unless we want to dredge the bottom of the Tallahatchie River for it, we're never going to see it again."

Silvie stared at her. "You don't mean—"

"What else could have happened to it?"

"Your father knew where it was kept?"

"Of course he did. The only surprise is that he didn't take it sooner, to pay for his gambling and drinking and women." Amethyst put her face in her hands. "It was my only hope, Silvie. What am I going to do now?"

Silvie sat in silence for a moment, then put her hand on Amethyst's arm. "Daddy will help, Amethyst. I know he will."

Amethyst choked back tears. "I know he would, Silvie. But Bick Littleton hasn't spoken to Mama since the day she married Daddy and the only Averys left are distant cousins. If I can't ask them for help, I certainly wouldn't ask your father. We can't take charity."

Silvie looked hurt. "It's not charity. We're family—a lot closer family than the Averys or the Littletons."

"Yes, we are." Amethyst squeezed Silvie's hand and felt strengthened, somehow, by the warmth of the touch. "I don't know what I would have done without you these past six months. And I'm probably going to need your help in the future. But I can't take your family's money."

"All right," Silvie conceded. "We'll talk about that part later. For now, what can I do?"

Amethyst shook her head and clenched her jaw so tightly it ached. There was no point crying over a brooch that was gone forever—even if it had been her only link to her grandparents and her only hope for a way out of this financial mess her father had left them with. There had to be another way.

A desperate determination began to flow through her veins. The first thing she had to do was get this paperwork sorted out so she knew exactly what she was dealing with. Then she and Silvie could make a plan. What kind of plan, she wasn't sure. For right now they would just take it one step at a time.

———•◦•———

"It's worse than I imagined," Amethyst moaned.

Silvie glanced down at the stack of papers in front of her, and her stomach churned. She felt helpless in the face of this dilemma, and she didn't like the feeling one bit. Amethyst was her best friend. They were like sisters. She knew her father would lend—or give—any amount of money to help get Amethyst and her mother out of debt, but she also knew that Amethyst would resist with her last breath taking what she called "charity."

The girl was proud, that much was certain, and her pride was both an asset and a liability. It made her strong, determined. But it also made her bullheaded and stubborn.

"Look at this!" Amethyst went on. "Bills dating back more than two years ago. For renovations—the plumbing for the bathrooms and electrification of the house. For a stud horse named Benedict, an animal I've never even heard of. And what's this one? A hundred dollars for a new suit and a brass-headed cane?"

Silvie winced. "You got records of any of these bills being paid?"

"Not a one." Amethyst shook her head. "Who in his right mind pays a hundred dollars for a suit?"

"Musta been made out of gold." Silvie shrugged. "Too bad we can't bury him in it, but there's nothin' left to bury."

Amethyst threw the bills onto the pile in front of Silvie. "I cannot believe he did this. I see it with my own eyes, but I don't believe it." She looked at Silvie, and tears spilled over. "We'll have to sell the house."

"You are not selling this house." A wave of determination rose up in Silvie, and she grabbed Amethyst's hand. "Look at this."

"At what?"

"At our hands. Mine's brown, yours is white."

"So?"

"So that's the way it's been for generations. Your grandfather built this house."

"Correction. *Your* grandfather built it."

"They did it together," Silvie amended. "They were friends. Like us. They defied tradition and built not only a house, but a family. Your family and mine. Together. And what they created was not just a pile of bricks and lumber, but a home. A heritage. We're not going to let that go. Not if I have anything to say about it."

"What other choice do I have?"

"We'll figure out something. God will see us through."

Amethyst snatched her hand away. "Don't talk to me about God, Silvie."

"You believe in God. I know you do."

"I did. Once. But you tell me—how much evidence have you seen that God is the least bit interested in what's happening to me and Mama? God didn't keep Father from leaving us alone and destitute. God didn't lift a hand to change my father's profligate ways. What did we do to deserve this? Nothing. It was Father's doing, and we're left to clean up the mess. No, Silvie, I'm not about to go begging to God—or anyone, for that matter—for help. I'll figure this out for myself."

Silvie didn't respond. In truth, she had nothing to say. She didn't believe that God had abandoned Amethyst in her time of need, but it did *look* that way. And no amount of talking would change Amethyst's mind about it. The only thing that might move her was some kind of miracle—an unexpected circumstance that would turn things around.

Please Lord, her soul implored, *let it be so.*

———•◦•———

Amethyst inhaled the savory scent of beef stew with carrots and onions and potatoes in a rich brown broth. *Thanks to Uncle Enoch,* she mused as she stirred the stew, *at least we won't starve.*

That was one benefit to living on the land. Even in winter they had vegetables put up from the garden and meat from the smokehouse. The chickens still thrived, providing eggs and frying hens. The root cellar was full of white potatoes and sweet potatoes, and the cupboards were lined with Mason jars filled with canned beans, black-eyed peas, carrots, corn, and beets.

Amethyst had never seen her father take a hoe to the corn rows, or help with grinding the meal or slaughtering hogs or smoking the hams and bacon that hung on meat hooks in the dark, fragrant log building out back. She had never once witnessed her mother anywhere near the kitchen on canning day. But still, miraculously, they always had good food, and plenty of it.

Now that Amethyst was running the household, she knew where it came from. Enoch and his family kept them supplied, sending one of the fieldworkers in to stock the pantry without a single note of fanfare. That, too, she suspected, might be called charity, but she wasn't in any position to quibble over semantics. It had probably been this way since her grandparents died—the responsible black landowner quietly taking care of the irresponsible white gambler's family.

What an irony, Amethyst thought. Her own father had been honored among the townspeople as the "master" of the Noble lands, while Enoch was simply tolerated and given a grudging kind of respect as "a credit to his people." Translation: still a Negro, and in many people's minds still a slave, but at least one who wasn't lazy or shiftless.

Amethyst was pretty sure that most of the citizens of Cambridge had no idea that Enoch was the rightful owner of Silas Noble's land. They undoubtedly viewed him as an overseer, the manager of her father's holdings. And Abe Noble had probably allowed—even encouraged—the misconception. He might not hold the title, but Abe Noble had the image and the name, and that was what was really important.

Silvie came into the kitchen and opened the oven door to check on her cornbread. "Almost done," she murmured. "It may be more convenient, but I still contend that cornbread is never as good in this modern oven as it was when it was baked in the wood stove."

Amethyst turned and grinned. Silvie's constant lament about the new kitchen was that everything tasted better cooked on the old wood stove. She actually still used it for baking cakes and pies. "The stove's out on the back porch, and there's wood in the kindling box. Be my guest."

"Too late now," Silvie sniffed. "Where's your mama?"

"If the cornbread's done, go ahead and serve up the stew," Amethyst answered. "I'll go get her."

Amethyst made her way up the stairs, sighing as she went. Mama would, as always, be in bed with the quilt pulled up over her and that vacant expression on her face. Sometimes she would come down and join Amethyst and Silvie for dinner, but more often Amethyst had to make the trek up the stairs twice—once to inform her that dinner was ready, and a second time to bring her a tray. "I declare," Amethyst murmured as she reached the top step. "It's like having a baby, but without any of the benefits of being married." What those benefits were, Amethyst couldn't imagine. She certainly hadn't seen much in her parents' relationship to recommend matrimony.

She paused at the bedroom door and knocked softly on the doorpost. "Mama? Can you get up and join us? Dinner's ready. It's your favorite—beef stew and cornbread."

No answer.

The room was dark, but that wasn't unusual. Mama usually slept a lot, and sunset came early in December. Amethyst walked to the bedside and turned on the table lamp.

"Mama?"

The figure under the covers didn't move or speak.

"Come on, Mama. You've been here all day. You need to get up and move around a little."

Amethyst gently tugged at her mother's shoulder. Still no response.

"Mama! Wake up."

She pulled a little harder, and a bare arm flopped out from under the covers and landed, palm up, on the edge of the bed.

It was blue and rigid.

———◦•◦•◦———

According to Dr. Noah Ramsey, Pansy Noble had died in her sleep. "I've seen it before, I'm afraid," he told Amethyst. "A wife loses her husband suddenly and unexpectedly—or even after a long illness—and something in her just gives up. Your parents were very close, I assume."

"Of course," Amethyst answered woodenly. What good would it do to tell him the truth?

"There's a special bond between loving spouses," Dr. Ramsey continued. "Almost as if the dead husband summons his wife from the other side." He gave her a consoling look and patted her on the shoulder. "I think she just decided it was time to go, time to be with him again. But you can rest in the knowledge that the two of them are together now . . . forever."

Amethyst stifled a laugh. Amid the swirling chaos of her emotions, all she could think about was how her father must feel at this moment. It had taken him years to get away from Mama, only to have her invade his blissful eternity after a brief six-month respite.

"Serves him right," she muttered under her breath.

The doctor blinked. "Excuse me?"

"Nothing. I was just thinking how right it was, for them to be together again."

Then the truth hit her with the force of a physical blow. She was an orphan. Alone in this house. Alone in the world. Seventeen years old, without parents, without an education, with a mountain of debts and not a nickel to her name.

Silvie put an arm around her shoulders and drew her close. "It'll be all right," she whispered.

But Amethyst knew better. It wouldn't be all right, no matter what Silvie said.

Nothing short of a miracle would make it all right ever again.

23
The Gift

December 25, 1917

Rain had been falling steadily for five straight days. The clock ticked loudly, echoing through the empty house. Four-thirty.

Amethyst walked to the window and watched as the drops slid down the wavering glass panes. Her stomach rumbled, and she thought briefly that she should go to the kitchen and heat up some of the leftovers Silvie had sent home with her from the family dinner at noon.

Christmas had been a somber celebration this year—the gathering of the Warrens in the big house Silvie's grandpa Booker had built during the Reconstruction. The only white face among them was Amethyst's, and although the wild turkey Silvie's brother had shot was delicious, nobody had felt much like eating. Conversation was stilted and formal; no one dared broach the subject they were all thinking about.

One week ago today, they had stood in a semicircle in the white cemetery adjacent to the old Rivermont Plantation and buried Amethyst's mother. Even though her father's body had never been recovered, a joint headstone served for Abraham Noble and his wife, bearing the ironic inscription, *United for Eternity*. Next to the mound of mud that covered her mother's coffin lay a third plot, unused. Waiting for Amethyst. Calling to her, beckoning from beyond.

It would be a welcome relief to answer the summons. Just to lie down and go to sleep and let peaceful death free her from the burden of going on with life.

But Amethyst knew, deep in her soul, that she couldn't—wouldn't—give in so readily. The path that lay before her was a difficult, lonely one, but something inside urged her on, promised her that she would be all right, that she had the inner fortitude and courage to face whatever lay ahead. She had no idea where this assurance came from, but she believed it. It was a truth that tolled in her spirit like a bell, its low, solid note vibrating through the very core of her being.

Amethyst watched as a single droplet of water, separate from the others, made its languid track down the far corner of the glass. She saw herself in that raindrop, alone on a journey that no one else could share, and a knot of apprehension twisted inside her. Where would she find the money to pay the taxes on the house, and the bills her father had left behind? How would she manage? The future stretched out before her, bleak and empty as the winter sky, and a thrill of fear ran through her.

I have to quit thinking like this, she reprimanded herself. She had to have faith, had to trust that inner voice. She had to believe—if not in God, then in her own strength and resourcefulness. She was determined not to be like her mother. She would not simply lie down and give up. She would fight—whatever fighting meant—for a life of her own, a life of meaning and significance and fulfillment.

The solitary raindrop paused in its downward slide, then began to move again. But before it hit the windowsill, a second raindrop appeared, then a third, then a fourth. They merged into one, shot down the windowpane, and landed with a resounding splat on the sill.

Amethyst gazed at the pattern created by the splash of water against glass. It looked like a star—like the cut-glass star that hung over the créche on the mantel.

The star that had led others before her to their destiny.

The attic was dim and musty. When Noble House had been electrified, no one had thought to put a light up here. At dusk, with the rain pouring down, Amethyst could barely see the stacks of trunks and boxes and old furniture that had accumulated over the years.

She lit a kerosene lamp and placed it on a rickety table just beyond the stairs. Yes. That was better. At least she wouldn't trip and break a leg.

She wasn't really certain what she was looking for. She had no conviction that she would find anything of value, anything that would help her out of the financial mess Father had willed to her as his legacy. But it was Christmas Day, and she was alone. What better time to seek some kind of connection with her ancestors?

Amethyst didn't know nearly enough about her grandparents, Silas and Pearl Noble. She knew the common history shared between the Nobles and Warrens, of course, but she needed more. Something deeper. Something more . . . personal. Her father had always been reluctant to talk about the past, as if he had something to hide. He had told her only that her grandpa Silas had been a doctor during the Civil War, and had been assisted in his practice by her grandma Pearl. Amethyst didn't ask many questions; it was abundantly clear that there had been some kind of falling-out between Father and Grandpa Silas. And if she had learned anything as a child, it was to tiptoe around Father's anger as if avoiding a bed of fire ants.

She took the lamp in one hand and began making a circuit of the attic. For an hour she sorted through boxes of old books and moth-eaten clothing, finding only a few ratty medical texts that no doubt had belonged to Grandpa Silas. The dust and mold filled her nostrils and made her sneeze.

"This is ridiculous," she muttered, coughing and gasping for air. "Somebody should have burned this stuff ages ago."

She set the lamp on the floor, struggled to her feet, and attempted to brush the grime of decades off her dress. But just as she leaned down to retrieve the lamp, her heel caught in the hem of her gown and set her off-balance. She put a hand out to steady herself, and a tower of boxes went down in a clattering crash.

"Amethyst? Are you all right? Where *are* you?"

Silvie's voice drifted up from downstairs, and Amethyst felt a warm rush of relief wash over her. "I'm in the attic," she called. "Can you give me a hand?"

After a minute or two Silvie's brown face appeared in the small doorway. "What in the name of Saint Peter are you doing?"

"I have no idea," Amethyst responded with a grin. "Just poking around, I guess."

"Law, you look like a chimney sweep." Silvie doubled over with laughter. "Or like you're all made up to do a blackface vaudeville act." She held out her arms and rolled her eyes. *"Mammy!"*

"Would you stop, please?" Amethyst motioned to the overturned boxes. "I need help here, not humor."

Silvie climbed into the attic chamber and stood up. "It's a mess, that's for sure."

"An understatement if I've ever heard one. Could you help me pick up these boxes and stack them—" Amethyst looked around. "Over there."

"All right." Silvie raised one eyebrow and pointed at Amethyst's filthy dress. "But don't 'spect this chile to be doin' none of your laundry, missus." She chuckled and began moving boxes to the corner.

"Silvie, look!" Amethyst took the lamp and sat down on the floor behind the fallen boxes.

"What is it?"

"It's a trunk—a very old one, if the rust and dirt are any indication." She wiped a hand across the front, revealing faded white letters. "S. *Noble*. Silvie, this must have belonged to my grandfather!" She struggled to open it. "The lock is rusted shut."

Silvie looked around and found a corroded hammer in an old toolbox near the chimney. "Here, try this."

Amethyst gave a few halfhearted taps on the lock, but it didn't budge.

"Hit it hard."

"How hard?"

"Pretend it's your father."

Amethyst rared back and swung the hammer with all her might. "We got it!" she shouted as the lock sprang open. "Let's see what's in here."

"That looks like a medical bag."

Amethyst opened it and peered inside. "It is—all kinds of tools, and little vials of drugs, I'd guess." She lifted a brittle stethoscope from the bag and held it carefully in her hands. "Imagine—my grandfather might have used this to listen to my heartbeat the night I was born."

"What else?"

"A picture. And here's a whole set of leather-bound books." She pulled out a volume from the set, opened it, and positioned the lamp so she could see. In a fine, angular hand, the name *Pearl Avery* was inscribed inside the front cover. The first page was dated May 1, 1854.

"Oh, Silvie, I can't believe it!"

Silvie reached around her and retrieved a second volume from the trunk. "It looks like a diary of some sort—a journal."

"My grandmother's journals," Amethyst breathed. "Apparently she started this one shortly after she and Grandpa Silas met."

"And what's this?" Silvie's hand closed around a framed photograph. She held it close to the lamp so that both she and Amethyst could see it. "Am I seeing right? Abraham Lincoln?"

Amethyst peered at the picture. "It is. And it's autographed!"

Silvie sat back on her heels and stared at Amethyst. "This is worth a bucket of money."

"What are you talking about?"

"A personally autographed picture of President Lincoln? Do you have any idea how much this would bring?"

"No, I don't," Amethyst answered. "But it doesn't matter. I wouldn't sell it—not in a thousand years." She stared at Silvie, flabbergasted that her friend would even consider the monetary worth of the photo.

"And I don't suppose you could use something like this to get a loan, either?"

"Forget it, Silvie. I'm not selling it. This is my heritage, my link to the past, to people whose blood runs in my veins. I can't explain why, but I feel a sense of attachment to Grandpa Silas and Grandma Pearl, a connection I never felt with my own parents."

An odd look crossed Silvie's face, as if she knew why Amethyst felt that connection, but she said only, "My daddy would really love to see this."

"We'll show him tomorrow. For now, I want to get these journals downstairs and clean them up a little bit."

"Wouldn't hurt to do a bit of cleaning on yourself as well," Silvie quipped.

"I guess I can manage that, too. Are you staying the night?"

"I thought I would, if that's all right."

Amethyst reached out and gave Silvie a hug, smearing her with cobwebs and dirt. "It's always all right. Are you hungry?"

"I could eat."

"Then let's get downstairs, get washed up, and heat some of that turkey and dressing. We've got a lot of reading to catch up on."

Enoch Warren turned the Lincoln photograph over and over in his big hands. "Amethyst, this is a real find. A treasure."

"I know. I can't believe it was stuck away in the attic like castoff junk."

A shadow flitted across Enoch's face. "Your father never got on well with Silas, I'm afraid. Or with me."

Amethyst nodded. "I know. It was because Grandpa Silas gave you most of the land, wasn't it?"

"Partly. But it started a long time before that. Abraham was always— well, not like Silas."

"You mean he was a drunkard and a gambler who never took any responsibility and never thought about anyone but himself."

Enoch chuckled. "Amethyst, sometimes you can be just like your grandmother."

"Should I consider that a compliment, Uncle Enoch?"

"In my mind, most certainly. She was a gentle, loving woman, but she was known to speak her mind, and she could be stubborn as a mule sometimes."

Silvie elbowed Amethyst in the ribs. ". . . we know you came by it honestly."

Enoch's handsome face took on a faraway expression. "My daddy idolized Abraham Lincoln," he murmured. "I remember the Emancipation, you know. I recall the night we escaped, out through the root cellar into the woods. It was the night your father was born. We got to freedom, all right, but Daddy never could adjust to living up north. Once the war was over, he determined to come back. Silas and Pearl were still here, still helping folks. Silas and Daddy formed a partnership of sorts, with

Daddy taking charge of the land and crops." He ran his fingers over the picture frame. "I remember seeing this picture hanging on the wall in the log cabin room. But I was too young to think much about it. Now I guess I'm old enough to appreciate it—and its connection to my people."

"I understand. I feel the same way about the things I found in the attic, especially Grandma Pearl's journals."

Amethyst watched Enoch's face and saw the longing in his eyes. She understood the expression all too well—it was the same emotion she had felt when she discovered Grandpa Silas's trunk and the treasures inside. All her life she had fought against shame—humiliation over her father's dissolute ways, embarrassment at her mother's simpering weakness. Isolated and at odds with her own family, Amethyst Noble had never belonged anywhere. But now, she had evidence of her roots, a heritage, a birthright—one that made her proud rather than ashamed.

She had told Silvie that she would never sell the photograph, but in that moment Amethyst knew that she could *give* it away—as a gift to Uncle Enoch. She loved him, and had always felt his love and understanding in return. He had been so good to her, and to her parents—looking after them, never asking for anything in return. It was the least she could do. And surprisingly, she felt no sense of loss at the idea of giving up the Lincoln photo. After all, it would still be in the family.

"You keep the photograph, Uncle Enoch. As a gift. A Christmas present."

He shook his head vehemently. "I can't accept this. It's much too valuable." He paused, and a light came into his eyes. "But I would like to buy it."

"Buy it?" Amethyst stammered. "I couldn't take your money, Uncle Enoch."

"Of course you could. You have something of value, and I have the money to pay."

"It would be charity, and you know it."

"I know nothing of the sort," he snorted. "I'll tell you what, Amethyst. I'll pay you for it now, and when you get on your feet, I'll let you buy it back."

Amethyst considered this for a moment. She did need the money—however much he offered. Taxes were due on the house next month, and at some point she would need to devise a plan to repay her father's creditors. It wouldn't exactly be a handout—more like a loan, with the Lincoln picture as collateral.

"All right," she sighed at last. "But only if we agree that it's temporary."

"Agreed." Enoch went to his desk and made out a bank draft. "Thank you," he said as he handed her the check. "I'll treasure it, you can be sure. Now, let Silvie pack up some more of that ham and turkey for you. We've got far too much."

Dodging the worst of the mud puddles, Amethyst dashed back to the house with Silvie's basket over one arm. She was soaked to the skin, but she didn't care. Just yesterday she had felt detached and orphaned, cut off from life. This morning she was surrounded by love, by the warm acceptance of family, and by the awareness of a proud and illustrious past.

Shaking the rain off, she went to the kitchen, set the basket down, and pulled Uncle Enoch's bank draft out of her coat pocket. When she unfolded it, her knees buckled and her breath caught in her throat.

"No!" she whispered to herself. "I can't believe it."

But it was true. Enough not only for the taxes, but to pay off every single bill Abraham Noble had left behind, with money to spare.

Laughing and crying at the same time, Amethyst moved with shaking hands to unpack the food and put it away. She felt as if she were flying apart, and yet had the sensation of being more *whole* than she had ever been in her life.

It was nothing short of a miracle.

She stopped suddenly, arrested by the thought. Maybe God *did* answer prayers—even prayers that had not yet been prayed. Perhaps the Almighty *was* looking out for Amethyst Noble, as Silvie insisted. If this was a gift from heaven, the Lord had certainly cut the timing pretty close. But she guessed you had to take the miracle as it came, without complaining about how or when it arrived.

Then she looked down into the bottom of the food basket.

Surrounded by carefully wrapped slices of cornbread, the photograph of Lincoln gazed back at her. A ray of light illuminated the face and made the warm dark eyes seem to come alive.

Amethyst turned her head toward the window. The rain had stopped. The sun had come out. She felt as if she were waking from a long, long sleep.

She lifted her eyes to the ceiling. "I don't know if you did this," she whispered, "but thank you."

There was no answer. Nothing but the sunshine warming her back.

Still, it felt like the hand of someone who loved her, and she smiled.

24
The Gambler

May 1918

Smoke filled the back room of the Beale Street Tavern and cast a thick blue haze over the six men seated around a table covered with green felt. It was barely one o'clock, and already the army suckers were lined up to hand over their mustering-out pay. These fellows were barely old enough to shave; it would be like shooting fish in a barrel. Avery Benedict smiled to himself and shuffled the cards one more time. The stuffed shirts at the bank were right: war was good for the economy—especially his.

"Good afternoon, gentlemen," he said in a voice as smooth as oil. "I'm Avery Benedict. Welcome to the Beale Street Tavern. You've all got your drinks, I see, and we've got Violet here"—he pointed toward the well-endowed barmaid in the corner—"to keep us supplied. The game is five-card draw. Who's in?"

"We're all in, Benedict," one burly sergeant growled. "Just deal the cards, will you?"

Avery knew the fellow—a no-neck, no-brain gorilla who went by the name of Sligo. He had been at this table yesterday, a loser every hand. Today, however, he was not alone. At his side sat a younger man, badly scarred, and evidently uncomfortable with being in an establishment such as this.

"Sligo, let's get out of here," he urged, even before the first hand was dealt. "You can't win; you know that. And you're nearly broke as it is."

"Shut up, kid," the sergeant growled. "I feel lucky today. Lend me a few bucks, and I'll pay you back. Half of whatever I win."

"I don't think so," the young man hedged. "I've got to pay for my train fare, and—"

Sligo turned to him, and his tone softened. "I know, kid. Just twenty bucks. You'll get it back, with interest."

Reluctantly the young man handed over the money and shook his head.

"Now, just go sit over there, out of the way. Amuse yourself with the barmaid. In a coupla hours we'll both be rich."

Avery looked at the clock. It was nearly four, and things weren't going well. Sligo's luck had changed, as he had predicted, and Avery was nearly tapped out. The gorilla had turned out to be a shill.

Avery could have kicked himself. Grandy, the owner of the Beale Street Tavern, was always warning him to watch out for guys like Sligo. Grandy didn't gamble himself, but he had agreed to a tenuous partnership with Benedict. Avery got the room and conducted the game with his own money, and Grandy got 10 percent of the winnings.

Avery should have seen it coming—Sligo had lost too much too easily the day before. He had been far too certain of sending this ape home with empty pockets. Letting his vanity get the best of him, Avery had let down his guard. Now his money was almost gone, Sligo was staring him down over the last hand, and everybody else around the table sat in silence, watching to see what he would do.

Sligo's massive thumb rippled over the stack of bills that lay in front of him. "It's my draw," he muttered, laying two cards facedown. "Two."

With a rush of relief, Avery dealt out two cards and looked at his own hand. He held two pair, jacks and eights. If Sligo was drawing two, he couldn't have much of a hand. Besides, Avery had a jack and an ace stashed behind his french cuffs—insurance for just such an occasion. He had Sligo where he wanted him now. Avery couldn't lose. "One for me."

"Where'd you get a name like Avery, anyway?" Sligo drawled, giving him a leering grin.

"It was my mother's maiden name," Benedict answered as he made his draw. He toyed with the card, leaving it facedown, while his mind spun. The idea had come to him in a moment of panic, when he was asked for his name and couldn't use his real one. Avery, from his mother's family, and Benedict, from that stallion he had purchased and then lost in a faro game before he ever had a chance to get it home.

"Sissy name," Sligo was saying, trying to rattle him. "Pansy name."

At the word *Pansy*, the bottom dropped out of Avery's stomach. Just the mention of the name sent a chill through him. "Let's just play the game, shall we?" he suggested, forcing a smile.

"I ain't the one who's taking all day."

Avery peered at his draw card. Another jack. He suppressed a chuckle. It was much more satisfying winning in an honest game, especially against a guy like Sligo. "Your bet."

Sligo eyed him. "How much you got left, prissy-boy?"

Avery looked down at his full house. "Don't worry about my pot, Sligo. Just place your bet."

The sergeant pushed his stack of bills to the center of the table. "Three hundred."

A gasp went up around the table.

"You know I don't have that much," Avery protested.

"Call or fold."

Avery looked into Sligo's eyes and held his gaze for a full minute. At last he put a hand into his pocket, and Sligo braced as if he expected a gun. "Easy, man," he chuckled. "I'm just getting this." He displayed a heart-shaped amethyst surrounded by pearls, then tossed it on top of the stack of bills. "That should cover the bet."

"What'd you do, Benedict? Knock off your old lady?" Sligo laughed, and everyone else joined him. Then Sligo said, "No deal. I ain't got no use for that. Besides, one of them pearls is missing."

"Sell it, then," Avery answered. He knew, of course, that Sligo would never have a chance to sell it; the brooch had been his good-luck charm for ages. He had lost it and won it back a dozen times, but always it ended up where it belonged, in his pocket, his little piece of security when the money ran low.

Sligo narrowed his eyes. "You calling me, then?"

Avery straightened his vest. "I am. Show your cards."

Sligo put down three tens and held the other two cards in his hand.

"Sorry, pal. The luck of the draw." Avery spread out his full house and began to rake in his winnings.

But Sligo stopped him with a meaty paw. "Not so fast." He twisted his face in a one-sided grin and laid the fourth ten faceup on the table. "Guess it ain't your day, *A-very*," he laughed, emphasizing the name with a mocking drawl.

He lifted his glass in salute, downed his drink, and tossed the amethyst brooch to his buddy. The young man got to his feet and came over to the table.

"Let's go, Sarge."

"I told you, didn't I?" he gloated. "Stick with old Sligo, and you'll end up a rich man!" He clapped his friend on the back and stuffed wads of bills into his pockets.

Avery winced as the fourth jack, still stuck up his sleeve, cut into the flesh of his left wrist. If only he hadn't been so quick to put down his cards, so eager to scoop up the pot. If only he had been a little more patient, a little less arrogant. . . .

But all the *what ifs* in the world couldn't help him now. He could only watch in silence as both his money and his good-luck charm disappeared through the back door of the Beale Street Tavern.

25
Pearls of Wisdom

———◦•※•◦———

June 1918

Through the open windows Amethyst could hear birds singing and squirrels chattering in the big magnolia tree beside the driveway. Spring always brought her hope—a new year, fresh with fragrant blossoms and unimagined possibilities.

On the wall between the roll-top desk and the doorway to the dining room, the photograph of Abraham Lincoln gazed placidly at her. She would probably never be able to repay Uncle Enoch, but she wouldn't insult him by attempting to return the picture to him. Besides, she liked to see it hanging there. It gave her a sense of completeness, as if it belonged here, as she did. As if the Noble legacy had finally come full circle.

Being alone in the house wasn't so bad, really. Aloneness wasn't the same as loneliness, and once Amethyst got used to being the sole inhabitant of Noble House, she discovered she actually enjoyed the solitude. It was much more peaceful now, without the constant arguing and bickering she had endured as a child. The sharp memory of those agonizing years had faded in the past six months, and now the house held echoes of the loving relationship between Grandpa Silas and Grandma Pearl, rather than the embittered battles between her own parents.

A good portion of the change, she thought, had to do with Pearl's journals. When she had first discovered them, Amethyst had intended to go through them from start to finish without stopping—a project that would have taken several weeks, even if she had done nothing else. But as she began to read, she realized that she would benefit much more by taking her time, absorbing the beauty of the words and trying to put into practice the wisdom that was her grandmother's bequest to a granddaughter she never knew.

What she had learned had changed her life. In the past six months, Amethyst Noble had set out on a different path, and deep in her heart lay the desire to emulate the woman whose soul was poured out upon those pages.

For one thing, the woman's faith in God was like nothing Amethyst had ever experienced. Grandma Pearl believed in God, that much was evident. But her faith had little to do with church or rules or maintaining an image of what religious people thought a Christian *should* be. Pearl Noble had a mind of her own, and used it. And to her way of thinking, a Christian's responsibility was to follow, on a daily basis, the kind of life Jesus exemplified. It didn't matter that others thought her strange or unfeminine or even rebellious. What mattered was that she responded to God's calling upon her life.

Amethyst pulled the first volume from the bookshelf next to the desk and opened it to a passage that had become a favorite. Her eyes scanned the page, and once more she found herself inspired and encouraged by the words of her strong and opinionated grandmother:

Many of the townspeople, especially the plantation owners and their wives, turn their heads when I walk down the street. Yesterday Mrs. Baldwin from Magnolia Acres actually crossed the street to avoid me. I could tell by the pinched look on her face and the way her nose elevated when she caught a glimpse of me that she did not care for my attire. A lady, I've been told, does not go about town in dungarees and boots. But the clothing suits me and is appropriate for the work I do. In those preposterous crinolines, I couldn't even enter the narrow door of a slave cabin, for heaven's sake!

The new doctor at Rivermont, Mr. Silas Noble, doesn't seem the least bit concerned about the way I dress. He is the first man I've ever met who truly looks on the inside, not at the outward appearance. It's a godly trait, and one I honor and respect in him. We worked together last week when one of the Rivermont

slaves was ill, and although he says little, I can tell that he appreciates my com-
mitment to the health and well-being of the Negroes. Once he even compli-
mented me, saying that he had never met such a selfless and sacrificial person.

I wonder if he has any idea that what he interprets as selflessness is actually
simple obedience? I am only doing what the Lord has given me to do, and I find
no real sacrifice in it. Is the loss of social acceptability a sacrifice? I hardly think
so, not when I have received back a hundredfold in personal fulfillment and sat-
isfaction. When will people who call themselves Christians—especially the
slaveholders who justify their abomination with selected scriptures—realize
that true faith in God doesn't mean accepting certain tenets, but living in a
manner which glorifies Christ and reflects the love of Jesus in the world?

Jesus, after all, didn't give so much as a thought to how the social and polit-
ical leaders of his time perceived him. He simply went about doing good, gath-
ering the outcasts of society, and loving them into a place of healing and
wholeness. To believe is to care. To care is to do. . . .

Amethyst ran her finger over the faded ink and repeated her grandmother's words: *"To believe is to care. To care is to do."* Every time she read
those words, or even thought about them, she felt a surge of pride and
inspiration rise up in her heart. *That* was the way she wanted to live.
That was the way she wanted to be remembered—as a woman of conviction and passion, a woman who gave herself to something bigger,
something finer. A woman who heard the whispered call of the Almighty
and responded with determination and joy.

Amethyst chuckled to herself. Six months ago, when she had
protested to Silvie that God had abandoned her, she couldn't have
imagined herself even thinking like this. But something had happened
deep in her soul. What she once would have called *accident*, she now
called *miracle*—finding her grandparents' treasures in the attic, receiving the money from Uncle Enoch to get her out of debt, reading
Grandma Pearl's journals.

Faith had sneaked up on her when she wasn't looking. Her eyes had
been opened to see that sometimes the "accidents" of life—what people
called luck or good fortune or even destiny—might just have their
source in a Divine hand.

Perhaps it was simply a matter of perception. You could look at your circumstances and think yourself lucky, or you could see beyond the event and acknowledge a deeper purpose, a hand of guidance, a gift from the Creator of the universe.

This she had learned from Pearl's journals. But she had found something else there as well. Something she hadn't expected.

Reality.

Grandma Pearl was not the kind of believer who had her head in the clouds. She was a realist who knew—and freely admitted—that life could be bittersweet, that pain accompanied joy, that prayers often went unanswered, that sometimes God seemed very far away.

The journals reflected it all—times of vacillation and confusion, anger with God, deep disappointment, heartache, agonizing loss and fierce longing. With a radical vulnerability, Pearl Noble had poured out her soul on these pages, holding nothing back. Woven into the fabric of her faith were many diverse strands—love and rage, devotion and doubt, skepticism and praise. Grandma Pearl related to God with complete candor, evidently believing that the Lord was strong enough and wise enough to take anything she could dish out.

It was this reality that had compelled Amethyst to reconsider what faith was all about. And she had decided, at long last, to put her trust in the God who looked back at her from the pages of her grandmother's journals.

Still, this left her with a dilemma. No matter how inspired she had been by her grandmother's authentic faith and the stories of her life with Silas, Amethyst couldn't simply embrace truth and stop there. *To believe is to care*, Grandma Pearl had written. *To care is to do.*

Amethyst believed. She cared. But what on earth was she supposed to *do*?

She had prayed, timidly at first, and then with more conviction, that the Lord would show her how her life could have meaning and significance. That God would give her some indication of what her own calling was and how she should live it out on a daily basis.

So far, no answer had come. The bills had been paid, the taxes taken care of, and Amethyst felt settled in Noble House, which she now claimed as a haven of spiritual refuge and security. Still, there had to be something more. Some purpose beyond her own comfort and freedom from anxiety.

With a sigh Amethyst put the first journal back in its place and drew out another. She had just finished reading about Silas and Pearl treating the war wounds of Robert Warren, the plantation owner, and about how the slave Cato earned his freedom by burning Rivermont to the ground. The image seared her mind; she had been to the ruins of Rivermont, stood between the charred columns, and imagined the grandeur and glory of the place. Now all that was left was ancient rubble flanked by blackened chimneys—a grim reminder of the high cost of prejudice.

Amethyst picked up where she had left off the day before:

> *Dear Silas's honor got the best of him in the end. Despite his misgivings, he treated Colonel Warren with all the skill and passion he had to offer, and kept the poor man alive until he could say his good-byes. I never liked Warren much, and his wife Olivia seemed to me the worst kind of mindless Southern belle, but still my heart broke to watch their final farewell. How would I feel if it were my beloved husband on his deathbed? Devastated, I'm sure, and woefully abandoned.*
>
> *Warren's death, however, is undoubtedly not the last we will see. Because of this terrible war, there will be much more heartache to come, I am certain, and even as I dread it, my soul is at peace. For I feel deep in my spirit that this is only the beginning, that perhaps God put us here, like Esther, for just such a time. Perhaps we will be given the strength and wisdom to bring healing to some, and to those who cannot be healed, to bring serenity in dying. There is a time to be born and a time to die, a time to laugh and a time to mourn, and the best we can do is trust that God will give us the grace for each separate time.*
>
> *Whether black or white, whole or maimed, healing or dying, every man or woman deserves a chance at dignity. Perhaps that is the greatest gift we can offer to those who come to us—to treat them as the magnificent creations of God that they are.*

Amethyst held her place with her finger and leaned back in the tall oak chair. *Dignity.* The very word resounded in her soul. She had seen, up close, what it meant—the self-respect and presence of Enoch Warren, the way he had instilled that confidence in his family. And she had seen its opposite, too, in her own father. People might be stamped with the likeness of the Creator, but they had a choice whether or not they would live up to that image. No matter what society did to them, no matter how others might perceive them, those who knew their own worth had the inner strength and conviction to live in bold obedience.

Just as her grandparents had done.

As Amethyst prayed she herself might do.

———

"Do you want another piece of chicken?"

Amethyst pointed toward the platter, and Silvie grimaced. "Not me."

"That bad, is it?" Amethyst grinned. "Well, maybe you should stay here permanently. Then you could do the cooking."

"I've already had two. How much approval do you need?"

"As much as I can get. Especially until I figure out what I'm supposed to do with my life."

"Been reading your grandmother's journals again?" Silvie raised an eyebrow.

"A little every day."

"And you still got no answer."

Amethyst shook her head. "I'm trying not to be impatient, but God seems to be taking his own sweet time answering this prayer. I don't even know what I'm looking for."

"Well," Silvie said with a shrug, "I suppose you'll know it when you find it. Just remember that God's will ain't necessarily *one thing* you're intended to do. It's more of an attitude, being open to see the possibilities."

"That's just the problem. I don't *have* any possibilities."

"You could go to college, like you always dreamed."

Amethyst laughed. "Not without money, I can't. Besides, I'm not sure that college is the place for me—at least not at the moment."

"Well, when you find out what your place is, let me know, will you? And while you're at it, send up a prayer for me, too."

"I take it things are not going well at the hotel restaurant."

Silvie rolled her eyes. "I been cooking there for over a year. Everybody loves the food, and it's a good job—for a colored woman." She gave a self-deprecating shrug. "But Mr. Mansfield, he's getting worse by the day. Follows me into the supply room, and once he tried to lock the door."

"Silvie, this sounds dangerous."

"It is. But what can I do? You know what's gonna happen if a Negro woman publicly accuses a white man of inappropriate behavior. I'll get fired—or worse."

"Have you thought about quitting?"

"And do what? Live off Daddy for the rest of my life?"

"He wouldn't mind. You'd be a big help to him."

"Yes, he would mind. When Mama died four years ago, he made it real clear that he didn't need a caretaker. He raised me to be independent, he says. And even though I'm still living under his roof, I have my own life, and he has his."

"What about living under *my* roof? I'd love the company."

"And I'd love being here. You know that. But I gotta earn a living, and that still leaves me with a predicament about the job." She paused. "Let's not talk about it right now. I promise I'll be careful, and I'll start looking for another position. Fair enough?"

"I suppose so," Amethyst conceded. "Do you want to hear what I read in Grandma Pearl's journal today?"

Silvie nodded and gave a little chuckle. "I can't believe how much you've changed since you got your hands on those books."

"They're quite inspirational, I have to admit. Today I read about dignity. It reminded me of you."

Amethyst went on to summarize her response to Pearl's journal, reading a few passages aloud. When she finished, she looked up at her friend. "So, what do you think?"

Silvie didn't answer for a moment. "Dignity," she said at last. "I suppose it is a matter of the heart, of the soul—what's inside a person. But I wish we lived in a world where people didn't have to fight for the kind of respect your grandparents believed in."

"So do I," Amethyst agreed. "And I wish I knew what to do about it."

Silvie frowned. "Do you really think one person can change the world?"

"I hope so. Grandma Pearl certainly believed it, and Grandpa Silas—"

Amethyst stopped and held up a hand. "Did I hear a knock?" A faint rapping sounded again. "Somebody's at the door."

"I wonder who? It's nearly dark."

Amethyst slanted an amused glance at her. "Well, we won't find out just sitting here, will we?" She went to the front door, with Silvie on her heels, and opened it to find a man standing on the porch with a bulging canvas bag at his feet. Dressed in an army uniform and holding a cane, he had his face turned to the right, as if something in the yard had caught his attention.

In the dim light, Amethyst could barely make out his profile. She turned the switch for the porch light. He had sandy hair, a wide brow, and a square chin that jutted out just a little. Not handsome, but nice-looking.

"Miss Noble?"

"Yes. May I help you?"

He kept his face averted. "My name is Harper Wainwright. As you can see from the uniform, I've just been discharged from the army, and I'm in need of a place to stay."

Amethyst frowned over her shoulder at Silvie, who shrugged. "I'm sorry, Mr. Wainwright, I believe you may have been misinformed. Noble House is not a boarding establishment. But there are several places I could recommend—"

He turned toward her, and Amethyst felt Silvie's fingernails dig into her arm. She stifled a gasp.

The entire right side of the man's face was a mass of puckered scars. His right arm was twisted, and his right leg bent at an odd angle. "I've tried other places," he said quietly. "No one will take me." He shuffled his feet around and leaned on the cane. "Forgive me if I've disturbed you. A gentleman in town suggested I come here. 'Try Noble House,' he said. 'It's just the kind of place you might find a welcome.' Although, now that I think about it, the man was laughing oddly, as if it were some kind of private joke." His blue eyes flashed. "I suspect the man was no gentleman after all."

"Are you from Cambridge, Mr. Wainwright?" Amethyst asked, trying with all her might not to stare at his disfigured face.

"My family homestead was way out in the country," he answered, "but they're all gone now. Besides, if I'm to find a job, I need to be in town."

Amethyst chuckled. "When my grandfather built this place, it was out in the country, too. Seems the town has grown up around us." She hesitated. "Still, I'm not sure—"

He smiled—a crooked, distorted half-grin. "Don't worry, Miss Noble. I have money to pay room and board. My mustering-out wages, you know. And unlike our friend who recommended you, I assure you I *am* a gentleman."

Amethyst looked at him, and for a brief moment her heart took her beyond the scars to the face of a sensitive man whose soul as well as his body had been wounded in battle.

"Could you give us just a moment, Mr. Wainwright? Please, have a seat in the swing. We won't be long."

She shut the door behind her and turned to Silvie. "Dignity," she whispered.

Silvie nodded. "Looks like God has spoken."

"Finally. But I can't do this alone. Are you with me?"

Silvie thought for a minute. "I didn't like working for Mansfield anyway. Count me in."

"A boardinghouse—for people who can't find a place of peace anywhere else. Sounds like something my grandparents would approve of. We could divide up the back parlor and make two rooms, and—"

Silvie clapped a hand over Amethyst's mouth. "We can plan later. Right now there's a man sitting on the porch swing waiting to find out if he has a bed for the night."

Amethyst opened the door. "Mr. Wainwright?"

"I'm still here." He struggled to his feet and came to the door.

"Come in, and bring your things. I'm Amethyst Noble, and this is my friend—and business partner—Silvie Warren."

Wainwright shook hands with them and gave a little bow. "Miss Noble, Miss Warren. It's a pleasure to make your acquaintance."

"We were just about to have dessert and coffee," Silvie said smoothly.

"But perhaps you haven't eaten yet. Do you like fried chicken?"

He smiled again, showing that crooked grin. "My favorite."

"Then follow us to the kitchen. We'll warm up some dinner for you." Amethyst started to lead the way, but a light touch on her arm stopped her.

"Thank you," he responded in a choked voice. "You're an answer to prayer. I never thought I'd find a place like this, a place where I could be afforded a little dignity."

She turned and looked directly into his face, studying the scars and the gentle countenance behind them. "Someday, Mr. Wainwright, when we know each other better, I'll tell you whose prayers have been answered tonight."

26
The Freak

———◆◇◆———

"Are you deaf as well as stupid?" Tarbush yelled, moving so close that Harper could smell his fetid breath and see decay festering on the far right molar in the man's mouth.

Harper took a step back, more for relief from the stench than for protection. "No, Mr. Tarbush. I am neither deaf nor stupid. I am simply looking for a job, and I have the skills you need to—"

"Skills? Don't talk to me about skills, boy! I got eyes, ain't I? Any fool can see that you ain't got the strength to do a man's job." He closed the gap between them, keeping his gaze focused on the good side of Harper's face. "My answer is no, and that's final. Now get along with you. Go back to wherever you came from." Tarbush's mouth twisted in a leering grin. "Maybe come Halloween, you can find yourself a job—at least for one night. And you won't even have to buy a mask."

Harper turned to go. His heart lay like a dead weight in his chest, but mentally he reprimanded himself for the hope that had brought yet another disappointment. Tarbush might be stubborn and ignorant and foulmouthed, but the truth was, he wasn't much different from the dozen other employers Harper had approached over the past two weeks. Some were less offensive, to be sure, but their answer was always the same: *No*.

In fact, Harper had to admit that he preferred Tarbush's crude candor to the thinly veiled disgust of the more polite ones. At least with Tarbush he knew where he stood. The man couldn't stand to look at him, couldn't believe that a fellow as scarred and broken as Harper Wainwright might have something of value to offer to his construction business—or to society in general. *Freak*, Tarbush had called him. *Nobody's gonna hire a freak.*

Harper limped along Main Street toward Jefferson Davis Avenue, where Noble House stood. As soon as the big two-story house came into view, his spirits began to lift. Here, at least, he didn't have to cover his face. Here he didn't have to apologize for who—or what—he was. Here he had meaningful work, even if it only bought him room and board.

And here he had the blessing of Miss Amethyst Noble's company.

Harper thrust the pleasurable thought from his mind. Amethyst was a lady, and no real lady would give a second thought to the likes of him. She was always nice to him, of course, pleasant and hospitable and even friendly. But he couldn't let his heart run away with his head. He would only be setting himself up for more disappointment, and he had experienced quite enough of that emotion since returning from the war. Besides, what did he have to offer her? A broken body? A wounded soul? A future filled with constant ridicule?

Harper let his mind drift back to the year before his enlistment, when his thoughts were consumed with the affections of another woman. Dorothea, his beloved, his betrothed. The fairest flower of the Mississippi Delta. He had adored her, written love poems to her, sent her letters every day from the front. And she had responded in kind, proclaiming her love for him and her eager acceptance of his proposal of marriage.

When he had been released from the hospital and discharged, Harper had gone directly to her, hoping against hope that she could find the inner resources to deal with the difficulties that lay ahead for them. Love, he had been told, could overcome the worst of challenges. Love conquered all. Love gazed with full acceptance at the inner soul, not at the outer appearance.

It had taken only the briefest of moments for Harper to realize that all the world's platitudes about the power of love were so much drivel. One glance at Dorothea's face told him everything—the way she averted her eyes from his twisted features, the way she tittered with that high, nervous laugh when she couldn't think of anything to say, the way she resolutely steered the conversation away from any discussion of their impending wedding.

In the end, he had given her the easy way out. Rather than making her face her feelings, he had lied, telling her that he himself had second thoughts about rushing into marriage.

They had parted with the promise that once Harper was settled and had a job, he would write to her, and they would begin afresh to explore their relationship and see where it led. But neither of them, Harper knew, had any intention of keeping that promise.

The problem with a broken heart, he discovered, was that it didn't break cleanly, with a nice even edge that could be glued together so that the seam barely showed. It splintered like crystal stemware into a million tiny shards—sharp fragments that could never be reassembled, invisible slivers that cut you even when you couldn't see them. Rather than take on the impossible task of fitting them back together again, it was better just to sweep up the pieces and toss the lot into the trash.

That's what Harper had done—or so he thought, until he came face to face with Amethyst Noble. From deep in the recesses of his soul, his discarded heart began to beat again—faintly at first, and then with more assertiveness. Despite his best intentions, he couldn't seem to control the way his pulse accelerated when she came near. His stomach fluttered, and his blood pounded in his ears. And all the while his mind was shouting, *No!*

This inward battle was, he knew, far more dangerous than any enemy fire he had faced at the front. And the potential for being hurt—even maimed for life—was greater, too. He could live with his physical disabilities, could look himself in the mirror every morning and see a man rather than a monster. As long as he kept his emotions closely guarded, he might be able to live a relatively fulfilled existence. But if he gave his heart free rein, he was bound to end up as scarred on the inside as he was on the outside. He had taken a chance on love once, and it turned out to be a thorny, pain-ridden path culminating in a devastating dead end. He wasn't about to go down that road again.

He paused at the sidewalk leading up to Noble House and gazed at the big white planter house. Two weeks, and already he thought of it as home. His place of safety and refuge, a healing sanctuary for his soul. . . .

"Freak!"

The shout behind him drew Harper's attention, and he turned. Three little boys, not more than eight or ten years old, stood on the other side of Jefferson Davis Avenue pointing and yelling in high-pitched voices.

"Freak! Freak! Freak!"

Instinctively Harper brought his hand up to the scarred right side of his face. He took a step toward the children and motioned for them to come closer.

"I'm not a freak," he said in a low voice, hoping to calm them. "I was scarred in the war, you see, and—" He lowered his hand and reached out toward them.

Three sets of eyes grew round as saucers, and an expression of horror twisted the grimy little face of the oldest one.

"You ARE a freak!" the boy yelled. "You're mean and nasty and EVIL!"

"What's your name, son?" Maybe Harper could reason with this child, find a way to make him listen.

The lad puffed out his chest with obvious pride. "Billy Tarbush," he answered with a sneer. "What's yours? Scarface?"

Harper winced inwardly as the disheartening truth registered in his mind. Then, out of the corner of his eye, he saw the boy reach down and scoop up a handful of rocks from the side of the road.

"No, wait—" he began.

But it was too late. The Tarbush boy sent a stone flying in Harper's direction, and the younger ones, taking their cue from the leader, followed suit. "Freak!" they hollered. "Get out of town, you freak!"

A jagged rock found its mark, hitting just under Harper's left eye. He recoiled from the blow and felt a warm wetness oozing down his cheek. But when he put his fingers to the wound, he was surprised to find the blood mixed with his own tears.

"Go home, boys," he murmured sadly as he turned and moved out of range of their missiles.

That old poet was right, he thought as he walked slowly up the side-walk. *Stone walls do not a prison make*. A broken body and a burned face could incarcerate as well as the stoutest iron bars.

Exhaling a ragged sigh, Harper pushed back the tears and wiped the blood from his cheek. This was his lot in life, his cage. He hadn't done anything to deserve such imprisonment, but none of that mattered now. Win or lose, he had no choice but to play with the hand fate had dealt him. If he kept to himself and shored up the vulnerable places of his soul, he'd be all right.

Even a freak could learn to be strong.

27
Pharisees and Publicans

———◆———

Harper Wainwright proved to be a godsend in more ways than Amethyst could have imagined. Despite his bad leg and crooked arm, he turned out to be an absolute genius when it came to renovations. Single-handedly he divided the back parlor into two smaller apartments, each with its own sitting room and small sleeping area, and a shared bathroom. Then he set to work on the coach house, and before Amethyst knew what was happening, she had five rooms available for rent.

"So, what do you think?" Harper asked as he put the finishing touches on the sign and attached it to the lamppost in front of the house.

Amethyst stood back and admired his handiwork. It was a carved wooden plaque, painted white with green letters that matched the shutters.

NOBLE HOUSE
Quality Room and Board for Patrons of Distinction

"I think it's perfect," she declared. "Absolutely perfect." She hesitated for a moment, then asked the question that had been plaguing her for weeks. "Harper, you applied for a job at Tarbush Construction, didn't you?"

"Yes."

His voice was low, and his tone said he'd rather not talk about it, but Amethyst pressed on. "I don't understand. I've watched you work around here. You can do anything. You've got a real gift for building and renovation. Why on earth wouldn't Mr. Tarbush hire you?"

Amethyst watched as a cloud passed over his features. He turned the scarred side of his face away from her. "I believe Mr. Tarbush had . . . ah, no available openings at the time."

"That's nonsense!" she blurted out. "On the square yesterday I heard him complaining about his crew. He had just hired three new men, he said, but they were lazy white trash who didn't know a hammer from—" She stopped suddenly and felt heat rise into her neck. "Well, you know."

Harper gazed to one side but did not respond.

Amethyst felt a white-hot stab of rage run through her. "Do you mean to tell me that he refused to hire you because of the way you *look*? That is the most absurd thing I've ever heard. Why, you could work circles around him and most of his crew, and do a better job at it, too!"

Harper cleared his throat. "But that's not the issue, is it?"

"Then tell me, please, what *is* the issue?"

He turned and faced her squarely. "Look at me, Amethyst. Really look. What do you see?"

"I see a kind and gentle man who's an absolute wonder when it comes to building things."

"Maybe. But what Tarbush sees is a freak, a deviant who frightens children and causes women to faint. What he sees is a liability to his business."

"Then he's a fool."

Harper gave a crooked little half-smile. "You're a strong woman, Amethyst—and, I might add, an opinionated one."

"So I've been told."

"But you don't understand the way of the real world. You expect people to respond out of compassion and kindness. They don't, you know. They usually react with selfishness and bigotry. They see somebody like me, and they're disgusted. Or they walk away with a smug sense of superiority, thanking God in heaven that they're not like me."

"The Pharisee and the publican," Amethyst mused. "But which one was justified in the eyes of God?"

"God's judgment doesn't matter," Harper responded flatly. "At least not down here on earth. Someday, maybe, it will. But right now I have to deal with people who don't much care what God thinks of their reactions."

He paused for a moment, and a look of pain crossed his face. "You know what the townspeople are saying about you, I suppose."

"That we're running a freak show?" Amethyst gave a little snort. "They can talk all they like. It's my house and my decision." She grinned at him. "Last week a fellow down at the hardware store confronted me. Said I had obviously inherited my grandfather's penchant for taking in strays and mutants. I considered it high praise."

"You might not, if you were the stray or the mutant."

The rebuke stung, and Amethyst fell silent, considering his words. She had gone into this venture with a certainty that the Lord had called her to it, but clearly she had a lot to learn.

At last Harper broke the silence. "I think I may have found a couple of new boarders for you," he said as if the previous exchange had never happened. "I ran into them yesterday while I was job hunting. One, named Pete Hopkins, lost both legs and is in a wheelchair. The other, Rodney Powell, was blinded in an explosion. Think you can take them on?"

Amethyst jumped to the challenge, grateful for the change of subject. "If you don't mind sharing the bath, we could put Mr. Powell in the other parlor room. It's small and compact and easy to get around in. Mr. Hopkins could take one of the rooms in the coach house. How long would it take you to build a ramp to the back door?"

"One day should do it, if we have enough wood for the job."

"I'll tell Silvie to stock up the pantry. Bring them on."

Word got around faster than a scandal with the preacher. Six weeks after the renovations were complete, Amethyst had a full house—five men, all casualties of war whose lives had been turned upside down by their disabilities.

Amethyst mentally ran through the list. Pete Hopkins, the amputee, was a huge, bearded fellow with an infectious laugh and a quick wit. Steven Bird, in braces and on crutches, never got the point of Pete's complex stories and always had to have them explained to him. Larry Summers, with one arm gone and the other hand distorted into a claw, needed help feeding himself—a task Silvie readily accepted with grace and good humor. Rod Powell jokingly complained that since he was blind, he should have Silvie's help, too, although he was quite adept at anything he tried and quickly learned the layout of the house as well as his own apartment.

And Harper, of course. Dear Harper. Without so much as a word of discussion, he had adopted the role of man of the house. He made repairs, looked for ways to improve the place to make life easier for the others, and appointed himself Chairman of Morale. In Harper's presence, no one could use the word *crippled* or descend into self-pity. Amethyst had seen him, on various occasions, joke, cajole, or shame the men into accepting their situations and making the best of them. And he took every opportunity to remind them all how blessed they were to have a home like Noble House.

Before long, everyone adjusted to the schedule and began to settle in. The problem was, they seemed *too* settled, to Amethyst's way of thinking. They were underfoot all the time—playing chess in the front parlor, raiding the pantry for midnight snacks, singing along as Rod Powell played popular tunes on the piano.

At last she sat down with Harper to have a little talk.

"Harper, I don't mean to be hard-handed, but these fellows have to find work. I'm not worried about getting paid, mind you—I know they have their pensions, and no one has been late with the rent. But they're—well—"

"They're driving you crazy?"

"I wouldn't have put it quite that way, but yes."

Harper leaned across the dining room table. Amethyst couldn't fail to notice how he turned his face away, or sometimes put a hand up to cover his scars. The realization disturbed her; she wanted him to feel accepted and cared for. She wanted them *all* to feel that way, of course, but—

But Harper Wainwright was different.

Amethyst had tried to tell herself that she simply appreciated all he had done to get Noble House ready for its new mission. She reasoned that she would naturally feel closer to him than to the others—after all, he had been the first to arrive at her door and had been here the longest. And he was, as she had told him on numerous occasions, gentle and kind and infinitely competent.

But that wasn't the whole truth.

She had never been in love, and wasn't sure she'd recognize the emotion if it came up and smacked her in the face, but she was beginning to think that her feelings for Harper Wainwright represented more than mere friendship, or appreciation, or sympathy. The way she tended to get flustered around him—the way her insides fluttered uncontrollably. The way her eyes sought him out in a roomful of people. The way her heart pumped a little faster when she heard his distinctive limping step coming across the front porch. She felt deliriously wonderful and sick to her stomach all at the same time.

The problem was, Harper had given absolutely no indication that he shared any of those feelings. If anything, he avoided her gaze and limited his contact with her to meals, when everyone else was there, or times like this, when they had a particular problem to solve. He wasn't cold or unfriendly toward her; he simply treated her with the same courtesy he offered everyone else. It was as if he were locked away somewhere, in a world she could neither enter nor understand, as if—

"Amethyst? Are you listening?"

Amethyst looked up. "I'm sorry, Harper. What were you saying?"

"I was saying that the fellows *are* looking for work. Rod thought he had convinced Mr. Mansfield at the hotel restaurant to hire him to play the piano during the dinner hour, but apparently the job fell through at the last minute. Pete and Steve and the others have been in town nearly every day, following up every lead they can find. But it's the same old story—nobody's hiring, not for any kind of work at any wage. Not in town, not at the college."

Amethyst struggled for a moment to clear her mind and focus on Harper's words rather than the strange, soft expression that filled his eyes.

"So," she said after a minute or two, "what we're dealing with is not just a few isolated bigots, but a whole town paralyzed by prejudice."

"So it seems."

A rush of energy exploded through Amethyst like fire in her veins, sweeping aside any personal concerns. She recognized the sensation immediately—the exhilaration of the challenge. The intoxication of the Cause. A massive injustice was happening, and she couldn't—wouldn't— sit idly by and let it go on. It was time for action.

"Give me a few days," she said with a slow smile. "I think I just might come up with a plan."

"What kind of plan?"

"Something my grandparents would approve of," Amethyst answered cryptically. "A Pearl and Silas Plan."

28
In the Lion's Den

———◆◆◆———

August 1918

Amethyst sat in the front row of a small semicircle of chairs and tried to maintain her composure as the Town Council gathered for its monthly meeting. At the front of the room, a long table with five leather chairs sat empty. Behind her, she could hear the murmuring of voices as a few people milled around finding seats. Once or twice her ears caught a mention of her own name, but she refused to turn around and give the gossips the pleasure of knowing they had irritated her.

Precisely at seven o'clock, a side door opened and the mayor entered, followed by the four councilmen. Amethyst narrowed her eyes and looked them over. Rube Layton, the mayor, a fat, flabby man with a flush complexion, took the center seat and cleared his throat. His head sat directly on his shoulders without benefit of a neck, making him look as if he were perpetually being lynched by his own necktie—an apt image, Amethyst thought, given the grunts and growls that punctuated any sentence he spoke.

To his right sat Will Tarbush, owner of Tarbush Construction. Tarbush had not gained a seat on the council because of his innate intelligence or civic pride, but because of the power his construction company gave him in the community. At Tarbush's elbow, whispering in his ear and pointing in her direction, was Ollie Ferrell, an oily fellow with a face like a weasel who ran the hardware store on the square. Completing the council were Marshall Avery and Lyle Constable. Marsh, a shirttail cousin on

Grandma Pearl's side of the family, was current owner and operator of
Avery's Mill. Lyle managed the Feed & Supply down on the south end
of University Avenue. Amethyst didn't know either of them very well,
but Lyle was a salt-of-the-earth type, and Cousin Marshall certainly
came from a good bloodline. She held out hope that she might be able
to appeal to their sense of decency.

Mayor Layton pounded a wooden gavel on the tabletop and let out a
series of growling noises—a totally unnecessary action, since the few
townspeople who sat scattered out in the room had already quieted
down. "Order!" he roared, hammering the gavel harder. "This meeting
of the Cambridge Town Council will come to order."

Marsh leaned in toward him and whispered, loud enough for everybody to hear: "Rube, I think we're already orderly enough."

A titter went through the crowd, and Rube's face flushed even redder,
if that were possible.

"Ahem. Yes, well. We'll begin with Councilman Constable reading the
minutes of the last meeting."

Lyle Constable fumbled for his notes and let his eyes rest on
Amethyst for a moment. Clearly, her presence here had them all a little
ruffled. "We, ah, decided to hire Trey Hayward, Johnny's oldest boy, to
cut the grass and trim the shrubs in the courthouse square—ten dollars
a month, out of the general budget." His gaze searched the pages in
front of him. "And, uh, we voted to have this year's Labor Day picnic in
the grove at the college—with the approval of the dean, of course. And
I guess that's about all."

"No, that *ain't* all," Tarbush objected, leaning forward to throw a menacing look in Constable's direction. "It's right here in Ollie's ledger—he's
the treasurer, you know. We also voted to buy a new flag for in front of
the courthouse and have the statue of the Confederate soldier cleaned."

"Uh, yeah, I guess we did." Lyle shuffled his papers nervously. "Oh, I
got it." He held up a page and nodded. "Sorry."

"You're sorry, all right," Tarbush muttered.

The longer Amethyst watched Tarbush, the less she liked him. Perhaps
it wasn't a Christian sentiment, but she couldn't help it. Of all the nerve,
to call down his fellow councilman in public—and unless she missed

her guess, it wasn't the first time. Lyle Constable's reaction spoke volumes about how often he had to take this kind of treatment.

She had fully intended to come into the meeting with cannons loaded, ready for a fight. But now Amethyst began to rethink her strategy. If she stood up and accused them all of bigotry, they would simply turn a deaf ear to her. Marsh and Lyle might listen, but they only represented two votes out of five. At the very least she had to find the mayor's soft underbelly—he was the swing vote. But maybe there was a way to convince all of them, even nasty old Tarbush, without them knowing they were being convinced. . . .

People around her shifted in their seats, attempting to hide their boredom while the council went through its mind-numbing agenda: the garbage problem behind the hotel restaurant; the need for a new streetlight on Main and Third; the question of getting a new Baby Jesus to replace the one stolen last Christmas (tabled until the September meeting); a resolution to require Neta Parkinson to remove the ladies' undergarments from her window display at the La Femme House of Clothing.

At a quarter to nine, Mayor Layton pounded his gavel, waking half the spectators from a sound sleep. "If there's no new business from the floor, we'll adjourn."

Obviously he didn't expect any, or wanted to close down the meeting as fast as possible before anyone had a chance to raise any real concerns. But Amethyst was too quick for him. She jumped to her feet and said, "Mr. Mayor, I have some business I'd like to discuss."

Will Tarbush glared at her from his side of the table. "Rube, she's out of order!"

"No, Mr. Tarbush, I am not." Amethyst raised a sheaf of papers. "According to the city charter, any resident has the right to appear before the Town Council and bring an issue for consideration."

Rube Layton narrowed his piglike eyes at Amethyst until they almost disappeared. "She's right, Will."

"But she's a . . . a woman!"

Amethyst batted her eyes and smiled at him. "Very perceptive of you, Mr. Tarbush."

The mayor gave a rumbling chuckle, and a wave of laugher moved through the room. *Good*, Amethyst thought. *Laughter disarms people.*

"The charter makes no limitation upon the gender of any person who wishes to speak. With your permission, Mayor Layton?"

The mayor cleared his throat and nodded. Amethyst stood up and faced the council.

"Cambridge has long prided itself on its civic heritage," she began. "A heritage of community, where we all help each other and care about each other." She fixed her gaze on Ollie Ferrell. "Remember, Mr. Ferrell, when Widow Nance got a leak in her roof, not two weeks after she buried her husband? As I recall, you provided the materials to fix it at no charge, and even went out there and helped put on the new shingles yourself."

Obviously surprised, Ferrell scrunched his ratty little face up in the imitation of a smile. "Yes'm, I did. It was the right thing to do."

"Indeed it was. It was a very generous act. And you, Mr. Tarbush—" Amethyst turned to look into the man's eyes. "When lightning took out the steeple of our church, you sent a crew over to rebuild it, did you not?"

Tarbush's chest puffed out, and he showed his yellow teeth in a grin. "Well, sure. I've been a good Presbyterian all my life. Donated the wood, the nails, the paint, everything."

"My point exactly. This is not just a town; it's a community. During the drought of 1915, Mr. Constable there provided feed for most of the county's cattle—on credit, at no interest—to get the farmers by until the rains came again. When the river flooded a few years back, most of the men in this town went down in the middle of the night to fill sandbags for a dike. And everyone knows how much you, Mr. Mayor, care about the people of this town. You've set the example for the citizens of Cambridge to take the Good Book seriously when it says, 'If your neighbor is hungry, feed him; if he thirsts, give him drink.' Isn't that right?"

Rube Layton leaned back in his chair, a smug expression on his fat face. "Of course, Miss Amethyst. That's what my leadership as mayor is all about—helping make Cambridge a fine, attractive place to live, a place where people feel they belong."

"Yes, Mr. Mayor, I'm certain that's true," Amethyst agreed. "And I'm equally certain that you will be shocked to know that some of our citizens *don't* feel as if they belong. That they feel like outcasts, when they haven't done a single thing to deserve such treatment. The fact is, some of our fellow townspeople have made Cambridge a very disagreeable place to live."

Rube sat up straight and focused his eyes on her. "Who would do such a thing? Every citizen of Cambridge has the right to be treated with respect, and if they're not, I want to know about it. I won't tolerate such behavior in my town."

Amethyst smiled. She had him right where she wanted him. "I'm glad to hear you say that, Mayor Layton. According to Mr. Tarbush, at the last meeting you voted on several important issues—purchasing a new flag for the courthouse square, cleaning up the Confederate soldier that stands in front of the square as a symbol of Cambridge's civic pride. What would you say if I told you that other soldiers—men who went to war to defend our way of life here in Cambridge—have been ostracized from its society and refused jobs for which they were qualified?"

Forgetting all about his gavel, Layton pounded his meaty fist against the table. "I'd say that Cambridge isn't that kind of town! I'd say that we'll make it right, no matter what it takes!"

Caught up in the momentum, Will Tarbush got into the act. "You're golldurn right we will! It's high time this council did something important, 'stead of just sittin' around on our duffs talking about picnics and trash!"

"Amen to that!" Ollie Ferrell squeaked.

So far, neither Marshall Avery nor Lyle Constable had uttered a word, and suddenly Tarbush seemed to notice their silence. "What about you wimps?" he yelled, leaning over the table and craning his neck to glare at them. "Ain't you gonna say anything?"

Marsh fixed his gaze directly on Amethyst and gave her an almost imperceptible wink. "Yes indeed," he answered Tarbush. "I'm going to make a motion that the council adopt a resolution. Are you ready, Lyle?"

Lyle Constable poised pen over paper and nodded.

"Be it hereby resolved that the Town Council of Cambridge, Mississippi, enacts this local ordinance: that no citizen shall without warrant be denied

employment, lodging, or any public service, or be subjected to any degrading or disrespectful behavior. This resolution is to be called the Good Neighbor Statute, and any violation of it is to be reported directly to the Mayor's office, where action will be taken against the perpetrators in the form of monetary fines and/or revocation of business licenses. You got that, Lyle?"

Constable nodded. "Got it."

"All in favor?" the mayor roared.

"Aye!"

The vote was unanimous, and a ripple of applause ran through the spectators. Amethyst figured no one really understood the significance of what the council had just done—except for herself and Marsh Avery. They were just glad to see the council doing *something*.

"All right, people, calm down," Rube Layton yelled. "This ain't no dog and pony show."

"Mr. Mayor," Amethyst said, giving a gracious little curtsy, "may I express to you my gratefulness for the strength of character and integrity you have all demonstrated here tonight."

"Why, you're welcome, Miss Amethyst," Layton responded with a silly grin. "Happy to oblige. That's what we're here for, after all—to make sure everyone in our fair town has an equal chance at life, liberty, and the pursuit of happiness. And may I say—"

He was about to go on with his bombastic speech when Amethyst held up a gloved hand to stop him. "Mr. Mayor, could I ask one more teensy little favor?"

"Why, yes ma'am. Ask away."

"I'd like to have some copies of this resolution. For the historical value of this action, you know. Might I pick up, say, ten copies at your office on Monday?"

He tugged at his lapels and nodded. "Monday will be fine, Miss Amethyst. And the resolution will be posted in the newspaper first thing Monday morning. We want all our people to know how the council is working on their behalf."

"You're doing a fine, fine job of it, too," Amethyst cooed. "And now, if you'll excuse me, I'll take my leave."

Amethyst could feel the eyes of the five councilmen on her back as she turned to leave the room. *They're pleased as puppies with themselves,* she thought. *And by the time they figure out what they've done, it'll be too late.*

Come Monday, there would be work for everyone.

29

The Sheik and the Spinster

---◆·※·◆---

November 1923

Harper Wainwright sat behind his desk at Bainbridge Metal Works and slowly turned the pages of the annual ledger. It was still six weeks until year's end, but he didn't need to wait for the December accounts to be able to tell Mac Bainbridge that profits were up again—this time by 18.5 percent.

In the five years Harper had worked for Mac, earnings had increased every year. He had begun as a metalworker out in the plant, and within a year had been promoted to plant supervisor. At first the men resented his promotion, but when they discovered he could find ways to make their jobs easier and more efficient, they came around. No one had called him "Scarface" in over a year—except for the new fellow hired last month, and he only did it once. The other workers had jumped on him like a cat on a June bug, and Harper himself hadn't had to say a single word of reprimand.

Because of Harper's efficiency and the new techniques he had discovered through a dedicated study of the business, Bainbridge Metal had never been in such good financial shape. Mac had originally wanted to pocket the profits, but Harper had convinced him that raising salaries would benefit everyone. And it had worked. Every man on the plant floor knew that hard work meant increased profits, and increased profits meant a raise in the hourly wage. There were no slackers at Bainbridge Metal. Nobody complained. Now guys were lining up to apply for jobs, and Mac had a waiting list longer than his brand-new, luxury-model Pierce-Arrow.

Harper gave a satisfied chuckle and closed the book. Five years, and he had not yet lost the joy of coming to the plant every day. When a man had to fight for the right to work, Harper supposed, he appreciated it more. It was one of many things he was grateful for during this season of thankfulness.

When he opened the top drawer of his desk to replace the ledger, the corner of a yellowed sheet of paper caught his attention. He drew it out and sat back in his chair, smiling to himself. The original copy of the Town Council's "Good Neighbor Statute"—he had brought it with him when he came for his initial interview with Mac Bainbridge. He ought to frame it, Harper thought, and hang it on the wall. A reminder of Amethyst Noble's courage and dedication.

Amethyst would say that she had only followed an old family recipe—two parts pride, three parts shame, and a dash of feminine wile. But whatever methods she had used, she had gotten the job done, and all of them had benefited. Rod Powell had created quite a following for himself, playing the piano down at the hotel restaurant. Mansfield, the owner, took credit for "discovering" him, of course, and when a dance hall manager from Memphis stopped in and offered Rod double his salary to play six nights a week at the Riverview Palace, Mansfield nearly had a fit of apoplexy. But Rod went to Memphis anyway, married some nice girl, and now had two children and a successful career.

Pete Hopkins had landed a job at the Feed & Supply, working alongside Lyle Constable. Although confined to a wheelchair, Pete could do just about anything except reach the top shelves. He talked Constable into hiring Steven Bird as their accountant, and when the owner decided to sell, the three of them purchased the business in equal shares.

Even Larry Summers had done well for himself. With Silvie's encouragement, he had gotten himself a claw arm and learned to use it so deftly that nobody thought of him as being crippled anymore. He went to work as a telephone operator—quite a novelty, being the sole man in a "woman's" domain. He and his new wife now lived in a little house down at the end of Main Street and were expecting their first baby in the spring.

Harper fingered the faded paper and sighed. Thanks to Amethyst and her Good Neighbor Statute, all the original fellows who had taken refuge in Noble House had found a place and created a new life for themselves. All except him.

He had a good job, of course, and friends in the plant. He could walk down the street without being stared at or called names. Even Will Tarbush had changed his tune—once he saw how successful Mac's business was getting, he came to see Harper in private and offered him a sizable bonus to jump ship and come over to manage Tarbush Construction.

Harper didn't take the bait, of course. Tarbush was still a bigot and a fool, with a heart as hard as old oak planks. The man hadn't changed; he had only conceded to the power of the almighty dollar. Besides, Harper was happy where he was, and the money didn't mean that much to him. The only disappointing aspect of his life had to do with his personal relationships. Specifically, his relationship with one person.

Amethyst Noble.

For five years Harper had kept his feelings for Amethyst to himself. They were friends—good friends, to be sure—but that was all. Every Christmas they exchanged little tokens of their affection; every Sunday they attended church services together. Twice a year or so they'd drive up to Memphis or Sardis Lake for a daylong outing. But other than a squeeze on the arm or a pat on the shoulder, Amethyst gave no indication of wanting their relationship to change in any way. And so he could not tell her the truth.

The truth was, he loved her. He respected her. He adored her. And he couldn't tell her—not even now, when he was a successful plant manager. He couldn't take the chance that she would not share his feelings, couldn't risk losing the friendship that they had developed. Some things had changed for the better in Cambridge, Mississippi, and for that he was grateful. But Amethyst Noble being courted by Scarface? It was too radical even to imagine.

Harper gave a sigh and replaced the paper in the desk drawer. It was almost quitting time, and he needed to make one last pass through the plant before going home.

Home, where Amethyst and Silvie were undoubtedly hard at work on their Thanksgiving dinner. Home, where he felt safe and honored and even loved—but not in the way he wished to be loved. Home, where every time he looked around, he was reminded of what he couldn't have.

Silvie put the finishing touches on the corn casserole and slid it into the last remaining nook in the icebox. "Law, hon, do we really need both pumpkin and mince pies? We got that huge coconut cake, you know."

Amethyst turned and grinned at her, her arms dusted with flour up to her elbows and a smear of pumpkin on her nose. "Harper likes both kinds. And it's Thanksgiving, Silvie. We're not going to scrimp at Thanksgiving."

"Whatever you say." Silvie reached a hand to Amethyst's face and swiped off the pumpkin. "Who all's coming?"

"The two of us, Harper, and Uncle Enoch of course. Pete and Steven, and the Constables. Larry and his wife. Two of the new boarders will be here—Gil and John; the others are going to their families, I think. Oh, and Dinah Johnson, the girl Neta just hired at La Femme. She's new in town, and nobody should be alone on Thanksgiving."

"Is she prepared for this crew?"

"I think so. I told her it was a very special group of people."

Silvie watched as Amethyst worked on the pies. The woman's face fairly glowed with anticipation. "You just love this, don't you?"

"What?"

"Doing up big for a whole lot of folks. Puttin' on a fancy spread."

Amethyst laughed. "I always think I love it, until I get about halfway into it. Right now my feet are killing me."

"Then sit yourself down and let me finish the pies. I can spice up pumpkin as well as you can."

"Better," Amethyst countered, "but you know I like to do this part myself."

Silvie narrowed her eyes and adopted a singsong tone. "Somethin' special for *Harper*?"

"What's that supposed to mean?" Amethyst sank into a chair at the kitchen table. "Here, now you can finish with the pie crusts. I need a break."

Silvie took over and arched an eyebrow at her friend. "When are you going to tell him, Amethyst?"

"When am I going to tell who what?"

"Don't play coy with me, girl. It's been five years, for heaven's sake. I ain't blind."

Amethyst kicked off her shoes. "I have no idea what you're talking about."

"Of course you do. I'm talking about Mr. Harper Wainwright." Silvie pounded the rolling pin against the dough with a vengeance. The girl could be so dense sometimes. And so stubborn.

"What about him?"

"You're in love with him, that's what about him," Silvie snapped. "Far as I can tell, you have been for maybe four years or more. Don't you think it's about time the two of you got honest with each other?"

Silvie kept on rolling the piecrust, but Amethyst didn't respond. At last she turned to see Amethyst with her head down on the table. "Look at me, girl."

Amethyst lifted her head, and Silvie saw shiny tracks on her cheeks. "Are you crying?"

Amethyst shook her head and sniffed. "Of course not."

"You are! Why? Is it something I said?"

"It's—it's *everything!*"

"Ah, don't take on like that, hon." Silvie abandoned the rolling pin and went to sit next to Amethyst at the table. "I didn't mean to hurt your feelings."

"You didn't," Amethyst gasped. "It's just that, well—"

She paused, and Silvie patted her hand. "Go on."

"He's been here five years, Silvie. And all that time he's been a perfect gentleman—"

"And you wish he wouldn't be quite such a gentleman? You wish he'd just corner you up against the wall and kiss the livin' daylights out of you?" Silvie grinned, and Amethyst rewarded her with a halfhearted smile.

"Not that, exactly. I just wish he'd do *something*—give me some indication of the way he feels about me. If he feels anything at all, that is."

Silvie closed her eyes and prayed for patience. When she opened them again, Amethyst was staring off into the distance. "Listen to me," she said firmly. "That man has been boarding here for over five years. For most of those years he's had a well-paying manager's job at Bainbridge's. Don't you think he could afford to live in his own house if he wanted to?"

"I suppose," Amethyst answered in a whisper. "But a lot of single men prefer boardinghouses—you know, having their meals prepared for them and all."

"Well, I gotta admit my cooking is near to impossible for a man to turn down," Silvie said with a chuckle. "But I don't reckon that's his primary motivation for staying."

"You think he's staying because of me?"

Silvie rolled her eyes. "What do you think?"

"I don't know! And you can stop prodding me to confront him with my feelings for him—and I'm not admitting I have such feelings, mind you. When it comes to romance, a lady does not approach a gentleman."

"And since when are you a *lady*?" Silvie tried to keep the derisive snort out of her voice, but she didn't succeed.

"You don't think I'm a lady?"

"Oh, for pity's sake, Amethyst. You went all by yourself and confronted the Town Council. You fought for justice for these men, and look what happened. You're a woman of courage and dignity and strength. Just like your grandmother."

Silvie watched as a change came over Amethyst's face. The tears dried, and an expression of determination filled her eyes. "You're right, Silvie. I *am* like my grandmother, and proud of it. People accused her of not being a lady, either." She hesitated and took a deep breath. "But this is different. What if Harper doesn't feel the same way about me? What if he only thinks of me as a friend? I do care for him—and I don't want to lose our friendship over a silly misunderstanding."

"It's a risk," Silvie agreed. "Maybe you're right; maybe it's better not to know."

"How can you say that? If I let fear keep me from finding out, I may be throwing my whole future away! I thought you had more gumption than that, Silvie. I thought you, of all people—"

Suddenly Amethyst looked up into Silvie's eyes and began to laugh. "You are so bad. You threw out the bait, and I took it, didn't I?"

Silvie chuckled. "Like a catfish on a cricket."

"All right. I'll think about it. But no promises, understand?"

"It's your life." Silvie shrugged, then turned back to her piecrusts so Amethyst couldn't see the smile that would not be contained.

———•·•·•———

"That was a wonderful meal." Harper gave a satisfied sigh and leaned back in his chair. "I declare, you two ladies are the finest cooks this side of the Mississippi."

Everyone around the table nodded in agreement. Nearly every bowl and platter had been scraped clean, right down to the tiny little roses on Grandma Pearl's good china.

Amethyst got up and began to clear the table. "You all go into the parlor. I'll clean up a little and then we'll serve coffee and dessert." Silvie rose to help her, but Amethyst shook her head. "You did most of the cooking, Silvie. I'll see to the dishes."

Silvie slanted a look at her and winked. "I do believe I'll take you up on that offer." She chuckled. "Harper, why don't you give Amethyst a hand? Earn your keep around here."

Amethyst felt a thrill of trepidation run through her, and she impaled Silvie with a withering glance. "That's not necessary," she said lightly. "I can handle it."

Harper laughed and pushed his chair back from the table. "I'll be happy to help."

"We can all help," Pete offered, reaching from his wheelchair and piling a stack of plates on his lap. "Most of us lived here, after all, and we know where everything goes—"

"No you don't!" Silvie snapped, jerking the plates out of his lap and thrusting them in Harper's direction. "You're guests now," she went on in a more moderate tone. "Just you relax in the parlor, and Amethyst and Harper can take care of it."

Amethyst grabbed Silvie by the elbow and hustled her into the kitchen. "What do you think you're doing?"

"You're drawing blood, girl," Silvie complained as she jerked her arm away. "I'm giving you your chance—now take it!"

Just as Amethyst was about to respond, Harper poked his head through the doorway. He looked at Amethyst, then at Silvie, then back to Amethyst. "Should I come back later?"

"Of course not, silly, come on in." Silvie steered him toward the sink with his load of dishes and narrowed her eyes at Amethyst. "I'll be in the parlor if you need me."

With that, she was gone, and Amethyst found herself alone in the presence of the man who made her heart pound. She could have throttled Silvie. Couldn't Harper hear her pulse racing, see the slow flush that she felt creeping up her neck?

Her reaction made no sense, of course. This wasn't *The Sheik*, and he wasn't Rudolph Valentino. What did she expect, for him to throw down the dishes and sweep her into his arms, then ride away into the desert night on his golden stallion?

The image almost made her laugh. Romance—at least the kind of romance they showed in the movies, with Douglas Fairbanks as Robin Hood rescuing his Maid Marian—didn't happen to people like Amethyst Noble and Harper Wainwright. The two of them would never be a silver screen hero and his lovely damsel. They were what they were—a spinster landlady and a scarred ex-soldier.

"Something funny?" Harper put the dishes in the sink and turned to her.

Amethyst shook her head, then raised her eyes to meet his. He didn't flinch or turn to one side. His gaze held hers, and he smiled—that endearing, crooked, one-sided grin. She didn't see his scarred cheek, or his bent leg, or his twisted hand. Just his eyes, soft and blue, looking at her with an indefinable expression.

Amethyst didn't know how long the moment lasted. She was caught there, trapped in his gaze, unable to speak a word.

"If you'll hand me a bowl, I'll pull what's left of this turkey off the bone," he said in a low voice.

She didn't move. When he reached around her to open the cabinet, his hand brushed her arm. A flame shot through her.

"Harper—" she began, barely able to catch her breath.

His hand stopped in midair. "Amethyst—"

"I—I don't know how to say this," she stammered.

He looked at her again, intently, then his eyes widened. "You, too?"

She leaned against the stove. "Yes."

He blinked at her. "For five years," he managed, his voice quiet and husky, "I've hoped, dreamed—even prayed—that you might come to feel something for me other than friendship. But I never thought I could be worthy—"

Amethyst laid a trembling finger across his lips. He flinched a little and shut his eyes as her hand moved to the scarred side of his face, exploring the tight, drawn skin, caressing the crevices left by the burn. His skin felt cool under her fingers—not hard and brittle, the way it looked, but smooth ridges of scar tissue that gave a little under the pressure of her touch.

"You avoided me," she murmured. "For so long you wouldn't even look at me."

"I was afraid," he admitted in a ragged voice. "Afraid of my own feelings. Afraid you'd reject me. Afraid of being hurt again, with a pain that would have been so much worse than any physical wound."

He put an arm around her shoulders, and Amethyst leaned in toward him. It wasn't the ladylike thing to do, an inner voice reprimanded her, but she couldn't help it. This was the moment she had waited for, and if she let it pass her by, she would never forgive herself.

"God willing, there will be no more wounds," she whispered. "At least not from me."

His other arm went around her and drew her close. "We're supposed to be doing the dishes," he murmured into her hair.

"The dishes can wait." Amethyst raised her face to him. "Promise you won't hide from me ever again."

"I promise."

He tilted his head, and Amethyst felt his warm breath against her cheek. When their lips met, she could have sworn she heard the pounding of hooves and the call of night birds in the desert.

What she really heard was Silvie's voice through the kitchen doorway. "Well, thank you, Jesus! It's about time!"

30
The Wedding Gift

March 1924

Amethyst strolled casually through the aisles of Hartwell's Grocery, glancing at Silvie's list and doing a quick mental calculation. Forty or fifty guests, she figured. The ham and turkey were already baking—one in the new oven Silvie complained about all the time, and the other in the old wood stove on the back porch. By this afternoon, the layers for the wedding cake would be cooled and ready to frost, and the bread would be finished. All she needed was a sack of sugar, a good selection of fruit for the salad, and some of those little pastel-colored candies to decorate the table.

"Gordon," she called as Hartwell passed by in his stained apron, "is there any chance you've got some strawberries?"

"Local ones won't be in till later in the season, Miss Amethyst," he said. "My supplier brought me some from down in Florida yesterday, but they're not cheap."

She smiled and patted him on the arm. "I only plan to do this once, Gordon; cost is no object."

"Yes ma'am!" He grinned at her. "They're in the cooler out back. I'll go get 'em for you. How many do you need?"

"As many as you've got."

Amethyst stood there, inspecting the apples and bananas, while she waited for Gordon to return with her strawberries. The market was nearly empty, and from behind her, she could hear the whispered voices of two women, hidden from view on the other side of a display of oranges.

"Can you believe it? She's really going to do it. She's going to marry that . . . that *man*."

"That *monster*, you mean. Do you suppose she's . . . kissed him? I couldn't stand the thought."

Amethyst felt a knife twist in her gut. After all this time, she should be accustomed to people gossiping about her, but to hear the man she loved called a monster—

"You don't suppose they'll try to have children, do you? Can you *imagine*?"

"I know. Even if the poor babies did turn out to be normal, what kind of life would they have, looking at that and having to call him 'Daddy.'"

"Well, what else would you expect, Edie? She must be nearing thirty, and she lives all alone in that big house with that colored woman and those deformed boarders. Who else would have her?"

"Twenty-four," Amethyst corrected in a firm voice.

The voices fell silent.

"Twenty-four," she repeated. "I turned twenty-four years old last week."

Amethyst stepped around the grocery display and found herself looking into the weak, watery eyes of Edith Layton, the mayor's wife. Edith's companion, a shriveled little woman named Beatrice Manning, stood with her gaze fixed on her shoes.

"My husband-to-be, Mrs. Layton," she said with ice in her voice, "is not a monster. He is a kind, gentle man with a loving and tender heart—qualities you must find impossible to comprehend, given your own marital status." She let her eyes rove up and down Edith Layton's frame and thought briefly that the woman reminded her of a sausage stuffed a little too generously into its casing. At last her gaze came to rest on the woman's floury, pockmarked face. "If it's any of your business, we love each other deeply, and that love is not dependent upon physical appearance."

Edith Layton's eyes bulged out, and a vein in her neck went rigid. "Well, I never!"

"No, I don't suppose you have," Amethyst countered. "But I sincerely hope you do, someday."

Gordon Hartwell had returned with the strawberries, and he stood there with a look of terror on his face, as if he feared a catfight might reduce his store to rubble. "I'll—I'll just charge this to your account, Miss Amethyst," he stammered. "Want this stuff delivered?"

"That would be lovely, Gordon. Thanks so much."

Edith and Bea gaped at Amethyst as she pushed past them.

"The wedding is tomorrow at four-thirty," she called over her shoulder with a smile. "You're both invited, if you'd care to come."

When she had put on fresh sheets and sprinkled them with the fragrance of lilacs, Amethyst smoothed the quilt on the ancient four-poster and smiled. She had spent her last night in this bed alone. And contrary to convention, she was not the least bit apprehensive about sharing it with Harper Wainwright.

She gave a little chuckle and plumped up the pillows. A real lady, she thought, would show some trepidation about her wedding night—or at least *pretend* to be nervous. But then, as Silvie had pointed out to her on numerous occasions, she was not and never would be a real lady. She was Pearl Noble's granddaughter after all.

Amethyst went to the tall wardrobe, took out her wedding gown, and hung it on the door. It was a beautiful dress—white satin, with a high neck and simple lines, a touch of lace, and seed pearls sewn into the bodice. The only thing missing was—

She took in a breath and stifled a rush of tears. She had told herself she would not get emotional about the thought of Grandma Pearl's brooch. After all, the brooch had been gone for years. Yet despite her best intentions, she felt saddened by its loss, especially today. This was her wedding day, and she knew from Pearl's journals that on the night of her birth, her grandpa Silas had pinned it on her baby blanket and prayed a blessing upon her. That blessing had been fulfilled in a hundred ways, and she was grateful. Still, she wished she could walk down the aisle with the heart-shaped amethyst at her throat. . . .

She glanced at the clock on the bedside table. It was 3:15—time she started getting ready.

But she couldn't seem to settle down to the task. She wandered into the bathroom and stared at herself in the mirror. She rearranged a shelf, went back into the bedroom and smoothed the comforter for the second time, then finally left the room altogether and went upstairs.

On the courting porch above the main veranda, Amethyst gazed down into the front yard. Chairs had been set up on the grass, and a wide white runner spanned the walkway. At the end of the walk, an old man stood gazing up toward the house. Probably one of the workers Harper had hired to set up, she mused. Well, he could be proud of his handiwork. The place looked absolutely wonderful.

Her eyes followed him for a moment or two as he made a slow circuit of the yard and came toward the porch. He was thoughtful, at least, making sure not to track up the white runner with his boots. As he drew closer, she could see him more clearly—gray hair, a grizzled beard, a haunted, empty expression about the eyes. His jacket was worn thin at the elbows, but underneath he wore a satin vest, stained and ragged, with a button missing—almost as if he had once had money but had since fallen on hard times. Poor old fellow. It was just like Harper to give a job to a man down on his luck.

As Amethyst watched him disappear under the porch roof, she was suddenly overcome with an awareness of the richness of her own life. How petty she had been, shedding selfish tears over not having Grandma Pearl's brooch to wear! A pang of remorse jabbed at her heart, and she offered up a prayer of gratefulness, asking God to bless that man, whoever he was. The old fellow could obviously do with a blessing or two. From now on she would try to keep him and those like him—those less fortunate—in mind whenever she was tempted to take for granted all the Lord had given her.

She went back down the stairs and into the dining room, where Silvie's cousin Esther was setting out food for the reception. "Can I do anything to help?" she asked as Esther came in bearing an enormous tray of baked ham.

"Law, no, Amethyst!" Esther reprimanded. "This is your wedding day, and your guests will be coming in less than an hour. Now get on back in there and get dressed!"

Amethyst gazed around, feeling totally useless. "Has anyone seen Harper?"

"He's been in and out, gettin' in the way just like you're doing now. But don't you be looking for him, neither. Don't you know it's bad luck for a bride to see her groom on their wedding day?"

Amethyst meandered into the parlor, where every horizontal surface, it seemed, was stacked with wedding presents. The wide mantel over the fireplace had disappeared under an avalanche of white boxes and bows, and gifts were stacked on all the tables and in the corners of the room. Only the small marble-topped coffee table had been left empty, so guests could place their cups and plates on it during the reception. But now even that space bore a gift.

Amethyst sat down on the love seat and picked up the small, delicately wrapped box. She should put it with the rest of them, she supposed, but instead she scrutinized it, turning it over in her hands. It was covered in satiny paper and tied up with a gold ribbon. The tag read, *Amethyst.* Not *Mr. Harper Wainwright and Miss Amethyst Noble,* like the others. Just *Amethyst.*

"Girl, what are you doing out here? Why aren't you dressed?"

Amethyst looked up to see Silvie glaring down on her. "Well, good afternoon to you, too," she chuckled.

"Don't you 'good afternoon' me, missy! Do you know what time it is? Get in there and get that wedding gown on. We still have to fix your hair."

Amethyst held up the box. "What is this?"

"What is what?" Silvie stared at her as if she had lost her mind. "It's a wedding present, I'd reckon."

"But who's it from? And why does it only have my name on it?"

"Amethyst, I don't know. And right now I don't really care. You need to get yourself—"

"I'm going to open it."

Silvie rolled her eyes and gave a long-suffering sigh. "All right, then, open it." She came to sit on the love seat with Amethyst. "But don't blame me if you're late for your own wedding."

Amethyst untied the bow and removed the wrapping, then lifted the top of the box and gave a little gasp.

"Lord, have mercy," Silvie breathed.

It was a heart-shaped amethyst brooch, a little larger than a quarter, surrounded by small pearls.

"Your grandmother's amethyst," Silvie murmured. "How on earth—?"

"No, it's not my grandmother's, although it's almost exactly like it. The one I lost had one of the pearls missing."

Silvie reached out a finger and stroked the table of the stone. "It has to be a gift from Harper. Nobody else would give you something like this."

"Harper never knew about the brooch," Amethyst protested. "I never told him."

"Then that man must have one direct line to heaven," Silvie countered. "You are going to wear it, aren't you?"

"I certainly am. But I need to talk to him about it first."

"You can't." Silvie tugged at her arm. "For one thing, you don't have time. For the second, it's bad luck—"

"To see your bridegroom before the wedding. I know. Esther already told me. I guess it will have to wait, then." Amethyst gazed at the brooch, and tears filled her eyes. "It's beautiful. But somehow I wish a pearl *were* missing. I wish it were my grandmother's."

"And you're sure it's not?"

"How could it be? It's impossible. Grandma Pearl's brooch disappeared years ago with Father." She shook her head resolutely. "Well, I guess we'd better get moving. Don't want to be late for my own wedding."

Then she turned the gemstone over in her hands. On the back, in tiny, cramped writing, were engraved the words: *Sincerity, Purity, Nobility.*

Noble House had never looked so festive—except, perhaps, the day Grandpa Silas and Grandma Pearl celebrated their wedding on this same front porch. The walkway was lined with budding azaleas, and yellow daffodils surrounded the base of the massive magnolia tree. Dogwoods and redbuds bloomed profusely. White ribbons and huge bows swagged between the tall square columns. Pots of gardenias flanked the steps, sending out their delicate fragrance on the afternoon breeze.

If Amethyst lived to be a hundred—as she resolutely hoped she would not—she doubted she would ever experience a day quite as perfect as this one.

Uncle Enoch and several of his friends had rolled the piano out onto the porch, and Rod Powell, who had come down from Memphis for the occasion, played softly as the guests gathered. At 4:15, Amethyst slipped from the bedroom and went around to the back porch to await the cue for her grand entrance.

"Do I look all right?" she asked Silvie for the hundredth time. Her hands went to her neckline, as if to assure herself that the amethyst brooch was still in place.

"You look wonderful. The brooch is perfect." Silvie adjusted the flowing skirt of the wedding dress and stood back to admire it. "I don't think I ever really thanked you for choosing me as your maid of honor."

"Who else would I ask?" Amethyst huffed. "You've been my best friend since we were babies."

"You sure you want me to stay on after today?"

"Of course I'm sure." Amethyst put an arm around her friend's shoulder. "Silvie, Noble House is *our* home, not just *mine*. And it's also our business. I wouldn't know what to do without you."

"I just thought—"

"Well, don't," Amethyst interrupted. "Harper and I will take the big bedroom downstairs, and everything else will remain exactly the same. Besides, I need you here to manage things while we're gone to New Orleans for our honeymoon. We'll be back in a week."

Silvie ducked her head. "I guess I was wondering if, once you were married, Harper might not take over running the boardinghouse."

Amethyst let out a laugh. "And be underfoot all day while you and I are trying to get our work done? Heavens, no. He's keeping his job with Bainbridge Metal. We're in love, Silvie; we're not joined at the hip."

The two embraced, and Amethyst whispered, "No more talk about leaving, all right?"

"All right." Silvie brushed aside a tear.

"And by the way, you are absolutely stunning in that dress."

Silvie did a graceful little pirouette. "Do you think so?"

Amethyst looked her over. She had always known her friend was beautiful; she just hadn't thought about it much. But today, in the lovely flowing gown, with the pale blue tulle against the soft toffee shade of her skin, Silvie looked positively radiant. "You're a knockout. That blue is perfect with your coloring. I almost wish I'd put you in a gunny-sack—you're going to steal everyone's attention from the bride."

Silvie was about to respond when Enoch appeared around the side of the house. "We're ready."

Amethyst took her bouquet from her maid of honor and linked her arm through Enoch's crooked elbow. "A colorful wedding," she quipped. "Just like Grandpa Silas and Grandma Pearl's."

Enoch smiled down at her. "Your grandparents would be proud of you, Amethyst."

Amethyst touched the heart-shaped brooch at her throat. "I know, Uncle Enoch. Believe me, I know."

The chairs in the front yard were nearly filled, and the white runner up the sidewalk had been strewn with rose petals. Enoch, Silvie, and Amethyst made their way around the back of the crowd and stood waiting behind the magnolia tree until the music began.

Amethyst scanned the crowd. Pete Hopkins sat on the porch in his wheelchair, taking up his position as best man. Steven Bird was on the front row with Lyle Constable and his family. Larry Summers and his wife were there, as were the last of Grandma Pearl's clan, including Marshall Avery and his family. All the black Warrens had come, with children and grandchildren in tow. The white Warrens, descendants of the original plantation owner, remained conspicuously absent. Brown faces and white; men, women, and children; the blind and the sighted; folks in wheelchairs and braces and crutches side by side with people of strong limb and active body.

As it should be, Amethyst thought. *As God intended it to be.*

Her gaze rested for a moment on two ridiculous hats—one bright blue, with an artificial bird perched on the wide brim, the other deluged in flowers. *Who?* she wondered, and then one of them turned.

It was Edith Layton, spiffed up to the nines in a blue silk dress that made her look for all the world like the fat bluebird on her hat. The woman beside her had to be Beatrice Manning.

Edith caught her eye and gave a brief wave, her expression a composite of pained humiliation and abject shame. Amethyst waved back, offering her most brilliant smile. On impulse, she left Enoch's side and slipped over to where the two women sat.

"Thank you for coming," she said softly, letting her hand come down lightly on Edith's shoulder.

"I—oh, my, I—" Edith jumped and squirmed in her seat. "Amethyst, I—I don't know what to say. We had no right to be gossiping like that, and—"

"Shhh," Amethyst interrupted her. "It's all right. You will stay for the reception, won't you?"

"We hadn't planned to." Edith shook her head. "We didn't exactly think we'd be—"

"Welcome?" Amethyst chuckled. "Look around, Mrs. Layton. Everyone's welcome here."

The comment brought a wan smile to Edith Layton's face, and Amethyst's heart warmed. "Do stay, please. I'd like you to meet Harper—*really* meet him."

"I'd like that," Edith murmured. "Thank you."

Amethyst heard the music stop for a moment; then the strains of "Jesu, Joy of Man's Desiring" floated out on the breeze. "That's my cue," she whispered. "I'll see you both later."

Silvie glided up the walk, a bouquet of pale blue hydrangeas in her arms, the very portrait of elegance and beauty. Amethyst stood watching, her arm linked through Enoch's. When she looked up at him, she saw an expression of pure bliss on his handsome black face.

"She is lovely, isn't she?" Amethyst murmured.

He nodded. "Yes, she is." Enoch squeezed Amethyst's arm. "Both my girls are."

The music crescendoed, and Amethyst began the long walk down the open-air aisle. This wasn't a house of worship—many of the guests would not have been welcome inside the walls of the Presbyterian church, were she worshipped every Sunday. But it was a holy place nevertheless, as holy as any sanctuary. As she raised her head and saw Harper smiling at her from his place on the porch, Amethyst's breath caught in her throat.

The congregation stood in her honor. On the porch, Pete Hopkins raised himself up on his powerful arms, lifting himself off his wheelchair; he stayed that way until everyone else sat. As Amethyst came forward, he nodded and grinned at her, and she thought she saw a single tear track down his cheek and lodge in his beard.

From that moment on, however, she had eyes only for Harper. By now she had memorized every crevice of that dear face. She let her gaze linger on his scarred cheek, his crooked grin, the way his right eye twisted upward when he smiled. And with the transcendent sight that looks into the soul, she saw only beauty—the splendor of love realized, the glory of two hearts made one.

The vows went quickly. Amethyst's mind was so full of Harper that she could barely remember what she said. But as the minister pronounced them man and wife and Harper leaned down to kiss her, she knew that the words didn't matter. What mattered was the gift God had given the two of them.

Harper's blue eyes held hers as he drew near. And then, just as his lips touched hers, he murmured, "Thank you for being my miracle."

The sentence resounded in her soul, a mighty bell ringing with the solemn toll of truth. It was the kind of sentiment, she was certain, that Grandpa Silas might have uttered to Grandma Pearl. She would never forget it, nor would she forget the look of pure love in his eyes as he said it. In that moment, as she lifted a brief, silent prayer of gratitude, she could almost feel her grandparents smiling down upon them. Approving their union, sharing their joy.

Amethyst looked up into her husband's eyes. "And thank you," she whispered, "for being mine."

31
Revelation

———◆◗❖◖◆———

Amethyst turned back the comforter and lay across the bed with a sigh. She was exhausted, and extremely glad they hadn't planned to travel to New Orleans until tomorrow afternoon.

"Harper," she ventured as he came and sat beside her, "who is this person?" She pointed to the first page of the guest register, where a practically illegible name was scrawled on the first line.

He read over her shoulder. "I have no idea."

"Not a friend of yours?"

"I can barely read it." He chuckled. "What does it say? 'A. Birecled'? Never heard of 'em."

"I thought maybe it was the man you hired to set up for the wedding."

"I didn't hire anybody. Enoch and his sons took care of everything." Harper tried to close the book and take it away from her, but she held on. He frowned. "What man?"

"This afternoon, about an hour before the wedding, I went out on the courting porch, and there was a man down in the yard. An old fellow, with gray hair and a beard. He looked as if he'd been through some hard times—you know, expensive clothes, but ragged and worn."

"I don't know any such man."

Amethyst laid the book aside, pushed the vision of the old man out of her mind, and snuggled close to her husband. *Husband.* She liked the way that sounded, liked the idea of being his wife. Not that she would ever be a traditional wife, of course. She had never been traditional in any way, and had no intention of starting now. But being married to Harper felt so right. As right as anything she had ever done.

Her gaze drifted to the wardrobe, where her wedding dress hung on the door, still adorned by the amethyst-and-pearl brooch.

"Tell me about the brooch, Harper. Where on earth did you find it?"

A shadow flitted across his face. "Do we have to talk about that now?"

Amethyst narrowed her eyes and scrutinized him. "I'd just like to know, that's all. I had one like it once, a long time ago. It had belonged to my grandmother, and was supposed to be mine on my wedding day. It just seems so—well, so miraculous—that you found one like it when you didn't even know."

"Your grandmother had one, you say?" His voice was low, muted.

"Almost exactly like it—except that one pearl was missing."

He was silent for a long time.

"Harper? Is something wrong?"

"One pearl was missing from this one." He sighed. "I had it replaced before I gave the brooch to you."

His words fell into Amethyst's heart like leaden pellets. "This brooch was missing a pearl?"

"Yes."

She thought about the inscription on the back: *Sincerity, Purity, Nobility.*

"Harper, where did you buy it?"

"I didn't want to tell you. I was a little ashamed, I guess. I didn't buy it, Amethyst, I *won* it."

Harper felt his neck burn red with embarrassment. Here he was, on his wedding night, confessing to his wife of eight hours that he had obtained her wedding gift in a gambling parlor. He would have let the subject drop right then and there, but she wouldn't leave it alone.

"You *won* it?" She jerked at his arm, and her eyes flashed fire. "You'd better tell me the whole story, Harper Wainwright. Immediately."

He sighed and nodded. "All right. I won it in a poker game—or rather, my friend Sligo did. He was my sergeant overseas, and we got discharged at the same time. We ended up in Memphis, at this little tavern. He got into a poker game and didn't have any money, and so I staked him—"

"The brooch, Harper," she said through gritted teeth. "What about the brooch?"

"I'm getting to it. The guy running the game thought he had a sure thing—a full house, as I recall. He bet everything, including this brooch, against Sligo's three hundred dollars." He paused, remembering. "Sligo had four tens."

Amethyst stared at him blankly. "That beats a house full, I gather."

"A full house," he corrected. "And yes, it does. The guy was furious, but what could he do? He gave Sligo the brooch, and Sligo gave it to me."

"And it had a pearl missing when you got it."

"Yes. I kept it for years; I don't know why. Sligo was killed in a bar fight two weeks later—maybe it was just the sentimental attachment to my friend. But there was something else, too—something about the brooch itself. Whenever I looked at it, I couldn't help thinking there was more to it than just a pretty trinket. It always seemed—I don't know, alive, maybe—as if it had a heart of its own, and a history. When we fell in love, I decided to give it to you as a wedding present; I figured it was a lot more valuable than anything I could afford to buy for you. But of course I wouldn't give it to you with a pearl missing."

He stopped and searched her face.

"Are you angry?"

Amethyst blinked. "For what?"

"That I would give you the winnings from Sligo's poker game as a wedding present."

"No," she said, her voice trailing off absently. "No, Harper, I'm not angry. . . ."

•••••

And she wasn't. Baffled, maybe. Confused, most certainly. But angry? No, she wasn't angry.

"It was the most valuable thing I had ever owned," he went on. "At least I think it's valuable."

"It's valuable all right. As priceless as the one who wears it is to the one who gives it."

Harper shook his head. "Excuse me?"

"My grandmother's journals. That's what Grandpa Silas's grandmother told him about the brooch."

"Then it truly is precious," he murmured, stroking her arm. "You know I love you, don't you, sweetheart? That I'd never do anything to hurt you?"

"Yes, I know." Despite his tender words, Amethyst could not keep the tears from her eyes.

"Then why are you crying?"

She took a deep, shuddering breath. "Harper, do you know the name of that gambler? The one who bet the amethyst brooch?"

She waited while he searched his memory. "Yes, I think I do. Sligo made fun of his name, baiting him, trying to make him give away his hand. Said it was a prissy name. No, that wasn't it. A *pansy* name."

A chill ran up Amethyst's spine. "A pansy name? What was the gambler's response?"

"He seemed a little agitated, I think, but he tried to hide it. His name was—wait, it'll come to me. Benedict. Yes. Avery Benedict."

Amethyst shut her eyes, and every muscle in her body stiffened as the truth washed over her. *Avery. Benedict. Pansy.*

She grabbed up the guest book and flipped to the first page. "Look again." She pointed to the name scrawled on the top line.

"Benedict!" Harper said. "A. Benedict!" He furrowed his brow in a frown. "But why would a gambler from Memphis sign his name in our wedding book?"

"The man I saw from the courting porch this afternoon," Amethyst whispered. "That poor, bedraggled fellow. That was your gambler. Avery Benedict. My father."

32

Generations

———◆◆◆———

December 1927

Amethyst sat by the fireplace in the log cabin room and cuddled baby Conrad against her breast. Even now, two months after his birth, he still seemed like the greatest miracle she had ever witnessed. Such a perfect little miniature, with his tiny fingers and toes, his enormous blue eyes, that deep dimple in his right cheek. The dimple, Harper told her, proved him a Wainwright, even though the scarring on his own face had eradicated his dimple forever.

She gave a deep sigh and stroked the baby's velvety head. Surely Harper's mother had held him this way, gazing into his eyes, thinking him the most beautiful baby who had ever drawn breath.

Amethyst let her mind drift as she watched the misting rain outside the window. It was nearly Christmas, and Harper had been nagging her for the past two weeks to tell him what she wanted as a Christmas present. But she simply couldn't think of a single gift that would make her life more complete. She had a home and family, friends and love, a sense of God's presence in her life, and a calling that gave significance and meaning to each new day. What more could any woman want?

Silvie had been apprehensive that once Amethyst and Harper married, everything would change at Noble House. But marriage had not altered the calling. Now the three of them worked together to provide a place of refuge and dignity for people rejected by society. And nobody called Noble House "the freak show" any longer.

Ten years. It had been ten years since the day Amethyst had sat in this very chair and wondered what would become of her now that her parents were gone and she was alone. But she hadn't been alone—not really. The spirit and legacy of her grandparents had survived. Through Pearl's journals, she had been challenged and transformed, shown the direction her life was to go. And even when she hadn't known it—if truth be told, even when she *resisted* it—God had been at work in her life to bring her to this place.

She only had one regret.

Her father.

Since the day of her wedding more than three years ago, Amethyst had been haunted by the vision of that bedraggled, decrepit shadow of a man who had appeared on the lawn. Given the story Harper told her of the amethyst brooch, the man *had* to be her father, and yet if he were, why had he not spoken to her? Why had he simply signed the guest book and disappeared?

In the year following their marriage, Harper had done his best to find the man who called himself Avery Benedict, but to no avail. Once more, he had vanished like the morning mist. Sometimes Amethyst wept over him. Sometimes she raged at him. Occasionally she wished he had never come back, so that she could consider him dead and push him out of her life forever. But he was always there, in the back of her mind, staying alive in the image of a broken-down old fellow in a ragged satin vest.

It was infuriating. He never truly went away, and yet he was never there.

After a while, Amethyst thought she had forgiven him. She had tried, anyway. She had rationalized his behavior, attempted to understand. But in the end, she had always returned to the one overwhelming emotion that assailed her every time she conjured up his image in her mind—anger.

What kind of man would leave his wife and daughter to take up a new life as a gambler under a different name? What kind of man would return on the day of that same daughter's wedding and then disappear again without a word?

Avery Benedict. Every time she thought of the name, Amethyst tasted bile in her throat. He had taken Grandma Pearl's maiden name and exploited it as an alias for his life of indulgence and debauchery. What gall! What self-centeredness!

And yet he was her father. No matter what he had done, no matter how vile his life had been, he was still her father. Something in Amethyst longed for him to know how blessed she was, what a wonderful man she had married, what a beautiful baby grandson he had.

The conflict tore at her every time she allowed herself to think about him. What if he showed up again? How would she react? Would she let the full force of her righteous anger blow him to kingdom come, or would she be so relieved to see him that she would forget her rage altogether and fall into his embrace like a devastated little girl whose daddy had finally come home?

Amethyst had no idea how she would respond. She wasn't even sure if she would want her infant son to become acquainted with his grandfather. Abraham Noble—or Avery Benedict, as he called himself now—wasn't exactly the kind of model Amethyst would want Conrad to emulate. And given what he had done to her, the man surely did not deserve a second chance.

Little Conrad stirred in her arms, and her eyes drifted to his innocent cherub face. A wave of remorse washed over her, and her heart sank like a stone in the river. It was almost Christmas. The season of second chances.

If God had blessed her so much, how could she not find one tiny space in her heart to plant a seed of forgiveness?

Harper leaned against his desk at Bainbridge Metal Works and braced himself against the pain. It crested over him, sending scalding needles of agony through every nerve ending, and then subsided, leaving him breathless and sweating.

Everything was in order, thank God. Amethyst and Conrad would be provided for. She would still have Silvie, and Noble House. She was a strong woman, a determined woman. She would be all right.

It just seemed so *unfair.*

He had been to a doctor, of course—three of them, to be exact. None of them knew precisely how long he had left. A few months if he was lucky. A few days if he wasn't. But all of the doctors agreed that his heart wouldn't hold out much longer. There was nothing anyone could do.

Harper didn't believe in luck. When the first physician had informed him of his condition, he had prayed that he might live long enough to see the birth of his child. That prayer had been answered over two months ago. Now he asked God to let him live through Christmas.

He felt a little like Abraham, bargaining with God over the destruction of Sodom. But Abraham's life hadn't been on the line. Harper's own prayers were undoubtedly more passionate than Abraham's. And although he wasn't sure he was as righteous as the Father of Nations, he wasn't banking on his own deservedness, but on grace.

So far, grace had held him up.

He hadn't told Amethyst. Initially, he had kept the information from her because of her condition—an expectant mother didn't need the additional anxiety of knowing that her husband was dying. After Conrad's birth, she had been caught up in the duties of motherhood and accepted without question his excuses that he was just tired, or that he had a touch of influenza.

Only Mac Bainbridge knew that after today Harper would not be returning to work. He just needed to finish preparing the salary drafts for the month. The men shouldn't have to wait for their pay just because his heart was giving out on him.

He arranged the paychecks in a zippered cash envelope and placed them in the safe where Bainbridge could find them. Detailed instructions for the running of the plant were in the top right-hand drawer, clearly labeled. If Harper had done his final tasks well, Mac would have all the information he needed to make a seamless transition to whoever was hired to take his place.

Amethyst would believe it when he told her Bainbridge had given him a few weeks off. After all, he worked hard, and he hadn't taken a day off since the week they went to New Orleans for their honeymoon. He smiled to himself at the irony of the situation. Most people did not take a vacation to die.

Harper was ready to go—in spiritual terms, anyway. He had made his peace with the Almighty years ago, and had enjoyed a blessed and fruitful life. No longer did he curse his scars and his physical disabilities—he barely thought about them any more. Amethyst's love had made all the difference.

Two years ago, before he knew about his heart condition, before Conrad had even been conceived, he had told Amethyst in a tender moment that he could die a happy man, knowing that once in his life he had been truly loved. It had seemed the right thing to say at the time, a sentiment that came from the depths of his heart. Now the memory of the moment mocked him. Yes, he had been truly loved, and truly happy. But he wished with all his soul that he didn't have to die.

In the beginning, he had begged to be healed, convinced that God would honor his prayer. When it didn't happen, he prayed to be gracious. And the Lord had responded to that one. His great regret—besides having to leave the woman he loved so soon—was the awareness that he wouldn't live to see his son grow up and become a man.

Harper put his head down on his desk, and tears seeped from his closed eyelids. He was resigned to the reality of his situation. Apparently he had done what he had been put on earth to do, and soon his time would come. But surely his God would understand a few tears over what he was leaving behind.

A soft knock on the office door arrested his attention, and Harper sat up and swiped at his eyes. "Come in."

Mac Bainbridge opened the door and stuck his head around the corner. "How ya doin'?"

Harper forced a smile. "Pretty good, I guess. I'm about ready to leave."

Mac moved into the doorway and leaned one shoulder on the door jamb. His eyes focused on the floor, and he bit his lower lip. "I'm going to miss you, Harper."

Harper blew out a long breath. "Thanks."

"You know that opening we've got? The packaging job?"

"I thought you had about eight guys lined up for that."

"Well, yeah, I did. But it's not heavy work, and all the men who applied are capable of doing the harder stuff out in the plant. Anyway, there's this one fellow—an older guy, who needs a job but can't do the metal work."

"Mac Bainbridge, are you going soft on me?"

Mac laughed. "I dunno. Maybe I've just learned a thing or two from you over the years."

"So this older fellow—" Harper prompted.

"Well, he looks like he's kinda down on his luck and could use a break. Do you mind talking to him?"

"Me? Why?"

"You've done all the hiring here for the past twenty years, that's why."

"Nine. I've been here nine years, Mac."

"Okay. Nine. It just seems like twenty." Mac shrugged. "If you don't want to see him, I'll take care of it."

Harper thought for a minute. It seemed appropriate, somehow, that his last official act at Bainbridge Metal Works would be to help a discouraged man find a job and get back on his feet again. "All right, Mac. Send him in."

Mac disappeared, and Harper pulled an application form out of his filing cabinet. He was scanning through the questions when he heard a shuffling at the door and looked up to see a skinny, gray-haired man with a week's worth of stubble.

Harper motioned to a chair next to his desk. "Come in and have a seat, Mr.—"

The man didn't move. He just stood there, staring.

Harper turned the scarred side of his face toward the man and launched into his explanation. He had done this a hundred times over the past nine years. "Go ahead and get a good look; you'll be seeing this face a lot if you come to work here—" Suddenly he stopped. The truth was, the man *wouldn't* be seeing his face again. But he went on anyway. "I was wounded in the war and my face was burned. Don't let it bother you—it doesn't bother me."

The man said nothing. Harper looked up at him again. "Is there a problem?"

"I know you," the man mumbled. "I've seen you somewhere."

"I doubt it. I don't get around much."

The old fellow shuffled into Harper's office and dropped into the chair. "Yeah, I know you." He tapped a bony finger on his forehead. "I remember faces. And I'd sure remember that one. You were a lot younger, but—"

The voice was craggy and hoarse, but suddenly something registered in Harper's mind. His head snapped up. "Memphis?" he whispered.

"Yeah, I been in Memphis. Used to have a little business up there, once upon a time." The gray head nodded and the rheumy eyes fixed on Harper's. "Lost it, though, some years back. Had a streak of bad luck, I did."

"What's your name?" Harper asked, although the knot in the pit of his stomach told him that he already knew the answer.

"Benedict," the old man answered. "Avery Benedict."

Amethyst leaned back in her chair at the dining room table and gazed at the man who sat across from her.

Harper had brought him home, and now, with a bath and shave and fresh clothes, he almost looked like the father she hadn't seen in ten years. He had aged, of course—he would be sixty-two now, but he looked ten or fifteen years older than that, with ashen circles under his eyes and a sallow cast to his skin. He was pathetically thin, and the skin sagged around his bony neck.

He ate rapidly, refilling his plate twice and darting a glance at her as if to make sure it was all right to have seconds. For a long time neither of them said anything, but simply stared at each other with the guarded expression of two cats circling for a fight.

Amethyst waited, her mind spinning with accusations. She thought about her mother, buried under a headstone that bore his name, too. Thought about the day he left, claiming to be fulfilling his patriotic duty in the war that had left her husband scarred for life. Thought about her wedding day, and the way he had scrawled his name in her guest book and vanished again. There was so much she wanted to say to him, so much anger to express, so many questions that needed answering. And the most overwhelming question of all: *Why?*

So far, he hadn't offered a word of explanation about the day he left, hadn't said so much as "I'm sorry." He had just watched her out of the corner of his eye, averting his glance any time she looked at him. But she had noticed one thing that tugged at her heart—whenever his eyes rested on the amethyst and pearl brooch she wore at her throat, he blinked rapidly, as if trying to stem back a rush of tears.

By the time he had finished eating, all the fight had gone out of Amethyst. All she could feel was pity for an old man who obviously had been punished enough.

Maybe that was what forgiveness was all about, she mused silently. Not condoning or excusing or even understanding, but leaving to God the business of doling out justice or mercy. Clearly, her father had reaped the harvest of his misdeeds. He was old and sick and miserable, nearly starving, and unable to look his only daughter in the eye. He hadn't apologized or asked for her forgiveness, and maybe he never would. But Amethyst suspected that from the Lord's point of view, that didn't matter. Forgiveness wasn't based on the worthiness of the one who needed it, but on the grace of the one who extended it.

Amethyst looked at Harper and saw a strange expression in his eyes—an entreating glance, as if begging her to do the right thing. For a moment or two, judgment and compassion grappled for the upper hand in her soul. Then, with a sigh, she surrendered.

She went to the bedroom, lifted Conrad out of his crib, and returned to the table.

"Father," she said in a low voice as she held the baby out to him, "I'd like you to meet your grandson."

33
Hard Questions

March 21, 1993

He died?" Little Am protested, sniffing loudly and reaching for a tissue. "Harper died without ever seeing his baby grow up?" She frowned and shook her head. "That's not fair, Grandam. I'm beginning to hate this story."

Amethyst gazed at her namesake and gave a little chuckle. "Life is rarely fair, child. And it's not a novel or a movie, where you can write the ending to suit yourself. The good Lord knows that if I had been creating this plot, I would have let my dear Harper live to a hale and hearty old age. But yes, he died. On January 14, 1928, I placed Conrad on his chest, held both of them in my arms, and committed my husband to God's keeping."

"Weren't you mad, Grandam? I mean, really furious?"

"At whom?"

"At God, of course, for taking him away. God could have healed him."

"Yes, I suppose you're right. But the miracles we get in life aren't always the miracles we hope for. I was angry at first, certainly—at God, and at Harper, for leaving me. It's part of the process of grief. Eventually the anger subsided, the pain lessened, and I went on with my life."

Little Am dried her tears and gazed at her great-grandmother. "Did you ever get over him? I've heard that you never get over your first love."

"When love is real, you don't 'get over it' at all," Amethyst answered with a smile. "It stays with you forever, expanding your heart and enabling you to love others more deeply. Love is a gift, child, a grace."

Amethyst watched while her great-granddaughter pondered the words. She was too young to understand; she hadn't yet met someone who would enrich her life the way Harper had enriched hers. But her time would come, and when it did, Amethyst prayed that she would choose wisely.

"So," the girl continued, "Con never really knew his father. That explains a lot."

"Yes, I suppose it does," Amethyst mused. "But it doesn't explain everything. Conrad grew up—well, strangely. From the time he was old enough to understand, I made sure he knew all about Harper—what kind of man he was, what kind of principles he stood for."

"But it didn't take," Little Am said bluntly. "Grandpa didn't turn out to be anything like his father. He turned out more like . . . well, like his grandfather, Abe. Or Avery. Or whatever he called himself."

Amethyst felt herself wince. It was true, although she didn't want to admit it so boldly. Still, the girl was bright and perceptive, and she deserved to know the whole truth. "Yes," Amethyst said at last, "I guess Con did turn out to be more like his grandfather than like Harper."

"Did Abe stick around?" Am lifted her lip in a sneer as she uttered the name. Clearly she didn't like what she had heard about her great-great-grandfather, and Amethyst couldn't blame her. "Or did he pull his vanishing act again?"

"My father lived with us until the day he died," she answered quietly. "Eight years after Harper went."

"And you let him?" Little Am narrowed her eyes. "I can't believe it, Grandam. That man was poison!"

"Perhaps," Amethyst conceded. "But he was ill and unable to care for himself any longer. And he was also my father."

"By 'ill,' you mean he drank himself to death."

"I'm afraid so. He needed care, and I was the only one left to give it."

Little Am peered into Amethyst's eyes. "But you wish you hadn't."

Amethyst shook her head. The girl was much too precocious for her age. But she had started down this path, and she would tell the truth, even if it wasn't a truth she particularly cared to revisit.

"Conrad adored his grandfather. From the time he was old enough to exert his own will, he spent every available moment with the man. At first I thought it was a good idea—a fatherly influence, you know. Con wouldn't have a thing to do with Enoch Warren, and there were no other men in my life close enough to fill that role. Then he began repeating stories his grandfather told him—he thought Abe's tales about drinking and gambling were exciting and adventurous. He also began picking up on Abe's negative and demeaning attitudes toward women."

"So that's where he got it," Am muttered.

Amethyst shrugged. "I'm afraid so. Anyway, I tried to counter Abe's influence by telling Conrad about his own father, what a good and gentle man he was, how loving, and how righteous."

"I'll bet that had about as much effect as a snowflake in—"

Amethyst held up a hand. "I get your point. And you're right, although I'm not thrilled about your choice of images."

"Sorry, Grandam. Go on, please."

"By the time Conrad was six or seven, he had become the image of his grandfather, despite my best efforts. He got it into his head that the freewheeling life of a gambler was the most glamorous occupation on earth. He picked up the most awful language, too, and although he learned pretty quickly never to use it in my presence, I knew it was still part of his vocabulary. He couldn't seem to grasp concepts like honor and dignity and truthfulness, but he hung on his grandfather's every word. When people asked what he wanted to be when he grew up, he'd say, 'A blackjack dealer,' and laugh."

"That must have been embarrassing."

"I wasn't concerned so much about my own embarrassment as about my son's mind and heart. I tried to talk to my father about it, but he wouldn't listen, either. Stubborn as mules, both of them."

Little Am nodded gravely. "That sure hasn't changed. Grandpa Con quit drinking, but some of the other stuff he learned from Abe has obviously stayed with him." She bit her lip and sighed. "Do you wish you had done things differently—told Abe to hit the road, for example?"

Amethyst thought about the question she had asked herself a thousand times. "Sometimes I do, to tell the truth. But I was torn between loyalties—my son on one side and my father on the other. I felt as if I had a duty to my father, even though he had abdicated his responsibility to me years before."

"And if you were choosing now?"

Amethyst didn't hesitate. "I would choose my son."

———•••———

That night, in the quietness of the big house, Amethyst found herself unable to sleep. Her conversation with Little Am replayed in her mind, and a familiar anguish washed over her.

Could she have done better at protecting Conrad from his grandfather's negative influence? She might have refused to care for her father—thrown him out on his own, abandoned him as he had abandoned her and her mother. He certainly deserved it. Still, Amethyst had learned over the course of nine decades that a person reaped more spiritual dividends by offering grace than by exacting justice.

Her father had, in the end, asked her forgiveness. Amethyst had never been sure of his motives—by then he was dying, and he knew the end was near. But the damage to Conrad had been done. The boy had embraced the worldly legacy of his grandfather rather than the spiritual heritage of his parents.

She sighed and turned over, pulling the comforter around her shoulders. When all was said and done, she supposed, you simply had to trust God—both with your own life and the lives of those you loved. In this world there weren't even any easy questions, much less easy answers.

34
Round Three

March 22, 1993

Conrad looked around Judge Tweety Bird's office and fiddled with his watch. She was playing the waiting game again, and he didn't like it one bit.

"Honey, stop fidgeting."

Conrad glared at Mimsy. The leather band of his new watch cut into his wrist, reminding him with every pinch how much he missed the satiny gold of the Rolex. He hadn't gotten a quarter of what it was worth, but selling it and the Mercedes had bought him a little time. He had lied to Mimsy, too, telling her that the Mercedes was beginning to develop transmission trouble and that a mugger at Mud Island had stolen his watch.

He didn't feel guilty about the lies, just mildly disgusted that his wife would accept such a stupid story so readily. She didn't think to ask why the mugger hadn't taken his wallet and credit cards, or why he hadn't simply gotten the transmission fixed. She just swallowed it all and gave him a day's worth of sickeningly sweet consolation over his losses.

If she only knew. The clock was ticking down—Mario had called twice yesterday, and one of the clients whose money he had borrowed had been after him about the pension account. Conrad had actually put the client on hold, disconnected him, and then unplugged the telephone so it would look as if he were having trouble on the line. What would he stoop to next?

A phrase came back to him from deep in the recesses of his memory, some poem an English teacher had crammed down his throat years ago: "I choose never to stoop." He couldn't remember the poet or the context, but it was a sentiment that appealed to him. If Judge Dove would just get off her honorific behind and get this situation dealt with, he would never have to stoop again.

The door opened and Her Honor entered the room.

"I see you're here bright and early, Mr. Wainwright," she said as she rolled her leather chair into place behind the desk. "With good news for me, I hope."

"I'm afraid not, Your Honor," Conrad answered. "I spoke with my mother and tried to reason with her, but she is simply not capable of rational response. She is still holding my granddaughter hostage, and—"

"I wouldn't exactly call it *hostage*, Con," Mimsy interrupted. "Little Am is being well cared for and actually seems to be enjoying herself."

Con leveled an acid glance at his wife and then turned back to the judge. "I believe that time is of the essence here, Your Honor. There's no telling what my mother might do if she goes into one of her . . . ah, spells."

"Spells?" Mimsy squealed. "What in heaven's name are you talking about, Con? Amethyst has never had a spell of any kind in her entire life."

"Whose side are you on?" he whispered under his breath.

"Why, yours, of course," she responded, tempering her tone to match his. "I'm just trying to help."

"Well, don't help. Just keep quiet."

The judge pulled her glasses down her nose and stared at Conrad. "Mr. Wainwright, you say you've attempted to reason with your mother. Precisely how many times in the past week have you spoken with her?"

Conrad squirmed. "Ah . . . several, Your Honor."

"Several. As in five or six?"

"Not quite that many times." Con coughed loudly and cleared his throat.

"Three times? Four? A number, please."

Conrad lowered his eyes and fought to keep his composure. Male bashing, that's what it was. Give a woman power, and she'd use it against a man every time. It was something in their nature, like a praying mantis eating her mate before the act was even completed. Judge Harriet Dove might as well have skewered him onto a spit and lit the fire.

"Mr. Wainwright? I'm waiting."

"One," he mumbled.

"Speak up, if you please. Did you say 'one'?"

You heard me just fine the first time, he thought, but he didn't say it. "One, Your Honor."

"You spoke to your mother once."

"Yes, Your Honor." Entirely against his will, the *yes* came out with a vicious hissing noise, like the sound a snake makes as it prepares to strike. The hostility and disdain he had been trying to hide were not lost on the judge.

"You will keep a lid on your temper in this room," she commanded curtly. It reminded him of something his mother used to say to him as a child: *"You will not speak to me in that tone of voice."*

"Yes ma'am." There it was again, that sarcasm he was trying so hard to curb.

"You are an attorney, is that correct, Mr. Wainwright?"

"That is correct."

"Then I assume you know I can slap you with a contempt citation before you can blink twice."

Conrad felt a hot flush creeping up his neck and into his ears. "Yes, Your Honor."

"I'd advise you to watch yourself. I wouldn't think twice about doling out a hefty fine and a week in the county jail."

Mimsy leaned in and put a hand on Conrad's arm. He flinched at the touch, but suppressed the desire to jerk his elbow away. "Why is she so mad at you?"

She's not mad; she's enjoying herself, Conrad wanted to retort. But he couldn't risk saying that or any of the other uncomplimentary words that came to mind to describe Judge Dove.

Her Honor let out an exaggerated sigh. "All right, Mr. Wainwright. I'll be perfectly honest with you. I despise what you're doing here, and I strongly suspect you are not being completely candid with this court. But nevertheless, I have in front of me a motion to declare Amethyst

Noble incompetent, and much as I would like to throw you and your motion out onto the sidewalk on your respective derriéres, I cannot ignore my responsibility under the law."

A lightning flash of hope struck in Conrad's heart. "You're going to sign it?"

"Not so fast. I will sign nothing until I hear from all parties involved, face to face. I'm issuing an order for Amethyst Noble to appear before me in these chambers on Friday at 5:00 P.M. And I want your grand-daughter present for the proceedings as well. What's her name?"

"We call her Little Am," Mimsy piped up. "She's named Amethyst, after her great-grandmother."

"Certainly not my choice," Con muttered.

The judge ignored him. "Little Am."

Con jerked to attention. "But Judge, you don't really want to see her. I swear you don't."

"And why not?"

"She's—well, she's just a child. A teenager. She doesn't know what's good for her. She dresses all in black, with this ghastly white makeup, and—"

"How old is your granddaughter, Mr. Wainwright?"

"Seventeen. There's no telling what she might say or do, Judge."

"Is she mentally ill? On drugs? Unable to speak for herself?"

"No, Your Honor. At least I don't think so."

"Then she will appear before me. And that's final." Judge Dove signed the order and slid it across the table for his inspection.

Conrad picked it up and scanned it. "Does it have to be Friday?"

"Too soon for you?" The judge gave him a sly smile and held out her hand. "I can make it two weeks from Monday."

"No, uh, Friday's fine." He handed the order back to her.

"I'll have the sheriff serve the order, then. And I'll see you back here on Friday. Five o'clock. And don't be late." The judge got up from the chair and placed her hands squarely on her desk.

"And Mr. Wainwright?"

"Yes, Your Honor?"

"Let's let our little meeting on Friday be the end of this, all right?"

I can only hope, Conrad thought as he gave the judge an affirmative nod. *Or it may be the end of me.*

———————

"Well, well," Amethyst mused as she held the judge's order out for Little Am to inspect. "Looks like you and I will get our day in court."

Am took the paper and perused it. "A woman judge. Cool." She folded it up and handed it back to Amethyst. "You sure you're okay with this, Grandam?"

Amethyst nodded. "My own son wants to have me declared incompetent, take my house, and have me committed to a nursing home for the rest of my days. What do you think I should do about it, child?"

Little Am cocked her head. "I think you should fight like—" She paused and grinned. "Like crazy."

"Then we go before Judge Dove on Friday."

"Yeah, but why does she want to talk to *me?*" Am countered. "I'm just a teenager."

"You don't think a judge would be interested in what a teenager has to say?"

"Why should she be? Nobody else is."

Amethyst smiled and laid a hand on the girl's cheek. To her delight, Little Am didn't flinch or move away, but leaned into the caress as if hungry for a loving human touch. "I'm interested, child."

Little Am ducked her head sheepishly. "I know you are, Grandam. At least I do now. This time last week I wouldn't have been so sure."

The affirmation warmed Amethyst's heart. They had come a long way during their week together. "Now, I have no idea what kinds of questions Judge Dove will ask you," Amethyst went on, "but I have one for you."

"Fire away."

"What do you want to do?"

"About what?"

Amethyst sighed. "You don't have to stay with me until Friday. You've been here a week already. I know you probably miss your friends, and the mall, and whatever it is you do when you're not in school. What do you do, anyway?"

"You probably don't want to know." Am grimaced. "But some of it I won't be doing anymore."

"All righty, then," Amethyst said, employing one of Am's favorite phrases. "I guess we won't pursue that line of discussion. But if you want to leave, go back home, I won't ask you to stay. You have a life apart from your ancient great-grandmother, and—"

Amethyst stopped suddenly as Little Am's face sagged into a mask of dejection. "You don't want me to stay?"

The tone was plaintive, like the cry of an abandoned child—a feeling Amethyst remembered vividly, even after nearly eighty years. "Of course I want you to stay," she amended. "I just don't want you to feel obligated."

The girl's expression brightened, and she sat down on the hassock and motioned Amethyst into the chair by the fireplace. "Hey, I have to go back to school in a week anyway. I can wait a few more days to find out whatever's been happening while I've been gone. Now, where were we?"

Amethyst gazed with love and astonishment at the young girl who bore her name. Was this the same child who came to her door a week ago looking like a ghoul and skulking around with a chip on her shoulder? "You want more of the story?"

"You wouldn't dare stop after Harper's death, would you? That's a worse cliff-hanger than *All My Children*."

"*All My Children?*"

"It's a soap, Grandam. I wouldn't expect you to know about it."

"That's a relief. You're talking about television, I presume?"

"Yes, I'm talking about television. But yours is a much more interesting story." Am held up a hand. "Just a minute. I'm going to get a can of Diet Pepsi and come right back. Want anything?"

"A glass of tea would be nice."

In a couple of minutes Am returned from the kitchen with a pitcher of tea, a two-liter bottle of pop, tortilla chips and Oreos, and two glasses full of ice.

"You plan to be here a while, do you?" Amethyst joked, eying the supplies.

"As long as necessary." Little Am handed over a glass of tea and poured a diet drink for herself. When she was settled in the chair opposite Amethyst's, she waved a hand impatiently. "I'm ready. Proceed."

Amethyst took a long drink of her tea, leaned her head back against the chair, and closed her eyes. "Harper's death was hard on me, and taking care of Father until he died compounded the struggle," she said quietly. "But I got through it, and time passed almost without my realizing it. Before I knew it, Conrad was nearly grown. . . ."

Part 4

EQUALITY

———◆———

Let justice roll down like waters
and righteousness like an ever-flowing stream.

Amos 5:24

35
The Boarding House Boys

August 1945

Conrad sat in his upstairs room and stared morosely out the window. The afternoon sun slanted through the big magnolia tree, creating shifting shapes on the ancient Oriental rug at his feet. It was a beautiful afternoon—or so his mother had told him countless times in the past hour and a half. He should be "out playing."

Playing, she said. For pity's sake, he was seventeen years old! He would probably be forty before his mother realized he didn't *play* anymore. What he *should* be doing was marching home in victory with some gorgeous dish hanging on his arm, like the guys in the newsreels. But he had been too young when the war started, and now it was over.

Mother wouldn't have let him sign up, anyway. He would have had to lie about his age, and with this blasted round baby face of his, no one would have fallen for it. So he was left to sit here and stew while other guys got the girls and the glory.

He poked the toe of his shoe at a worn place in the rug and cursed to himself. If only he had been old enough to go to war, he wouldn't have to be stuck in this hick town for the rest of his life. Rumor was, the government was going to start handing out money hand over fist for veterans to go to college—money that could have gotten him out of here and into some kind of life of his own. But no, Conrad Wainwright would not be leaving Cambridge, Mississippi, anytime soon. Tomorrow he was supposed to go over to the university to register, and his mother acted as though he ought to be grateful for the opportunity.

Well, he wasn't grateful, and he wasn't going to pretend to be happy about the situation. He was pretty ticked off, to tell the truth. Mother accused him of pouting, but then she was a danged saint, the woman everybody loved, some kind of paragon of virtue. The original do-good-er. He was tired of listening to her spout platitudes about being thankful for what you had and sharing it with others, sick of her endless talk about God's blessings. *He* hadn't been blessed, or he'd be on the first train out of here. Instead, he was going to college in Cambridge. He was going to live at home, under the watchful eye of Saint Amethyst.

What he really should do is what Grandpa Abe had done—just disappear, take a new name, begin a new life somewhere else. Anywhere his mother couldn't find him.

It was a great idea, a vision that sustained him when he just couldn't stand it anymore. But deep down he knew he didn't have the nerve, and he sure didn't have enough skill at poker or blackjack to support himself.

Yet.

But maybe that would change.

The one redeeming factor in the situation was that Noble House seemed to be filling up with college students. Young men, mostly—guys only a year or two older than Conrad himself. Most of the ones he had met so far seemed like wimps—mamas' boys whose parents wanted them looked after and protected. They repulsed him, the little panty-waists, but he had to admit they would probably be good targets. A few games of five-card draw with these guys would fatten his wallet considerably.

"Conrad!" his mother's earnest voice called up the stairs. "Come down, please. It's almost time for dinner, and Silvie and I could use some help."

He let out a disgusted huff. A college man had no business serving in the kitchen and setting the table like a common busboy. Why couldn't that colored woman do it?

Con had grown up with Silvie, and Mother always insisted that she be treated like one of the family. But a servant was a servant. A nigra was a nigra, and no amount of social action or claims of equality would change that. Grandpa Abe had told him so.

He pushed himself up off the bed and started slowly down the stairs, dragging his feet with each step. Too bad things weren't like they had been in Abe's day. Then he would have been a landowner's son, rich and respected, with a fine bay horse and slaves at his beck and call. . . .

———————

Amethyst looked around the table and surveyed her new boarders. All four of them were young, and to be perfectly honest, she had balked at the idea of taking in college students. But times were hard and money was scarce. A person did what she had to do.

As she scanned the fresh faces, however, a new vision took shape in her mind. They were barely more than boys, most of them—only a little older than her own son. And although they tried hard to carry themselves like mature men, they had a rather lost look about them, like children whose mommies had gone away.

She knew the feeling all too well. At seventeen *she* had been alone—both parents dead, or so she thought—with a house to run and bills to pay. She didn't know how she would have survived without the support of Silvie and Uncle Enoch.

Maybe this was the new calling she had been seeking from God: to be mother to a group of fledgling young men who undoubtedly thought they didn't need a mother anymore. To help them find the right path—a path of honor and truth and compassion.

She waited while Silvie set a huge bowl of mashed potatoes on one end of the table and slid into her seat. A few eyebrows went up, but no one said anything. Clearly some of these boys had never sat down to a meal with a black person at the same table. All the more reason for them to be here.

Two or three hands reached for the food, grabbing biscuits and scooping up potatoes and peas. Amethyst watched in silence until, one by one, they looked up.

"At Noble House it is our custom to give thanks before every meal," she said quietly. A fork clattered onto a plate. Two of the new boys blushed bright red. Uncomfortably, they folded their hands and bowed their heads.

"Silvie, would you say grace, please?"

Amethyst saw a couple of shocked glances shoot around the table. Silvie cleared her throat, offered a simple prayer of thankfulness, and asked the Lord to bless each young man who shared their meal.

When the "Amen" was uttered, nobody moved. Nobody spoke.

It was the quietest meal the residents of Noble House had ever experienced.

"Is your mother *always* like that?" demanded Clarence Bogart, whom everyone called "Bogey." He was a gangly kid with hands and feet too big for his body—nothing at all like the famous star of the silver screen. But he seemed proud of the nickname and corrected anyone who dared call him Clarence. Conrad thought it was funny. And Bogey was the only one who had gotten up the nerve to verbalize the question everyone was asking silently.

"Like what?" Con was pretty sure he knew, but he liked seeing Bogey squirm.

"Well, so . . . so spiritual. Praying and all that."

"Yep," Con answered. "I'm afraid so. Get used to it."

His cynical response seemed to loosen up the others and give them permission to speak their minds.

"And that nigra woman—she always eats at your table?" This came from George Hatfield, a beefy, red-faced boy from the Delta.

"She lives here. Always has, since before I was born."

Jackie Rudolph, a pale seventeen-year-old with a bulging pimple on his right cheek, piped up. "Naw. You can't be serious."

"Yes."

Dooley Layton, from Natchez, was older than the rest of them by a year or more, and gave off an air of being worldly wise and sophisticated. His great-uncle, Rube Layton, had been mayor of Cambridge years ago, and his parents had sent him to the university so that he'd have family to keep an eye on him. According to Dooley, he didn't need anybody to wet-nurse him, and he had no intention of having any more contact with the Cambridge Laytons than was absolutely necessary. "Where I come from, white folks wouldn't be caught dead breaking bread with a nigger."

Con tried to keep the shock from registering on his face. The "N" word was expressly forbidden in his mother's household—Dooley would be out on his hind end quicker than a snake on a mouse if Mother got wind that he had applied it to Silvie. "Dooley, I wouldn't use that word in my mother's presence if I were you."

"What word? Nigger?" Dooley challenged. "You a nigger-lover, too, Wainwright?"

Conrad hesitated. It wouldn't do to get Dooley on his bad side so early in the game. He had to play it smooth, get along, if he wanted these guys to respect him. "Who, me? 'Course not. A nigra is a nigra, I always say, and nothing good comes out of letting them rise above their station. I was just warning you, Dooley—you want to stay here, you'd better keep your mouth shut around my mother, that's all."

"Don't sound like you and your mama got much in common,"

Con shrugged. "Not much," he said. "Not much at all."

The poker game turned out to be a weekly event. Dooley's apartment, in the converted carriage house, became their headquarters, and the five of them met every Saturday night. Con told his mother they were studying, and she left them alone.

Dooley was a pretty experienced cardplayer, and he and Con ended up having to teach George and Bogey how to play. Jackie claimed to have played before, but he kept trying to call wild cards every time he dealt.

"What kind of sissy poker do you think we're playing here?" Dooley snarled, dragging on a cigarette and sending a blue haze of smoke into the air. "There ain't no wild cards, Rudolph—how many times do I have to tell you? It's draw or stud, that's all. You wanna be a man, learn to play a man's game."

Once or twice Dooley had Jackie on the verge of tears, but he bucked up and played on. He even tried one of Dooley's Camels, only to choke himself and turn green when he attempted to inhale. For the most part, Con and Dooley took the pots, but Con could usually beat Dooley when it came down to the two of them. Like Grandpa Abe had taught him, he kept an ace and a jack under his cuff, and when things got tight, he could count on them to pull him through.

"So," Dooley asked one night as Conrad dealt the final hand, "just how old is this nigra woman Silvie?"

Con looked up. "I don't know. Old. Fifty, maybe. Why?"

"Fifty, huh? I don't think so. She's still one *fine*-looking woman." Dooley blew a lungful of smoke into Con's face and leered at him.

Con's heart dropped into his stomach. "What are you talking about?"

"You know what I'm talking about. Everybody knows black women want it all the time." He lifted one lip in a sneer. "Insatiable."

If Dooley had been talking about his own sister, Conrad could not have been more stunned. Silvie was a fixture in the house—she was like his aunt, except that he would have denied it if any of these guys had accused him of caring for her. And here was Dooley, making all kinds of lewd implications about her as if she were some kind of streetwalker.

"She's old enough to be your mother," he said lamely.

"But she ain't my mother, is she?" Dooley laid a couple of cards face-down. "I'll take two."

"I'll take four," Bogey said.

"Four?" Dooley laughed in his face—a sinister, menacing kind of laugh. "Bogey, you're hopeless." He turned back to Conrad. "Admit it, Con—you've noticed how sexy she is. Don't tell me you haven't."

"No, I haven't," Con stammered. "And you shouldn't, either."

"I *shouldn't*?"

"No, you shouldn't." Con narrowed his eyes at Dooley. "She's not that kind of woman. Besides, I thought you didn't like nigras."

"I don't like nigras buttin' in where they don't belong. I don't like nigras gettin' uppity and thinkin' they're as good as everybody else. But didn't you know, pretty-boy? It's an old Southern tradition, the master taking whatever slave girl strikes his fancy. They expect it. Shoot, they *like* it. That gal Silvie would fall all over herself to get her hands on a college man like me."

"She might get her hands on you," Conrad retorted, "but I wouldn't want to have to look at your face once she's done with you."

The other three laughed, but Dooley was not amused at being made the butt of the joke. He said not a word in response, but his jaw clenched until the veins in his neck popped out.

And Conrad suspected he might have made a big, big mistake.

"Miss Amethyst, can I talk to you?"

Amethyst looked up from her book to see Clarence Bogart standing in the doorway, his long arms and huge hands dangling awkwardly at his side. He reminded her of a young colt—gangly and gawky and not yet proportioned quite right. Someday he might grow up to be a reasonably handsome young man, but right now his development seemed halted at its most unattractive stage.

"Of course, Clarence. Come on in." She motioned him to the chair opposite hers. "What can I do for you?"

He glanced around the room nervously, as if afraid someone might overhear.

"It's all right, Clarence. We're alone."

"Yes ma'am. Well, I, uh—"

Amethyst's heart went out to the poor fellow, and she reached a hand in his direction. "Tell me what's bothering you, son."

At the word *son*, huge tears welled up in his eyes. He turned away and blinked rapidly. "I got something in my eye."

"It's okay, Clarence."

"No ma'am, it's not okay. I mean, I guess it will be, eventually, but right now it's not."

"What's not okay?" Amethyst asked, silently entreating God to give her wisdom—and patience. It might be midnight before he ever got the words out.

"College is a lot . . . a lot harder than I thought it would be. I—I ain't doing too good, especially in English."

Amethyst suppressed a smile. "I see."

"We gotta do this writing stuff all the time—essays, you know? I just don't get it. And I don't see what good it's gonna do me anyhow."

Amethyst restrained herself from launching into her speech about the benefits of clear and concise writing—heaven knows she had given it to Conrad enough times over the past twelve years or so. Instead, she said, "And what else?"

His eyes widened. "How'd you know there was something else?"

"Just a hunch. I *am* a mother, you realize."

"Oh, yeah," he answered, as if motherhood explained everything. "I guess . . . I guess I'm in a little trouble."

Amethyst closed her eyes and prayed. "A girl?"

"Oh, no ma'am, nothing like that!" Clarence grinned and shook his head. He almost seemed pleased with himself, grateful that she would think him capable of *attracting* a girl, much less doing anything about it. "I think I'm a little—" He paused, and his neck flushed a bright red. "Homesick."

She breathed a sigh of relief. "What can I do to help, Clarence?"

"I dunno. Just let me sit in here a while, I guess." He pointed to the book. "Whatcha reading?"

"Robert Frost." She cocked her head and took in his blank stare. "He's a poet."

The light came back into the boy's eyes. "Oh, yeah. I know that name. We hafta read some of his stuff and then write about it for English class." He shrugged his shoulders and looked away. "I don't understand poetry."

Amethyst smiled. "It's pretty simple, really. Just words, but in a different form than you're used to. Would you like to read some and then talk about what it means?"

"You mean like doing homework, when my mama used to help me?" She watched him closely as he fiddled with the top button on his shirt. Clearly this wasn't his idea of the way a college man should be spending his evening, and he was ashamed.

"Maybe. More just like two friends discussing a poem together."

"Well, okay." He brightened, and his lanky form relaxed.

"Tell you what." Amethyst rose and held out the book. "I think there are a couple of pieces of apple pie left over from dinner. I'll go get us pie and milk while you read a poem. Then when I come back we can talk about it." She gazed down at him, this innocent man-boy, and smiled. "What were you assigned to read?"

"Something about a road, I think."

"Ah. 'The Road Less Traveled,' I'd expect."

"Yes'm. That's it."

Amethyst flipped pages. "All right. Here it is."

He heaved a sigh of relief. "It's short, anyway."

"Yes." She chuckled. "It's short."

She left him to ponder over the poem and went out to the kitchen. What had the Lord gotten her into this time?

"'*Two roads diverged in a yellow wood,*'" she murmured to herself as she cut two slices of pie and poured the milk. "'*And I—I took the one less traveled by. And that has made all the difference.*'"

36
Bailey Blue

———◆◆◆———

April 1946

Silvie stacked the breakfast dishes in the sink and heaved a long, drawn-out sigh. "I declare, Amethyst, I believe those boys are gonna be the death of me yet."

"What do you mean?" Amethyst folded the newspaper and looked up at her. "They're barely more than children, Silvie. I know they can be a little wild and rough sometimes, but they're good at heart."

"You go on believing that, if you want to," Silvie muttered. "I'm gonna watch my back."

"Has one of those boys said something to you?" Amethyst leaned forward intently. "They should know by now that you're a member of this household just as well as I am. If any one of them has been rude to you—"

"It's got nothing to do with rudeness." Silvie shook her head and turned back to the dishes. Amethyst wouldn't understand, no matter how much she tried to explain it. For years, since they were little girls, she and Amethyst had lived like sisters. Amethyst had called her own daddy "Uncle Enoch," God rest his soul, and the two families had shared this land for generations. But none of that mattered beyond the doors of Noble House. Out there, in the real world, Silvie was a colored maid, and Amethyst a white lady.

No, the boys hadn't been rude to her—not directly, anyway. But she had seen the way that Dooley Layton followed her with his eyes, leering at her—never mind that she was old enough to be his mama, and then some. He had a look about him, that snobbish, superior expression some white men got when they looked at a black woman. It made her skin crawl. It was the same kind of look, come to think about it, that old Mr. Mansfield used to have years ago when she worked for him at the hotel restaurant. An expression that said, *You're mine for the taking, whenever I want you. You're property, and don't you forget it.*

And she had overheard some of their conversations—at least enough to know that all of them, Conrad included, regularly talked about Negroes in demeaning language. Only last week, an old Negro man had been shot over in Dudley County just for walking on the road in front of a white man's place, and the murderer hadn't even been arrested. The sheriff said the man had the right to protect his land, and that was the end of it. Conrad and his friends had laughed about it, saying it was a lesson to all of them to stay where they belonged.

Amethyst, dear heart that she was, would like to believe that slavery had ended eighty years ago. But Silvie's own daddy had been a slave, and had told stories about his terror of the pattyrollers. The beast was still out there, prowling around at night, only this time it wore a white sheet and burned crosses in people's front yards.

"Silvie? Are you listening?"

Silvie jerked back to the present. "Sorry, Amethyst."

"I asked if any of the boys have been rude to you. Because if they have—"

"No. It's just that—" She gave up, waving her hands in frustration.

Amethyst slapped one palm down on the table. "If you've got something to say, Silvie, why don't you just come out and say it?"

"Because you won't understand. And you won't like it."

"Try me."

Silvie heaved a ragged sigh and sank down in a chair opposite Amethyst. "All right. None of the boys have said a word to me, other than 'pass the potatoes.'"

"Then what's the problem?"

"That's just the point, Amethyst. They don't talk to me; they don't relate to me in any way except as a servant. A slave. They don't *see* me.

Except maybe for Dooley Layton, who looks at me as if he's ready to drag me out to the woods and have his way with me."

"You don't mean it! Silvie, you're nearly fifty years old!" Amethyst laughed out loud, then stifled her mirth when she saw that Silvie was not amused. "You *do* mean it."

"I mean it. I've seen the look before, and I'd recognize it if I was ninety years old."

"Well, I know you're still a beautiful woman, Silvie, but a college boy? Please!"

"It has nothing to do with my age, Amethyst, or whether or not I'm still attractive. It has to do with power—a white man's power over a black woman. Or over a black man, for that matter."

Amethyst blinked. "Race has never mattered in this house. You should know that."

Silvie struggled against her anger—not at Amethyst, particularly, but at the whole of society. "Outside this house," she said in a measured voice, "things are quite different."

"I don't understand."

Silvie picked up the newspaper and scanned the front page. "Remember the Negro man who got shot last week across the county line?"

"Yes."

"Did you know his murderer walked free? No arrest, no trial, not even so much as a slap on the wrist or a fine?" She laid the paper down in front of Amethyst. "Here's the story."

Amethyst looked at the newspaper for a full minute. "There's no story about that shooting."

"Exactly. That's my point, Amethyst. Black folks are invisible. Rape us, shoot us, beat us to death, drag us behind a car—it doesn't matter. We don't count."

"You count to me," Amethyst murmured.

Silvie felt her heart melt, and she reached out and patted Amethyst's arm. "I know that, hon. I'm not talking about you. I'm talking about—"

"About the Klan?"

"Yes and no. Sure, I'm scared to death of the Klan. I don't know a single black person in Mississippi who isn't. But it's not just the outright acts of violence that are dangerous, Amethyst. It's all those well-meaning, good-hearted people who just sit by and do nothing."

She paused and groped for words. Amethyst was her best friend, and she wasn't going to want to hear what Silvie had to say, but she had asked for the truth and deserved nothing less.

"What frightens me," she went on, "is the look in the eye of a boy like Dooley Layton. What terrifies me is the idea that eighteen-year-old boys would applaud the sheriff who let that murderer in Dudley County go free. What appalls me is hearing them say, 'He had it coming,' as if being a Negro were reason enough to kill someone."

"Conrad?" Amethyst asked in a strangled whisper. "My son said that?"

Silvie gritted her teeth. "He didn't say it," she amended. "He just laughed when someone else did."

Amethyst had been miserable all day, thinking about what Silvie had told her. She didn't know what to do with Conrad, how to talk to him or what to say. He never listened to her anymore.

If he ever did, she corrected herself.

What, she wondered, made a child rebel against everything his parents stood for? It was true that Conrad had not had a father to look up to, but Amethyst had done her best, teaching him about God, trying to instill faith into his heart, encouraging him to pray and learn to trust the Lord for himself. And he certainly hadn't grown up with racism and hatred—at least not from her.

His grandfather was a different story.

Abraham Noble, Amethyst knew, had lived and died a bitter, broken man. He blamed his dissolute life on everyone but himself—on his father Silas, who had seen into his character and hadn't trusted him with the Noble lands. On Enoch, who in his mind had taken his place as first son and rightful heir. On his wife and daughter for chaining him to a life he hated. As a young boy, Conrad had undoubtedly been influenced by her father's attitudes.

But she couldn't entirely fault Abe for the way Conrad had turned out. The boy could have decided in favor of his mother's faith rather than his grandfather's bitterness. He'd had a choice between grace and arrogance, between compassion and cynicism. Everyone did.

In the long run, she supposed, there was no explaining how those influences sorted out. Amethyst had done all she could do, and now that he was grown, she had to let go. She had no option except to pray, and keep on praying, that one way or another, the Almighty would reach down and turn her son's life around.

She only hoped Conrad wouldn't have to become like his grandfather before he embraced the truth.

The dinner dishes had been dried and put away, and Amethyst was just about to sit down with a book when she heard a knock at the door. She went into the front hall to find Silvie holding the door open, as rigid as if she had just been struck by lightning.

"Silvie? Who's there?"

The door opened a little farther and a man stepped into the hallway, holding his cap in his hand. He was a tall fellow, broad-shouldered and handsome, with soft dark eyes and skin the color of burnished oak. "Pardon me, ma'am," he said in a rumbling baritone as he caught sight of Amethyst. "I'm looking for Amethyst Noble."

A rectangular patch over his pocket read "BLUE." Amethyst let her gaze take in the navy uniform, the close-cropped black hair, the flashing white teeth. She had always thought Uncle Enoch was handsome, but this man gave new meaning to the word. No wonder Silvie was standing there dumbfounded.

Amethyst tugged at Silvie's elbow and reached around her to shake the man's hand. "I'm Amethyst. My married name is Wainwright, but people still tend to use my maiden name, even after all these years." She shrugged. "It's the South, you know. This is Silvie Warren."

Silvie finally managed to come to her senses and put her jaw back in place. "Hello."

"It's a pleasure to meet you, ladies," he said with a brilliant smile in Silvie's direction. "I'm Bailey Blue. I've just been discharged from the navy, and I'm looking for lodging in this area. Might you have a room available?"

Silvie took a deep breath, sort of a strangled gasp. "You're not from around here, are you?"

He laughed—a deep, mellow sound that filled the hallway like music. "No ma'am. I'm from Washington, D.C."

Suddenly Amethyst remembered her manners. "Come in, Mr. Blue."

"Please, call me Bailey." He followed them into the log cabin room and took a seat in one of the chairs next to the fireplace. "What a nice room. Very comfortable and inviting."

"Would you like coffee?" Amethyst shot a glance at Silvie, who nodded. "Won't take but a minute to make."

"I would, thanks."

Amethyst hustled Silvie into the kitchen, and as soon as the door closed behind them, Silvie grabbed the edge of the counter. "Can you believe that?"

"What? That he's gorgeous, or that he wants to rent a room here?"

"Both." Silvie sank into a chair at the kitchen table while Amethyst put the coffeepot on. "Do we have any of that chocolate cake left?"

"You must be dreaming. The boys wolfed down the rest of it at dinner tonight. And I don't have any more ration stamps for chocolate, either."

"Never mind the ration stamps. There must be something we can offer him."

Amethyst nodded. "We made teacakes for tomorrow with the last of the sugar, remember? They're on the top shelf in the pantry. I hid them so the boys wouldn't find them."

Silvie jumped up, retrieved the cookies, and began arranging them on a plate. Then suddenly she stopped and turned to Amethyst with a look of abject misery on her face. "What are we doing?"

"I thought we were making coffee and cookies for a new boarder."

"Amethyst, we can't!"

"Of course we can. We've still got that nice apartment on the back side of the house. And we could use the extra money."

"Amethyst," Silvie breathed, "he's *colored*."

"Well, I know that. What's your point?"

"Nobody bothers me because I've been here forever. I grew up here, and the whole town is used to it. But if we take him—"

"It will be exactly like it was when we took in Harper and the other fellows twenty years ago. This gossipy little town will buzz about it for a while, and then everything will settle down."

"It won't settle down, Amethyst. Don't you see?" Silvie shook her head and went on without waiting for an answer. "No, you don't see. How could you? Despite everything you've been through, Amethyst, you're still an innocent. You think you've seen trouble? You wait till you take that man into your house, and then real trouble will plant itself right on your front doorstep. Probably dressed in a white hood, with a torch in its hand."

"He seems harmless enough to me." Amethyst peered at Silvie. "I can't believe you don't want him here."

"It's not a matter of what I want. It's a matter of—"

"It's a matter of what's right," Amethyst interrupted.

Silvie stared at her. "Excuse me?"

"It's a matter of what's *right*," Amethyst repeated. "You told me this morning that the world was in desperate need of changing. Well, we've spent the last twenty years changing what we could, and I don't see any reason to stop now."

"You mean it?"

"Of course I mean it. And what could happen, anyway? Some rednecks could get their boxers in a twist because we have a black boarder. Let 'em."

Silvie let out a muffled laugh. "Amethyst, you are outrageous."

"And I enjoy it immensely. Besides, he seems like a perfectly cultured gentleman. It might do our college boys good to have a little of that influence in their lives. My own son included."

"Conrad won't like it."

"Conrad will learn to live with it."

Silvie bit her lip. "But what if there's trouble?"

"What kind of trouble could a nice man like that stir up? He'll probably be the quietest boarder we've ever had."

The more Bailey Blue talked, the more Amethyst liked him. He spoke in softly modulated tones, laughed easily, and had an incisive wit. Not to mention a bagful of nylons and chocolate bars.

"So, Bailey," she asked as she poured him another cup of coffee, "what did you do in the service?"

He ran a hand across his hair and chuckled. "What most black seamen do, ma'am. Swab decks, clean latrines, scramble eggs."

Amethyst frowned. "I don't know much about the navy and wouldn't recognize one uniform from another, but I just assumed you were an officer."

"And why would you assume that?"

"Because you're so—I don't know. Obviously educated, intelligent, articulate. Shall I go on?"

He laughed out loud. "I'd love for you to, but modesty compels me to ask you to stop." He fixed his dark eyes on hers. "I'm an attorney, ma'am. Howard University, class of 1940."

"An attorney!" Silvie's jaw dropped open again.

"That's right. But in the navy it doesn't much matter what a man did before he enlisted. If he's colored, that is. I was in the service almost three years, and I never once met a black man with a rank above petty officer."

"That's the stupidest thing I've ever heard," Amethyst blurted out.

"I agree. And so does the organization I work for."

He went on talking for a while about his experiences in the navy, and how difficult it was for a Negro man to gain the rank he deserved. His voice, low and subdued, was mesmerizing, almost hypnotic. Amethyst could have listened to him for hours.

Then suddenly something he said registered. "You mentioned the organization you work for?"

"Yes ma'am. That's why I'm in Mississippi. To try to act as catalyst for some long-overdue changes." He paused. "I'm with a group called the National Organization for the Advancement of Colored People. The NAACP. Perhaps you've heard of us. We're working on behalf of equal rights for Negroes—battling against job discrimination, violence, and the like. It's a wonderful cause."

Amethyst had heard of it, all right. And it was a wonderful cause.

Just not the cause she expected to come knocking at Noble House.

37
The Conspiracy

Conrad sat at the dinner table and shifted his chair as far as possible from Bailey Blue. He couldn't believe his mother had done this—taken in a Negro boarder without so much as asking his opinion. It was bad enough that she took in any boarders at all. It embarrassed him no end to be the son of a . . . a *landlady*. But at least until now she had kept to her own kind.

He stared at his plate and avoided Dooley's piercing stare. He would be held responsible for this, he knew. Dooley and the others would never let him hear the end of it, would pressure him to convince his mother to get rid of Bailey Blue. Silvie was help, so they could tolerate her. But they would never live in the same house with a colored boarder. And a Yankee lawyer, at that!

One glance at his mother, however, told him that she would never in a hundred years give that man the boot. She hung on Bailey's every word, laughing at his jokes and leaning toward him across the table. And Silvie! You'd think she was a love-struck schoolgirl, the way she kept eyeing him when he wasn't looking.

Conrad grunted under his breath. Silvie was nearly fifty, he was pretty sure. And a woman that age—especially a *nigra* woman—ought to know better. Her job was to keep this house running smoothly, to cook and clean and do laundry. Not to fall all over herself the first time a big buck showed her ten seconds' worth of attention.

Bailey threw back his head and let out a booming laugh at something Mother had said. Then he launched into an intense discussion—a *sermon*, really—about how life in the South was due for change, how the NAACP was determined to see Negroes take their rightful place in society.

Mother was nodding enthusiastically. She had always loved this stuff about social justice and the rights of the downtrodden. How many times had she told him the story of his own father—an outcast, a man who had to fight for the most menial of jobs and the most basic level of acceptance? She had intended the story to make him proud of his daddy, Conrad supposed, but in his mind, he was Son of Scarface, a freak who had frightened children and made women swoon, and the idea disgusted him. The very fact of his heritage made life an uphill battle for him. And now she had done the unthinkable—taken in a Negro man under her own roof.

Bailey was the only one talking. Mother and Silvie were mesmerized, apparently unaware that all the others were squirming in their seats. He cut a glance at Dooley and saw a dark rage building in his eyes. Then, suddenly, Dooley jumped up from the table so quickly that his chair clattered to the floor behind him.

"Dooley," Mother said mildly, with barely a glance at him. "Remember your manners, please."

"I'd like to be excused," he grated with menace in his voice.

"All right. Run along."

Dooley bolted for the door with George Hatfield and Jackie Rudolph close on his heels. Bogey sat glued to his seat, biting his lower lip nervously.

Con elbowed him in the ribs. "Let's get out of here," he whispered. Bogey nodded uncertainly, and Con stood up. "Excuse us, too, Mother. We've . . . ah, got some things to attend to."

"Don't you want to stay a while and talk?" she asked. "Bailey has had some fascinating experiences as an attorney, and—"

"No ma'am. Sorry. We—uh, we gotta go."

Con hustled Bogey into the hallway. The last thing he heard before the front door closed behind them was his mother's voice saying, "Let me tell you about my husband and my grandfather, Bailey. I think you would have liked both of them."

Amethyst wished Conrad had stayed a little longer. The boy might benefit from some contact with a man like Bailey Blue.

What an amazing life he had lived! Howard University Law School, third in his class. After graduation, he had worked with the newly formed NAACP Legal Defense and Educational Fund, as assistant to a prominent black attorney named Thurgood Marshall.

"Mark my words," Bailey went on. "It may take another twenty years, but Thurgood Marshall will be the first Negro appointed to the Supreme Court. He is a brilliant man, a man with a vision. Received his law degree at age twenty-five, and barely five years later became chief counsel for the NAACP. He's committed to seeing this nation embrace its responsibility for providing equal justice for all."

"And that's why you're here?"

Bailey nodded. "Our goal is to bring an end to discrimination against Negroes. At the moment, we're focusing especially on job discrimination and education—specifically the 'separate but equal' policy." He shook his head. "There can be no equality in separation. It's 1946, and black people still suffer in inferior jobs, with inferior housing, and their children get inferior education. We're refused the right to vote, relegated to the back of the bus, shot to death for setting foot on a white man's land." He paused. "I assume you heard about the killing over in Dudley County. It's a travesty in a land that claims to offer liberty and justice for all."

Amethyst nodded, thinking back to her own battle to give Harper and men like him a fair chance at a job—and further back, to Grandma Pearl and Grandpa Silas's work with the slaves before and during the War Between the States. It was the same struggle all over again—different faces, different circumstances, but the same conflict. When she had told Silvie that it was the right thing to do, taking in Bailey Blue, she had believed it, at least philosophically. Now her theory was going to be put to the test.

"I have to be honest with you, Amethyst," he said. "Most white people in the South don't like the NAACP very much. Local and state governments—and especially the Klan—oppose us at every turn. They're afraid of seeing the balance of power shift, terrified of losing the control they've held for so long. If you want to change your mind, I'll find another place to stay."

Amethyst looked across at Silvie. She had loved this woman for as long as she could remember—had played with her as a child, confided in her as a young woman, depended upon her during times of heartache. For more than forty years, they had been family. Sisters. And yet a wall stood between them, a barrier that neither of them talked about. They could not share a meal at a restaurant, could not sit together on a bus, could not even worship together. It was not, Amethyst was certain, the way God intended it to be.

"It will be a risk," she said softly, gazing into Silvie's dark eyes. "Is it a risk we want to take?"

Silvie's brown hand reached out and grasped Amethyst's white one. "What would your grandma Pearl do?"

Amethyst smiled, and a phrase from Pearl's journals surfaced in her mind: *To believe is to care. To care is to do.*

Years ago, those journals had set her on a journey—a quest to find her own way to faith, to discover the calling God had placed upon her life. Each time she thought she had found her direction, the one cause she was destined to embrace, the Lord set another challenge before her. Another stretching of her trust, another leap into the unknown.

"You're in the right place," she said to Bailey Blue. "And so are we."

⸺•⬥•⬥•⸺

Silvie lay in bed and watched the moonlight play in the shadows of the tree outside her window. Usually she slept soundly, but tonight her mind spun with turmoil. In the apartment next to her room, just a wall away, she could hear Bailey's soft snoring.

His words—his very presence in the house—had stirred something in her, something she had never named and couldn't quite understand.

Part of it, she supposed, was the fact that he was outrageously attractive. From the moment she had opened the front door and laid eyes on him for the first time, she hadn't been able to still the rushing of her pulse. His smile, his easy laugh, his wit and intelligence, the passionate intensity in his eyes when he talked about his work—everything about him captivated her.

There was no chance of a romantic relationship between them, of course. She had to put that out of her mind and not be a fool about it. She was easily fifteen years older than he was, and if she hadn't found the right man by this time, she wasn't likely to find him in a thirty-five-year-old lawyer. Clearly the good Lord intended her to be single, and for the most part she was satisfied with her life and didn't constantly nag God for more.

But Bailey Blue was offering more, and despite herself, Silvie found herself longing for it.

Over the years she hadn't given much thought to the status of Negroes in general, or herself in particular. It didn't matter that most of the white folks in town referred to her as "Amethyst's maid," even though she held equal shares in Noble House. She knew different, and that was what counted. Her daddy had taught her to hold her head up, to turn a deaf ear to ignorant people, to be proud of who she was and what she had accomplished.

Bailey, however, implied that having a thick skin wasn't enough. Not for her, not for the thousands upon thousands of black people who struggled to make a living and provide food and shelter for their families.

Equal rights. The phrase reverberated in her soul, and she knew instinctively the truth of Bailey's words. Negroes weren't slaves anymore, but they might as well be, for all the share they got in the kind of life white folks enjoyed. Simple liberties, like the freedom to walk down the street without the fear of being harassed. The right to vote and elect candidates who would represent their interests. The right to dignity and respect. Just the right to be seen, to be acknowledged as an individual with a personality and feelings and abilities.

Bailey had said that community leaders opposed the work of the NAACP. Why, she wondered, were white people so threatened by the idea of Negroes having equal rights? Were they afraid that coloreds would take over, the way the Pharaoh feared an uprising among the children of Israel?

Her heart latched onto the parallel. Yes, there were similarities here. Negro men in menial jobs, being browbeaten into submission by white overseers. Negro women trying to keep their families together and protect their children from abuse. An old black man in the next county shot to death. People lynched in the dark of night, their houses burned. Was there a Moses out there somewhere, preparing to face down the Pharaoh and demand, "Let my people go!"?

A cloud blew over the moon, plunging the room into darkness. A chill ran through Silvie's veins, and she pulled the quilt tighter about her shoulders. Amethyst was right—this was a cause worth fighting for. But there was more at stake than social acceptability. The price was likely to be higher, much higher, than a few nasty comments on the street or in the grocery store.

She closed her eyes against the blackness of the night, and an image arose in her mind—a multitude of Negroes, marching out of Egypt, singing a victory song. But the vision didn't end there. Behind them, across the desert wilderness, an army of approaching soldiers, trapping them as the Red Sea refused to part.

Pharaoh's armies, in white sheets and hoods, with burning crosses in their hands. . . .

Con felt his stomach twisting into knots.

Dooley stood in the middle of the small apartment, a baseball bat in his hands, slamming the bat against his open palm. "I say we go after the nigger now, tonight!"

The other three—George, Jackie, and Bogey—sat on the floor in a semicircle around Dooley. Bogey's eyes got wider and wider, as if they might pop right out of his head. George and Jackie watched each other cagily, each assessing the other's reaction.

"Keep your voice down!" Conrad hissed. "Do you want to wake the whole household?"

"They can't hear me over there," Dooley sneered in reply. "And if they do, so what? I can take two women and a nigger easy enough."

Con fell silent. Dooley was right—about the noise, anyway. The carriage house sat away from the main house, separated by thirty feet or more. It was a chilly night, and the windows would be closed. Nobody could overhear Dooley's plan.

"Wait a minute," he objected when he got up his nerve. "That's my mother you're talking about."

"Ah, take it easy, Wainwright. I ain't gonna hurt the old lady. It's that uppity lawyer I'm after. And maybe it's high time I showed that nigra gal what a real man can do for her."

Bogey started to speak, but choked on his own spit and began coughing wildly.

"Shut up, Bogey," Dooley commanded. "Now, who's with me?"

Nobody said a word.

"George? Jackie? Come on, you little wimps. You gonna let some highfalutin nigra from up north come in here and take over?"

Silence.

Con studied the faces in the room. Bogey wouldn't stand up to Dooley, but he wouldn't do anything stupid, either. He had too big a crush on Mother to do anything that might hurt or anger her. Jackie didn't have a brutal bone in his body—he couldn't even be aggressive in a poker game. It was George who was the wild card. George idolized Dooley, probably because Dooley was everything George didn't have the guts to be. As cowardly as he was, he might follow Dooley's lead just to prove himself. And if he followed Dooley, Jackie would follow him.

Dooley was furious, determined to break some heads and shed some blood. Con had to think of a way out of this—and fast.

"Hold on," he stammered. "Dool, we don't have to resort to violence here."

Dooley took two steps toward him and brandished the bat. "Aw, the mama's boy is losing his nerve. All talk and no action, eh, Wainwright?"

Con felt his knees buckle, but he stood his ground. "We can get rid of Bailey without beating the pulp out of him—and without risking going to jail."

Dooley gave a snort. "Ain't you heard, Wainwright? No white man goes to jail for defending himself against a colored."

"You don't know that. Besides, Bailey's a lawyer. He's got a lot of support behind him." Con felt himself growing bolder, and he returned Dooley's stare. "You got a lot of nerve, Dooley, but you're not too smart. The NAACP will be on you like white on rice if you mess with one of theirs."

Dooley faltered—Con could see it in his eyes, see the wheels turning in his mind. He pressed his advantage. "Your daddy wouldn't like it much if you ruined your chances for college just because you couldn't keep a lid on that temper of yours."

Dooley squinted at Con and let the bat fall to his side. "What you got in mind, mama's boy?"

Conrad hesitated. He was making this up as he went along, and wasn't quite sure what he was going to say next. But Dooley and the others were waiting. "Simple," he said, clearing his throat until an idea came to him. "We move out."

"What are you talking about?"

"If we move out, there won't be enough money coming in to continue to keep Noble House running. No boarders, no income. The boarding-house closes, and Bailey Blue is out on his duff."

"You're gonna shut down your own mama?"

Con considered this. It was brilliant, even if he did say so himself. For years he had bemoaned the fact that he had to live in a boarding-house with a landlady for a mother. She'd find something else to do, and he knew for a fact that she had enough money laid by for a few months at least. Besides, he wouldn't have to worry for a while—his tuition was paid up for the year.

"Yep," he said with a determined nod. "We'll all go—now, tonight. We've got friends who'll take us in. And when people in this town find out why we did it, we'll be heroes."

George and Jackie jumped at the plan. "Great, Con. Yeah, we'll do it. Count us in." Clearly they didn't want to go beating up on Bailey, and they'd grab at any idea that would keep them from having to lose face with Dooley.

Bogey looked as if his world had collapsed before his very eyes. "I don't know . . . well, all right. I guess."

Dooley eyed Con suspiciously. "You sure this will work?"

"Why wouldn't it? We'll put out the word around town and at school, and nobody will come near this place."

"All right. But if it don't work, I still got my bat. And I'll use it on you first."

Con suppressed a shudder. He believed it. Every word of it.

But he couldn't worry about that right now. He had packing to do.

38
Plan B

———◆·◆·◆———

Amethyst caught a glimpse of someone in the mirror and did a double take. Who was that old woman?

She approached the dresser and peered into the glass more intently. When had she become the person she saw in that reflection? Dark smudges under the eyes. Crow's-feet fanning out across the temples. Wrinkled, crepey skin draping the folds of the neck. Last time she had looked, she had seen a middle-aged woman—with a few lines here and there perhaps, but still with a spark in her eye, and with most of the wrinkles tracing the patterns of her smile.

Today, she didn't feel much like smiling. She hadn't slept for three nights straight, and her emotions were obviously taking a toll on her.

With both hands she pushed back the skin of her cheeks until the image in the spotted glass resembled the young woman she remembered. But the deception didn't last. As soon as she let go, the truth reasserted itself, arranging her features into the semblance of a woman betrayed by her only son and on the verge of financial ruin.

Her stomach clenched, and Amethyst gripped the edge of the dresser until the pain subsided. She took a deep breath, pushed away, and grim-aced at her reflection.

How Conrad could have done such a thing, she could not imagine. She knew he was the instigator, even though Bailey and Silvie tried to reassure her that perhaps it wasn't his idea at all. Maybe he had only submitted to peer pressure and gone along with the crowd.

But Amethyst knew better.

Clarence Bogart had told her so.

Poor Bogey. He had come to her under cover of darkness, weeping profusely and apologizing over and over again. At first Amethyst didn't know what he was talking about. Only when he had calmed down enough to speak without gasping did she learn that the college boys had left—all of them, including Conrad. Moved out in the middle of the night without a word of explanation. It was Con's idea, Clarence confessed.

In the fifteen minutes Clarence had taken to say good-bye, he had looked over his shoulder a dozen or more times. Clearly he had been intimidated by someone, although Amethyst hadn't been sure whether it was Conrad or Dooley Layton who was the object of his terror.

Still, amid the heaving and apologizing and fresh waterfalls of tears, Bogey had managed to get the fundamentals of the situation communicated. None of the boys would continue to board there, not as long as Bailey Blue was in the house. There had been talk of violence—once again Amethyst couldn't be sure who the source was—and if Bogey didn't go along with the plan, his own life would be in jeopardy. Something about a baseball bat and broken kneecaps—with all his sobbing, Clarence didn't make the details very clear, but Amethyst comprehended the essence of the threat.

The long and short of it was that Amethyst was left with a nearly empty house, very little money, one lone boarder, and the knowledge that her only son had been, if not the driving force of the betrayal, at least a willing participant.

Amethyst pressed her fingertips to her eyes. She had to pull herself together, had to make a plan. But she couldn't make her mind work, couldn't get any momentum of logical reasoning started. All she could think about was Conrad standing in the midst of those college students, conspiring against his own mother.

It felt like a death.

Amethyst had faced death any number of times over the past thirty years. Harper. Uncle Enoch. Both her parents. Her father, she thought cynically, she had buried twice. Every time, it had been painful. Every time, she thought her heart would never mend. With Harper, especially, she was certain she would grieve forever.

But the grieving eventually waned, the pain diminished, and life went on. She learned to smile again, learned to laugh. Learned to get through a day without the sudden rush of tears that came with the memories.

This was worse. Her son was not dead. She couldn't stand at his graveside and say good-bye, couldn't weep for him in the night and then at last let him go. She would live every day with the knowledge that he was still alive, close by, but separated from her by a vast chasm of deceit. She would pass him on the street, and he would turn his head, unwilling to meet her eyes. She would hear his laugh in the square, see him from a distance walking hand in hand with some young woman in the park. . . .

Amethyst shook her head and let out a snort of disgust. She had to stop this. Now. Conrad would have to bear the responsibility of what he had done. She couldn't change the situation, couldn't change him. All she could do at the moment was find a way to salvage everything she had worked for since she was eighteen years old.

What she would not do was evict Bailey Blue.

"But Amethyst, he's your son."

"Yes, he is, although at the moment I'm not particularly proud to claim him." Amethyst looked into Bailey's clear, guileless gaze and refused to back down. The pain she had felt at the news of Conrad's betrayal had metamorphosed into a deep-seated anger—partly at Conrad, partly at the state of the world in general. Nobody, her only son included, had the right to tell her that she couldn't rent to a Negro. Nobody had the right to intimidate a poor helpless boy like Clarence Bogart. Nobody had the right to coerce her into betraying her own principles. Nobody.

Those self-important little college boys no doubt thought she was just a weak, insecure woman who would collapse like a house of cards at the first sign of resistance. But they couldn't have been more wrong. Amethyst had her Grandpa Silas's courage flowing in her veins and her grandma Pearl's faith surging in her soul. What was right was right, and she wouldn't bend to the winds of prejudice. Not even if it cost her Noble House.

"I can find another place to live. You can get your boarders back."

Amethyst shook her head. "Do you think I want them back? Besides, Bailey, this is not about money, and you, of all people, should know it."

"Of course I know it. I've spent years putting myself on the line for justice. But that's just the point—it's my life, my career, my reputation. You took a chance on me because you believed it was the right thing to do, and I appreciate it. We need people like you—people with the courage to stand up for their convictions. But it backfired, Amethyst. And you shouldn't have to go bankrupt on my account. This is my cause, my battle. Not yours."

Amethyst sat there in silence for a moment, considering his words. This could all be smoothed over so easily. Without Bailey in the house, she would have boarders again—not the college boys, necessarily, but someone else. Someone . . .

White.

The truth struck her with all the force of a blow to the midsection, and the air went out of her lungs. That's what it would take to save Noble House. White boarders. "Acceptable" boarders, people who wouldn't challenge the status quo or incur the wrath of the citizens of Cambridge. It was so simple, really. All she would have to do was reject everything she and Silas and Pearl had ever stood for.

Amethyst looked at Silvie, who sat quietly with her hands in her lap, gazing at her. The woman had been a light in the darkness for Amethyst, the one person she could depend upon no matter what struggles or difficulties life brought her way. It was Silvie's hand she reached for when she needed support and consolation, Silvie's words that made her laugh, Silvie's incisive honesty that made her think. And they couldn't even share a cup of coffee together at a restaurant table.

Amethyst returned her attention to Bailey. "You're wrong," she said quietly. "This isn't just your battle. It's my cause, too."

"But Conrad—"

"Conrad has chosen his course. He's not a child anymore, and he will have to answer to God for the decisions he makes. I love him, and my door will always be open to him, but—" She paused and smiled at Silvie. "Only if it's open to you, too."

At last Silvie spoke. "So let's hear it, Amethyst."

"Hear what?"

"Your plan."

Amethyst chuckled. "What makes you think I have a plan?"

"You think I don't know you, girl? I can see it in your eyes. You're hatching something."

"Silvie and I have been together way too long," Amethyst said to Bailey. "She thinks she can read my mind." She paused and grinned. "But as a matter of fact, I do have an idea."

Edith Layton slid into the booth next to Amethyst and grabbed her elbow. The hotel restaurant was nearly full, and Edith's beady little eyes kept darting around the room. She reminded Amethyst of a fat little wren on the alert for the neighbor's cat. "Act natural," she whispered. "Pretend we're talking."

"Good afternoon, Edith," Amethyst said smoothly. "And unless I've missed something, we *are* talking."

"Don't 'good afternoon' me, Amethyst Noble," Edith hissed. "Just tell me it's not true."

"Going to give me the latest gossip?" Amethyst laughed. "Please do, Edith. I haven't heard a juicy tidbit for ages."

"Stop it! You know perfectly well what I'm talking about." Edith's voice was hushed, barely a whisper, but her mouth was so close to Amethyst's ear that the breath tickled. "It's all over town that you have five . . . ah, colored men living under your roof."

Amethyst pulled back a little. "Don't make it sound so salacious, Edith. I'm not running a brothel, for heaven's sake."

"Oh, dear, dear!" Edith fanned herself with a napkin. "Then it is true!"

"That I have five boarders? Yes, I do. Gentlemen, every one of them."

"Gentlemen? You call a bunch of nigra Yankees come down here to stir up trouble *gentlemen?*"

"They're lawyers, Edith. Educated, cultured attorneys. If they were white, you'd think I was living in a gold mine, and every unmarried woman from here to Memphis would be lining up at my door to get a peek at them."

"We're all aware of what they are," Edith spat out, her volume increasing with every word. "They're rabble-rousers from the N-double-A-PC."

"NAACP," Amethyst corrected. "The National Association for the Advancement of—"

Edith waved a hand. "I know, I know. Keep your voice down."

"Why?"

"Because it's a shame and a degradation, that's why. Amethyst, how could you?"

"How could I do what? Rent rooms? That's what you do when you own a boardinghouse, Edith."

"But to them? Everybody in town knows you're a little eccentric, Amethyst. When my husband, Rube, was mayor, he actually admired you for standing up to the town council and working to get jobs for those . . . those—"

"Freaks?" Amethyst supplied. "Like my husband Harper."

"I didn't mean it that way," Edith amended. "But that was different. They were—"

"White."

"They were veterans." Edith shook a finger in Amethyst's face. "They deserved jobs."

"And black people don't?"

"Of course they do. Jobs that befit their station in life, that is. But these nigra lawyers—"

"Bailey Blue is a veteran," Amethyst offered. "He served aboard a navy destroyer for two years during the war."

"Yes, but—wait, you're confusing me," Edith complained. "Now, where was I?"

"Confused."

"The point is, Amethyst, you simply cannot have those colored men in your house. A lot of people in this town just won't stand for it. And Rube isn't mayor anymore. He can't protect you."

"Do I need protection?"

"You might." Edith slid out of the booth, her gaze coming to rest on the second place setting. "Is someone joining you for lunch?"

"Yes. I'm expecting a friend any minute now."

"Try the barbecue chicken salad. It's wonderful." Edith patted Amethyst on the arm. "Please, think about what I've said," she whispered. "And consider yourself warned."

Amethyst was still mulling over her conversation with Edith Layton when she looked up and saw Silvie standing over her.

"I'm not sure this is such a good idea," Silvie muttered.

Amethyst pointed to the booth. "Sit." Silvie sat. "I, on the other hand, think it's a great idea. I think it's high time you and I had lunch together without one of us having to cook it."

"That's not what I mean, and you know it."

"Silvie, look at me." When Silvie met her gaze, Amethyst went on. "It's time for this to happen. Nothing ever changes in this world unless people take risks."

A shadow fell over them. Amethyst looked up to see a vaguely familiar face staring down at them.

"Hello, Miss Amethyst. Silvie." The waitress frowned. "You don't remember me, do you? I came to Thanksgiving dinner at your house. But it was a long time ago; I don't expect you to recall."

Amethyst peered at the woman. "Dinah? Dinah Johnson?" She grinned at Silvie. "Remember, Silvie? Dinah had just come to town, and was working for Neta at La Femme—"

"Of course." Silvie shifted nervously. "Nice to see you again."

"So what have you been doing, Dinah?"

"I've been working. Up north, in Virginia, just outside Washington."

"And what brings you back this way?"

"My . . . uh, my husband." Tears welled up Dinah's eyes. "He, ah—"

Amethyst opened her mouth to console the girl for losing her husband in the war, but something held her back.

"Found someone younger and prettier," Dinah finished. "Divorced me. I couldn't make it alone up there, so—" She shrugged. "Here I am."

Amethyst cringed, thankful she hadn't said something that made her look like a total fool. "I'm so sorry."

"Yeah, me, too. Sorry I ever met him." She swiped at her eyes. "Now, what can I get you?" She fixed her gaze on Silvie. "I reckon you're ordering something to take with you?"

"No," Amethyst said in a soft voice. "We're both having lunch. Here. Together."

Dinah's eyes widened. "I don't know—I—I don't think I can—I'll have to ask—"

"I'll have the barbeque chicken salad," Amethyst continued. "Silvie, what would you like?"

Suddenly the hubbub of conversation in the restaurant fell into silence, as if the lights had dimmed and the show was about to begin. Somewhere a fork clattered to the floor. A baritone cleared his throat. A soprano let out a little gasp.

Silvie cut a glance across the table, and her expression reminded Amethyst of a rabbit with one leg in a trap. "The same, I guess," she stammered.

A masculine figure appeared beside Dinah and snatched the pad and pencil from her hand. "Go serve your other customers," he snapped. "I'll take care of this."

Amethyst looked up. "Well. Mr. Mansfield."

She hadn't seen him up close in ages, since back in the days when Silvie had worked as a cook in his restaurant. The years had not been good to him. He was fifty or sixty pounds heavier than she remembered, his round, florid face crisscrossed with broken blood vessels until it looked like a road map. He rolled his eyes and tapped the pencil against the pad. "You know better than this, Miss Amethyst." One meaty finger pointed to a sign that said WHITE ONLY.

His gaze shifted to Silvie, and he made no attempt to hide the leering expression in his eyes. "You want something, gal?" He grinned at her and picked his teeth with the edge of a fingernail. "Naw. You never did know what you wanted, did you?"

The implication in his words was unmistakable. Amethyst was just about to respond to him when she caught a glimpse of Silvie's face. The scared-rabbit expression had vanished, replaced by a look of pure outrage.

"I'll have roasted Mansfield on toast, and a glass of iced tea," she said, her voice strong and clear. A titter of laughter dispelled the tension in the room, and someone in the back corner applauded.

He blinked. "Not in my restaurant, you won't. Now get out, both of you." He grabbed Silvie by the arm and hauled her bodily out of the booth. "And don't come back."

Silvie jerked her elbow from his grasp and turned to face him, so close that their noses were almost touching. "Mansfield, you're a bigot and a lecher, and not worth my time," she spat out, then raised her chin and addressed the whole restaurant. "And in case anyone's interested, there are rats in the kitchen."

Propelled by Mansfield's arm, Amethyst and Silvie found themselves out on the sidewalk in front of the hotel. But they were not alone. A mass exodus from the restaurant followed, nearly pushing them down in their haste to leave the establishment.

Amethyst straightened her collar and grinned at Silvie. "I think that went well, don't you?"

"Perfect," Silvie agreed, falling in step beside Amethyst. "I don't know about you, but I haven't felt this good for ages."

39
Nightriders

———◦•◦———

Amethyst usually slept soundly—the gift of a clear conscience, Silvie always said—but tonight she couldn't seem to relax. For three hours she drifted and dozed, awakening at the slightest noise from the creaking old house.

When the clock in the hall chimed two, she opened her eyes and stared into the darkness at the canopy over the bed. Strange, how the shifting of leaves in the moonlight reflected against the fabric. It almost looked like—

Amethyst sat up and squinted again at the canopy. An odd light, flickering and moving, as if from a candle flame. Then her nostrils caught the faint, dusky scent of wood smoke.

Fire!

She grabbed her robe, stuck her bare feet into her slippers, and ran toward the front door. Silvie met her in the hall. "Where is it?"

"I don't know. I couldn't sleep, and—"

At the same time they saw it—the eerie red glow coming through the windows of the parlor. Silvie pointed. "Outside!"

Amethyst flung open the front door, and her heart lodged in her throat.

On the front lawn, just beyond the big magnolia tree, a cross stood, engulfed in flames.

"Quick! Get a bucket!"

Silvie sprinted for the kitchen, and Amethyst ran out onto the porch, robe in hand, headed for the conflagration. Maybe she could beat some of the flames out before the fire spread.

Even from this distance, however, she could feel the heat. The smell of gasoline came to her on a wave.

"Fire!" she yelled, hoping to wake the boarders. But her voice came out weak and whispery, as if she were in a nightmare, trying to scream but producing no sound.

Then her eyes focused to one side of the burning cross, in a dark hollow where the moonlight could not penetrate the dense leaves of the magnolia. A circle of men, dressed in white robes and makeshift hoods, their eyes shadowed like ghostly apparitions. In the center of the circle, a dark figure huddled, its legs drawn up to its chest.

"Let it burn, Miss Amethyst," a rough voice commanded. "Consider this a warning. You ain't getting another one."

A cold bead of sweat traced down Amethyst's spine, and she shivered. Then the figure on the ground let out a horrible groan, and the fear turned to rage.

"Bailey!" she screamed, running toward him. "Bailey, are you all right?"

"Let him alone," another voice warned.

But Amethyst didn't listen. "Get out of my way, you idiot." She pushed her way into the circle and fell on her knees at Bailey's side. "What have you done to him?"

"We gave him what was coming to him. Nigger troublemaker."

She touched Bailey's face, and her hand came away streaked with blood. He had been beaten badly, but she was pretty sure he would live. She struggled to her feet and faced down his attackers.

"Big men, are you?" She shoved one of them, hard, leaving a handprint of blood on his white tunic. "Big, tough men, with your bats and ax handles, half a dozen of you against an unarmed man. Takes a lot of courage, doesn't it, Billy Tarbush?"

The one she had pushed took a step back. "I—I ain't—"

She moved closer, until she could see his panicked look through the eyeholes of the hood. "Don't try to deny it; I know your voice. And I know your daddy, too. He's been an ignorant bigot for as long as I can remember. Looks like that apple didn't fall too far from the tree."

She swung around. "And you, John Layton! You should know better! Your grandfather was mayor of this town for years, and he would never have condoned this!"

On she went around the circle, identifying each one of the attackers by name. Did they really think they could get away with this? Hide in the dark and beat a helpless man senseless just for the color of his skin?

She came to the last one, a tall, skinny fellow holding a blood-spattered baseball bat. She peered at him. Something about him was familiar, but she couldn't place him. Then she looked down at his shoes—scuffed brown oxfords with one lace broken and retied in a knot. Shoes that had been under her own dining room table; shoes she had stumbled over in the parlor when he forgot and left them there. Dooley Layton, John's cousin.

She whipped out a hand and snatched off the hood. "You!"

Dooley glared at her. "He had it coming," he repeated lamely.

"Get off my property," she hissed. "All of you. I see any one of you within a hundred feet of my house, I'll call the sheriff."

"And what do you think he'll do?" Dooley sneered.

"For one thing, he'll cart your sorry behind back to Natchez, where your daddy will beat the living tar out of you," Amethyst retorted. "Don't forget—I can identify every one of you. You think I won't press charges? Try me. I've got a houseful of lawyers to represent me."

"You got a houseful of niggers, you mean."

Amethyst whirled around to see Rube and Edith Layton's grandson John standing behind her with a self-satisfied smile on his face. "Your grandpa would be so ashamed of you," she said. "And your grandmother warned me that something like this might happen, but I didn't believe her. What do you suppose she'll say when she finds out where you were tonight?"

"I'm a man—I'm old enough to do as I please."

"Old enough to get yourself killed, or hanged for murder." Amethyst gave a little snort. "You think you're all so powerful, dressing up in bed sheets like a bunch of goblins. If you were *real* men, and believed what you're doing is right, you wouldn't be ashamed to show your faces, and you wouldn't be running around at all hours of the night like little boys at Halloween. Trick or treat's over, boys. You're obviously too immature to be playing with matches, so take your toys and go on home."

One of them let out an ear-piercing whistle, and a dark pickup truck pulled up to the curb. The white-sheeted attackers climbed into the back, and one of them pounded on the top of the cab, a signal to get moving. But just before the headlights came on, Amethyst caught a quick glance at two of the figures inside the truck.

The one on the passenger's side, hanging his head and looking thoroughly miserable, was Clarence Bogart.

Between Bogey and the driver sat her own son, Conrad.

* * *

"Ow! That hurts!"

"Sit still, will you?" Silvie commanded as Bailey Blue squirmed in his chair. "If I don't get some antiseptic in this cut, they'll have to amputate your head."

"I'd probably feel better if they did," he muttered.

"We all would. Now stop whining."

Bailey laughed, then grimaced as Sylvie dabbed at the wound. "I'm sorry, Amethyst. This is all my fault."

Amethyst shook her head. "I'm sure my lunch with Silvie at Mansfield's didn't help the situation. Edith warned me, but I guess I didn't really think the Klan would come after us."

"Klan Junior, you mean." Bailey put a hand to his head and held the bandage while Silvie taped it on. "If that had been the real Klan, I'd be swinging from the magnolia tree."

"I wish you wouldn't talk like that." Amethyst winced.

"It's the way of the world, at least in the South," he responded. "That's why the NAACP is here."

"But what would cause those boys to do that?"

"Exactly what you told them, Amethyst—insecurity. They probably never even considered the fact that they could have killed somebody. They were trying to prove their manhood, trying to be tough. But they're not thinking for themselves, making a statement of their own. It's what they hear at home—that Negroes ought to keep in their place."

Amethyst fell silent, thinking. Bailey had sustained some pretty bad bruising on his arms and shoulders, and a couple of nasty cuts to the head. But it could have been much worse. He could have had internal injuries. He could have been in the hospital, or . . . the morgue.

She hadn't told anyone about what she had seen in the cab of that pickup. She wasn't sure she could admit to Bailey—or even to Silvie—that her own son had been party to the attack. Oh, he hadn't clubbed Bailey with his own hands or set fire to the cross, but he had been there. Even his presence among those boys testified to an implicit acceptance of such violence and brutality. She couldn't comprehend how the child of her own flesh could be so cruel, so heartless.

And she couldn't stop blaming herself.

Silvie sat in the passenger's seat with the window rolled down and the fresh spring breeze blowing in her face. Bailey drove slowly, as if relishing every flash of white dogwood in the woods, every scent of daffodils along the roadside.

"It's a beautiful afternoon, isn't it?" He slanted his eyes toward her. "Are you cold?"

"A little," she admitted, pulling her sweater closer around her shoulders, "but I like it."

"Spring is my favorite season," he went on, looking back at the road. "A season of rebirth, a time that makes me believe anything is possible."

She studied his face. The bruises were fading a little, but the angry gash in his forehead still had a bit of infection in it. When they got home this evening, she would make sure to clean it out and put a new bandage on it. It would probably leave a scar, but a few nicks and cuts just added character to a man's face. Especially a man as handsome as Bailey Blue.

"A nickel for your thoughts," he prodded, giving her a dazzling smile.

"Pardon me?"

"I figure they've got to be worth more than a penny." He smiled again, and her heart did a little jump-step.

"You'd be getting the bad end of that bargain," she retorted playfully.

"Oh, I don't know. The NAACP doesn't pay as well as private practice, but I'd wager a month's salary that anything on your mind would be absolutely fascinating."

Silvie smiled faintly—what she hoped was a mysterious, inscrutable expression—but she didn't respond. She wasn't about to tell him what she was thinking: the way her pulse raced anytime she heard his voice; how her mind wandered to him throughout the day; the feelings of terror and loss she had experienced when she saw the blood gushing from his head the other night. The truth was, she thought he was perfect. A man of character and integrity, a man of intelligence and honesty, a man who was giving his life to an important cause. And a man, she had to admit, who was as handsome on the outside as he was on the inside.

Not that physical appearance would have made a difference. Human beings looked on the outside, the Bible said, but God looked on the heart. Handsome or homely wouldn't have mattered; she could never be attracted to a man whose soul was not tender—both toward God and toward others.

But she *was* attracted to him. She couldn't help it, no matter how much she tried to reason with herself about the difference in their ages, their education, their life experience. He probably had a gaggle of women after him up in Washington. Younger, prettier women; educated, refined women. Not women who cooked and cleaned and ran a boardinghouse for a living.

Still, here she was with him, at his invitation—his insistence, really. Traveling the back roads of Cambridge County and talking to poor black men and women about their lives, their dreams, their fears. Encouraging them to attend the civil rights rally he and his colleagues were planning.

The white folks were right, she supposed. In some ways, Bailey Blue was a troublemaker. But it was trouble that needed to be made. Bailey had a gift for seeing into people's hearts, knowing what would stir them to action. He had a way of calming their fears, convincing them that there was power in numbers. So far more than a dozen Negro families had agreed to take part in the rally.

One old man, a ninety-nine-year-old former slave named Jabeth, had kissed him on the cheek and thanked him for coming. "I's been prayin'," he murmured in a palsied voice, "prayin' I wouldn't die before I saw the comin' of the Freedom Train." He gripped Bailey's hand and held on tight while tears streamed down his wrinkled face. "Bless you, boy. Bless you."

Silvie found herself easily caught up in the charisma Bailey emanated. Surprisingly, the attack on Bailey—what he jokingly called "The Night of the Klan Babies"—made her even more determined to join his cause, to take a risk that might just make the world a better place.

Bailey's mellow, taunting voice interrupted her thoughts. "It's taken me forever to get you to myself, and there you sit, refusing to talk to me."

Silvie turned. "I'm sorry. You were saying something?"

He gripped his chest and let his head sag against the steering wheel. "You really know how to hurt a guy. And all this time I thought I was such a charming fellow."

If you only knew, Silvie thought. Aloud, she said. "My fault. I was drifting. Please, go on."

He brightened. "Well, as I was saying—back when you weren't listening—I was beginning to fear I'd be an old man before I got any time alone with you. You haven't been avoiding me, have you?"

Silvie frowned. "Why would you think that?"

"Because you never really talk to me, that's why. You're always busy. It's not because I'm a lawyer, is it? Some people hate lawyers."

Silvie let out a little laugh. "No, I don't hate lawyers."

"That's better. You have a wonderful laugh, you know. Like music."

Suddenly Silvie realized that the car wasn't moving, and she looked around. He had pulled onto a dirt road—just two tracks through the grass, really—and parked alongside a small lake. A white bird with long legs was feeding in the shallows.

"This is one of my favorite places." He sighed, leaning back against the seat. "I found it not long after I came here, on one of my trips out to the country." He gazed at her and pointed toward the lake. "That egret and I have become pretty good friends. Want to meet him?"

Silvie nodded, feeling a strange mix of euphoria and nervousness wash over her. "What did you call it?"

"It's a snowy egret. I call it Buster."

The ridiculousness of the name attached to such a gracious bird made Silvie laugh out loud. "Buster, huh?"

"Yep. We're pals."

He got out of the car and came around to her side, opening the door for her with a gracious little bow. "Milady."

Silvie giggled. How long had it been since anyone had opened a car door for her, held her coat, treated her like a lady? Probably never. In Cambridge, she wasn't a lady. She was the nigra maid who kept the boardinghouse for Miss Amethyst. But now, here, with Bailey, she felt as if she might be an African princess, born to royalty and nobility.

He took her elbow and led her down a narrow path to the water's edge. The sun was beginning to set, casting red and purple hues across the water. She sat on a fallen log, and he settled himself next to her.

"I can see why you love this place," she whispered. "It's so peaceful."

He pulled a small tin out of his pocket and held it up. "Sardines. Buster loves them."

She stared at the sardine can, and a pleasant realization worked its way into her consciousness. "You *planned* to come here? With me?"

"Guilty as charged. Yes, I planned it. And definitely with you." Deftly he snapped the key off the back of the can and unrolled the top. The egret's head jerked around, and he surveyed them with an unblinking eye. Bailey tossed a sardine in the bird's direction, and its long neck darted down into the water to retrieve it.

When the sardines were gone, Bailey went to the edge of the lake, washed out the can, and laid it on the log to dry. The bird stretched its long neck and nodded in their direction, as if bestowing a kind of bene-diction.

"I feel God's nearness here," Bailey said quietly. "As much as anywhere I've ever been, including church."

Silvie nodded. "I expect in your line of work, a sense of the Lord's presence must be hard to come by."

"Because of the violence, the animosity?"

"Yes."

"I see what you mean. But actually, it's quite the contrary. Every time

I look into the trusting face of a little black child and hope for a better future, I confront the face of God. I see God's tears in a mother who has lost her son to the Klan. I feel God's touch in the hand of an old man like Jabeth. Sometimes I even think I hear God weeping over all those created in the Divine image who have not yet tasted freedom. The fact is, I couldn't do this job if I didn't sense God's presence in it. It's a calling, not just a career."

"I know how you feel." The words came unbidden, and Silvie bit her lip. She felt like a silly little fool, comparing what she did to his important work.

But his response couldn't have surprised her more. "I was certain you would understand, certain you would feel the same way."

"You were?" she blurted out. "How?"

"I can see it in your eyes, hear it in your voice. And I'm aware of the history of Noble House, what you and Amethyst have done. You know what it is to take a risk for something you believe in. You know what it means to give people the dignity and respect they deserve."

Tears welled up in her eyes, and she could hardly speak. Over the years she had not received much appreciation, except from Amethyst. Not many people knew, or acknowledged, that she was more than Amethyst Noble's nigra maid. And as much as she tried not to let it hurt, the truth stung. She had been invisible for so long that it stunned her when someone looked into her heart.

"Thank you," she managed at last.

Bailey turned to face her, his eyes locking on hers. "Silvie, I've never met anyone like you. You're so gentle and giving, yet you have a backbone strong as an iron rod. I don't know quite how to say this, but—"

She composed herself and gave a little chuckle. "And you call yourself a lawyer?"

"I know, I'm supposed to be good with words. I guess what I'm trying to say is that I've waited all my life to find a woman like you."

Silvie stared at him. Was it possible he was saying he was *interested* in her? No. It couldn't be. She had misunderstood him, and if she responded seriously, she really would look like a fool. "Well," she quipped, "that's to be expected, since you haven't lived very long."

A shadow passed over his handsome features, and he frowned. "I know. There are a few years' difference in our ages, but I don't think that should matter if two people are meant for each other."

"Meant for each other?" she repeated stupidly.

"Yes, I—oh." He stopped suddenly. "You must think I'm an idiot. Of course. You have someone in your life. I didn't know, but it stands to reason, as beautiful and sensitive as you are."

"Someone in my life? You mean a *man*?" Silvie let out a donkey bray of a laugh, then clapped a hand over her mouth.

"You don't?" He leaned forward eagerly. "Well, that's—that's *wonderful!* Not wonderful for you, of course, but wonderful for me. What I'm trying to say is—well, you know."

She crossed her arms and gazed at him. "No, I don't know. Exactly what *are* you getting at, Bailey?"

He took a deep breath. "You're going to make me say it, aren't you?"

"It would solve a lot of confusion, yes."

"All right. Here goes. I think I'm falling in love with you, and I want to know if you'd be open to the idea of pursuing a relationship." He said it in a rush, as if expelling all the air in his lungs would give his words more emphasis. Then he sat back and took in a deep breath. "I want to get to know you better, Silvie, but what I know already tells me that we could build a life together. Work together. Do great things in this world. I've never met anyone I felt so at home with, so complete with. All I ask is the chance to love you."

The sun had almost set, and the reflection in the water cast a ruddy glow over his face. He looked as if he were lit from within by some celestial light. And perhaps he was.

"You're sure?" she whispered as his eyes searched hers. "You're sure it's me you want, not some pretty young thing from up north?"

"Yes."

She leaned closer to him and felt his lips touch hers—a brief, velvety kiss that left her with the promise of more. When she drew back, he was smiling, suppressing a laugh.

"What's the matter? Do I kiss funny?" Silvie narrowed her eyes at him.

"Of course not. You kiss wonderfully." He pointed in the direction of the lake. Buster, the egret, was staring at them as if thoroughly offended by their public display of affection.

"Guess he doesn't appreciate kissing." Silvie chuckled.

"I wouldn't, either, with a beak like that." Bailey turned to him. "Get your beady little eyes off my woman, fish-breath. This one's taken."

Silvie peered at him. "She is, is she?"

He took her hand and squeezed it gently. "I certainly hope so."

"Well, Buster, you heard the man. Go find your own girl."

With a haughty tilt of his head, Buster unfurled his wings and flew into the sunset.

40
Second Chances

Silvie hummed to herself as she put bacon on to fry and slid a pan of biscuits into the oven. She consciously tried to contain her joy, but it just kept spilling over when she wasn't watching. Who would have believed that at the ripe old age of fifty, Silvie Warren could have found love?

God would have believed it, that's who, she thought. All these years she had trusted in a Deity who specialized in wonderful surprises. She had seen miracles happen to other people, and had rejoiced with them. She had even been instrumental in the romance between Amethyst and Harper. And yet when the miracle happened in her own life, it caught her unawares. She had never expected anything like the gift God had given her in Bailey Blue.

Silvie had been content as a single woman. She had a purpose for living, and she knew—even if others didn't—that her work, her calling, had eternal significance. She had been happy. But she hadn't known, not until the past three weeks, that life could be so completely beautiful.

Funny, what love did to a person. Just the awareness that Bailey cared for her had put a new lilt in her voice, a spring in her step. The little aches and pains that came with growing older—the twinge in the back, the creak in the knees—seemed to have vanished overnight. She felt like a girl again. Young, desirable, and full of promise.

Silvie took the bacon out of the pan and placed it on a towel to drain. Why, she wondered, did it take the revelation of human love to make her feel this way? Since she was a little child, she had known that God loved her, and she loved God. But somehow the Lord's acceptance of her didn't have the same effect. She felt God's presence—most of the time, anyway. She knew that her soul lay in the Almighty's keeping. And yet it had taken the human touch to bring God's love into focus.

When she first thought about this, she felt a little guilty. Was her faith so weak that she needed a flesh-and-blood person to confirm the Lord's love to her?

But what had Bailey said? *Every time I look into the trusting face of a little black child . . . I confront the face of God. I see God's tears . . . feel God's touch . . . hear God weeping.*

And then she remembered: Jesus. The ultimate revelation of the nature of God didn't come down from on high in a booming voice or a declaration from angels, but in a human body. Flesh and bone, arms and legs, a face, a heart, a mind. A person who could reach out to others, smile, embrace, laugh, cry. And love.

She had encountered it before, this presence of Christ in human form. She just hadn't had the words for it. Her father's touch held the gentleness of God. Amethyst's faithfulness reflected the Lord's own commitment to her. Harper's scarred face revealed the Lord's wound-edness and compassion. And Bailey? Well, Bailey's declaration of love for her brought it all into startling clarity—love that could look beyond age or appearance or a hundred other barriers and see into the heart.

Over the years she had discovered bits and pieces of her soul reflected in the eyes of those who loved her. Some of the people in her life challenged her mind and caused her to think. Some aroused her heart with laughter or tears. Others stretched her spirit and enabled her relationship with God to deepen and grow.

Bailey touched everything. For the first time in her life, she felt entire and whole, even though she had never been aware of incompleteness before. He was her soul's connection.

"Hmmm. A beautiful, intelligent, godly woman who also cooks." A resonant chuckle came from behind her. "How lucky can one man get?"

Silvie felt his arms go around her, and she elbowed him in the ribs. "Luck has nothing to do with it."

"How right you are." He nuzzled the back of her neck. "You are a gift, my darling. Straight from the heart of God."

She craned her neck and grinned at him. "You make me burn my biscuits, and we'll have to reconsider this relationship."

Bailey gave her a quick kiss on the cheek and released her. "Ooh, that's a threat I'll take seriously. Besides, I don't know how I'd start my day without a biscuit from my true love's hand." He poured himself a cup of coffee and leaned against the counter. "How's life in the big house this morning?"

"I'm doing just fine. I'm not so sure about Amethyst."

The grin faded from Bailey's face, and he frowned. "How long has she been this way? Three weeks?"

"Ever since the Night of the Klan Babies." Silvie gazed at him. The bruises had faded, and only a faint, shiny scar remained from the cut on his forehead. It was Amethyst who hadn't healed.

"And she hasn't talked to you about it?"

"Not a word. I've always respected her privacy, Bailey, always figured that when she was ready to talk, she'd come to me. But I've never seen her so downhearted, and I'm worried about her."

Bailey nodded. "I don't know her as well as you do, but I suspect there's something she's not saying. Do you think she might be fearful of another attack?"

"I suppose that might be part of it. Things have been so quiet. I don't want to go borrowing trouble, but I keep thinking they're out there, waiting. It makes my skin crawl."

"Maybe that's all it is with Amethyst, too."

"No. There's something else. Something she's not saying. She tries to hide it, but she's acting almost the way she did when Harper died. Like she's grieving."

"Perhaps you should talk to her."

"Maybe I ought to." Silvie took the biscuits out of the oven and slid them onto a plate. "Hand me that bowl of eggs, will you?"

Bailey passed the eggs and watched as she put them in the skillet to scramble. He picked up a slice of bacon from the platter. "You're reluctant to get into this conversation with Amethyst. Why?"

Silvie kept her eyes fixed on the eggs as she stirred them. "I don't know."

"You do know. Tell me."

"All right." She let out a sigh. "I feel a little . . . well, guilty. Guilty for being so full of joy when she's so miserable."

Bailey gave a low chuckle and came to put his hands on her shoulders. "Amethyst loves you, Silvie. No matter how she's feeling, she won't begrudge us the happiness we've found."

"You're right, of course." Silvie nodded and leaned back against him. The warmth from his chest infused her with strength and determination. "I'll talk to her. Right after breakfast."

Amethyst lay on the bed and listened as the low murmur of voices reached her from the dining room. She should be out there helping Silvie serve breakfast and clean up the dishes. But she couldn't face them. Any of them.

Especially Bailey, with his probing eyes and questioning glances. Especially Silvie, who for her sake was trying hard not to look so happy even though she was obviously in love. *The girl should be enjoying this*, Amethyst reprimanded herself. *Not tiptoeing around on eggshells trying to keep me from feeling worse.*

Amethyst remembered, as vividly as if it were yesterday, how she felt when Harper first declared his love for her—euphoric, as if the pieces of the world had finally fallen into place and she knew at last where she belonged. She couldn't have hidden it if she tried. But she didn't have to try. Silvie had been a model of support, encouraging her to relish every insane moment of this new love, laughing with her, listening dutifully to every recitation of how wonderful Harper was.

And Amethyst wanted to do that for Silvie. She felt no envy over her friend's relationship with Bailey—on the contrary, she approved heartily. But right now it was hard for Amethyst to rejoice over Silvie's blessing. Not because she was jealous of it, but because she had something else weighing on her soul.

Conrad.

Ever since the night of the attack, Amethyst had not been able to rid her mind of the image of her own son in the cab of that pickup truck, aiding and abetting those hooligans who had beaten Bailey and burned a cross on her front lawn. Her failure as a mother haunted her, gnawed at her. Where had she gone wrong?

For three solid weeks she had wept and prayed, begging God for an answer. She had confessed every sin she could think of, and a few she wasn't sure she had ever committed. She had waited and listened, searched the depths of her soul, berated herself for real and imagined offenses. And still, she could find no peace.

It had to be her fault, somehow. Wasn't a parent to blame when a child went wrong?

When Conrad had moved out, taking the other college boys with him, Amethyst had told Bailey that he was an adult and had to answer to God for his decisions. She had meant it at the time, but this was different. This wasn't just some adolescent prank, some foolish choice her boy had made under the influence of a group of his peers. This went to the very heart and soul of who he was as a person, what kind of man he was becoming.

She didn't want to admit that her only son was turning into a racist, and yet the reality of what she had seen ate away at her like a cancer. Grief consumed her. Every time she thought her tears were spent, a fresh wave of remorse rolled over her like the incoming tide. And through it all, the Lord seemed strangely silent.

———•·•·•———

She awoke to a faint knocking on the door. The morning sun had shifted, and the house was silent.

"Amethyst?" Silvie's voice called through the door. "Are you awake?"

Amethyst sat up, her hands feeling for stray wisps of hair. She pushed the comforter into some semblance of order and patted at the sagging skin under her eyes. "Come on in, Silvie."

"Lord help us, hon, you look like death warmed over."

"Well, thanks for the compliment." She tried to keep her voice light, to maintain a semblance of normalcy, but she failed miserably.

Silvie plopped down on the bed and peered into her face. "We need to talk."

"I don't feel like talking." Amethyst averted her eyes. "Don't get too close. I—I think I might have some kind of influenza."

"You're a bad liar, Amethyst. Always have been." Silvie raised one eyebrow. "Not enough practice, I'd expect."

"All right," Amethyst conceded, "so I'm not sick. Is it a crime to want a little time to myself?"

"I don't know; I'll have to ask Bailey. He's the lawyer."

In spite of herself, Amethyst smiled. "You two getting along all right?"

"Smooth as butter." Silvie returned the smile. "He's—well, he's very nice."

"Nice?"

Silvie grinned sheepishly. "Okay, he's wonderful. Magnificent. The most incredible person I've ever met. Not to mention devastatingly handsome."

"That's better." Amethyst shifted on the bed and pulled her dressing gown around her.

"But I didn't come in here to talk about Bailey."

"I know you didn't. You want to know why I've been cloistering myself away for the past three weeks."

"That would be a start."

Amethyst felt tears rising in her throat, and she choked them back. "I can't talk about it, Silvie. Not to you. Not to anyone."

"We've always talked about everything."

"I know. But I just—" She couldn't go on; the tears came in a rush, and she began to weep.

Silvie put her arms around Amethyst and held on tight until the wracking sobs subsided. It was so good to be embraced, to feel Silvie's hand stroking her hair, to hear her hushed voice whispering, "It's all right, hon. Let it out. I'm here."

"I've done everything—" Amethyst's voice came out strangled and weak, but she pressed on. "I've tried to be obedient, to be faithful. I've prayed and confessed and tried to listen, but nothing—" She heaved in a deep breath. "I just don't understand how God could let this happen."

Silvie waited until Amethyst had regained control, then stroked a gentle hand across her forehead. "Can you talk about it now?"

Amethyst gulped down a painful lump in her throat and nodded. "I think so. I guess I need to."

"All right. Let's start at the beginning."

Amethyst stared past Silvie's shoulder and watched as the clock on the mantel ticked away a full minute. Where was the beginning? How could she make Silvie understand when she herself didn't?

"Is this about the attack on Bailey?" Silvie prodded.

"Yes and no." Amethyst bit her lip. "It's about that night—something I haven't told you, or anyone."

"Go on."

In fits and starts, Amethyst got the story out—how she had seen Conrad in the cab of the pickup; how angry she felt that her own father had planted seeds of ungodliness in her son's heart. How she had been trying, for the past three weeks, to get an answer from God, to find some peace, to figure out what she had done wrong.

"I can't understand," she concluded, "why God would let something like this happen. I did everything I knew to raise my son as a faithful, God-fearing boy. But apparently I failed, and he's turned out more like Abe than like Harper . . . or me. That's why I couldn't tell you—I couldn't face your reaction to the truth. My son—with the Klan! Oh, Silvie, I am so sorry!"

Fresh tears came, and Amethyst began to sob again. Once more Silvie held her and waited out the storm, but this time her embrace was not quite so tender. At last Amethyst lifted her head. "What am I going to do, Silvie?"

Silvie regarded her with a measured gaze. "What do you want from me, Amethyst?"

"I don't know. Nobody can help, I realize. I just—"

"No, that's not what I meant," Silvie interrupted. "It's a straightforward question. What do you want? Do you want me to sympathize, or do you want me to be honest with you so we can get to the bottom of this?"

"I want to know what you really think. I want honesty, of course."

Silvie straightened up and gave Amethyst a knowing look. "All right. The first thing we need to decide is who's to blame."

Amethyst blinked. "Excuse me?"

"Well, so far you've blamed yourself, your father, and God. We need to sort out who's really responsible for Conrad's actions."

Amethyst considered Silvie's words. She was angry with God—both for allowing this to happen and for remaining silent when she needed an answer so desperately. She was furious at her dead father for the influence he exerted over her son. And she raged at herself for not being the kind of mother who could have prevented such a turn of events.

"I guess I'm the only one to blame," she whispered after a while. She felt sick and miserable and ashamed, and although she was willing to take responsibility for her faults, she still couldn't understand where she had gone wrong. Silvie had always been candid and logical and wise; maybe she could help figure this out.

"What about Abe?" Silvie prompted.

"My father certainly had a negative effect upon Conrad," she mused. "Con adored him, and he absorbed a great deal from his grandfather before I realized what was happening. But Abe died when Conrad was just a boy. I should have been able to do something to alter that influence."

"And what about God?"

"Do I blame God, you mean, for the way Conrad turned out?"

Silvie nodded and pressed her lips together. "Couldn't God, who is supposed to be Father to the fatherless, have intervened? Couldn't God have counteracted Abe's influence in Con's life?"

"I suppose so, but—"

"But you blame yourself. You're angry with God, and you're angry with your dead father. But still you're the one who is responsible for Conrad's choices." Silvie peered at her, waiting for an answer.

Amethyst's heart felt like a lead weight in her chest. "I guess I am."

Silvie sat back on the bed. "I'm impressed."

"Impressed at what?"

"Impressed that you have so much power over other people's lives. I never knew."

Just briefly, Amethyst felt like a bug in a jar, being scrutinized and inspected. She didn't like the feeling one bit, but she suspected that Silvie was probing toward an important revelation. "And your point is?"

"This is not about you, Amethyst. It's not about how good a mother you were, or what kind of mistakes you think you've made. It's about Conrad."

"I know, Silvie. But I'm his mother, and—"

"Tell me about *your* mother."

Amethyst frowned. "You know all about my mother. She was a weak, self-centered person who didn't have an ounce of backbone."

"And your father?"

"He was a drunkard and a gambler who abandoned his family and ruined his life."

"And you turned out to be a compassionate, deeply spiritual woman who is committed to serving God and helping others," Silvie whispered. "How do you suppose that happened?"

Amethyst paused. She was beginning to understand. "Because I chose a different way. Grandma Pearl's journals helped me find my way to faith. Grandpa Silas's life became a model for the kind of person I wanted to be."

"Exactly. You *chose*. And so did Conrad." A soft light came into Silvie's eyes, and she smiled faintly. "We can't change other people, Amethyst. We can't even change ourselves. Only God can bring about the change and growth that need to happen in our lives."

A spark of anger flared up in Amethyst's heart. "Then God could have changed Conrad."

Silvie shook her head. "You know better. Even God doesn't force change upon people. We have to invite it. We have to want it." She shrugged. "Sometimes we're not aware that we want it. You weren't, when you first began reading Pearl's journals. But God knows our hearts and responds accordingly."

"You're saying I don't bear any responsibility for what Conrad has become?"

"I'm saying neither of us can know what Conrad *will* become. You were a good mother, Amethyst, a loving mother, a model of integrity and honesty. But you have to let go. Your son is nearly a man now. He makes his own choices, and he will have to live with them. You can't change him, can't force him to become the person you have in mind for him to be. All you can do now is pray that someday, in his own way, he will invite God to work in his life."

"You're not angry that Conrad was involved in the cross-burning?"

"Of course I'm angry, and for the same reasons you are. But I don't blame you. You're his mother, hon, not his conscience."

For the first time in three weeks, Amethyst felt the burden of sorrow lift from her shoulders. She looked deep into Silvie's eyes and saw something else there—the gaze of a loving God, who wept with her when she cried.

She drew Silvie into a firm embrace. "How did you get so wise?" she murmured.

Silvie leaned back and grinned. "Comes with the territory," she answered. "After all, I've lived with you for years."

41
Dixon Lee

———◆◆◆———

"Amethyst, there's someone here to see you."

Amethyst looked up from the cutting board. Her fingers reeked of onion, and her hair fell in ragged wisps around her face. She pushed at a stray lock with the back of her hand. "Silvie, I'm not exactly dressed for receiving. Look at me—blue jeans and one of Harper's old shirts. Who is it?"

"The new preacher at the Presbyterian Church."

"Dixon Lee Godwin?" She frowned and waved the knife in Silvie's direction. "What's he want with me?"

"White folks don't often tell me their business," Silvie quipped. "Besides, you are a member of his congregation."

"He's only been in town a month. I'd barely recognize him on the street."

Silvie shrugged. "Maybe he's eager to get to know his flock."

"Can you tell him this is not a good time? I'll give him a call and invite him to tea." She went back to dicing the onions.

"He seemed very insistent. Agitated, I'd say."

"Oh, all right." Amethyst flung the knife down and pulled the apron over her head. "But somebody needs to tell this fellow that it's impolite to drop in unannounced." She looked down at her jeans and stained shirt and grimaced. "He'll just have to take me as I am."

Silvie grinned and picked up the knife. "Don't we all?"

Amethyst went into the parlor to find the Reverend Dixon Lee Godwin perched uncomfortably on the brocade settee. She had only seen him in the pulpit, where he cut an imposing figure. Up close, she thought he looked a little like Abraham Lincoln—very tall, with gangly legs and enormous hands. He had that same angular jaw and jutting brow, but his face was clean-shaven and his hair graying at the temples. *A fine figure of a man,* she thought. *Born to be a preacher.*

"Reverend Godwin," she said as she approached him with her hand outstretched. "Please forgive my appearance. I wasn't expecting company."

He stood, towering over her, and gave a formal little nod. "I apologize for barging in on you like this. I know you must be busy—"

Amethyst shook her head. "Nonsense. When you run a boarding-house, there's always work to do. You finish breakfast and start dinner." She caught a strong whiff of her hands and wrinkled her nose. "It's just your misfortune to arrive when I was slicing onions."

Amethyst sat down and motioned for him to resume his seat. "To what do I owe the honor of this visit, Reverend Godwin?"

He blushed a little and ducked his head. "Please, call me Dix. I'm not much accustomed to the *Reverend* label yet; I just completed seminary, you see. This is my first parish. Until four years ago, I was a salesman in Sioux City, Iowa." He lifted his shoulders in a gesture of surrender. "I received the call late in life, I suppose."

Amethyst smiled. She liked this affable man. He was humble and self-effacing, not at all caught up in the pretensions of being "a man of God."

"Well, I have no doubt that the Lord did call you to ministry. I've heard you preach."

He smiled, and a deep dimple creased his left cheek. "Thank you. Coming from you, that's a real compliment."

"Coming from me?" She cocked her head and looked at him quizzically.

"I didn't mean it quite in that way," he hedged. "It's just that you have a reputation for being a person of . . . ah, uncompromising faith."

"Meaning I'm bullheaded and stubborn."

He threw back his head and laughed. "Apparently you also live up to the other part of your reputation. Being unflinchingly candid."

Amethyst pressed her lips together. "Hmmm. Yes, that, too."

Godwin leaned forward and laced his long fingers together. "Actually, that's why I've come to see you."

"Because I'm bullheaded? Or because I'm honest?"

"Both, really. I'd like to talk to you about your, ah, perspectives. On the Negroes."

Amethyst sat for a moment and watched him. Clearly he was uncomfortable, yet she did not discern in his expression any evidence of disapproval. "Just what, precisely, do you mean, my 'perspectives on the Negroes'?"

He cleared his throat. "Miss Amethyst—"

"Just Amethyst will do."

"All right. Amethyst. It's well known around town that you have several colored men, lawyers from the NAACP, boarding here at Noble House."

Amethyst felt her temper begin to simmer, but she said nothing.

"And, well, I am your pastor," he stammered. "Part of my calling is to be concerned about the safety and well-being of my parishioners."

Again she waited. Let him squirm.

"You are, after all, a single woman, with no one to look after you," he went on lamely after a moment. "As leader of the church, I have a responsibility to—"

"*Reverend* Godwin," she interrupted, glaring at him, "forgive me for being *unflinchingly candid*, but I have been looking after myself for a number of years now. I am perfectly safe in my own home, and if you're here to tell me I should evict my boarders, you're wasting your breath. And your time." She stood up. "If there's nothing more—"

Godwin remained fixed to his seat. "Please, sit down," he said in a quiet voice. "I didn't come to pick a fight."

"Then why did you come?" Amethyst remained standing and placed both hands on her hips.

"I came to talk to you about the Negro situation."

"The Negroes are not a 'situation,' Reverend Godwin. They are *people*."

"I couldn't agree with you more. Forgive me; I misspoke. I'm—" He ran a finger around his collar. "I'm a bit nervous."

Amethyst watched him for a minute, then took her seat. She felt a little sorry for him, but she couldn't let pity get in the way of standing her ground. "I'm listening."

"As I said, this is my first pastorate. Already I have had a number of people coming to me, concerned about the church's response to what is happening in this town. People are frightened, Amethyst. All they see is that a group of outsiders—these NAACP lawyers—have come to Cambridge to stir up trouble. And trouble is being stirred up. Witness the— ah, incident—that occurred here several weeks back."

She bit her tongue to curb the caustic response that leaped into her mind. *Incident.* Bailey savagely beaten. A cross burned in her front yard. *Incident, my foot.* And who, she wondered, were the *troublemakers* in that little scenario?

"I am quite familiar with the *incident*, as you call it," she answered, consciously governing her tone of voice. "Those NAACP lawyers are here for one reason and one reason only—to do what they can to improve the lot of Negroes in this county. If we didn't have a problem, Reverend Godwin, they wouldn't be here. And as long as hooligans in sheets are running around the countryside terrorizing innocent people, Mr. Blue and his colleagues are welcome in my house."

Godwin gave her a despairing look. "I understand," he said plaintively. "Things *do* need to change. Black people are being oppressed and terror- ized—sometimes even killed. I abhor what's going on. As a Christian, I cannot in good conscience stand by and let it happen without offering some response. But isn't there some other way? Some way to make changes more gradually, without inciting people to violence?"

Amethyst thought about this for a moment or two. Then she looked Godwin straight in the eye and said, "You really want to know, don't you? You're really struggling with what the Christian's response should be."

He nodded. "Yes, I am."

"Jesus said, 'Blessed are the peacemakers,'" Amethyst mused softly. "And yet Jesus also stood up to the Pharisees and confronted them with their pride and arrogance. It's the dilemma of all who would follow

Christ, I suppose—when to make peace, and when to take an unpopular stand and refuse to budge. Tell me this, Reverend Godwin—how long are you willing to sit back and wait for change to occur?"

He frowned at her and lifted his shoulders in a shrug.

"Another ten years? Twenty? Fifty? A hundred?"

"I'm not sure what you mean."

"Slavery ended more than eighty years ago. In those eighty years, living conditions for many Negroes have become worse, not better. Black people get inferior jobs at less pay and are treated as second class citizens. Many fear for their safety, even their lives, because they've seen their neighbors beaten and lynched, their houses and churches burned to the ground, if they dare to stand up for their own dignity. How long do they wait? Until the Ku Klux Klan decides, out of the goodness of its heart, to stop hating and embrace their black brothers and sisters? Until the Jim Crow laws vanish from the books by some miraculous act of God?"

She shook her head. "If you wait for that, Reverend Godwin, you'll be waiting forever. People don't lay down their prejudices because it's the right thing to do. They won't stop killing and beating and oppressing and insulting until the law isn't on their side any longer. This isn't the Negroes' struggle, Reverend. It's a struggle that concerns all of us."

As Amethyst spoke, she began to realize that the words she was saying weren't just for his benefit, but for hers as well. She had believed them for a long time, but speaking them aloud confirmed their truth in her, heart and mind and soul. With the words came a determination of conviction, a power she had not known before.

"Bailey Blue says there is strength in numbers," she finished quietly. "But there's also strength in diversity. I believe the Lord has called us to reconciliation—not just reconciliation with God, but with one another as well. God commands us to gather the outcasts and welcome them in. And that means those of us who are not among the outcasts—us white folks, who have privilege and power and prestige—must lay down our power, must willingly share it with those who have none. No one is free while anyone is in chains."

When she finished, Godwin was leaning forward in his seat, intent upon every word. "Do you want to preach this Sunday?" he asked with a grin. "My pulpit is open to you anytime."

Amethyst chuckled. "I believe I'll leave the preaching to the professionals."

"Too bad." He got up and extended a hand to her. "Thank you. You've given me a great deal to think about. And now I'll let you get back to your work."

"You're welcome, Reverend."

Amethyst walked with him to the door, and he stood on the porch, obviously reluctant to leave. Finally he straightened his jacket and turned to her. "I have a request of you."

"Certainly."

"Pray for me," he said earnestly.

"I will," she promised. "Anything in particular?"

He nodded. "Pray for direction. Pray for wisdom. We have a lot of challenges ahead of us."

Amethyst smiled and waved as he walked down the sidewalk toward his car.

We, he had said.

"Lord," she whispered as she shut the door behind him, "give Dixon Lee Godwin what he needs most." She rolled her eyes heavenward and grinned. "Wisdom. Direction. And a kick in the pants every now and then."

"Amethyst, come look!"

"I'm busy, Bailey." Amethyst was sitting on the piano bench, trying to replace the bulb in the hideous piano light. She hated the lamp—a miniature bronze statue of Michelangelo's *David*, his upraised hand holding a fringe-trimmed, lurid pink shade. It had once been a gas lamp, but had been electrified along with everything else in the house. Every time she looked at it, she felt the overwhelming desire to put a tiny little diaper on the shepherd-king's midsection. But the lamp had belonged to Grandma Pearl, and she couldn't bear to part with it. Sometimes taste had to take a backseat to sentimentality.

She peered into the socket. "This bulb is broken off—Bailey, would you mind going to the kitchen and getting me a potato?"

Bailey stared at her. "A potato? But we just had dinner."

"Not to *eat*." Amethyst let out a long-suffering sigh. Men could be so dense sometimes, and evidently a law degree rendered a man totally useless when it came to simple household tasks. "You slice the potato, see, and press it down over the broken bulb. Then you can unscrew it without cutting yourself—"

"Never mind that. Come look."

Amethyst got up and went over to the window. "All right, Bailey, I'm here. What am I looking at?"

She peered through the ancient glass and rubbed at her eyes. "These old windows distort everything. Is that someone out in the yard?"

It was almost dusk, but beyond the big magnolia tree she could see a figure bent over a rake, scratching at the ground. "What on earth?"

She headed for the door with Bailey right behind her. In her haste, she slammed the screen door against the side of the house, and the figure in the yard jumped a foot and a half off the ground

"Miss Amethyst!" His voice squeaked, as if he had just hit puberty and was still a part-time soprano.

"Bogey?" she called. "Clarence Bogart, is that you?"

"Yes'm." He moved a couple of steps forward, out of the shadow of the magnolia. "I—I'm sorry to disturb you. I thought I could just—"

"What are you doing?"

He held the rake at arm's length and hung his head. She looked past his shoulder to where a large blackened circle stood as witness to the Night of the Klan Babies. The burned grass was gone, the hole filled in where the cross had been planted. Next to the magnolia tree sat a small bag of grass seed.

—•◦•—

"So you thought you'd just sneak over here and repair my lawn without anyone knowing it?"

Bogey flushed a bright red and lifted his shoulders until they met his earlobes. "Yes'm. It was kinda stupid, I guess."

"It was very thoughtful," Amethyst corrected. "But why?"

Amethyst knew why, but Clarence Bogart didn't know she knew. He had no idea she had seen him in the cab of the truck next to Conrad. Clearly he had come as an act of repentance, an attempt to clear his conscience, and she needed to give him the chance to unburden himself.

"It—it wasn't thoughtful," he objected. "It was—" He stopped suddenly, and tears filled his eyes.

"Go on," Amethyst prompted gently.

"I was here, Miss Amethyst—the night the boys—" He broke down and began to sob.

"The night Dooley and his friends attacked Bailey and burned the cross?"

Bogey nodded miserably. "I—I'm so sorry, Miss Amethyst. I didn't mean to—I mean, I didn't want to. They made me come." He looked up at her with a pleading expression.

"Did they?"

He shook his head. "No ma'am. I coulda said no. It was Dooley's idea, to put a scare into you, I guess. I didn't know they were gonna beat anybody up."

"I believe that," Amethyst said.

"Anyway," he went on, "it just kinda happened. Everybody was getting rowdy, and Dooley, he was pretty out of control. Kept yelling about how the niggers were trying to take over—beg your pardon, Mr. Blue."

Bailey waved a hand. "Forget it."

"And so when everybody lit out and piled in the truck, I went along for the ride. Nobody dragged me along, I guess. I coulda refused, but—"

"But they would never have let you hear the end of it," Bailey supplied.

"No—ah, I mean, no, sir." He eyed Bailey cautiously. "Still, I wished I'd never got in that pickup. If I had it to do over again, I'd slit their tires."

"They'd have found another truck," Bailey commented. "Bigotry never lacks for transportation."

Clarence took a deep, shuddering breath. "I'm really sorry, Miss Amethyst. And you, too, Mr. Blue, for what they did to you. I didn't hold the bat, but I'm just as guilty." With fear in his eyes, he held out a shaking hand. "I hope you can forgive me. I swear I'll never do anything like that again as long as I live."

Bailey shook his hand and clapped him on the shoulder. "I accept your apology, son. Do you understand why racism like that is wrong?"

As Bailey carried on a conversation with Clarence Bogart, Amethyst watched the two of them. Clarence visibly relaxed, and even laughed a time or two at Bailey's easy humor. She had to credit the poor boy for his apology. It took a lot of courage for him to show his face again and admit outright what he had done.

She only wished it were Conrad.

Would it ever be her son, sitting in this parlor, having this kind of conversation? She could only hope and pray.

An hour and a half later, after a glass of milk and two pieces of Silvie's mixed-berry pie, Clarence stood to go. He put his bony arms around Amethyst's neck and hugged her until she could barely breathe. "Thank you," he said. "I can't tell you how much better I feel."

"I do too, Clarence. You come back anytime, all right?"

"I'd like that." He ducked his head sheepishly. "I've missed you, Miss Amethyst."

"I've missed you, too, Clarence."

"Oh." His eyes darkened. "There's one more thing I need to tell you. Con was there, too."

"I know, Clarence."

"You do?"

"I saw both of you in the truck that night."

"You knew? And you still let me in your house?"

Amethyst nodded. "Everybody deserves a second chance, Clarence."

He bit his lip. "Well, Con, he's really sorry, too. He kinda got swept along with it the same way I did. We've talked about it. He didn't want to come, either, but he has a hard time standing up to Dooley."

"And a hard time facing his mother, apparently."

"Yes'm. I guess so. He didn't know I was coming over here, though. I didn't tell anybody."

"Well, I'm glad to know he regrets what he did. I just wish he'd tell me."

Bogey's face took on a hopeful expression. "Maybe I could talk to him—"

"No," Amethyst interrupted. "I'd rather you didn't. If he's going to come, he needs to come on his own."

"I guess I understand that. I just wanted you to know he's sorry."

Amethyst felt a lump rise up in her throat, and she turned her head. "Good night, Clarence."

"Good night. Oh, and Miss Amethyst?"

"Yes?"

"You'll need to keep that grass seed watered for a few days."

Amethyst nodded. The way she felt at the moment, she could water it with her tears.

42
Trial by Fire

July 1946

Bailey stood next to the Confederate soldier in the courthouse square and looked out over the group assembled on the grass. It wasn't a bad turnout, given the fact that this was the first public civil rights rally ever held in Cambridge, Mississippi.

He estimated about two hundred, not counting the state police who lined the perimeter of the square and the white onlookers who stood on the sidewalks behind them. Across the pillars of the courthouse stretched a banner that read "FREEDOM AND JUSTICE FOR ALL." A small platform had been erected in front of the steps, and several folding chairs awaited the arrival of the dignitaries—four black pastors from local churches, each of whom would speak for a few minutes, urging their congregations to commit themselves to the cause.

"You're the man in charge?"

Bailey turned to see a large man in a shiny black suit and white shirt, accompanied by a teenage boy. "Yes, sir, I suppose I am."

The man pumped his hand and smiled broadly. "Well, I just want to congratulate you and say Godspeed. This is good work you're doing here."

Bailey looked from the man to the youth. The lad had a keen, intelligent air about him. His dark eyes darted everywhere, taking it all in.

"My boy and I have come a long way for this," the man went on. "I'm the pastor of a church in Atlanta."

"Atlanta?" Bailey grinned. "You have come a long way."

"This is my son, M. L.," the man went on. "He's just finishing up his second year at Morehouse College. He's going to be a preacher, like his daddy and his granddaddy."

Bailey focused on the lad. "Second year in college? How old are you, son?"

"Seventeen, sir." The boy spoke quietly, confidently.

"Yessir, he's a smart one, he is. Skipped two grades in school. We're real proud of him."

"As you should be." Bailey caught a glimpse of Silvie and Amethyst waving in his direction. "You'll have to excuse me, I'm afraid. We're about to start."

"You go right on, son. And God bless." The preacher moved into the crowd, but the boy laid a hand on Bailey's arm.

"This is my calling," he said. His voice was firm, determined.

Bailey looked into the young man's eyes and saw a depth of wisdom and compassion he had rarely seen in people twice the boy's age.

"It's my dream," he went on. "Equality for all God's people."

"Then you keep right on dreaming, M. L." Bailey gripped the boy's hand. "The cause of freedom needs people like you."

He had a sudden, unaccountable urge to throw his arms around the lad and hug him. But before he had a chance, the young man turned to follow his father and disappeared into the throng.

———◦•◦———

There weren't many white faces in the crowd, and they tended to cluster together. From the platform Bailey could pick out Amethyst, standing next to Silvie, and just behind them, Dixon Lee Godwin, the new Presbyterian minister. Clarence Bogart looked intensely uncomfortable, sticking close to Amethyst like a little lost boy. But at least he was here, and Bailey couldn't have been more pleased.

Absalom Smith, the minister from the African Methodist Episcopal Church, gave a long-winded invocation, and shortly after the first speaker began his impassioned plea, more flashes of white caught Bailey's attention.

White robes. White hoods.

A knot twisted in Bailey's gut, and he sent up a silent supplication for peace. So far the Klansmen hadn't done anything—they just stood there, a menacing presence on the outskirts of the crowd.

Then one of them raised a fist. "Niggers, go home!" he yelled at the top of his lungs. "This is our town, and we aim to keep it!"

"Go back to Africa, where you belong!" another screamed.

The speaker, a huge man with jet-black skin and a barrel chest, pointed a meaty finger in the direction of the Klansmen. "Who brought us here?" he challenged. "Who made us slaves?" He turned his attention to the crowd. "The time has come for the slaves to be set free!"

The audience cheered halfheartedly, but clearly most of them were intimidated by the appearance of the Klan. Women clutched their children closer. A few began to edge away from the gathering.

"We'll set you free, boy!" the Klansman yelled. "Free at the end of a rope!"

"Just a minute!" a commanding female voice rang out.

Bailey turned his head, and his heart sank. With one hand on Goodwin's shoulders for support, Amethyst had climbed onto the base of the Confederate statue and was waving her free arm for attention. *No, he entreated silently. Amethyst, no!*

"Keep out of this, Miss Amethyst," the Klansman shouted. "This ain't your fight."

"It *is* my fight," she retorted. "It's the fight of every decent, peace-loving person in this country." She pointed at him. "You, Will Tarbush! What do you stand to lose if Negroes are given equal rights under the law? Nothing except the opportunity to put your foot on some other man's neck. That's what's at stake here—not another person's equality, but your sense of superiority. And the good Lord knows, Will, if that happens, you won't be superior to *anybody!*"

A titter of nervous laughter ran through the assembly. Tarbush took a step forward. "You shut up, Amethyst! We all know what you are, you nigger-loving—"

"You sit in church behind me every Sunday," she went on, "but what good has it done you? You thrive on hate, and you've taught your son

Billy to be just like you. Look at yourself, Will Tarbush. You think you're a big man, a powerful man, because you have the power to prey on the helpless. But you're mean and ignorant and miserable. I pity you."

Will Tarbush jerked off his hood and glared at Amethyst. Even from this distance, Bailey could see the hatred in his eyes. "This ain't over yet."

Bailey watched as the state police closed ranks around the Klansmen, and he breathed a sigh of relief. The local authorities had promised him that if he wouldn't call in the federal troops, they would see to it that there were no incidents of violence, and apparently they intended to keep their word.

The Klan gradually dispersed, shouting obscenities as they left, and the rally resumed. But much of the enthusiasm had drained from the crowd, and a pall of apprehension overshadowed all of them for the remainder of the day.

Bailey suspected that Will Tarbush, in his own perverse way, had spoken the truth.

This wasn't over yet.

Amethyst stood staring at the spectacle. She was seeing it with her own eyes, but she couldn't believe it.

An enormous red truck blocked the entrance to Jefferson Davis Avenue. Water gushed down the driveway and ran in rivulets along the street. Men in rubber jackets and helmets milled around, their big boots crushing through the flower beds. Thick hoses snaked across the lawn, mauling the shrubbery.

Noble House was on fire.

Or at least it had been. By the time Amethyst, Bailey, and Silvie arrived, most of the damage had been done. The outer walls, though charred, still stood, and the left side, where the old log cabin had been built, seemed untouched. The conflagration had been contained before the flames reached the upper level, but the right side of the house on the first floor looked to be gutted. The front parlor had been reduced to a mass of rubble. There was smoke and water damage everywhere.

Amethyst blinked. Her eyes were gritty, but tears wouldn't come. "Who would do such a thing?"

"I think you know who," Bailey muttered.

He was right, of course. Most of the townspeople had been in the courthouse square all afternoon—a few of them attending the rally, the others watching. Except for the Klansmen, who after Amethyst's tongue-lashing had slunk away like the cowards they were.

A light touch on Amethyst's shoulder arrested her attention, and she turned to see Dixon Lee Godwin standing beside her.

"Don't say it," she warned.

"Don't say what?"

"Don't say, 'I warned you.' Please."

He gazed at her with an expression of compassion and pain. "After today—being at the rally, and now this—there's only one thing I can say."

Amethyst closed her eyes and waited. "Then go ahead, if you have to."

He cleared his throat. "I think—I think you're the most courageous person I've ever met, Amethyst. I want to help. And I want to be your friend."

"Courageous?" She let out a shuddering sigh and shook her head. "Some people would call it pure obstinacy. And maybe they're right, if this is what it gets me."

The fire chief walked by, his muddy boots making squishing sounds on the soaked ground. When he saw Amethyst, he stopped and removed his hat. "I'm sorry about this, Miss Amethyst," he said as he wiped a sooty hand across his face. "We done our best."

She forced a smile. "You saved the house, Jake. I have you and your crew to thank for that."

"Yes'm." He pushed a lock of wet hair out of his eyes. "But Miss Amethyst, if I was you, I'd think twice before taking on the Klan again."

When he was gone, Dixon Lee took her hand and looked into her face. "And if you were to think twice, what would you do?"

"I suppose I'd do it again," she said. "Somebody has to stand up to them."

"It's a high price to pay for your principles."

"Other people have paid a greater price," she mused. "People have died, Dix. And more lives are likely to be lost before this is all over. Still, I believe it's a battle that needs to be fought."

"But is it a battle we can *win*?" he asked, his eyes searching hers. "It's a godly cause, and an important one, but you know how deep the prejudices run. Is it possible to change those attitudes, or even to stop the violence?"

She regarded him with a measured gaze. It was a legitimate question, one she had asked herself time and again. And at this moment, standing before the smoking ruins of Noble House, she wasn't sure she had an answer.

"I'm not doing it because it's *possible*," she whispered. "I'm doing it because it's *right*."

43

Grace Amid the Ruins

———◆◆◆◆———

I don't even know where to start." Amethyst shook her head and kicked the toe of her shoe at the charred remains of the parlor rug. It wasn't as bad as it might have been. Her bedroom furnishings reeked of smoke and were covered with a sticky residue of damp soot, but at least they were still intact. Most of the serious damage had been confined to the front parlor. The only piece of furniture left standing was the old piano. Its finish had been bubbled by the searing heat, and it would have to be completely restored, inside and out, but it was salvageable.

Jake, the fire chief, had showed her the central flash point where the fire had started—a huge oval of black in the center of the parlor. "Gasoline, or maybe kerosene," he said. "Pour it on the rug, strike a match, and—*poof!*"

There was no doubt who was responsible. Amethyst's bedroom drawers had been rifled, and on the mirror over the bureau, a message had been scrawled in lipstick and baked hard by the heat: *Niger Lovver. KKK.*

Evidently, bigots couldn't spell.

Bailey and the others had been working since sunup, hauling debris out to the yard, raking through the rubble. Silvie looked like a charwoman, and Dixon Lee Godwin could have been black himself, for all the smoke and grime that covered his face. They were good people, these friends of hers. People who would stand with her no matter what.

Amethyst tied a bandanna around her hair and slipped on a pair of gloves. She might as well get to it. Probably the best place for her to begin was sorting through her personal things in the bedroom. Nobody else could do it. But first she was determined to remove that message of hate from the mirror.

She went out on the porch and waved Bailey down. "Does anyone have a toolbox?"

"Around back, I think," Bailey answered. "What do you need?"

"A scraper of some kind. To get the lipstick off the mirror."

Bailey went to track down a putty knife while Amethyst waited on the porch. But before he could get back with the toolbox, a caravan of cars and pickup trucks pulled up to the curb. People kept piling out, two dozen or more of them. Men in dungarees and coveralls, with tool belts slung around their waists. Women carrying covered dishes and loaves of bread and pies.

Rube and Edith Layton led the way.

"Mornin', Miss Amethyst," Rube said formally.

"Good morning, Rube, Edith." Amethyst narrowed her eyes and peered at them. What were they doing here?

"We've come to help out, if you could use a hand or two," Rube went on. "Now, I'm not the mayor anymore, but I've still got a stake in how this town treats its citizens. And I've still got a little influence, too." He took off his cap and ran a hand through his thinning hair. "We're not saying we agree with your stand, Miss Amethyst. You gotta know that. But none of us"—he waved toward the crowd assembled behind him—"think a lady like you deserves this."

"A lady like me?" Amethyst suppressed a smile. "Time was, nobody in Cambridge would have called me a lady."

He ducked his head. "Well, you are, in my book, anyway."

Amethyst wondered, just briefly, if these people would have offered the same support and aid had she been a Negro. But before she got a chance to say anything, Bailey appeared from behind the house with a paint scraper in his hand.

"Morning, Mr. Layton," he said, eyeing Rube warily. In his old khaki work pants and a T-shirt stained with sweat and soot, he could have more easily been taken for a poor dirt farmer than a Washington lawyer.

Layton looked Bailey up and down. "Good morning, Mr. Blue." He held Bailey's gaze. "I've got a work crew here, if you'll just tell us what you need done."

Bailey moved forward and extended a hand. "We appreciate that, Mr. Layton."

Rube Layton's gaze darted to his wife, who gave a curt little nod. Hesitantly, he reached out and shook Bailey's hand. When he drew his hand back, it was smeared with black grime.

"Hmmm," he mused. "It *does* rub off."

Bailey threw back his head and laughed. "Only temporarily. It'll wash."

The tension was broken, and everybody began talking all at once.

"We brought food," Edith added, holding out a fresh apple pie.

The women clustered around Amethyst, and the men, taking their cue from Rube Layton, gathered near Bailey to get instructions.

Amethyst watched in awe as white farmers and builders and one former mayor went off to work side by side with a group of NAACP lawyers. *Miracles do happen*, she thought to herself.

Sometimes they just came in inscrutable ways.

———•••———

Dixon Lee Godwin sat on a pile of rubble in the backyard and drank down a cold glass of lemonade. All morning, as he had worked with a dozen other men clearing out debris from the parlor and repairing the interior walls, he had engaged in a silent dialogue with his God.

It was more like a monologue, really. Dix had asked a lot of questions, but gotten little response.

For one thing, he wanted the Lord to tell him what he was supposed to do. His mind and heart swirled with a mass of conflicting thoughts and emotions, and he couldn't for the life of him sort it all out.

He had been obedient, hadn't he? After his wife's death, he had left a moderately lucrative sales job and a comfortable home to go to seminary—at an age when most men were beginning to think about retirement. He had spent what little savings he had on tuition and living expenses, and once he was done, he had said yes to a pastorate in

Cambridge, Mississippi, when he would rather have gone back home to Iowa.

He had sacrificed a lot to respond to the Spirit's call. Yet he felt isolated, lonely, and unsure of himself. Didn't God have a responsibility to him in return—at least to answer him when he prayed?

But he had received no answers.

The congregation at First Presbyterian had accepted him, he supposed. They smiled and shook his hand on their way out of the service, told him he had preached a lovely sermon. He fit right in, they said. Perhaps they thought it was a compliment.

But he hadn't become a pastor to fit in, to deliver sermons that made people comfortable. He had gone into the ministry because he was engaged in his own search for truth. The spiritual life wasn't about being ready for heaven, but about reflecting the character of Christ here on earth. It was about growing, deepening, grappling with the difficult questions of real life, discovering how the power of the living God intersected with human life. Unless he challenged his congregation to enter into that exploration for themselves, he had failed.

And at this moment, Dix felt like an absolute and utter failure.

Not a single member of his church had showed up to offer help and support to Amethyst in her time of need.

The people who came, in fact, weren't for the most part churchgoing folks at all. Rube Layton and his wife attended church off and on—they were Episcopalian, he thought. But from what he could tell through the conversations that went on among the other men, few of them gave the first thought to religion. They were not here because they had any spiritual motivation. They just saw a need and met it.

Dix also knew that Rube Layton and his crew didn't necessarily agree with Amethyst's position on civil rights. The man had made that pretty clear, and yet here he was, taking orders from Bailey Blue, laughing and talking and working side by side with a bunch of Negro attorneys. At one point Dix had asked him why he had come, and Rube just shrugged and said, "When a neighbor needs help, you get off your duff and lend a hand."

Why, Dix wondered, didn't his parishioners respond like that? Were they simply oblivious to the Lord's command to feed the hungry and clothe the naked and help those in trouble? Or were they so concerned about appearances that they couldn't get their hands dirty?

The truth was, he was ashamed of his congregation.

And he was ashamed of himself.

Ever since his first conversation with Amethyst about her perspectives on "the Negro situation," Dix had felt like Jacob, wrestling with the angel through a very long night. He knew she was right, that as a Christian—especially as a Christian pastor—he couldn't sit idly by and wait for change to happen. He had heard about the death camps in Germany, about the Jews and Europeans who had been annihilated in German ovens. He had read about the trials going on in Nuremberg. And the question haunted him: *If he had been an Aryan pastor in Germany, would he have stood up against Hitler and his purification plan?*

Some Christians had resisted. Dix had heard about those who had hidden Jews in their basements and attics, defying Hitler and his gestapo and risking their own lives to save the innocent. Some had escaped. Others, along with those they had rescued, had died in concentration camps or been impaled on the point of a Nazi bayonet.

He hoped . . . wished . . . begged . . . that if he had been offered that opportunity, he would have been brave enough to seize it. He just didn't know for sure.

Just last Sunday, the epistle lesson had been taken from Hebrews 11, and when he had stood to read it, he could barely get the words out: *By faith they subdued kingdoms, wrought righteousness . . . escaped the edge of the sword, out of weakness were made strong. . . . But others were tortured, stoned, sawed in two, slain with the sword. . . .*

The words tore at his soul . . . taunted him. All of these saints, Dix recalled with a flash of humiliation, were approved as faithful unto God—whether they were victorious or not. The outcome didn't matter. It was the motivation that counted in the sight of God.

Not because it's possible, Amethyst had said, *but because it's right.*

What was the difference, he wondered, between what happened in Germany and what was happening here, now, in Mississippi? The death camps were worse, certainly, in terms of the sheer horrifying numbers of the slain. But the principles were similar: a dominant, powerful group inflicting cruel, even deadly sovereignty over those they perceived as inferior.

Guilt crested over him in a wave. He didn't need a voice from heaven to tell him the answer.

There was no difference.

The fact was, he had not been an Aryan Christian in Germany, facing down Hitler's storm troopers. The choice to aid and rescue Jews had not been given him. But he was a white Christian in the South, and all around him black people—human beings, created in the Divine image—were being harassed, beaten, burned out, even killed, simply because they weren't members of the "correct" race. A Klansman's noose had the same effect as a Nazi's rifle.

For weeks Dix had been praying about what he should do, what his response as a pastor and a Christian should be. Now even the prayers he had offered shamed him. Of course God hadn't answered him. The answer had already been given, centuries ago—in the example Christ set by embracing the outcasts of society, in the way God extended love and acceptance toward all. In the cross that hung behind him every Sunday when he stepped into the pulpit.

He had been praying for the wrong thing. He had asked for wisdom, for direction. But he had his direction. What he needed was the backbone to follow it.

He set aside his glass of lemonade, put his head in his hands, and prayed. But this time his prayer was different: *Lord, give me courage.*

He barely had time to get the thought out when a voice broke into his consciousness. "Dix? There are some people here to see you."

He glanced up to see Amethyst gazing down at him. She looked ridiculous—soot-covered from head to toe except for one little swipe on her nose. Wisps of graying hair stuck out in all directions from beneath her bandanna. Without warning, a fierce longing overtook him—to hold her in his arms, to tell her he was sorry for being such a coward and ask her forgiveness. The idea shocked him, and he tried vainly to push it aside.

"Dix? Are you all right?" She put a hand on his shoulder, and a rush of warmth pulsed through his veins. He pushed up from the pile of debris and smiled down at her. "I am now. Someone wants to see me?"

She nodded and led him around to the front of the house, where a group of his parishioners stood in a cluster next to the magnolia tree. For a split second his heart soared. Then he took another look.

It could have been a board meeting. Most of the leadership of his congregation had assembled on Amethyst's front lawn. And from the expressions on their faces, Dix could tell they hadn't come to help. They had come to confront.

The church moderator, a venerable, white-haired old man by the name of Edward Shoemaker, stepped forward. "We'd like an explanation," he said tersely.

Dix watched him guardedly. "An explanation about what, Ed?"

"About what you think you're doing. We were under the impression we had hired a pastor, not some kind of civil rights activist. We're not sure we approve of the idea of you attending rallies put on by the NAACP, or associating with people who do." The old man slanted a reproving glance in Amethyst's direction. "Your place is in the church, doing the job we pay you to do."

Dix suppressed a smile. *Well,* he thought, *I guess some prayers are answered more quickly than others.* He lifted his head and looked Shoemaker straight in the eye. "Being a pastor is not a job," he corrected, "it's a calling. And the first responsibility of that calling is to be obedient to God. My second responsibility is to be a model of Christlikeness among you."

He paused and took a deep breath. "I have something to confess to you—to all of you. I haven't been the kind of model I'd want you to follow."

An expression of relief swept over Shoemaker's face, and a wave of murmured assent went through the group. "Well, Pastor, we accept your apology," the old man said. "We had hoped we could resolve this and put it behind us."

Dix held up a hand. "Allow me to clarify. I have long believed that prejudice of any kind is wrong, an affront to the Almighty. I just haven't had the courage to stand up for that conviction, to put my life and

reputation on the line for it." He waved off Shoemaker's attempt to interrupt him and continued. "We have a choice before us—to follow the
example of Christ, or to live by the standards our society sets for us. I,
for one, intend to do the former. So you need to know that from now
on, First Presbyterian will be a church that welcomes all God's people
without regard to the color of their skin. You can go or stay as you see fit,
but if you stay, expect to have your preconceived notions challenged, and
expect to see your pastor taking a stand whenever justice is denied to
any human being."

Shoemaker stood there for a minute, his jaw slack and his eyes wide.
Then, without a word, he turned and left, with the others trailing in his
wake.

Dix watched them go, then looked down to see Amethyst holding his
hand.

"Do you think you'll get fired?"

He didn't withdraw his hand from hers. It felt good, this human
touch, this connection. As if, at long last, he belonged.

"I don't know." He shrugged. "Maybe. But at least I'll have my integrity."

Amethyst stood in front of the bureau in her bedroom. She had been
through every drawer, looked everywhere she could think of.

The amethyst brooch was gone.

She had found the velvet box she kept it in—tossed carelessly under
the bed, smeared with soot and spotted with water. And empty.

She sank into the small rocker by the window and bit her lip to hold
back the tears. So far she had done pretty well handling her shock and
grief over the fire. No one had been killed; no one had gotten hurt.
"Things can be replaced," she had told Silvie.

And she believed it. Despite all appearances to the contrary, blessings
were already beginning to emerge from this misfortune. Friends had ral-
lied around her in her time of need. It appeared that the folks Rube
Layton had brought to help were beginning to view Bailey and her other
boarders as individuals rather than as stereotypes. And Dix Godwin had
discovered courage in the midst of his own spiritual crisis.

But to lose Grandma Pearl's brooch! Amethyst shook her head. It was too much. . . .

Hot tears, dredged up from the deep well of her soul, broke through her resolve and spilled over. She wept silently, clutching the velvet box to her chest. For a long time—she didn't know how long—she sat there, rocking and crying.

Then she heard a noise—a small, faint gasp.

"Mother?"

She blinked back her tears and turned to see Conrad standing in the doorway between the parlor and her bedroom.

"Mother, are you all right?" He ran to her and knelt on the floor beside her. His arms went around her, and he pressed against her the way he had done when he was a little boy and needed comfort. But this time he was comforting her. "Don't cry," he whispered over and over again. "Please, don't cry." But he was crying, too, choking on his sobs, mumbling something about being so, so sorry.

Amethyst dropped the velvet box and laced her fingers through his hair. She held him that way, caressing his hair, until he got control of himself and looked up at her.

"Mother, what's wrong?" he asked. Then he laughed at himself and swiped at his eyes. "That was a stupid question, wasn't it?"

She gazed down at him. He had Harper's eyes, and one little dimple that was the Wainwright legacy. It tore at her heart, seeing him again. He had changed so much in such a short time. Her little boy had become a man.

"The brooch," she said quietly. "Grandma Pearl's amethyst brooch. It's gone."

A stricken look came over his face, followed by a shadowed, inscrutable expression. He pulled away from her and sat cross-legged on the floor, lowering his face so that she could only see the crown of his head. A shock of hair stood up, that unruly cowlick she had combed down a thousand times when he was a child. Now she smoothed at it again, but he brushed her hand away.

"I should have come sooner," he said, his voiced laced with misery. "I wanted to, but—" He paused, took a deep breath, and raised his eyes to meet her gaze. "I'm sorry, Mother. Sorry for everything."

She wanted to ask, *Sorry for what?*, to encourage him to confess, to begin the process of healing and reconciliation.

"You know I was here the night Dooley and the others burned a cross in the yard," he went on after a minute or two. "Bogey told me you had seen us."

"Yes."

"I wanted to come then, I really did."

"Because you had participated in such a horrible act, or because Clarence Bogart told you I saw you?"

He shrugged. "Both, I guess."

Amethyst sighed. At least it was an honest answer.

"I was there, but I didn't mean for anybody to get hurt. And now this—" He waved a hand at the devastation that surrounded them.

"The fire wasn't your fault, Conrad."

"No, but—" He shook his head. "I should have come long before now. You probably hate the sight of me."

"Conrad, I could never hate you. You're my son. I love you. I'll always love you."

"But you wish I were more like my father, more like your grand-parents, and less like Grandpa Abe."

At first Amethyst tried to deny it, but she knew he was right, and the truth stung. "Is that what you think?"

He nodded. "It's all I've heard, all my life. My great spiritual legacy, the models I should emulate. But I don't know if I can be like them—or like you. I don't even know if I *want* to be. It's not always easy, being the son of a saint." He gave a brief, wry smile, and then his expression sobered again. "Still, I'm sorry for hurting you. Sorry for the stupid things I've done. And I'm sorry about the brooch."

He got to his feet and looked down at her. "I need to go talk to Bailey. And then I'm going to pitch in and help clean up this mess." He shrugged. "I'm not much of a handyman, but I guess I can carry wood and fetch water."

Amethyst rose and pulled her son into a close embrace. He wasn't a child any longer. He was nearly grown. She had done her best to sow seeds of goodness and faithfulness and truth in his life. Whether they took root or not was up to him, in the choices he would make for himself. He would always be her son, and even if he disappointed her, she would always love him. But the course of his life was not hers to decide.

As she let him go, she felt a burden lift from her soul. Whatever kind of man her son became, it was between him and God now.

44
The Offering

September 1946

From her accustomed place in the fourth pew on the left, Amethyst watched as Dixon Lee Godwin entered from the side door of the sanctuary and stepped onto the platform. She had always thought he cut an impressive figure in the pulpit, but her perception of him had changed over the past few months. No longer did she merely see a tall, rugged-looking fellow with hair graying nicely at the temples or hear the low, vibrant tone of his voice as he spoke.

She had looked into his heart, had heard the resonance of conviction that reverberated through his soul. She had watched him put his beliefs into action with passion and determination, had seen him take a bold, unflinching stand for justice.

And she loved him.

The organist had begun the prelude—a soul-stirring rendition of "Great Is Thy Faithfulness." Amethyst closed her eyes and sang the words in her mind: *All I have needed, Thy hand hath provided. Great is Thy faithfulness, Lord, unto me.*

When she opened her eyes and looked down the pew, she was reminded again of the truth of those words. To her left sat her son, Conrad, with several of his buddies from the university. Con turned to Clarence Bogart and whispered something that made Bogey smile. At the far end, much to Amethyst's surprise, hunched Dooley Layton with his head down and his eyes fixed on the floor.

Dooley looked a bit the worse for wear this morning. His right cheek was bruised, his lip was cut, and a bandage hid most of his nose. Clearly the boy had been in a fight—and pretty recently, if his wounds were any indication.

Then Conrad reached for a hymnal, and Amethyst caught a glimpse of his right hand. The fingers were swollen and a little blue, the knuckles skinned down to the flesh.

She grimaced, but before she could get Conrad's attention, the organist began playing the introductory bars of the first hymn. She rose to her feet and slanted a glance at her son. Con was pointing at the order of service, and he and Bogey were elbowing each other and grinning.

Amethyst took up her own bulletin and scanned it. Dix's sermon title this morning was "Fighting the Good Fight."

Well, that boy is in for a good talking-to, she thought automatically. Then she remembered. She had given him up to God. Amethyst didn't approve of fighting, but Con had to make his own decisions now. And if he had been duking it out with Dooley Layton, maybe he had a good reason.

When the hymn had ended, Dix stood up, faced the congregation, and smiled. His eyes lingered on Amethyst for just a moment, and she felt a warm flush creep up her neck.

"I want to welcome you all to this service of worship," he said. "Especially those of you who are worshiping with us for the first time." His gaze focused on the back of the church. "Some of you, I see, are still waiting to be seated. Please, come down front and join us."

All eyes turned, and a hush fell over the congregation.

It was Bailey Blue, gripping Silvie's hand. Behind them, a cluster of black faces surveyed the crowd.

Amethyst's heart jumped in her chest. She held her breath. And then, without a word, Bailey and Silvie came down the aisle and slipped into the pew next to Amethyst. The others scattered throughout the congregation.

Behind her, Amethyst heard a rustling noise and turned to see Will Tarbush getting to his feet. A tall Negro man, with his wife and two little children in tow, had just invaded Will's pew. He slammed his hymnal

into the pew rack, squeezed past the man and his family, and lurched
out into the center aisle. "I didn't come to church to sit next to no coloreds," he declared at the top of his voice. He stomped down the aisle,
made his exit, and slammed the door behind him.

No one moved. No one spoke.

Dix picked up his Bible from the pulpit and cleared his throat. "In the
gospel of John, chapter 6, Jesus presented some very difficult teachings
to those who were following after him—teachings that seemed to fly in
the face of their long-held traditions. Some of the disciples, verse 66
tells us, left him and no longer followed him. Interestingly enough,
Jesus did not go after them and beg them to come back. Instead, he
turned to his disciples and asked, 'Will ye also go away?' It's as if the
Lord were saying, '*If you want to leave, now's your chance. Make your decision to stay or go.*'"

His gaze swept over the congregation, and with a surge of pride
Amethyst saw the expression of fearless conviction in his eyes. "We face
that same decision today, this moment," Dix went on. "Whether we will
bend to the teachings of Christ and let our hearts be changed, or hold
on to attitudes from the past. If you want to leave, now's your chance."

Someone in the back coughed. Feet shuffled. Papers rustled. But no
one moved to go. Not even Dooley Layton, who still sat at the end of
the pew with his eyes downcast.

Dix looked around. "Fine. Now, let's all rise and greet one another in
the peace of Christ."

Amethyst stood up and turned to Silvie. "The peace of the Lord be
with you," she said.

Silvie's arms went around her, and they stood there hugging while
others milled around them, shaking hands and murmuring welcomes.
It was a familiar embrace, one Amethyst had experienced many times
over the past forty-five years. And yet here, today, in God's house, it
seemed warmer somehow. More significant. More right.

"I feel like I've waited for this day forever," Silvie whispered in
Amethyst's ear.

"So have I," Amethyst responded. "It's about time."

Amethyst had difficulty focusing her attention on the rest of the service. She rarely drifted when Dix was preaching, but this particular morning, with Silvie's hand clutching hers, her mind swirled with memories.

How would Silas and Pearl have felt, she wondered, if they could see her at this moment, sitting in the house of God next to Booker's granddaughter and her handsome, educated husband-to-be? Her grandparents had longed, prayed, given their lives' energy for such a time as this. Amethyst suspected—she hoped, at least—that from their vantage point in the presence of God, they would know that their labors had not been in vain.

In her mind's eye, she could envision the two of them, standing on the front porch of Noble House, hand in hand, just as she and Harper had stood on the day of their wedding.

She could see Harper, too, but in her vision his crippled limbs were straight and strong, the scars on his face erased by the power of love. The dimple in his cheek deepened as he smiled, and his blue eyes radiated joy. She could almost see him wink and nod to her, as if offering a benediction on the growing love between Amethyst and Dixon Lee Godwin. Harper would approve of Dix, she knew instinctively. She had put her grief behind her and moved on, but Harper would always be a part of her, reaffirming the truth that it was the heart, not the outward appearance, that mattered in the sight of God.

Other faces paraded through her mind. Black and white, scarred and smooth, old and young. Some, like Silvie and Dix, graced her life today. Others, like her grandparents and Harper, had already finished their course. But each of them had influenced her own path, helped direct her along the road she had walked.

Pearl's journals, Silas's healing touch, Booker's faith. These were the first footpaths, the original legacy of the Noble name. Enoch's dignity, Silvie's faithfulness, and Harper's love had led her further down the way. And now people like Dix and Bailey had come into her life, confirming the birthright of those early years and illuminating the passages that still lay before her.

Everything fit. When she turned and looked behind her, Amethyst could see the pattern, the winding roads and intersections of lives that had led her to this place and this time. Her grandparents' bequest: *Sincerity. Purity. Nobility.*

Unconsciously, Amethyst's hand went to her neck, and her throat tightened. The brooch was gone, but the heritage Silas and Pearl had left behind need not die.

Let the legacy live on, she prayed silently. *Let what we do here, now and in the future, honor those who came before us and serve as an example for those who follow. . . .*

A rustling around her caught Amethyst's attention. She opened her eyes and looked up. The sermon had ended, and the organist had begun the opening strains of the offertory hymn.

> *When peace like a river attendeth my way,*
> *When sorrows like sea billows roll.*
> *Whatever my lot, Thou hast taught me to say,*
> *It is well, it is well with my soul.*

Silvie caught her eye and smiled at her, and Amethyst didn't need to ask what Silvie was thinking. They had known peace like a river and sorrows like sea billows. They had endured inward struggles and outward conflicts. But they had come through it—together. They had grown. They had learned. They had found a place of belonging, and the love that comes from the deepest heart of God. It was well with their souls.

The offering plate came down the row, and Amethyst fumbled in her bag for her tithe. She frowned at Conrad, who was jiggling the brass plate in front of her and grinning. Couldn't the boy be just a little patient with his old mother? Then she looked down.

Amid the crumpled bills and coins, she caught a flash of color. Something shiny, set in gold. Something purple. With trembling fingers she pushed the bills aside. Then she saw it.

An outline of tiny pearls. In the center—shimmering, vibrant, reflecting back the lights in the sanctuary and pulsing as if it had a life of its own—a radiant, heart-shaped brooch of deep amethyst.

And one of the pearls was missing.

45
Amethyst's Heart

March 25, 1993

Little Am leaned forward eagerly, a glint of excitement illuminating her dark brown eyes. "So the amethyst heart returned to where it belonged. That's so cool." She grinned. "And even cooler that my grandfather beat the tar out of Dooley Layton for it."

Amethyst held up a hand. "Maybe. I never found out exactly what happened, but that was my understanding as well. Although Conrad never told me, I assumed that Dooley was part of the Klan group that broke in and set fire to the house. Since he had lived there, he would have guessed where to look for anything of value."

"But what happened to the missing pearl?"

"I'm not sure. I suppose it must have come loose when it was in Dooley's possession." Amethyst shrugged. "It's appropriate, though, considering what my grandmother said about the brooch when Silas gave it to her."

"Something about human nature, wasn't it?"

"Yes. She said the missing pearl served as a reminder of the human condition—beautiful, yet flawed. Priceless, even in its incompleteness."

"And you never had the pearl replaced."

"No." Amethyst shook her head. "It seemed fitting, somehow, to leave it as it was."

"Did he ever apologize to you? Dooley, I mean."

"No." Amethyst shook her head. "That's the sad part. He might have found a place of peace if he had just owned up to what he had done and asked forgiveness. I heard rumors some years later that he died in prison, but I don't know for certain."

"Yeah, but we know how my grandfather turned out."

"Try not to be too hard on Conrad, child." Amethyst sighed. "He had a difficult time, growing up without a father, and he's made some questionable choices over the years. But I have to believe that deep down, he has a good heart. He's just never let it take priority over his wallet."

Little Am sat in silence for a moment. "I guess so," she conceded at last. "Still, I don't agree with his values."

Amethyst gazed at her great-granddaughter, and a warm rush of love and pride coursed through her veins. This girl would do all right. In her own way, she would take up the family legacy and live out the prin-ciples Amethyst had tried to instill in Conrad. *Sincerity, Purity, Nobility.*

It was ironic, really. Less than two weeks ago, when the family had gathered for her ninety-third birthday, Amethyst had looked at the girl and seen a rebellious teenager. Now she saw the future of the Noble name. The mantle had fallen upon Little Am's shoulders, and Amethyst could only release her to God and trust that the girl would find her path and live out the heritage she had been given.

She felt a little like Simeon in the temple, watching, waiting for years to see the coming of the promise. Maybe this was why the Lord had let her live so long.

"And so you married Dixon Lee Godwin," Little Am was saying. "I wish I had known him."

"I wish you had, too, child. He was a wonderful man, a godly and just man. Although I have to admit that I never really fit the role of a pastor's wife."

"Because you didn't play the piano and teach Sunday school?" Little Am grinned.

Amethyst laughed. "Partly. But mostly because I couldn't manage to keep my mouth shut."

"You? Opinionated?" Little Am rolled her eyes. "I'm shocked, Grandam."

"Actually, I have to give Dix credit. He never tried to force me into that mold. And to tell the truth, he didn't fit most people's idea of what a minister should be. He had a pastor's heart, and he loved and cared for his congregation. But he also had a passion for justice, and he stepped on a lot of people's toes."

"But he never got fired?"

"Miraculously, no. I think the members of First Presbyterian—most of them, anyway—realized that change was inevitable, and were glad to have someone in leadership who could guide the church into a peaceful, Christ-centered response."

"Seems to me that's what the church should be," Little Am declared solemnly. "But so far all I've seen of church is a bunch of rules and regulations, people putting on a religious act to impress each other."

"I know," Amethyst said. "It's easy for a church to get caught up in numbers and buildings and rules. But there are churches out there that serve as agents of justice and truth in the world. Places where people are encouraged to find their own relationship with God, and live out that relationship in action. And sometimes you find church without a building, in connection with other people who share your faith and values."

"You mean like what Grandma Pearl wrote in her journal: '*To believe is to care. To care is to do.*'"

"Exactly. You have been listening, child!" Amethyst smiled wryly. "I thought all teenagers had five-second attention spans."

"Most of us will listen," Little Am countered, "if we're given something worth listening to." She gave Amethyst a grin and a wink. "So, finish your story. Once you married Dix, you didn't keep running the boarding house, did you?"

"Not officially. Once Bailey and Silvie married, they moved into Uncle Enoch's house. Then, during the sixties, when the Civil Rights movement was in full swing, some of Bailey's lawyer friends stayed at the house when they came to Mississippi. But by then, Dix and I didn't really need the money, and the work had become too much for me. We kept the apartments and used them for what Dix called 'sanctuaries'— places for people to stay when they needed temporary housing. Over the years we took in five or six unwed mothers, as well as a number of battered women and their children. Helped a few homeless people find jobs and get on their feet again." She paused, her mind drifting to those days. "A lot of laughter and tears. A lot of precious memories, and a few minor miracles."

"Then it's no wonder you don't want to give this house up," Little Am mused. "I can't believe my grandfather wouldn't understand that."

"I believe he does understand it, on some level. But at the moment he can see nothing except his own financial problems, and the fact that I'm ninety-three and bound to go ahead and die sooner or later."

"But he doesn't have the right to—"

"We're not sure yet what he has the right to do. That will be up to the judge when we meet with her tomorrow."

Amethyst watched as Little Am's jaw clenched and a determined look came into her eye. "Well," she muttered fiercely, "we'll just have to see about that, won't we?"

March 26, 1993

At 4:45 on Friday afternoon, Conrad sat once more in Judge Dove's chambers. The timing of this meeting could not have been worse. Everybody knew that judges became surly and uncooperative on Fridays, especially at five o'clock, when they wanted to be out of their robes and starting to relax for the weekend.

Her Honor probably did it deliberately, he mused. Setting him up for the kill.

Mimsy fidgeted in the chair next to him, and this time the office was a bit more crowded, with Mother and Little Am wedged into the extra chairs that had been brought in for the final showdown.

Con eyed his mother warily. She seemed calm, even a little complacent. Not at all ruffled to be appearing before the judge.

And his granddaughter! Much to his dismay, the girl had shown up looking not at all like a ghoulish figure out of a horror movie. She was wearing neat navy slacks with a bright fuchsia blouse, and had fixed her hair and put on subdued and tasteful makeup. Why couldn't she have been her natural self and arrived looking like a freak?

He studied Little Am's demeanor as she conversed quietly with her great-grandmother. The two of them were getting along like mashed potatoes and gravy, he thought sullenly. And the girl looked positively smug, as if she were privy to some fascinating secret.

A sudden thought struck him, and his stomach turned to lead. What if the two of them had cooked up some kind of plan to get on the judge's good side? Mother had, after all, kept the girl to herself for nearly two weeks. Little Am might be bullheaded and independent, but two weeks was surely long enough for Am to be influenced by Mother's brainwashing.

No. He pushed the thought aside. His granddaughter was just like every other teenager in the country—only interested in herself, or in malls and boys and television and computer games. You could dress her up, but that didn't change her essential nature.

Judge Dove entered, smiling and nodding cordially at Little Am and Mother and Mimsy. When she turned to him, however, her countenance sobered and her eyes narrowed.

"Ah, Mr. Wainwright. We meet again."

"Yes, Your Honor."

She glanced pointedly at her watch and cleared her throat. "Well, let's get on with it."

Conrad winced. He knew it was a mistake, having this meeting on a Friday afternoon. But he hadn't been given much choice in the matter.

"Mr. Wainwright, I'm waiting."

Con snapped to attention and faced the judge. "Right. Well, Your Honor, as I told you before, my mother is ninety-three years old and lives alone. She is not an invalid, as you can see, but she is getting on in years. What if she fell and broke a hip, or left something cooking on the stove and set the house on fire? I'm only interested in what's best for her."

"And you think it's best for your mother to be in an assisted-living facility."

"For her own good, yes. I've already made arrangements at a state-of-the-art place near Memphis, where we would be close by and could keep an eye on her."

The judge pulled her glasses down to the tip of her nose and peered over the frames. "You've made arrangements. Don't you think that's a bit premature, Mr. Wainwright? Or do you think *I'm* so senile that I already made my ruling and forgot what I decided?"

Conrad felt a cold sweat break out on his forehead, and he jerked a handkerchief from his pocket and blotted his brow. "It's a—ah, a preliminary arrangement, Your Honor. Purely tentative. Nothing set in stone."

"Ah. Well, it's good to know I'm not losing my mind." She gave him a chilly glance and turned to Little Am and his mother. "I'd like to hear from you, Miss Amethyst. You are, as your son has stated, ninety-three years old?"

She nodded. "I am."

"I must say you don't look ninety-three."

"I'll consider that a compliment, Your Honor."

"All right, now—" Judge Dove looked down at the paperwork in front of her. "Mr. Wainwright here contends that you are no longer able to care for yourself. What do you have to say about that?"

Conrad held his breath. *Please,* he begged, *please let her say something outrageous.*

Amethyst watched out of the corner of her eye as Conrad fell silent and waited for her to speak. His face bore an expression of desperation, as if willing her to give the judge one reason, just one, to rule in his favor. If she did, Noble House would be gone forever. Con would have money in his pocket to pay off whatever debts he owed and live high on the hog for the rest of his days, and she would end up in a nursing home until she died of sheer boredom. A lot was riding on her answer to Judge Dove.

She felt a movement at her side as Little Am reached to squeeze her hand. It was all the encouragement she needed.

"Certainly, Your Honor, I believe I am still capable of caring for myself. As you can see, I haven't yet killed myself, and I'm not completely addled—at least no more than I have a right to be at my age. But I'm sure most elderly people would say the same thing. I simply urge you not to put my future in my son's hands simply because I'm old."

"You're not accusing me of age discrimination, I hope," the judge said tersely.

"Not in the least." Amethyst considered her next words carefully. "But you must admit that our society *does* prejudge the elderly. The universe revolves around youth, and often the wisdom and experience that can accompany gray hair and wrinkles are altogether ignored."

"Your reputation has preceded you, Miss Amethyst," Judge Dove interrupted. "You're something of a crusader, I believe. But please spare me the agism rhetoric and let's concentrate on the issue at hand." She shuffled the papers and picked up a pen. "There are a few questions that need to be answered."

Amethyst nodded.

"First, you are the sole owner of the property at 4236 Jefferson Davis Avenue, is that correct?"

"Yes."

"Your legal name is Amethyst Noble Wainwright Godwin?"

"Yes."

"Widowed?"

"Twice, Your Honor."

"Conrad Wainwright is your only son and heir to the property?"

"Only son, yes. Heir? That remains to be seen."

Judge Dove suppressed a smile. "Did you or did you not lock your doors and threaten your son with a shotgun?"

"I did. But it wasn't much of a threat. The gun wasn't loaded. I don't even own any shells for it."

The smile widened. "Do you have a mortgage?"

"No, Your Honor. The house has been in my family for more than a hundred years."

The judge's eyebrows went up. "Ah, yes. Your house is that grand old planter home, with green shutters and white columns."

"That's the one, Your Honor."

"Hmmm. You're to be commended for keeping it up so beautifully. Most of the other stately homes in the area have been taken over as law offices." She slanted a scathing glance at Conrad. "Do you owe back taxes?"

"No, Your Honor. I always pay my bills on time."

By now the judge was reading questions perfunctorily, checking off boxes on her list. "Ever been arrested, or convicted of a crime?"

"Yes, Your Honor."

"Ever been—" Judge Dove stopped suddenly. "What did you say?"

"I said yes, I have been arrested. Several times."

Out of the corner of her eye, Amethyst saw Conrad's eyebrows shoot up into what was left of his hairline. His lips twitched, as if doing a little victory dance.

The judge laid down her pen and leaned back in her chair. "Let's hear about that."

"The charge, if I remember correctly, was disturbing the peace." Amethyst took a deep breath.

"*You?*"

"I'm afraid so, Your Honor. I was arrested five—no, six times, I believe, between 1960 and 1965. Spent a few nights in jail, too."

Conrad couldn't restrain himself any longer. "I never knew about this, Mother. Why didn't you tell me?"

She turned and leveled her gaze on him. "As I recall, you were too busy building your practice in Memphis to call your mother."

This time the judge chuckled out loud, then sobered herself, made a few quick notes on her pad, and went on. "You were in your sixties at the time of the arrests?"

"That's right."

"What in heaven's name did you *do?*"

"I parked myself on the courthouse steps and refused to budge. I participated in a sit-in at a lunch counter in Jackson. I protested in Birmingham, and marched in Selma and Washington, D.C."

Judge Dove leaned forward. "Really? I was a junior in college in 1963, and I went to the Washington march, too. Were you there for the 'I Have a Dream' speech?"

"Yes. I remember being on the left, about halfway down the reflecting pool. I was standing on the ledge of the pool, and my husband, Dix, had his arm around my waist to keep me from falling in. I looked down into the water, and I could see the reflection of all those people standing out in the August heat, cheering—"

"Could we take this little trip down memory lane later?" Conrad interrupted with a growl. "Maybe the two of you could go out for dinner this evening and catch up on old times."

The judge slapped her hand down on the desk. "One more word out of you, Mr. Wainwright, and you'll be having dinner from a tray slid through the bars of your cell."

She turned back to Amethyst. "Obviously, your arrests will not be held against you when I render my judgment. The Civil Rights movement was an important cause in the history of this nation, and I applaud your participation in it. Dr. King's speech, in fact, was the turning point in my decision to enter law school." She turned and cast a withering glance in Conrad's direction. "If you had been the loving, concerned son you paint yourself to be, you'd have known that your mother was in jail."

"Yes, but—" Conrad stammered.

"Still," Judge Dove went on, ignoring him, "my own mother is getting up in years. If she were your age, Miss Amethyst, I might not want her living alone, either."

Amethyst closed her eyes and fought back tears. Her heart felt like a stone in her chest. She was going to lose Noble House. It didn't matter if the judge put the proceeds from the sale in trust for her. She didn't care about the money. She only wanted to live and die in the home where Pearl and Silas had lived, where she had loved and married two exceptional men, where her memories sustained her and her heritage surrounded her.

She heard a shuffling sound and opened her eyes to see Little Am leaning forward in her chair.

"Your Honor?"

The judge looked at Little Am. "Ah, yes, the granddaughter."

"If I may, Your Honor," Am said politely, "I'd like permission to say something."

Conrad jumped to his feet. "No!"

Judge Dove shook her head and gritted her teeth. "I warned you, Mr. Wainwright. I'm fining you one thousand dollars for contempt."

"A thousand dollars? But—"

"No buts. One question—answer it with a yes or no. Is this young woman your granddaughter?"

"Yes, Your Honor."

"Not exactly the teenage mutant you described."

"No, Your Honor—I mean, yes, your honor. She, uh, doesn't usually look like this. It's an act, put on for your benefit."

"Perhaps you could learn something from her, then, about putting on an act for my benefit. Being respectful might be a good place to start."

Conrad shut his mouth and sat down.

"Now," the judge went on, turning back to Little Am. "Let's hear what you have to say."

———⊷⊶⊷———

Am had thought this was a great idea when she came up with the plan. Now she wasn't so sure. This Judge Dove was a powerful lady, and Am felt a little intimidated in her presence. Still, this was something she had to do—not just for Grandam, but for herself. It was probably impossible, this scheme she had come up with. Con and Mimsy would never go for it, not in a million years, and they were still her legal guardians. But Grandam had said something that had stuck with her, something that gave her the guts to go on.

I'm not doing this because it's possible, she reminded herself, *but because it's right.*

"Well?" Judge Dove prompted. "Let's hear it, young woman."

"I'm seventeen," Am began haltingly. "A junior in high school. I turn eighteen in September. Ever since I was a little girl and my parents were killed in a car wreck, I've lived with Con and Mimsy. And they've been good to me, I guess. Mimsy smothers me a little, but that's just her way."

She turned and cast an apologetic glance in Mimsy's direction. "Anyway, I appreciate all they've done for me, and I love them and all, but—"

The judge was leaning forward, listening intently. "Go on."

"But I'd like to live with Grandam. My great-grandmother." Am looked in Grandam's direction. She was dabbing at her eyes, and Am wasn't sure if Grandam was upset with her or happy about the suggestion.

She hurried on before she lost her nerve. "My great-grandmother didn't know I was going to suggest this," she said. "And Con and Mimsy may not be too happy about it. But what I'd like to do is move in with Grandam as soon as school is out. That's only a couple of months away. I can finish my senior year in Cambridge, and then go to the university here. I'll be in the house with Grandam, so Grandpa Con won't have to worry—"

She paused and cut a glance at him. His face was red and his eyes were beginning to bug out. He looked as if he might bust an artery at any minute. "It would solve a lot of problems, wouldn't it, Judge? Grandam wouldn't have to live alone, and she wouldn't have to give up her house, either."

"I won't have it!" Con sputtered. "I won't have my own grand-daughter turned against me."

"I'll be eighteen by the time school starts next fall," Am said quietly. "I guess then I can make my own decisions—as long as Grandam wants me."

Judge Dove's expression softened, and she gazed at Am with wide, soulful eyes. "But what about your school? Your friends in Memphis? I don't know many teenagers who would willingly transfer during their senior year."

Am shrugged. "I guess I'm not like most teenagers."

"No, I guess you're not." She turned to Mimsy and Con. "You, Mr. Wainwright, have made your position perfectly clear, so you keep your mouth shut. Mrs. Wainwright, do you want to add anything to this discussion?"

As usual, Mimsy had that deer-in-the-headlights expression on her face, but when she glanced at Con, it turned to a look of determination. "I love my granddaughter," she whispered. "But I'm not so sure my husband has the right motives in all this. If Little Am wants to live with her great-grandmother and keep an eye on things, I won't stand in her way."

Way to go, Mimsy! Am thought to herself.

"Well," Judge Dove declared briskly, "it seems as if a compromise has presented itself. Mr. Wainwright, your motion to have your mother declared incompetent and have yourself named as her power of attorney is denied, and you are ordered to pay court costs, as well as your thousand-dollar fine, to the bailiff on your way out. Miss Amethyst, is this agreement acceptable to you—to have your great-granddaughter come and live with you for the foreseeable future?"

Am turned toward her great-grandmother. Tears were streaming down Grandam's cheeks, but she was smiling.

"It's more than acceptable," she said with a nod and a chuckle. "It's cool. Way, way cool."

Epilogue

———◆◆◆———

March 2, 2000

Am Carpenter stood leaning on the rail of the courting porch and watched the moonlight play against the leaves of the ancient magnolia tree.

"Tired, I bet," her husband, John, whispered in her ear.

"Exhausted. We've had a lot to deal with these past few weeks."

"You want to come in and change clothes?"

Am looked down at her black dress, now rumpled from the activities of the day. One rhinestone button, jerked loose by an infant hand, dangled by a slender thread.

"In a little while. I need a few minutes alone, I think."

"I found this." He reached over her shoulder and handed her a manila envelope. In the dim light she could make out her name, written on the front in a shaky hand.

"Where?"

"In the freezer, under some packages of fish. When Mimsy and I were putting away some of the casseroles." He squeezed her shoulder. "She and Con are staying overnight. They've already gone to bed. I'll be inside if you need me."

She felt his lips kiss the back of her neck, and heard the screen door shut behind him. Bracing one hip against the porch rail, she opened the envelope. But she already knew what she would find. She had looked everywhere for it—everywhere except in the freezer, of course.

With trembling fingers, she slid out the contents: a single page of pale lavender paper and a battered velvet box.

The amethyst brooch.

In the moonlight, the deep purple of the heart-shaped stone looked almost black, and the pearls surrounding it took on an ethereal luminescence. She didn't need to read the inscription on the back; she knew it by heart. *Sincerity, Purity, Nobility.*

She picked up the note and held it so that the moonlight spilled over the page.

My dearest child,

Forgive me for hiding this from you. I've never hidden anything else, but I didn't want you to bury it with me. I was afraid you might try, and by that time I wouldn't be able to argue with you any longer.

Unless you cook a lot of fish in the next few weeks, by the time you read this, I'll be gone. Everything goes to you, of course—to you and that dear husband of yours, and that glorious, miraculous baby.

I won't tell you not to grieve, for grieving is natural and healthy. But I will remind you that I've lived a full and blessed life, and these last years with you have been a gift greater than any I ever could have imagined.

And I couldn't imagine, either, what a strong, generous, godly woman you would grow to become. You've always made me proud. Just remember that you have the Noble blood running in your veins, and a legacy from your spiritual and physical ancestors. Pearl and Silas, Booker and Enoch, Silvie and Bailey Blue, Harper and Dix. And myself, of course, for what one old woman's history is worth.

Spend freely on those around you—the love, the commitment, the passion, the faith. Give everything willingly, from the deepest resources of your soul. You will find your own way, I have no doubt. And all of us will be cheering you on.

I love you—

Grandam

Am swallowed hard and managed a smile. *One's going out, while another's coming in,* she thought. Barely two weeks shy of her hundredth birthday, Amethyst Noble had gone to sleep, and sometime during the night had slipped silently, without fanfare, into the next world. But she had lived long enough to hold her great-great-grandson in her arms.

Am went to the screen door and peered in. "John," she called, "would you bring the baby and come out here for a minute?"

After a moment her husband appeared at the door with the sleeping infant in his arms. "He's so beautiful," John said as he joined her on the porch. "Do you think I'll ever get over being amazed every time I look at him?"

"I hope not." Am took the child and cuddled him next to her breast. He stirred, but did not awaken. "There's something we need to do."

John nodded, and together they went to the porch railing, where a ray of moonlight pierced the thick branches of the tree. Am pinned the heart-shaped brooch onto the baby blanket and lifted the child toward the light, high over her head in the manner of the slaves. "We commit this child to the Almighty," she whispered, "and name him Silas Noble Carpenter."

Her husband's low voice joined her as she continued the prayer they both knew so well. "May he draw from his heritage the faith and love of his ancestors, and may he live a life worthy of his name and his calling."

Despite the chill of the spring night, a sudden warmth spread across Am's shoulders. A familiar touch, delicate and comforting. But when she turned to look behind her, no one was there. John was standing at her side, his elbows resting on the porch rail.

Am lowered the baby into her arms and gazed at him as he slept on. The moonlight shifted, and as she watched, the amethyst brooch seemed to come alive, pulsing in rhythm with the infant's deep, even breathing.

"Live, little Silas," she murmured. "Live under the blessing of your heritage. Find your way to truth, no matter what it takes."

And the amethyst heart winked back, as if in silent benediction.

Book Group Discussion Guide

———◆◆◆◆———

1. This novel begins in the present and then employs the narrator's flashbacks to relate the Noble family's history. What do you know about your ancestors—their families, faith, daily life? If you had the chance, what would you ask your great-grandparents, and how could their stories help you live your life today?

2. In the first chapters, we see an alienated, frustrated teenager in Little Am, who hides behind her "ghoulish" attire and indifferent attitude. Over the course of a few days spent alone with her great-grandmother, Little Am sheds her protective armor to reveal the lively, engaging young woman beneath the dark clothes and the sullen expression. What factors brought about such dramatic change? Has something like this happened to you or someone you know? What can the oldest and the youngest members of your family (neighborhood, church) contribute to each other's lives? Discuss ways you can help nurture good cross-generational relationships.

3. What is the significance of the amethyst brooch? What if it had been a ruby pendant, a string of pearls, or a diamond ring?

4. Discuss the real family heirloom at the core of *The Amethyst Heart*.

5. There are several romantic subplots woven throughout this story. Which one appealed to you the most and why?

6. Though World War II (1939-1945) is more familiar to most of us, it was World War I (1914-1918) that set the tone for what one writer has called "this terrible century." Horrific new modes of combat (chemical weapons, air attack, trench warfare) resulted in unprecedented casualties. Many soldiers who survived the war returned home scarred beyond recognition—some with missing limbs, some wearing masks to hide freakishly disfigured faces. In *The Amethyst Heart,* battle-scarred veteran Harper Wainwright is called "freak" by town boys, turned down for jobs, and is rejected by his girlfriend. Yet Amethyst Noble falls in love with him. Why do you think she is able to look past Harper's deformities? What is it about his character that makes him a heroic figure in this story?

7. The fictional setting of Cambridge, Mississippi bears a resemblance to the real-life town of Oxford, home of the University of Mississippi. In 1963, James Meredith became the first African-American student to attend classes at the school, but that historic enrollment was marred by violence when an angry crowd of white segregationists (including students) confronted National Guard troops called out by then-President John F. Kennedy. Against this backdrop of 19th century disharmony, the black-white relationships in *The Amethyst Heart's* Cambridge present a striking foil. How does this anomalous situation help us to view the present with hope?

8. In the chapter called "The Offering" we are privy to the inner thoughts of Amethyst Noble in September, 1946, as she takes part in the first racially-integrated service at Dix Godwin's church. Thinking back on her family history and recent events in her own life, she ties her thoughts together in this sentence: "Everything fit." Does "everything fit" in your own story? If not, how can you learn to see patterns of God's design in the "winding roads and intersection of lives" in your own family history?

9. Is Amethyst Noble the hero of this story? If so, what are her most admirable qualities and how did she acquire them? Who else can be considered a hero/heroine in *The Amethyst Heart*?

10. Why does Conrad fail to "come around" the way Little Am did? Does this less-than-happy ending for his story bother you, or is it satisfying? Why do you think he turned out the way he did, given his family heritage and good parenting? Do you think the author uses Conrad's story to illustrate our fallen nature, or to show how a child can absorb negative influences despite the family's best efforts? Does the author leave room for redemption in Conrad's life, or is she content to leave those questions unsettled? How or why?

11. What does this book teach us about the value of remembering the past? Does it present that lesson forcefully or with finesse? What other lessons does it have for the reader? Are there any particular ways in which the story moves you to do something different in your own life? Which character do you find most inspiring and why?

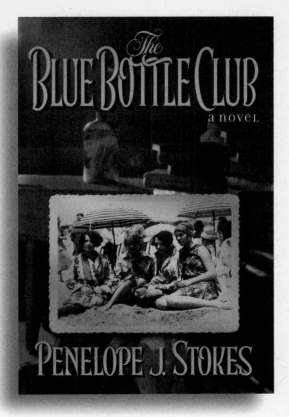

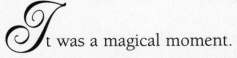t was a magical moment.

In the dim stillness of the Camerons' dusty attic, with their dreams captured in
a cobalt blue bottle, the four friends joined hands and reached out toward
the unknown. "We commit our dreams to the future," Letitia said quietly.
"To the future," the others echoed.

Letitia dreams of marriage to her high school sweetheart. Mary Love hopes to
become a famous artist. Wealthy Eleanor aspires to help those in need as a social
worker. Adora, the preacher's daughter, yearns to be a Hollywood film star. Will
the fulfillment of their dreams bring them happiness? Or will they awake from
their dreams to find destinies yet unimagined?

"Keep your eyes—and your heart—open."

🔟 WORD PUBLISHING
www.wordpublishing.com